FIRE FROM THE SKY: ASHES

Creative Texts Publishers products are available at special discounts for bulk purchase for sale promotions, premiums, fund-raising, and educational needs. For details, write Creative Texts Publishers, PO Box 50, Barto, PA 19504, or visit www.creativetexts.com

FIRE FROM THE SKY: BOOK 11: ASHES
by N.C. REED
Published by Creative Texts Publishers
PO Box 50
Barto, PA 19504
www.creativetexts.com

ISBN: 978-1-64738-031-1

FIRE FROM THE SKY: ASHES

N.C. REED

For those gone ahead.

Until we see you again.

FOREWORD

There are always many people to thank who will never see their names on the cover of a book like this. People who have helped me make a book better, or more accurately, people who helped shape me from boyhood, and fostered the imagination that allows me to do this.

One man I think I have neglected is an English Lit teacher at Memphis State University that I had the privilege to learn from many, many years ago (yeah, I'm that old). William Robert Williams was an incredible teacher who fostered a student's writing abilities like no other teacher I ever encountered, anywhere. While I had already started writing before I met him, the impression he left on me was such that I would go out of my way after that first semester to take any class he taught, or just to run in to him so I could speak with him. That's odd behavior for me, to say the least. That was how much of an impression he left on me, and on many other students that he taught over the years. I doubt I will ever forget one day in class when I heard him calling my name rather loudly and snapped to attention only to find out that I had fallen asleep in class. He apologized for waking me but explained that my snoring was interfering with his ability to teach the class. (I had worked thirty-six hours of the past forty-eight and was at the end of my endurance. I was still in uniform, in fact, having come to class straight from work at the state prison in Memphis. Fun times, fun times.) Even when he had to embarrass me, he did it with a class and a style that no teacher I have had before or since managed to match. He taught me not only that I could write, but that I could do well at it. All I had to do was apply myself, and bleed on the page. To write as I lived.

Thank you, Mister Williams, wherever you may be now.

NC Reed

FIRE FROM THE SKY

Dramatis personae

THE SANDERS FAMILY AND FARM

GORDON SANDERS – CURRENT PATRIARCH OF THE SANDERS FAMILY

ANGELA SANDERS- WIFE OF GORDON SANDERS, MOTHER OF THEIR THREE CHILDREN

ROBERT SANDERS – OLDEST SON OF GORDON AND ANGELA

PATRICIA SANDERS- WIFE OF ROBERT SANDERS, MOTHER OF THEIR TWO CHILDREN

- ABIGAIL SANDERS – OLDEST CHILD OF ROBERT AND PATRICIA
- SAMANTHA WALTERS – ABIGAIL'S BEST FRIEND, CURRENTLY LIVING WITH THE SANDERS
- GORDY SANDERS – YOUNGEST CHILD OF ROBERT AND PATRICIA

ALICIA TILLMAN – ONLY DAUGHTER OF GORDON AND ANGELA, SECOND CHILD

RONNY TILLMAN – HUSBAND OF ALICIA TILLMAN, FATHER OF THEIR THREE CHILDREN

- LEANNE TILLMAN – OLDEST OF TWINS BY TWO MINUTES
- LEON TILLMAN – YOUNGEST OF TWINS BY TWO MINUTES
- CLAYTON 'FUSSY' TILLMAN – NEWBORN ADDITION TO THE TILLMAN FAMILY

CLAYTON SANDERS – YOUNGEST SON AND CHILD OF GORDON AND ANGELA

LAINIE HARPER – CLAYTON'S GIRLFRIEND

GREG HOLLOWAY – CHILDHOOD BEST FRIEND OF CLAYTON AND JAKE SIDELL. DEPUTY SHERIFF OF CALHOUN COUNTY, NOW LIVES WITH GORDON AND ANGELA

JAKE SIDELL – CHILDHOOD BEST FRIEND OF CLAYTON AND GREG HOLLOWAY. MECHANIC AND BUSINESS OWNER, NOW LIVES ON THE SANDERS' FARM WITH HIS SEVEN-YEAR-OLD DAUGHTER JACQUELINE (JAC)

- JACQUELINE SIDELL – DAUGHTER OF JAKE SIDELL WITH HIS LATE WIFE, KAITLIN

MEMBERS OF CLAY'S OLD UNIT

JOSE JUAREZ – CURRENT SECOND IN COMMAND OF CLAYTON'S SECURITY DUTIES FOR THE FARM

MARTINA SANCHEZ – JOSE'S FIANCE

- ROBERTO SANCHEZ – SON OF MARTINA SANCHEZ, 8

- Rae Sanchez – daughter of Martina Sanchez, 6

Shane Golden – considered third in command, normal go-between for the group and new people

Jody Thompson – sniper for the group

Nathaniel 'Nate' Caudell – scout for the group

Cristina Caudell – Nate's wife

- Baby John Caudell – Nate and Cristina's newborn son, less than a year old
- Kaitlin Caudell – Nate's older sister, and Registered Nurse
- Nathan Caudell – Kaitlin's son, 16

Stacy Pryor

Kevin Bodee

Tandi Maseo – medic

Ellen Kargay – Tandi's girlfriend

Mitchell Nolan

Beverly Jackson – Mitchell's girlfriend

- Jonathon 'JJ' Jackson, Beverly's son, 14

Xavier Adair

Friends of Gordy's worked into the unit

Zach Willis

Titus Terry

Heath Kelly

Corey Reynard

Kurtis Montana (newly arrived with Shane's group, but normally fitted with the other teens)

Amazon Squad (but don't call them that)

Talia Gray

Kim Powers

Amanda Lowery

Danica Bennet

Freda Fletcher

Devon Knowles

Petra Shannon

Heather Patton

Eve Albert

Jena Waller

Mikki Reeves

Gail Knight

Savannah Hale

Carrie Jarrett
Eunice Maynard
Carol Kennard
Janessa Haynes

ORIGINAL HILLTOP COMMUNITY AND OTHER NEWCOMERS

Gary Meecham – gunsmith, sharpshooter, one of the group leaders
Dixie Jerrolds – schoolteacher

- Ashton Jerrolds – Dixie Jerrold's son, 7

Marcy George – 'emancipated teenager' 17
Samuel Webb – current 'patriarch' of the surviving Webb family members
Luke Webb – brother to Samuel
Seth Webb – Brother to Samuel – 16
Lila Webb – Sister to Samuel – 15
Daisy Webb – Widow of Micah Webb
Jasmine Webb – Widow of Matt Webb
Darrell Goodrum – blacksmith
Carlene Goodrum – wife of Darrell and mother of their three children

- Anthony Goodrum – son, 16
- Jamey Goodrum – son, 10
- Cara Goodrum - daughter, 8

Victoria Tully – former National Guard member, EOD specialist
Byron 'Brick' House – friend of Leon the Elder with murky past
Terri Hartwell – veterinarian student caught by the Storm, now part of the Sanders' Farm
Olivia Haley – 17, classmate of Gordy's, orphaned by Storm, now living with Gordon and Angela

- Caroline – sister, 7
- Libby – sister, 5

Amy Mitchell – rescued from attack soon after Storm

- Lisa – daughter,9

Janice Hardy – 18, came with Lainie Harper, has an eidetic memory
Callie Weston – rescued from attack on the farm

- Carl – son, 4

Tammy Denmark – rescued from attack on the farm

- Diane – daughter, 3

NEW MEMBERS OF HILLTOP COMMUNITY

Kandi Ledford – former 2nd Lt., U.S. Army

SIENNA NEWELL – FORMER 1ST LT., U.S. ARMY
VIRGIL WILCOX – FORMER SSG, U.S. ARMY
JAYLYN THATCHER – SURGEON, FORMER CAPT., U.S. ARMY

- RODDY THATCHER – HUSBAND OF JAYLYN, TRUCK DRIVER

CLIFFORD LARAMIE – FUEL TRUCK DRIVER
MOSES BROWN – BUTCHER/MEAT CUTTER
TRUDY LEIGHTON – SHANE GOLDEN'S COUSIN

- GWEN PAIGE – TRUDY'S GIRLFRIEND

MILLIE LONG – TEEN PICKED UP BY SHANE'S GROUP ON THE WAY EAST, NOW LEON SANDERS GIRLFRIEND
DOTTIE GREER – HUSBAND JAMES, TRUCK DRIVER, WORKING WHEN STORM HIT, INVITED TO LIVE AT FARM

- HELENA – DAUGHTER,8
- QUENTIN – SON,7

EVELYN LACEY – SOAP MAKER

JORDAN
CLEM PICKETT – NEWLY ELECTED MAYOR
CLINT DAWSON – MILITIA LEADER
BEN DRAPER – ECONOMIC LEADER
DOREEN MILLIGAN – ECONOMIC LEADER

LEWISTON
VAN BRONSON – DEPUTY SHERIFF
MARVIN SEWARD – MAYOR
WALTER GOGGIN – DEPUTY SHERIFF

NATIONAL GUARD CONTINGENT
MAJOR ANDREW WHITTEN
CAPTAIN LAKE ADCOCK
1ST LIEUTENANT TRIANA FLORES
2ND LIEUTENANT FARON GILLIS
1ST SERGEANT HEWIE MAXWELL
SERGEANT FIRST CLASS SHAUN GLEASON
STAFF SERGEANT LOWELL MARTINSON
SERGEANT TED DEERING

Author's Note: Those listed as part of the Hilltop Community may or may not actually be staying on the Hilltop at any given moment. All are listed with them as either those who arrived at the farm just before the disaster struck, or were invited to stay afterward, and are not part of the Sanders' family group or extended family (or part of Clay's old outfit at the Troy Farm). For instance, Brick and Janice live in Leon's old house due to their connection to Leon but were not a part of the Sanders' group beforehand.

TABLE OF CONTENTS

CHAPTER ONE 1
CHAPTER TWO 12
CHAPTER THREE 18
CHAPTER FOUR 29
CHAPTER FIVE 41
CHAPTER SIX 53
CHAPTER SEVEN 63
CHAPTER EIGHT 72
CHAPTER NINE 84
CHAPTER TEN 94
CHAPTER ELEVEN 103
CHAPTER TWELVE 113
CHAPTER THIRTEEN 122
CHAPTER FOURTEEN 131
CHAPTER FIFTEEN 144
CHAPTER SIXTEEN 155
CHAPTER SEVENTEEN 169
CHAPTER EIGHTEEN 182
CHAPTER NINETEEN 192
CHAPTER TWENTY 202
CHAPTER TWENTY-ONE 214
A NOTE FROM THE AUTHOR 229

CHAPTER ONE

"Roy Lee, nobody cares about you making shine," Greg Holloway said for the fifth time.

"Then why are you threatening me?" Roy Lee Fitz demanded.

"Nobody cares anymore that you make shine, Roy Lee," Greg said patiently. "Nobody even cares anymore if you sell or trade the shit away. Feel free to open your little bar and sell good shine. No license or anything right now. Don't know about the future, but I don't make those sorts of decisions."

"But *this*," he indicated the setup that Fitz had running, "I care about. You know damn good and well you can't run this *through a radiator*! You'll be poisoning half the people in Calhoun within a week!"

"It ain't killed nobody yet," Fitz replied sourly.

"That you know about," Greg amended. "There's only one reason for you to have these strung together, and we both know it. You're running whiskey through them because it's faster than using a worm. You want to do that? Go right ahead. But if I hear of you selling one *drop* of it for anything but fuel, I will come back here and blow this barn, and you, clear up to Murfreesboro. You get that?"

"Fuel?" Fitz looked confused. "You mean like gas?"

"No, moron, like lighter fluid," Greg shot back. "Of course, like gas, you idiot! Even if it's poison to drink, it will still mix with gas or even diesel and make it stretch further. For that matter, I'll buy it for the Sheriff's Department to use in our vehicles, provided you want something I can give you in return. We can use it to stretch our fuel supply and keep you from blinding half the people in Juniper while we're at it."

"I ain't never blinded nobody, neither," Fitz said, just short of surly.

"That you know about," Greg amended once again. "You'd never have done this when Leon was alive."

"No, cause then he'd send that crazy ass grandson o' his down here to beat me half to death and blow my shit up," Fitz growled. "But ain't he dead now?" he asked, less surly than before.

"Yeah, he is," Greg sighed. "Died earlier this year. Hated to see it."

"Me too," Fitz agreed. "He was hard to deal with, but Leon was a good old man, and his word was as good as a bar o' gold. We'll miss him for sure."

"Well, you can honor his memory by making sure no one drinks this shit," Greg told him flatly. "I'm serious as a heart attack here, Roy. I got more than enough trouble on my plate without finding ten dead drunks killed by drinking lead laced moonshine. You want to open a bar and sell shine, you make it the right way or not at all. Hear?"

"I hear ya," Roy nodded. "Just can't make as much that way is all."

"Then you'll be able to charge more because there's not much of it, right?" Greg smiled. "As for this," he waved to the barn around them, "figure out what you want to keep making however much of this you can. So long as it's high enough proof to burn in an engine, and again assuming we can make a deal, either I'll buy it for myself, or let the Guard commander know that he can try to make a deal for it. You won't lose anything that way. But remember what I said, because I'm not playing. I see one shot of this radiator fluid sold for whiskey and I've got a pound of C4 with your name on it. Now do we have an understanding, or do I need to go ahead and start laying explosives?"

"No, no, no," Fitz raised his hands in supplication. "I can live with that. But I can't make much more for right now. I don't have the materials for it. Maybe we can work out some kind of a deal for that?" he scratched his jaw, whiskers bending under the pressure.

"Maybe we can," Greg nodded. "Let me know what you need, and I'll see if I can get it, but only for fuel. And then only if it will burn. Don't try to sell me water or make me look bad by selling the Guard water, either."

"I wouldn't do that, man," Fitz sounded hurt. "If I tell you I'll do something, then I'll do it. Just 'cause I don't like it don't mean I won't do it, Greg."

"I'm counting on that, too," Greg agreed. "Cause if I thought you'd lie to me I'd be setting charges in here right now. As it is, I'm taking a huge gamble on you. Don't make me regret it."

"I won't, I swear," Fitz raised a hand. "I didn't think about trying to sell you high grain alcohol for fuel supplements. But what are we using for money nowadays?"

"Still working on that," Greg admitted. "That's why I asked about what you'd want in trade. I'm sure there's something that you need or want, right? If I can in good conscience give it to you, then I'll make a deal with you for it. It looks like you're right at a hundred gallons here."

"Give or take," Fitz nodded. "I don't have exactly proper measurements until I bottle it up."

"Well, save your bottles for the good stuff and just pump this into a tank," Greg ordered. "Use an old farm tank for it, should be fine. I'll get up here as soon as I can to get it, or else send someone else. Meanwhile you be thinking on what you need for it. And don't make me come back up here because you're selling this garbage like it's the straight goods."

"I already said I won't, man," Fitz sounded put upon. "I said it, then I'll do it. Besides, you done gave me a whole new set of ideas," the man grinned crookedly.

"I don't know whether to be proud, or be scared," Greg sighed, shaking his head as he walked back to his Hummer.

"You've had this trouble before?" Amanda Lowery asked, walking beside and a half-step behind him.

"Not like this," Greg shook his head. "The Old Man used to ride herd on this kind of thing. With him gone, people like Roy Lee want to start cutting corners. Leon would never have stood for that."

"We're talking about Leon Sanders here, right?" Amanda wanted to verify that. "By which we are not referring to that cute kid in the radio room. Right?"

"Right," Greg opened his door to step into the Hummer. Amanda climbed behind the wheel, having drawn the 'official driver' duty for the day.

"So, the elder Sanders was some kind of criminal tycoon, then?" Amanda asked, starting the Hummer even as Greg motioned to the MRAP behind them that they were leaving.

"Tycoon is stretching it I'd imagine," Greg shrugged. "More of a godfather type. Made sure people toed the line and didn't do anything stupid. Like, you know, running shine through old car radiators strung together on a barn wall."

"And the 'crazy ass grandson o' his' that our budding distillery owner mentioned?" Amanda asked once she had backed out of the drive and put them on the road.

"Now who do you think that would be?" Greg snorted.

"Well, I am assuming it was Clayton Sanders," Amanda shrugged. "Only he doesn't seem all that crazy to me. Granted my experience around him has been limited."

"He's fine so long as everyone is peaceful," Greg promised. "It's when this kind of crap gets out of hand that he gets annoyed. And before the lights went out, rumor had it that he did Leon's customer service, so to speak."

"Customer service, huh?" Amanda snorted. "I guess that's as good a euphemism as any. At least he's not as scary as Xavier or Zach."

Greg's laughter filled the Hummer for the next several minutes as they continued down the road on patrol.

-

Clayton Sanders winced as his ear suddenly had a sharp, ringing sensation. He ran a finger into his ear, shaking it slightly, as if that would help relieve the irritation.

"Problem?" Jose Juarez asked, seeing Clayton's apparent discomfort.

"Ear's ringing," Clay told him. "Somebody talking about me, probably."

"Now who could that be?" Jose laughed. The two men were watching as their newest recruits went through a series of fire-and-maneuver drills under the watchful eyes of Nate Caudell and Stacey Pryor. The only missing members were Amanda Lowery and Petra Shannon, both of which were on patrol with the Sheriff.

Clay could rarely hide a smile at the idea of Greg being Sheriff. It wasn't so much that his friend was actually the Sheriff, but the memory of the look on his face when he found out he'd been appointed to the post by the region's military commander. Under the provisions of Martial Law, the regional commander had the authority to appoint people to such offices and hadn't hesitated to make Greg, the sole surviving member of the pre-Apocalypse Sheriff's Department, the new high Sheriff.

"They're doing good," Jose noted, missing the sly smile that flashed across his Boss' face.

"They are indeed," Clay agreed. "I think at this point we could leave the safety of the farm in their hands, so long as they were leavened by a couple of the older hands. We shouldn't need it, but if we do, it's good to have that option."

A month had passed since members of the farm had ventured to Lewiston to hunt down and kill a team from further south that was sniping at the town as well as abducting and killing townspeople. They had done so not at the request of Captain Adcock, the area commander for the National Guard force responsible for their part of the region, but because a rifleman had killed a girl known to at least three of the teenagers on Clay's team, including his nephew.

That trip had also brought with it the discovery that the 'Armies of God', something that Clay had indeed begun to sweat about, were nothing more than guards and convicts from a private prison in north Georgia. True, there were at least some 'converts' out there who were singing the praises of the 'Great Worthy Boaz' or whatever the hell the prison chaplain called himself, but it wasn't an army. Or at least, no army had appeared.

What had appeared, attempting to shake down Lewiston for their food and other supplies, was a loose team of former prison guards and prisoners. While the group had caused a good bit of damage and fear, along with no small amount of pure panic, it had taken less than two days for a small team from the farm to find the undisciplined and poorly led group and eliminate all but a handful, who they had delivered to Captain Adcock on their way out of the woods and on their way home.

Discovering that there was no actual 'Army of God' made up of mad zealots looking to kill the heathen who refused to blah, blah, blah, had not been the only unexpected benefit from that small job. Almost forty good horses, complete with saddles and tack, had been seized by the team as 'spoils of war', and added to the farm's growing herd of horses. Knowing horses would be big business in the future, those in charge of growing the herd were glad to see new blood brought to the group. Clay was glad for the horses, but even more so for the saddles and other gear. Atop of that had been a mass of weapons and ammunition, which would be added to their growing stockpile of weaponry taken from the bodies of their enemies to be used later on as trade goods.

In all honestly, despite his not wanting to accept the mission, it had turned in to a rather profitable venture.

In the month since then, Greg Holloway had firmly established the return of the Sheriff's Department and had discovered that there were more survivors in the area than had been previously believed. Or perhaps *feared* was a better term. Most of the farm had feared that those people gathered in Jordan were perhaps all that remained of the county's former residents. Greg's patrols, however, had found several groups that had escaped the raiders that had plagued the entire area before Clay and his men had eliminated them as well. Most of those people, hardy country folk, were doing pretty well if not flourishing. Greg had talked to many of them and taken notes of their needs. With so few vehicles still operating, or even on the road, Greg's patrols had become a sort of 'trading post' for people out and about.

If someone had an item they wanted to get rid of, they told Greg. Likewise, if there was an item they needed, they told Greg. The new Sheriff then could often manage to put deals together for people, and every so often a gun truck would be pressed into service to make a run and move material around from place to place. While this arrangement could likely never become permanent, it was working for now, and had been a big boost in the popularity of the new Sheriff. Always a plus to have the voters behind you, Clay had told Greg with a smile.

Adcock had visited once in that month, advising him that Whitten had decided, barring any new problems, that they would start spreading their forces into the small winter garrisons by the first week in November. A little less than three weeks from this very day, in fact. At that point, Clay's appointed teachers would begin teaching Adcock's soldiers to ride and care for horses. Those lessons, a few meals when and where the farm could spare the means, and a place to post a small force to help have men available close to where they might be needed had been beneficial to the farm on several levels.

The chief benefit was the addition of sixteen trained and experienced soldiers to help defend the farm. A farm that had become extremely popular and important to the soldiers in general thanks to at least two great meals and the friendly reception they had received.

The second benefit, easily as important as the first in Clay's eyes, had been assistance in 'looting' what was left of some building materials and home furnishings to erect new lodgings for the people of the farm. A two-story barracks-type building that would double as a defensive position in case of attack had been constructed on the western side of the hilltop square to house the sixteen young women who were now finishing their training to become part of the security forces for the farm. The bottom floor would be for bunks, while the top would be for defensive uses, but could also double as a recreational area for the women, especially during winter when board games and card games would be most of the available recreation.

Along the eastern side of the square were six new cabins, each with three bedrooms and a large sitting room, as well as a partial loft area. The cabins could be used for individual roommates or for a family dwelling either one. People from both groups would make use of the facilities and mess hall in the square.

A single, separate cabin, smaller but still with four rooms and a loft, was constructed for Evelyn Lacey, now permanently known as 'the Goat Lady' behind her back. This cabin was placed to the west of the three large buildings on the Troy farm, with fencing giving her goats a good five acres of fenced safety to roam in, along with her two Aussie Shepherds. A creek running through the area would provide water, and Clay had already had a small pond scooped out near the center with a rock dam to slow the flow of water and fill the pond for the goats.

Lacey used the goat's milk, among other items, to make soaps, lotions and other goodies that were immensely popular among most all the women on the farm. It was in fact that popularity with one Lainie Harper, Clay's live-in lady love, that had prompted the effort to move Lacey, lock, stock and dogs, to the farm. The cabin had ample living space as well as providing a workshop for her services.

The final new construction lay on the eastern side of the Troy farm, and was like the dorm erected for the young women on the hill. A roughhewn two-story construct to house the soldiers that would be garrisoned on the farm over the winter, complete with a private room for their NCO, Sergeant First Class Sean Gleason, another for a visiting officer, and an upstairs area for both defense and recreation.

The addition of the second floor had been made after the success of the women's dorm on the western side. The same thick walls were added to the soldier's barracks, making it a solid defensive structure to make a stand in. In the future, whenever soldiers were at the farm, this was where they would stay.

Some were less than enthused by the presence of the soldiers, that fear sparked by a group of raiders posing as soldiers who had ravaged several small communities in the area during late spring. Clay well understood that unease, which was why the young women in particular, all victims to one degree or another of those same raiders, were as far as possible from the soldier's barracks. Some contact between the two groups was inevitable, given that the farm had taken responsibility for training the soliders to ride, but Clay was determined to keep that contact as limited as possible. If the ladies wanted to meet with the soldiers they could, but it would be on their terms. That was the best compromise Clay could come up with, and even Beverly Jackson, the resident psychologist, had agreed.

"-ready…you haven't heard a word I've said, have you?" Jose's voice broke through Clay's train of thought.

"What?"

"That answers that question," Jose sighed. "I was basically saying that I think they're ready. They're trained well enough to work in the field if they decide they want to. I think they'll do fine here at the farm."

"Sounds good," Clay nodded approvingly, attempting to get back into his 'command presence' voice. "Good job."

"Thanks," Jose commented dryly. "What are you going to do now?"

"I guess go look through the new haul and see what's there," Clay shrugged. "I'm really starting to think of building a general store across the road. It would mean allowing people access to the farm, but it might be worth it. Think it over and see what you decide."

A final benefit from the visit to Peabody with the National Guard detail was the discovery that the ravaged town was apparently abandoned. Clay couldn't blame the former residents for that. With over half of the town in ashes and the rest ravaged by repeated gun battles, what remained bore only the slightest resemblance to the town he remembered from before the lights went out.

While Clay hated to see his hometown look so destitute and ghostly, it did allow his teams to collect anything and everything in town that they could make use of or possibly trade away. Some would look upon them unfavorably for that, but it couldn't be helped. Leaving supplies and equipment to rust away to ruin was too wasteful. Even things like tin roofing taken from buildings that were burned hollow on the inside was something the farm could use.

Oddly enough, the schools had not fallen victim to the fires, nor had they been used as shelters, something Clay could only attribute to the public's fear of staying in town during the violence. The schools had netted books, paper, writing utensils and other education needs for the growing number of children on the farm, as well as the contents of the library. The high school, designed as an emergency shelter during a remodel only a decade before, had produced fifty army cots with thin camp mattress pads. While not the most comfortable things in the world, they were much better than a cold floor.

It never ceased to amaze Clay the things that were overlooked, abandoned or unused in a time of such great turmoil and destruction. It was possible that those fleeing the fire or the violence or both simply didn't have the time to gather much. On top of that, with no working vehicles to speak of, carrying off large or heavy items would have been impractical if not impossible.

Clay truly hated the level of destruction that had come to Peabody in particular and the entire county in general. While he knew from Whitten and Adcock that other areas had it worse, much worse in the case of the larger cities, this was his area. His home, his family's home for generations. Much of the ruin he had seen through the county had played a role in his childhood, or his teen years. Many of those who had perished had been known to him, if not friends, and even those he didn't know were known to his family.

He shook those thoughts away. It did no good to dwell on them. It didn't fix the problem.

Nothing would fix the problem.

-

"I have no idea how our ancestors didn't end up going naked or dressed entirely in fur," Angela Sanders declared abruptly as she paused in her efforts to spread wet flax across an unused portion of pasture in order for it to dry.

Once harvested, the flax had to be soaked for two weeks, give or take, until the outer and inner strands of the fibrous plant could be easily separated. That had been accomplished. Now, the plants had to be dried. Sun-dried was the preferred method, spread across the grass to allow the water to drip and drain away from the plants.

After that it would have to be regathered and tied into bundles and stacked to allow the drying to complete, and prepare the flax for 'stutching', or the process of separating the inner and outer layers. At its very basic, it meant gathering a bundle of plants and beating the stuffing out of them with a flat stick to break apart the inner fibers. That process would continue with something called 'crimping', which would further break the inner fiber down. It was from those inner fibers that they would get what the Scottish had called true linen.

While it had become highly industrialized by the mid-20th century, the farm lacked that industry themselves, and so were reduced to using old tried and true methods found by the Duo of Leanne and Leon Tillman on the internet before the lights had gone out.

As it turned out, it was an incredibly involved and labor-intensive process.

"Well, fur would be hot to wear in summer, I guess," Lainie mentioned, pausing to wipe a slight sheen of sweat from her forehead. While it was no longer truly hot, it was still warm enough to work up a sweat with such exertion.

"And hard to come by if you weren't able to hunt very well," Dottie Greer agreed, working further down the line of plants to make sure they were spread thinly and able to dry.

"I'm just saying this is a very involved process," Angela noted.

"I thought you had seen this done before," said Amy Mitchell, her arms full of wet flax as she made her way to the end of the line to start anew.

"No, I've seen spinning and looming done before," Angela corrected. "But with cotton. We grew cotton when I was a girl and it was something my mother… actually it was more my grandmother doing it, really," she amended, remembering those long-ago days. "They made thread, or yarn, really, I suppose, which they then either spun down finer for thread or else weaved into cloth in order to make clothing. This," she waved to the flax all around them, "is a completely different material, but the spinning and weaving process is much the same. But instead of cotton, this will produce linen."

"Linen being much lighter and more breathable than cotton," Greer opined. "Hence the name 'linens' for bed clothes and what not."

"Exactly, yes," Angela nodded. Sighing, she prepared to return to her work. "But I fear this is something we may as well get used to doing. It will be years if not decades before any kind of industrialized material making returns to this area."

"Way to cheer everyone up, Angela," Lainie chuckled.

"It's a gift," the older woman laughed along with her.

-

Dixie Jerrolds fought the urge to sigh as she looked around her at the sheer number of childen she was responsible for. While she did have assistance with them, she was the only teacher and was forced to take the role of authoritarian. It wasn't that she minded the work in itself. She had always wanted to teach, ever since her freshman year of high school. She never even considered another line of work and had devoted herself to being the best of her vocation.

But she had never imagined that she would end up with so many children of so many different ages, all at one time. She had gained an incredible amount of respect for the teachers of old, who had taught multiple grades in the same one-room school during the nation's early history. Trying to separate the lesson plans for children of wildly varying ages was already a task, never mind having to watch out for so many children.

There were a few high points of course. Today for instance. It was a gorgeous fall afternoon, and they were all outdoors, different age groups spread accordingly over blankets on the ground. She went back and forth between groups as the children read from their schoolbooks and answered questions on small chalk board rather than paper. While the older children had found that oddly challenging, the younger children had loved using the chalk.

"Miss Dixie, why did it take so long for the United States to have a Constitution?" Lila Webb asked. "Even after the Revolution was ended, it took years to have a real government."

"Well, Lila, technically we did have a real government in the form of the Continental Congress," Dixie reminded the teen gently. "But one of the problems with that was that the Congress didn't meet on a regular basis, and it was the only real branch of government on the federal level. There was as yet no Supreme Court, no President of the United States, there wasn't even, technically, a United States, save in form."

"So, what made them decide that the first government wasn't working?" Nathan Caudell asked, clearly interested now that the subject had been raised.

"Because it wasn't working," Dixie replied with a smile. "Consider that the Congress could print money, but it wasn't worth anything. It had no value behind it and only the promise of a weak and somewhat disorganized government. If they borrowed money, how did they pay it back? Who could they borrow from to start with? There was also the issue of taxes. How would the states be assessed for taxes, and how would they pay them? That tax money would be how the Congress could pay soldiers, who were the most unifying part of the nation at that time. Former soldiers who had fought the British were the first to oppose any sort of infringements and often revolted against even a hint of tyranny in local governments. It was that threat more than any other, I would say, that kept many otherwise crooked politicians honest in those days."

"Sounds like we could have done with some of that ourselves," Anthony Goodrum noted. "Before things turned off, you couldn't watch television without seeing where some politician or another had been a crook, or was accused of it, anyway."

"Sadly, dear, I'm afraid you're right, at least where the news is concerned," Dixie noted.

"Well, at least we don't have to worry about all that now, do we?" Lila Webb looked at her classmates and then back to Dixie. "Everything has pretty much fallen apart, hasn't it? When the lights went out?"

Dixie didn't know how to explain to Lila and the others that Lila was both right and wrong at the same time. That sometimes the teacher didn't have the answers.

She was saved from having to develop that answer by a commotion from the small playground behind her school children.

-

Callie Weston and Tammy Denmark had arrived at the farm under far from ideal circumstances, being used as a shield for a planned attack on the farm and its occupants. Trying to protect their own children, they had gone along with a group of women carrying children taken from others as a cover to infiltrate the farm.

They had almost lost the right to remain by not speaking up and telling the soldiers protecting the farm about the plan, but a last-minute reprieve had seen them assigned to live in a purpose-built building to care for the small children now left without parents and unable in most cases to even provide their proper names.

Two other women had received that same blessing but had thrown it away to follow Malitha George in her crusade against Trudy Leighton working in the orphanage. Both Callie and Tammy considered that to have been the stupidest decision ever made, especially when considering that Trudy was great with the kids and easy to work with. Today, for instance, she was at the orphanage with the smallest of the children, all still in diapers, while Tammy and Callie had brought the older children who were still not yet of school age down to the playground to enjoy this beautiful day.

A fate filled decision that would change a great many things on the Sanders' farm.

CHAPTER TWO

"Miss Tammy, Bobear got bited by a worm."

Tammy Denmark looked at the bright face of the little girl known as Marie and almost smiled. Marie couldn't say 'Bobby', she always said 'Bobear'. But what else was-

The sound of a crying infant drew her attention away from Marie. She looked across to the swing set and saw Bobby sitting on the ground, crying loudly. She could see something slithering away from him through the grass and her stomach clenched.

Bited by a worm?

Tammy raced to where Bobby sat screaming, hoping she would find anything but puncture marks. She would be disappointed.

Little Bobby, whose real name, age or parents was unknown to any of them, had an obvious snake bite on his little right arm, already beginning to swell. Looking up in the direction she had seen the snake crawling away, she saw Zach Willis walking toward them.

"Snake!" she called to Zach. "There's a snake! Kill it, Zach! It bit Bobby! I need to know what it is!"

Zach immediately began searching the grounds, moving to intercept the path that Tammy had pointed out for him. Tammy, meanwhile, jerked Bobby up from the ground and started for the clinic, yelling for Callie as she ran.

"Callie! I'm taking Bobby to the clinic! Be careful! He's been snake bit!"

"Got it!" Callie called back, immediately gathering all the children up into a close group so she could watch them better. Lila got up at once to go and help, as did Nathan and Anthony. Dixie, and her assistant for the day, Gwen Paige, began doing the same thing with the younger children among those who were school age.

"Do you think they can help him?" Dixie asked Gwen quietly as the two met briefly.

"Depends on what bit him," Gwen replied just as quietly. She was about to say more when she saw Zach Willis in the distance, raise a foot and stomp down hard before drawing his knife. He knelt, knife sawing at an unseen object, before he stood again, having speared something with the point of his knife.

"To the clinic!" Gwen pointed for him in answer to his unasked question. She called to him so Callie could stay quiet around the very alarmed smaller children.

Nodding to her in thanks, Zach trotted that way.

"Stay away from over there until I can check it!" he called, jabbing the thumb of his free hand toward the spot where he had apparently killed a snake. "I'll be back in a minute."

Gwen waved an acknowledgement, not trusting herself to speak just now. There was only one reason that Zach would be carrying the head of a snake that was thought to have bitten a child.

-

"Help!" Tammy ran through the clinic doors cradling Bobby, who was beginning to tremble and had stopped crying. Just as she reached the doctor, Bobby threw up, the contents of his stomach emptying onto them both and the floor below.

"What happened?" Jaylyn Thatcher had happened to be closest to her and took the child, moving toward a bed.

"He was snake bit!" Tammy told her, following. "I saw, I think I saw, the snake moving away. I asked Zach to see if he could kill it. But when I saw the punctures…." She trailed away, as if her voice had simply stopped.

"You did the right thing," Jaylyn assured her as Patricia Sanders moved to assist her. They quickly had Bobby wrapped in a pressure cuff and were checking his other vitals. Patricia cleaned the remnants of his vomit from Bobby's mouth as Jaylyn attempted to check his blood pressure. The sound of the door opening drew Tammy's attention and she saw Zach Willis standing inside, his knife in his hand.

"It was a copperhead, Miss Jaylyn," Zach said tonelessly. "He was bit by a copperhead."

"His pulse is too high and hard to find," Patricia noted even as Jaylyn acknowledged Zach's announcement.

"His arm is already swelled," Jaylyn replied. "His blood pressure is far too low. I don't-," She cut off as Bobby began spasming then convulsing on the table, almost as if he was in the midst of a seizure.

"How long ago was he bitten?" Patricia asked Tammy.

"I don't know for sure," Tammy admitted. "Another child told me he had been bitten by worms, and before I could work out what she meant, Bobby started screaming. I ran to him and saw the punctures and the bleeding, and had already seen the snake moving away, so I grabbed him and ran here as fast as I could."

"Is he allergic to bee stings?" Jaylyn asked Tammy, who made a helpless shrugging gesture at the question.

"I have no way of knowing, Doctor," she admitted. "I don't even know who he is. None of us do."

"Even for a child, this is-," the doctor stopped talking as she realized that she could no longer feel Bobby's heartbeat.

"He's not breathing," Patricia told her, forcing Bobby's mouth open to see if his tongue was obstructing his airway. What she saw alarmed her.

"His throat is closed, and his tongue is swollen! His throat is completely shut and even his mouth tissue is swelling!" she said urgently. "He's in anaphylactic shock. He must be allergic to the venom. Even in a small child this venom should not be so fast acting, otherwise."

"We have to perform a tracheotomy," Jaylyn decided at once. "It's the only way we can make sure he can breathe." She grabbed a scalpel and began probing Bobby's throat area for the proper spot.

"Jaylyn," Patricia said softly, but the doctor didn't answer, continuing to look for the right spot to make her incision.

"Jaylyn," Patricia reached out and took the doctor's hand in her own, stopping her. Jaylyn looked up at her.

"He's gone," Patricia said gently. "His pulse and his blood pressure are both gone. His little lips are blue, and it's spreading. His throat is completely closed, and his esophagus is swelling well below where we could perform a trach. The venom had to have hit an artery or a vein, and he had to have had some type of allergy to the venom. It's too late. We're too late."

"Can't you do anything?" Tammy didn't quite yell, her hands making motions of all kinds around her.

Jaylyn Thatcher sighed, dropping her head.

"No," she admitted softly. "I don't know what the cause was, but this was too fast. We should have had time to work. This was so fast, even epinephrine might not have been fast enough. Even if we had known to use it, which we didn't." She pinched the bridge of her nose, clearly going over every move they had made since Bobby had come into the clinic, looking for something she could have done differently.

"I don't know how many snakebites I've treated over the years," Patricia's voice was gentle in opposition to Tammy's outburst. Calming. What her children called her 'Doctor Voice'.

"None of them, not one, has been like this," Patricia told them all. "I have seen allergic reactions, but never this severe. Usually it presents with hives, or an increase in respiration. And normally it's from food or bee stings. Not…not this," she motioned to the small, still body on the table. "I don't know what underlying medical problems he may have had, but there had to be something. Either that, or the venom hit an artery or vein and went straight to his little heart. I can't imagine anything else causing all this."

"The odds of something like this are…staggering," Jaylyn leaned back against the counter behind her. "Something like one in six thousand bites, maybe? I can't recall, and it doesn't matter anyway, but it's almost unheard of."

"He's…" Tammy couldn't finish.

"I'll help get the kids back to the orphanage," Zach said quietly. Patricia nodded her thanks as Tammy Denmark finally crumbled, the adrenaline of the last few minutes wearing off abruptly and leaving her weak and shaking.

"This is my fault," she said softly. "This is all my fault."

She would continue repeating it for some time as she herself went into shock.

-

"This is my fault."

Clay had been summoned to the clinic by Janice Hardin, who had heard all the loud voices while working her post in operations. While she didn't know what might have happened, she did know that 'Mister Clayton' very likely needed to know about it.

Having run to the clinic from looking over the latest items brought in by their scavenger teams, he had slid into the clinic just as Zach Willis was exiting. Zach had shown him the snake head and explained, so Clay had known what to expect when he entered.

He hadn't stayed long, noting that Patricia was rather concerned over Tammy Denmark, who appeared to Clay to have gone into shock. With a look at the small body that Jaylyn Thatcher was covering with a small cloth, Clay had turned abruptly and departed.

"This is my fault," he repeated as he sat in front of Building Two, staring across the road.

"How?" Jose asked him, having joined him as soon as he heard that school was dismissed for the time being.

"It just is," Clay settled for saying, but Jose was shaking his head.

"Your persecution complex is showing, brother," he told Clay softly. "It was a snake bite. He was allergic. It is a complete and utter tragedy, I agree, but hardly your fault."

"We're going about this wrong," Clay spoke as if he hadn't heard Jose at all.

"We're still teaching these kids as if everything is okay, or will be," Clay told him, finally tearing his gaze away from the horizon. "As if things will return to normal and we don't want them to be behind when it does."

"That…that is more or less true," Jose had to admit.

"That's a stupid thing to do," Clay stated flatly. "We should be teaching these kids to survive in the world they're facing now. Not in the world we've left behind. I should have seen that problem and dealt with it. Hell, the Old Man made sure to teach the Duo how to do things the old way. Everyone made sure they learned how to do stuff, how to be safe. It's not like I didn't know it needed doing."

"Clay, do you think any of the rest of us knew that, too?" Jose asked, frowning.

"Probably," Clay shrugged. "I'm not saying it's just me, necessarily."

"Yeah, you are," Jose challenged. "And I get it, man. I do. You're in charge, it's your place, and you feel responsible for everything that goes on here. It's something to admire you for, in my opinion. Most men do their best to duck responsibility, you know."

"But this, this is more like an act of God than some kind of fault," Jose told him, his voice sounding almost urgent. "A snake in a playground that eluded Bruce and that Kangal hound that was laying around. That both Bella and Petals missed too? Biting a child, probably the one child in the group even, who was allergic to the venom? Man, you can take blame for a lot, Clay, and if I thought you were to blame, I'd tell you, and you know that. But there is no way for you to take blame for something like this. Jaylyn already said the odds of this happening were thousands to one. Sometimes, brother, a thing just is."

"We still need to be doing things differently," Clay almost muttered, only half listening to his friend. "We need a new education policy. And we need it as soon as we can manage it, too."

"What kind of education are we talking about?" Jose asked, not quite hesitantly.

"Bobby probably tried to pick that snake up, thinking it was a toy or a pet," Clay replied. "If we had taught him better, he might not have tried."

"Clay, he was three, we think," Jose shook his head. "We don't know that for sure, and never will! You could tell him all day not to pick up a snake, and he might still do it!"

"It's not just that," Clay was already shaking his own head before Jose finished. "It's everything. Kids still need to be able to read and do math and know science, I get that. But we have to change things. From now on, they're going to need to know other things, and we haven't bothered teaching any of it. We have to fix that."

"What are you expecting to teach them?" Jose asked him. "Some of them are barely out of diapers, man."

"That is true, and we'll have to just experiment with it to see what we can get by with," Clay agreed. "But we have to start teaching these kids to *survive*."

"What do you have in mind?" Jose asked.

"How many of them could start a fire?" Clay asked him in reply. "How many could catch, clean and cook a fish? Skin a rabbit that they caught in a snare? Tan the hide into usable leather? Build a shelter in the woods? Do you not see what I mean? It's not just the snake, Pancho! That's just the tip of the iceberg that showed me what we've done wrong! Or at least haven't done right."

"Okay, okay, I get your point," Jose tried to soothe his friend. "So, we start using some of the school time to teach the kids anything they can learn about. We'll have to decide who gets that honor and then how to divide the kids up.

Some will be better able than others despite their ages. We'll have to be observant and make sure we're teaching at a level they can manage."

"We need to talk to Beverly about that, too," Clay nodded. "We need to make sure that we don't teach things to kids that are young enough to be disturbed by them. But at the same time, all of these kids have to get used to the idea of living a different kind of life."

-

"Understand that while I did study child psychology, that was not my field," Beverly Jackson told Clay. "That said, there are certain things that you will want to hold off trying to teach to the very youngest children. If you scare them with something, they could very well carry that fear with them into adulthood, and you'll never be able to rid them of it. Things that are scary must be approached with caution." She paused, clearly debating.

"I've been talking to the little girl who reported that Bobby had been bitten," she said finally. "We call her Marie. The commotion that surrounded Bobby has given her an instant fear of snakes, where none existed before this afternoon. She might have been hesitant, or even cautious, but not fearful. Now, she is likely to be petrified of snakes from here on in, and there is little we can do to prevent it besides trying to use things like touch therapy to help her get over her fear."

"That's where you present someone with what they fear, and allow them to get used to it, right?" Jose asked.

"Exactly," Beverly nodded. "And there is no way that Marie will be able to stand that for a while. When we do approach her with it, we will need a calm environment and a careful plan. The same would go for any child with that fear. In fact, we can gather the children that are afraid into a group. The fact that they aren't alone will lend them courage they might not find on their own."

"Okay," Clay nodded slowly, his mind already racing ahead. "We have to determine when each child would be ready for something like learning how to shoot or using a knife. At what age they could be exposed to blood when dressing an animal. Or when they could handle with having killed that animal, for that matter."

"Something like that will have to be done on a child-by-child basis," Beverly told him at once. "There is no set age for anything you're talking about. That's going to take some time, Clay. I will have to sit down with each child and talk to them about how they would feel if they participated in those things."

"They have to learn," Clay insisted.

"They won't learn anything if they're terrified," Beverly replied. "I'm telling you now; once you've put a fear into a child, it will haunt them the rest of their lives. We have to be careful."

"Then we'll be careful."

CHAPTER THREE

"I don't like this," Dixie Jerrolds said as she looked around the meeting table. Most of the adults, all of those who had their own children, along with those who assisted in caring for the children at the orphanage, were present.

"There's nothing to like," Clay shrugged. "It has to be done. We should have been doing it all along. We could see that in other things but looked right over it when it came to teaching these kids. It was a stupid thing to do, and I admit the responsibility in large part is mine. Changing it won't help Bobby, but it will, I hope, help the rest."

It was the day following the incident. That morning had been a somber affair of burying the small child's body. Everyone save those on watch had attended, and as Gordon spoke there was scarcely a dry eye in the crowd. More than one was heard to mutter about the unfairness of it all.

Now, after lunch, Clay had called the meeting to announce what he had decided had to be done.

"Children need an education," Dixie argued with the stubbornness one might expect from a professional educator. "They have to have it. Without it they will be at a disadvantage when they're out in the world!"

"What world, Dixie?" Clay asked calmly. "Which one? The one that those schoolbooks you're using were written for? Because that world is gone, and not a one of these kids will see it again, barring a miracle. They need to be taught how to get by, how to survive, in the world we're in now. And let's be honest here. This farm is likely to be the biggest part of the world they're likely to know. We've done our best to establish a safe, secure place for them to live, and even thrive, as long as we're teaching them how to be self-sufficient and provide for themselves." He paused for a moment, looking at the table where his hands were locked together, white at the knuckles from the strain.

"I'm not saying they don't need to know the basics," he told her finally. "They do. They need to know how to read, write and do math for certain. They need the sciences that we'll use. They need to know our nation's history, too, if for no reason other than as a reference. None of that is useless, and most of it is a necessity. I don't deny that."

"But from now on it has to be buoyed by skills and knowledge that they need to survive. I admit it might not have helped someone as young as little Bobby was, but it just might have led to an older child recognizing the danger and knowing what to do."

"That can be taught without undoing our entire school program!" Dixie insisted.

"You don't see the problem, do you?" Clay asked. "It's not about the snake. The snake led me to realize that we aren't teaching these children properly, that's all. We're teaching them for a world that no longer exists. We better stop doing that and start teaching them for the world we live in *right now*. A world where they need to know things that your school program isn't teaching. That isn't your fault," he raised a hand to stop her protest. "It's mine, and I guess Leon's somewhat." He paused again, searching for the words he needed.

"We thought we were so smart, having our own little school. And I suppose we would have been if things were going to straighten out and return to normal. But they're not. It doesn't do the kids a bit of good to keep them 'caught up' when there's nothing to catch up to. I can all but promise you that the teenagers at least have seen their last day in a high school. Peabody is a ghost town, even if the school building is somehow still standing."

"These kids have to learn how to make it in the world we have, not the one we had," he rammed his point home. "That means their education has to change. Period. If any of you can change my mind with something other than pro forma arguments, go right ahead." He sat back in his chair, waiting.

"I don't like it," Dixie repeated.

"You've made that clear, Dix," Clay assured her. "You not liking it doesn't change it."

"He's right," Beverly weighed in. "We want to try and let them have at least something of a childhood, of course. They need it in order to be happy and to grow into the kind of adults we want them to be. But Clay is right. While we do have to continue to teach the basics, and science is important to them, we also have to teach them to survive. We didn't have to do that just a year ago. Their survival was taken care of by society even when we as parents couldn't do it. No more. We have to see to it that they can take care of themselves."

"I agree," Gordon's voice was quiet. "When I was a boy, we were taught that way. I don't know how many schools still had an FFA program or FHA program, but when I was in school, it was all but mandatory and every school had them. Boys learned how to farm or care for livestock, how to manage a farm, do accounts, keep from being cheated, everything they needed to make a living from the earth. Girls learned to budget for a household, to cook, to sew, to care for children and everything else they needed in order to keep their homes running. Things that we don't usually bother with now, I suppose, with everyone working two jobs to keep up with the neighbors."

"We were taught trade skills," he continued. "Carpentry, machining, welding, auto and diesel mechanics. Typing, secretarial skills, nursing skills even, though nothing like today's nursing schools were, I'm sure," he looked at Kaitlin Caudell as he spoke. "We left school ready to be producing adults in society, even when we were still just seventeen. Sure, some went to college, and others joined the military. Some moved away and didn't come back. That's life. Things change, and always will. But we learned a lot more in school than math, reading and how to write."

"We had vocational school even when I was there," Clay nodded. "And there was still an FFA when I was there, but I don't remember about Home Economics, to be honest."

"There was," Ronny offered. Alicia was absent with their new baby, but Ronny had joined them.

"There was a huge fight between Alicia and Leanne over Home Ec," Ronny grinned. "Alicia wanted Leanne to be part of the FHA, and Leanne called it a 'misogynistic waste of time', and that was just to start. They argued over it all summer before her freshman year started until Ally gave up."

"All this means is that schoolwork will be slower," Jose commented. "Instead of the kids having class five days a week, it will be three, or sometimes two. It no longer matters how or when they learn the things they need, so long as they learn them. When the weather is bad and they need to be indoors, then classes can be full time again and progress faster. But when the weather permits, they need to be outside learning other things. In fact, there will be times when it will be better to use the classroom to teach them. It will be easier to get the basics down in that environment rather than throw them headfirst into the wild, so to speak."

"Just what all are you saying they need to learn?" Dixie asked.

"Everything," Clay replied. "Everything from how to identify a poisonous snake to how to identify poisonous plants. How to build a shelter if they're caught away from the farm or lost. How to get home if they were to be lost. For the older kids, and the others as they get older, how to track, kill and dress animals. How to run snares and traps for food and furs. How to ride a horse and care for it. How to care for the gear they need to ride the horse to start with."

"They need to know how to defend themselves. They need to learn how to operate the machinery we still have in case we can keep it running longer than we think. If we can't, then they need to know how to plow the ground with horses or mules so they can plant. They need to learn when crops are ready to be picked, and how to do it properly. How to can or dry food. How to sharpen a knife, or an ax, or a garden hoe. How to make those things if they need to. I could sit here all day going over a list and never cover it all," he admitted suddenly.

"I learned all that from my mother!" Dixie objected. "Some of it, anyhow," she added, reviewing Clay's list mentally even as she argued against it.

"We have an entire building full of children who no longer have that option," Clay reminded her. "Further, we have people now on this farm who didn't get that kind of education, and so can't pass it along to their children. They need to learn themselves, perhaps, but their children have absolutely got to know how. One day we'll all be gone, and they will be on their own. If we don't prepare them for that, we're dooming them to failure, and that failure will be ugly. If we care anything about them, we won't do that."

"He's right on that," Mitchell Nolan said, looking down at his boots. "We've seen it. Too many times. Kids left to fend for themselves and not know how. Parents dead before they could teach them anything. Left without the tools to work, sometimes without shelter and not knowing how to build any." He looked up; eyes bright.

"You don't want to do that to your children," he told the group. "Trust me. You may as well kill them yourself because that's essentially what you'd be doing, anyway. At least doing it yourself would be faster and more merciful."

"Stop exaggerating!" Dixie almost yelled at him.

"I'm not," Mitchell stayed calm. "Like I said, I've seen it. More than once. And it you think this nation is any different than those areas now, you're not looking. Think of how much we've already seen. Say something happens to us," he made a circular motion around the group. "Who do you think will step in and take care of the children that survive? Jordan? Doubtful, though they will be glad to strip this place bare you can bet, seeing as how some have already threatened it. Lewiston? How will they get there? And who there will care for them if they make it?" He shook his head.

"No, there's no exaggeration here, just hard facts. You think today was bad?" he asked her flatly. "Burying one child? Wait until you have to-,"

"Mitch, that's enough," Jose said softly. "It won't help. Let it go."

"You know I'm right," Mitchell replied.

"I do," Jose nodded. "I also know that it won't move us forward. Let it go," he repeated gently.

"I'm still waiting for that reasoned argument about why I'm wrong," Clay took the conversation back. "If I'm not getting one, then this is decided. We're doing this, and we'll start right away. Tomorrow, we'll start with anyone aged twelve and up, teaching them to identify trees and bushes, along with any fruit or berries that they produce. We may have other, easier classes for the younger children. We'll know that in the morning. If there's nothing else, we can adjourn."

"This is wrong," Dixie Jerrolds persisted. "You're going to end up hurting those children with this," she warned. "You'll be sorry you did it."

"I'm already sorry," Clay replied. "I'm sorry I didn't think of it before we had to bury a child that should have had a decent life ahead of him. That's on me, but I won't make that mistake again."

There was no further objection from the schoolteacher as Clay walked away from the table, shoulders hunched over and head down.

-

"Okay," Nate Caudell said, looking at a list he was holding. "Initial learning for the older kids, aged twelve and up: Orienteering, knife sharpening, plant identification, tree identification, venomous snake identification, tracking, trapping, killing and cleaning and then skinning game. Horsemanship, including care for the saddles and other gear involved in riding a horse. And," he looked up at the group, "I've added shooting to that list as well. We've already taught the kids sixteen and up, and we've had familiarization classes for the younger kids. Most of that familiarization was just different ways of saying 'don't touch that', though. We need to do better."

"We need a Stranger Danger program, too," Greg noted. He had been added to the planning sessions on his return. He had been shocked to hear what had happened, and more than a little surprised at the response.

"Hadn't thought of that, but we do," Nate added it to the list. "Most strangers have been dangers since the light went out, but that's just identification. You're talking about teaching proper responses, I imagine?"

"Yes," Greg nodded. "Child trafficking was a large problem before the lights went out, and it was growing. Now? I shudder to think how bad it is. Look at what we've seen here at home. Never would have imagined it. Never."

"Archery," Kevin Bodee offered. "Teach them now, while they're young. It will be easier to learn. I can teach them to make their own bows, and even their own arrows. It will be a skill that will stick with them, and one they can make use of in a number of situations."

"Another good one," Nate nodded, writing.

"Driving?" Mitchell asked.

"If time allows it," Clay agreed. "But I don't see any reason to make it a priority. Not much left to drive. Still, it's a useful thing to know." He shifted in his chair, mind running full speed ahead.

"We'll start teaching them how to care for the cattle and pigs, too," he told them. "Not right away. We'll have to give Dee, Sam and Terri time to get a class of some kind together, or at least decide how they want to proceed with the lessons, but they need to know that kind of thing."

"You know," Beverly Jackson spoke for the first time in this meeting, "it might be a good idea to get them involved in things like the flax preparations. Adding that, spinning and weaving as critical skills is planning for the future."

"Good idea," Nate was scribbling rapidly. "Hadn't even considered any of that."

"I don't want to be the downer of this little planning session," Lainie spoke up, a rare event in sessions like these, "but we need to take the girls aside and talk to them. By which I mean all of the girls who are of age or are nearly of age."

"About what?" Mitchell asked, then grunted as Beverly elbowed him in the midsection.

'What?" he demanded, looking at her. "I'm just asking!"

"You can't be that dense, dude," Tandi Maseo was chuckling. "She wants to talk to them about hygiene, and about a different kind of stranger danger I should imagine?" he asked, looking at Lainie.

"That was the idea," she nodded. "I know none of you 'guys'," she used finger quotes, "will want to hear this, but there will soon come a time when certain women's needs will be gone. We have until then to come up with a solution to that problem and have it ready to go when that happens. And that doesn't just include the girls, but all of us," she indicated the women in the group as she spoke.

"You're right," Nate said seriously. "We don't want to hear it," he grinned at her, unable to keep his straight face any longer. "But it's a valid point. With so many parents gone, someone has to fill that void. You want that job?"

"No, but it needs doing and it's my idea," Lainie sighed. "I'll deal with it," she promised.

"I will assist," Martina Sanchez promised.

"Me too," Beverly agreed. "There is something else we need to keep in mind, and that needs to be applied to your list as well," she looked toward Nate. "That is information overload. We will have to be very careful as we start all this. Ease them into it and vary the lessons. As you teach them one difficult thing, add a simple one, or even two that are easier, perhaps even fun. When you can, make it a challenge or a game, not where they compete against one another necessarily, but where they are perhaps challenged to a personal best. They need to have moments where they feel they are succeeding. If they don't see at least some winning, so to speak, they will become discouraged and start to give less than one hundred percent."

"No participation trophies for survival," Tandi remarked.

"I'm not talking about participation trophies," Beverly replied at once. "I'm talking about allowing them to build confidence in themselves. They *must* believe they can do this. You throw something too difficult at them right out of the gate, and they fail, then they will assume they will fail the next time as well. Organize your classes in a progressive order, easiest to hardest. Let them see improvement in themselves as they go along. Foster it. They'll need it."

No one disputed that statement. All could remember failures of their own and how those failures had affected them.

"This is enough for now," Nate declared, leaning forward. "Let's take the list we've got and start organizing it like Bev said. As we discover things we've missed, we can add them to the list. Now, first off, do we want to have any further breakdown in age groups? We've got…."

-

“What’s going on?” Amanda asked, looking at the crowd of people leaving Building Two. She and Kim Powers had just arrived for their training session with Xavier Adair. Zach was also there today, as well.

“The death of little Bobby has led to some changes in the education program for the children,” Xavier told her simply. “They were working to create a list of the more important things that the children must be taught for their survival. I presume they are finished, since they are departing. It is likely that they are going to be considering who will be instructing for each class and which classes are the most important to start with.”

“What are they going to teach them?” Kim asked.

“As I said, they will be teaching them how to survive,” Xavier raised an eyebrow. “Since I was not a participant in the meeting, I cannot say what, exactly, they have decided to teach, though I daresay I could make a handful of educated speculations.”

“How to identify venomous snakes, for one,” Zach stated, still looking to where the people from the meeting where moving away from the buildings.

“I have no doubt,” Xavier agreed. “None of that concerns us at that moment, however,” he turned to face his ‘students’. “Today, ladies, Zach has volunteered to be the victim as you learn better knife techniques and how to apply them.”

“I have?” Zach asked, surprised.

“You have, indeed, and we greatly appreciate it,” Xavier assured him. “Watch as I demonstrate the necessary moves for our first scenario. Remember that the exact moves I use here may or may not be needed, or possible, in whatever real-life scenario you may find yourself in. Learning these, however, will teach you to evaluate that as well, enabling you to choose your actions more effectively and, thus, make success more likely.”

“Do you always talk like that?” Amanda asked suddenly, blurting the question out without thinking.

“Like what, Miss Lowery?” Xavier asked politely.

“So…,” she struggled to think of how to describe it.

“Educated?” Xavier almost smirked. “With proper annunciation? Using correct English?”

“Yeah, Mavis,” Kim snorted behind her. “What’s wrong with how he talks?”

“Dammit, don’t call me Mavis!” Amanda snapped.

“Who or what is Mavis?” Zach asked suddenly. “This ain’t the first time I’ve heard that. And why is it such a sore spot?”

“She’s Mavis,” Kim snickered, pointing at Amanda.

“Mavis is my middle name,” Amanda told him, glaring at Kim as she spoke. “It’s an old family name, given to the first born in every generation. I was an only child, so I won that lottery.”

"What's wrong with it?" Zach asked her. "Why do you hate it?"

"I…nothing is wrong with," she replied, sighing. "I don't hate it. I don't. It's just…old fashioned. An old name that doesn't fit in with modern times. So, I don't use it. And I've asked others not to," she glared at Kim once more. "Repeatedly."

"I see nothing wrong with the name," said Xavier. "I agree it is an old name, but that simply gives it uniqueness, in my opinion. Originality. Something sorely lacking in today's times, incidentally."

"I don't see anything wrong it," Zach shrugged. "Just wondered why it garnered such a response when someone used it."

Amanda looked at each of them, trying to gauge whether they were having a joke at her expense. Neither seemed to be fighting off a grin or laughter, and both seemed entirely sincere.

"I took a lot of teasing over it when I was a child," she admitted finally. "I suppose it made me more sensitive to it than I should be. And I really don't hate it. Like I said, it's an old name in my family and I'm the one who got it. My cousins were all younger than me. I was always proud of it, and never minded it until I started getting teased about it. Mostly by other girls. Girls with names like Heather, Muffin, or maybe Kimmy," she glared at Kim one more time for good measure.

"Hey, that's a nickname," Kim laughed. "C'mon, Wheezer," she hugged Amanda suddenly. "You know I love ya more 'n my luggage," she laid on a thick southern drawl to make the old movie line ring true.

"Yeah, yeah," Amanda tried to be mad, but couldn't. "You are evil, and must be destroyed," she shot back, finishing off the scene from *Steel Magnolias* as both girls laughed.

"If you two are quite finished?" Xavier all but cleared his throat. "Now that we have solved the conundrum of who Mavis is, shall we move on?"

"Yes, sir," both girls nearly came to attention, turning serious.

"Excellent. Now, first, we look at approaching a standing enemy from the rear. A sentry, perhaps, or merely someone straggling behind his group. Ideally…."

-

"You know, this really wasn't your fault," Lainie said as she and Clay walked home.

"I suppose not," Clay admitted, nodding slightly. "Sure feels like it, though."

"I know," she lowered her head to lay on his shoulder. "You take so much on yourself, Clay. Too much, really. You aren't the only one who could or should have thought of things like that. There is a farm full of people who could have and didn't."

"That doesn't absolve me, though," he replied.

"Sharing the blame isn't absolving you, Cowboy," she raised her head again, looking at him. "It's being factual. You are not alone here. We all knew there were things that far too many of these kids didn't know, and I'm not just talking about the kids at the orphanage, either. A lot of our own kids don't know enough of those things, either. For that matter, some of the adults don't, either," she added with a wry smile.

"That's true," he agreed. "I hate this," he sighed. "I hate it has to be like this."

"We all do, but that doesn't change it, and won't help any," Lainie reminded him. "Clay, you've done a great job here. You and Leon, the twins, Gordon, all of you. You worked and worked and made a place for all of us to be safe, to preserve even a tithe of the life we had before all this started. I know this has hurt. It hurt all of us, and I think Tammy more than anyone, save maybe Jaylyn and Patricia."

"But as bad as this is, Clay, it doesn't wipe away all that good that you did getting us this far. It doesn't make what you've done, what you accomplished, any less valuable. Remember that Bobby and the others weren't even supposed to be here. Leon was the champion behind there even being an orphanage to start with if you'll recall. You were right there with him. So, stop trying to take all this blame for something that happens in nature. You literally had nothing to do with what happened. Do you blame Tammy and Callie for not watching the children close enough?"

"Of course not," Clay replied at once. "They were doing the best they could, I'm sure."

"See how quick you are to absolve the very people who were right there, while taking the blame on yourself?" Lainie closed her trap gently but effectively. "I don't blame them either, I'm just trying to make a point. There's plenty of blame to go around. Let the rest of us have a share."

Clay had no response to that, and she let him finish their walk in silence, thinking.

-

"This makes me afraid for Roberto and Rae, you know?" Martina said once she and Jose were alone.

"Of course, it does," Jose agreed with a nod. "It would any good parent, and you are an excellent parent, *mi corazón*."

"Flattery?" Martina raised an eyebrow.

"Truth," Jose corrected, hugging her close. "You're a wonderful parent. It is no surprise that you would be worried about your children after something like this."

"Is there no way to prevent this from happening again?" she asked him.

"Remember how difficult it was to prevent scorpions from entering a house in Arizona?" Jose asked her.

"Oh," realization showed on her face. "I should have known that," she admitted. "Not thinking straight as I worry, I suppose."

"Few of us do," he reassured her. "And think of it this way. For all the people here, and as far spread out as we are, this is the only time since we've been here that something of this nature has happened. According to Mister Sanders, no one on the farm has ever been bitten, either. It is just like walking through an empty lot in town, back home. 'Here there be rattlers'. Except now it's rattlers, copperheads and cottonmouths," he added with a weak smile.

"But no scorpions," she reminded him.

"Actually, they do have these little wood-," he had to stop as her hand covered his mouth.

"For today, there are no scorpions," she told him. "Give me that, even just for today."

"Fair enough," he smiled.

-

"That might have been the saddest thing I've even seen," Millie said dejectedly as she literally plopped into a chair in Operations. "I could cry again even now."

"It was a sad sight," Leon agreed. "Part and parcel of this life, though, I'm afraid," he added carefully. "But even Aunt Patricia, heck, even my grandfather can't remember the last time someone actually died from a snake bite in this area. Even without anti-venom, or with late application of the anti-venom, it's not common. Sure, it's serious and can cause all kinds of problems, but not such rapid death like Bobby suffered. Miss Jaylyn said the odds, by which she meant literal medical odds of something like this happening, are on the order of one in five thousand. Maybe a little more."

"And we got the one," Millie exhaled. "Figures."

Leon studied her for a moment, weighing what he wanted to say. Finally, he took the seat next to her, turning her slightly to look at him.

"Look," he kept his voice even. "I don't know exactly how much you know about this kind of life. I know you were a city kid, you said so yourself." She nodded her agreement at that.

"This life is hard," he told her flatly, if softly. "That's just a fact. Farm work in general is hard, dangerous work, but that's not what I'm talking about. Even in the best of times, which we all agree are behind us now, rural life like this is hard. People walk into yellowjacket nests, disturb a hornet's nest, one man rode into the water and hit a nest of mating cottonmouth snakes. We use machines that can kill you with just a second of inattention. We deal with animals that weigh as much as three thousand pounds and could kill us by just shoving us into a stall wall by accident. One guy west of here drowned in corn when he got trapped in a silo and no one could hear him scream as they filled it."

"What I'm trying to say is that this is not new," he concluded. "Not for us, anyway. I know that for a lot of you it is. My grandfather lost both his brothers before they even hit their teen years. It was common. My great-grandfather lost his little sister when she was eight. I don't think they ever were sure what killed her, just called it the flu and had done with it. This isn't really any different from that. Bobby either was allergic, which I know has happened around here at least once, or else Miss Jaylyn and Aunt Patricia are right, and the venom hit an artery and went straight to his heart. Either way, the rest of us have to get our heads on straight, because life will not pause while we grieve. It never does, but nowadays that means a whole new level of danger than it did just two years ago."

"Great pep talk, Ace," Millie sighed, trying to smile. "Really. You know just how to make a girl stop worrying."

"It's part of my charm," he smiled, albeit sadly. She reached out suddenly and hugged him tight. He felt her shake just a little as she did cry a bit more.

"Drowned in corn?" she said after a minute, her voice muffled by his shoulder. "Is that even a real thing?"

"It's also called suffocating," Leon admitted and despite the morbid subject she chuckled a bit.

"I would never have imagined that to be possible."

"Most people don't," Leon agreed as Millie sat back in her chair, drying her eyes. "Just like they don't go to the supermarket or the butcher and imagine a cow the size of Lance being the source of their steaks. I've read that the old Longhorn cattle out west would attack almost any man they caught on the ground, on foot. Cowboys who ended up on foot were at their mercy if they lost their gun."

"I've read that myself," Millie admitted. "So, what kind of snakes are there around here, and how poisonous are they?"

"Well, first off, they aren't poisonous," Leon clarified. "They're venomous. That's what makes deaths like Bobby's so rare. Around here, we see generally three kinds of…."

CHAPTER FOUR

"Can anyone tell me what this is?" Greg asked the assembled teens as he held a branch from the plant out the show the leaves and berries.

"That's a holly bush," Lila Webb replied.

"Very good, Lila," Greg smiled. Considering who her mother had been, it was no surprise that she would know her plants, berries and trees. "Why is it here, near the house like this?" he asked the group.

"It's used as a hedge, mostly," Anthony Goodrum supplied, raising his hand. "Lots of people plant them along roadsides to give them privacy. And as they grow together, they make a fairly good fence."

"All true," Greg complimented. "In fact, we're planting some along the boundary of the farm in areas where the livestock aren't allowed to roam. Why would we take that precaution?"

"The berries are poison," Lila said gently. "A few will make you very ill, but more than a handful could kill you."

"Right again, Lila," Greg praised. "I want you to take a look at the leaf, first," he told them as the group gathered closer, save for Lila, who didn't need this particular class, herself.

"Once you can identify the plant, then it doesn't matter if the berry is present or not," Greg told them. "You can identify the berry by the leaf of the bush or tree. Now, the interesting thing is that that while these berries can be deadly to us, they are a common source of food for birds and other wildlife. Sometimes people wonder why we don't destroy these plants, since they're so dangerous, but that's why."

"From a forestry perspective," Abigail Sanders mentioned as she happened by, "the plants themselves are something of a nuisance to our native species of plants, something that commercial growers ignore, unfortunately. Sorry, Greg," she waved as she carried on her way. "Just thought I'd toss that in there."

"Glad you did," he smiled at her. "Abigail worked for Forestry before the disaster, kids, and knows a lot more about that kind of threat than the rest of us would."

"Does that mean we're endangering the native plants by planting Holly along the border of the ranch?" Nathan Caudell asked, turning to look at Abigail's back. She stopped and looked back.

"No, because we're being careful and planting them only in areas where they don't border the forest. Or where the forest would be if not for the fire," she added. "Those trees will grow back, though, probably next year. When they do, the Holly won't be anywhere nearby. In a few years, the bushes and plants of all kinds and types that we're planting around us will form a natural fence that will help keep predators of all kinds away from us, and the animals."

"Neat," more than one voice mentioned at that news.

"I know, right?" Abigail smiled. "See ya, kiddos!" she waved as she turned again to head for the barn.

"Bonus lesson for today, kids," Greg told them, glancing at Abby's departing form. "Remember what she said, though, because it's important and we just may test you on it."

Groans accompanied the threat, to which he laughed and waved for them to follow him.

"Onward!"

-

"What do we do if we find something like this?" Lainie asked, smiling as she pointed to a rifle lying in the floor.

"Go tell a grown up!" a group of small voices replied.

"That's right," Lainie praised. "What about finding something like this?" she pointed to a butcher's knife, lying on the table in front of them.

"Go tell a grown up!" the reply was stronger this time.

"Great job!" she praised them again. "But let's say that someone asks you to hand the knife to them. What do you do then?"

No one spoke right away, so Lainie picked one child out of the crowd.

"Jac, will you go first?" she smiled at Jacqueline Sidell, Jake's daughter.

"I would say I'm not supposed to touch the knife," Jac replied, her voice steady if a bit subdued at being called out in front of everyone.

"Exactly!" Lainie beamed, heaping praise on Jac after putting her on the spot. "That's exactly right. Now," she looked at the class once more. "There may be times when someone you know, and trust, tells you to hand them the knife, that they need it and can't reach it. First, who could that be? How would you know that you could trust them?"

"It has to be someone in our group," Roberto Sanchez told her. "Someone that we know belongs here and has permission to use the knife."

"Very good, Roberto," Lainie smiled. "Very good. Everyone understand that? It has to be someone you know belongs here. Someone that has permission to use the knife. How do we know who that is?"

"If we can't s'posed to give them a knife, they'll be 'Danger'," Rae Sanchez piped up, determined not to be outdone by her brother. While she didn't speak as clearly as Roberto had, her point had been made. 'Danger' was the one-word title given to anyone that the children were not supposed to associate with. While it was unlikely that such an individual would be allowed to remain on the farm, the plan was to teach the children for every occasion.

"Very good, Rae," Lainie nodded. "But, everybody, what if it's someone we don't know?"

"Stranger, Danger!" every little voice cried out, and Lainie clapped excitedly for them.

"Yes! Very good! All of you! Now, I think you've all earned a cookie! What do you think?"

The cheers were louder this time.

-

"Abby," Greg Holloway said, walking up to Abigail Sanders. She looked up from where she was working on one of her family's tractors. Greg almost laughed at the smudge of grease along her forehead and down her left cheek.

"What?" Abby demanded, seeing him stifle a laugh.

"I just always forget what a tomboy type you are," he told her, leaning on a work bench along the wall of the shed. "Then I see you doing something like this, and your face covered in grease, and I remember you grew up chasing cows and driving tractors and bulldozers, and I can remember."

"Ha, ha," she almost muttered. "If you just came by to make fun-,"

"I'm not making fun, Abby," Greg promised, shaking his head. "I meant it as a compliment. You are far prettier than the average tomboy, and you usually work enough for two people. There's nothing about that to make fun of, I promise."

Blushing furiously at being called pretty by one of Clay's friends, Abby made a show of putting down the tools and parts she was working with and then took a rag and wiped her face and hands.

"Well," she looked at him once she was finished, "if you aren't here to poke fun at me, then what can I do for you?"

"You can teach the forestry class to the older kids," he said without any preamble. "I don't know why someone didn't think to ask you before. No matter how much some of the rest of us know, you know more. It's your trade, after all. I want you to teach the teens, at least, everything you can about trees, bushes and the ecology that goes along with them. The importance of having healthy plants and trees, and what that means to us. To them. And to the wildlife around us."

"I don't have time for that kind of crap," Abby was shaking her head. "And no one will want me teaching their kids, anyway, after the way I showed my ass when Sam and I were taking care of the kids at the Troy House. I screwed up over there, big time."

"That was a while back, Abby," Greg noted. "And you've done a lot for this place since then. Including organizing and leading the effort to save us from the wildfire. That counts for a lot, seems to me."

"It might," she nodded slowly, not looking at him. "I haven't checked, and don't intend to. I'd rather just forget all that, to be honest. But don't you forget that I just tromped all over Jody with my fat mouth, too. I admit I was mad when I did it, and I wasn't listening to him, but I still did it. So again, no one is going to want me teaching their children anything, I would imagine."

"Tell you what," he said suddenly, standing up straight. "You come with me tomorrow and teach the class yourself. I'll just hang around, maybe say something every now and again. See how you like it and see how the kids respond. It may be that you can't stand one another for all I know. Don't forget that the twins, JJ, Janice and Millie are all figured in there, somewhere."

"Great," Abby snorted. "With a lineup like that, no wonder you want to pass it off to someone else."

"I know, right?" Greg laughed. "But the real reason is because you're better qualified than I am, and because of my job as Sheriff. I really don't have the time to be occupied with a class like that and still do my new job. I've got too much to get organized as it is. But let's face it, Abby. You're damned near a forest ranger yourself. Probably only needed to finish a degree in something they'd accept to get there, weren't you?"

"Yeah," she sighed deeply at the loss of something so important. "The Old Man had promised me he would pull the strings to get me hired, but only if I could qualify for it on my own. But I would have insisted on that anyway," she shrugged. "I might accept the help to get a position, but not to qualify for it."

"That says a lot about you right there," he assured her. "Most people with access to Leon like that would demand that he just get them a job. You didn't." He paused, about to say something else, but she beat him to it, not realizing he was about to speak.

"Why do you have that kind of confidence in me?" she asked, looking at the ground beneath her. "I've screwed up time and again since all this started, Greg. Some of them were spectacular, too. And not all of them were just personal, either. Some of them hurt other people. If I were putting it in words that you and Clay would use, I'm a fuck-up. A big one at that."

"Why is that, Abby?" he asked her. She had unknowingly walked right into the discussion he wanted to have.

"Big mouth, impatience, arrogance, bad temper, take your pick," Abby was shaking her head. "I'm the whole package," she tried to joke, but it didn't help.

"Sounds like a pity party, Abby," he told her seriously. "What do you do when your tractor gets stuck?" he asked her before she could get wound up over his statement.

"I get it unstuck," she told him flatly. "But that's not the same-,"

"It's exactly the same," he cut her off firmly. "You fucked up. Your words, not mine. I'm sure Clay said it, too. Not my business, but I do know him. But just because you did it before, doesn't mean you have to keep doing it, Abby. It sounds like you know what your weaknesses are. If you know what's wrong with that tractor," he pointed to the machine she was working on, "do you just keep trying to use it the way it is?"

"No," she scrubbed at her face tiredly with her hands, leaving smudge marks along her face once again.

"You fix it, don't you," he stated rather than asked. "Just like you're doing right now. You already know where your problems are. You just pointed them out to me. Now, you don't work for me and I don't have any authority over you whatsoever, so this is just free advice, okay? Start fixing it. Ignore what's happened before and move forward. What already happened is done and gone, and you can't go back and change it. So, forget it. It's done. Move on. Concentrate instead on making the changes you need to make and on moving yourself forward."

"If you want to improve your standing among parents, then you can start by teaching their kids things they need to know," he continued. "Things they will carry into the future with them. Get a grip on your mouth, your temper, put your arrogance away for good, and learn the patience you need to make the changes you want. This is as good a place to start as any, and better than most. This is something that needs to happen for these kids to have a chance in this brave new world we're living in. You have an opportunity here to influence that, and to make a meaningful contribution that even your Uncle Clay will have to acknowledge, along with every other person on this farm, whether they like it or not."

"You think on that while you finish making sure that tractor can move forward into the future," he concluded, already walking slowly away. "If you decide I'm right, then meet me and the kids at Building Two tomorrow at ten o'clock. And if you do decide to do it, I will support you in every way I can, so long as you give it one hundred percent and don't give the kids attitude. Your call, though."

With that, he was gone, leaving Abby looking after him. She sat down, back leaning against a tractor tire, considering all that he had said.

She had always liked Greg. Had even harbored a crush on him for almost as long as she could recall. If the truth were told, she still did. While she had strong feelings for Jody, or once had at least, that tiny little flame for Greg still flickered even now, probably the cause of her blushing embarrassment when he called her pretty a few minutes before. She had never dared speak of it to anyone, lest Clay or Gordy find out and make her miserable over it.

The fact that Greg thought she would be able to contribute in such an important way was very meaningful to her. Abby knew that she had been a first class screwup since the Storm, or at least since soon after it. She regretted that, regretted the problems she had caused as well, but they were pretty spectacular screwups and she had never found a way to correct them.

Added to that was her equally spectacular breakup with Jody Thompson. If it could be called a breakup since they had never actually been a couple other than in name. She had made no secret of how she had managed to completely offend Jody, though as far as she was aware, he had spoken of it only to her father. Still, it was common knowledge, and Jody was well liked by most everyone on the farm, even by those who were afraid of him. The fact that she had hurt him would not have endeared her to any and would have alienated more than a few of them. Again.

Rubbing her face again, heedless of the stains she was leaving on her face, she took a deep breath, which ended up being released in a sob. The sound caught her by surprise as her throat constricted and her tears began to flow. The pain of thinking of all the mistakes she had made, the results of those mistakes, all that it had cost her and sometimes cost others around her, hammered at her with a force she had never encountered and she was unable to stop it.

Lying down on the hard ground beneath her, packed solid from years of heavy equipment moving across it, Abigail curled into a ball, pulling herself nearly into a fetal position, and began to cry in earnest, completely unable to control the action now that it had started. She couldn't remember the last time she had cried, let alone come completely undone as she had now.

She didn't know how long she remained there, replaying errors of every kind over and over in her memory, mindful that very few of them had been accidental or unintentional. Looking back, it seemed as if she had never cared what her actions might mean to others, or what impact they might have on the people around her.

She had always had confidence in her own abilities, probably too much so in many cases. That confidence, even when justified, had still led to her arrogant attitude. She was smart, strong and confident, and that had led her down a path where, in her eyes, she could never be wrong. Her decision-making skills were excellent; therefore, her decisions were always correct.

Arrogance, thy name is Abigail Sanders.

"Oh, God, how stupid can I be?" she said quietly even as she continued to sob. "I should be smart enough to know better! What is *wrong* with me?"

"What *is* wrong with you?" a new voice asked gently, and Abby sat up like a bolt, instantly rubbing at her raw face. Through tear dimmed eyes she saw Lainie Harper, of all people, crouching beside her, face creased with concern.

"Abby, are you hurt?" Lainie asked. "Are you injured?"

"Just my pride," Abby tried to play it off, moving to get to her feet. A firm hand on her shoulder kept her seated, however, as Lainie continued to look her over.

"Abby, this is more than pride," Lainie said quietly. "If I had to guess, I'd think you were on the edge of a breakdown, if not already into one. Do you want to talk about it?"

"No," Abby said flatly. "I don't."

"Fair enough," Lainie didn't push her. "But will you at least take a suggestion? One from someone who has suffered pretty much the same kind of break?"

"Sure," Abby snorted. "Got nothing to lose. Right?"

"Crying like this is a good stress relief, Abby," Lainie surprised her. "I know it seems like a weakness, but don't believe it. Letting all that pent-up stress and emotion out like this is good for you. Therapeutic in a way that few things are. Don't be afraid or ashamed to let those problems go, okay? And if you ever think you need someone to talk to about whatever it is, I can always listen without saying anything. I'm not Beverly, but I can at least listen."

"I doubt Beverly would talk to me, anyway," Abby tried to laugh but it didn't sound right to her own ears. "I don't blame her, either. I have no idea what is wrong with me!" she cried suddenly. Had it been loud it would have qualified as a wail, but instead it was merely a quiet, desperate sob.

"You know, Abby," Lainie's voice was gentle, "the world did just pretty much come apart at the seams not long ago. Most of our hopes, our dreams, are all gone now. Left behind in a burst of sunlight that took away almost everything. Maybe it's not what's wrong with you, but just how it's affected you. That's not the same thing, really."

"I was always over-confident," Abby was shaking her head. "Arrogant to a fault. I didn't, maybe couldn't, see it until now, but it was there."

"Abby, you were working in a position dominated by men," Lainie replied. "For a woman working in those conditions, I would think that confidence would be a requirement. I can't imagine what a woman as attractive as you are went through at the hands of all male crews like that, from sly remarks all the way up to actual physical harassment. You can't tell me that didn't happen, or that it didn't leave a mark on you, either."

Abby had already opened her mouth to reply when she pulled herself up short. Lainie had made a strong point, and while the older woman couldn't know it for sure, it had been accurate. She couldn't recall how many times a man had slapped her ass as he walked by her at the scene of a fire. While they did it to each other as well, it had been obvious that more than one of them had gone out of their way to make sure they were close enough to make that contact with her.

She had been called everything from tomboy to dyke because she had chosen to work in a field traditionally reserved for men. Never mind that she was better at it than many of the men were, or that she had proven time and again that she definitely had what it took to drive right into the face of a wildfire and do what had to be done. Despite that, it was a constant battle just to be acknowledged and accepted in her position, let alone given the due she had earned. Not just deserved but *earned.* Earned fighting fires and cutting trees and driving heavy equipment and so many other things that her job with Forestry had demanded.

No. It had never been easy. For all that she had enjoyed her job, even loved it, really, it had never been easy. Before the Storm, she had just accepted that as the normal state of things and always would be. Had taken whatever abuse had been doled out and laughed at it, since showing any other kind of reaction would merely invite more of the same.

"No, it happened," she finally replied, wiping her eyes even as she nodded. "I took it because I wanted to do that kind of work, and if I said anything it would have been ignored, even held against me. They were afraid to do very much because of the Old Man, but even he couldn't stop everything like that. So, I took it. I wanted to be a forest ranger, and I wanted it bad enough that I took it."

"And never said a word about it, I bet," Lainie said firmly. "That stress had been building on you for years, honey. Add to that all this," she waved her arm to encompass their present circumstance, "and that's quite an overload on you. It had to stop somewhere, and apparently this is it. What happened to bring this on? If you don't mind me asking or knowing."

"Greg asked me to teach forestry to the kids," Abby told her with a shrug.

"That's it?" Lainie showed surprise for the first time.

"I told him that as badly as I had screwed up in the last year, I doubted anyone wanted me teaching their kids anything," Abby barked a short laugh. "It started me thinking about everything I had done wrong in the last year, whether by accident or just because I wouldn't listen, or because I knew more than anyone else, or whatever," she made a shoving motion with her hand.

"We all make mistakes, Abby," Lainie pointed out. "It's not the mistakes you make that define you. It's what you do afterward. How you come back from them."

"How do I come back from how I acted with those kids at the Troy House?" Abby asked. "I didn't mean to do anything wrong. I didn't even realize what I was doing, exactly. I was angry and I wasn't paying attention. And how do I come back from what happened to John Barnes? And now from what happened between me and Jody? How do I 'move forward' after all that, Lainie?" She sounded almost desperate. As if she were pleading with Lainie to provide an answer.

The redhead sat down beside her, stretching her long legs out before her.

"Crouching down like that was getting to me," she smiled at Abby. "And how do you come back? From any of it? Just like you've been doing it, Abby. Hard work and a better attitude. More than one person had commented on how you were trying to walk a better road, so to speak. With John Barnes, I thought that had already been put to rest, no pun intended. Your behavior at the Troy House I would think you made up for with saving the ranch and our homes from the fire. There's no way we would have done that without your help and hard work, Abby. While we might have saved the homes and probably the barns, we couldn't have saved the fields, and maybe not all the livestock. You did good. Really good." She paused, looking at Abby closely.

"As for you and Jody?" she said finally, then shrugged. "Shit happens, kiddo. Sometimes we do it to ourselves, sometimes others do it to us. If you and Jody had that big of a blow-up, then maybe you weren't right for each other to start with, you know? It was plain that there were a lot of cultural differences the two of you would have to overcome as a couple. Maybe the fact that this happened was because it was too much to do."

"Or maybe it was because I have a big mouth and I'm too eager to take offense to even the simplest things," Abby replied. "It's almost as if I'm not the one doing it, sometimes. Like I'm standing outside, watching it happen, knowing it's wrong or going to go wrong, and still can't stop it. Like I can't control it."

"Is that why you've been avoiding the rest of us lately?" Lainie asked gently.

"Pretty much," Abby nodded. "I may not can manage to have a simple, civil conversation, but I can work. I can get things done that need doing. So, I do those things as a way to make my own contribution to this place. To do my part to keep us going. 'Moving forward' as more than one person has said to me," she almost snorted.

"Yeah, I've heard that one a lot, myself," Lainie sighed. "It's easy to say if you haven't had a rough ride or walk, but it's not so easy if you're trying to come back from the edge. Sometimes people who say that don't honestly know. I'm sure it sounds good to their ears, though," she smiled a bit sadly. "There's nothing worse than good intentions that go bad places."

"Never heard that one before," Abby almost smiled. "Makes a lot of sense, though."

"You think you might teach the kids about the woods?" Lainie asked her. "I mean, I sure can't do it. I don't know any of it myself. I can tell a pine tree from others, and a cedar tree by how it looks, but that's about it, to be honest."

"They aren't real cedar trees, you know," Abby said absently. "Not the ones around here, anyway. They're a type of cypress, for the most part. Cedars, true cedars I mean, aren't native to this region. There's a state park east of Nashville called Cedars of Lebanon that has a stand of transplanted cedars from Lebanon itself, where they are native. I doubt you care anything about hearing this," she laughed suddenly. "Sorry. I get carried away with that, sometimes."

"Which makes you perfect for the job," Lainie shrugged. "I honestly had no idea. I've been to that park and should have noticed that. I just went there for a picnic and a day off. I could have learned something if I'd applied myself."

"Most people never need to know anything like that," Abby said simply.

"For me it's never about whether I need to know," Lainie shook her head. "I *want* to know. I've always pushed myself to learn things, new things, wherever I could. I was always pushing, driving to make myself better. To make a better life for myself. Of course, as soon as I got it, the sun fell on me," she chuckled. "Had I known that was coming I guess I could have partied a little more, you know?" she grinned at her 'niece'.

"You don't really regret it, do you?" Abby asked her.

"Of course not," Lainie smiled. "And it wasn't as if it was wasted. Do I miss my old life?" she asked, leaning back on the large tire with Abby. "Yeah, I do. I miss going out. I miss being able to drive my car around the bypass. I miss the restaurants, the shows, the freedom of a big town that always has something to do. I miss it all, really," she sighed heavily. "I especially miss sharing all that with Clay. But I came out of it with something way better. There are a lot of people still there that are wishing they could trade places with me, assuming they're still alive. According to Adcock that's a big assumption, too. So, I can't really complain about how things worked out, can I? Yeah, it was a lot of hard work to get where I was, only to lose it just as I got there, but I did it. And, I made a lot of money, which I managed to spend getting myself set up decently before the lights went out. Not many of the people behind me can say that, either."

"I can't remember sometimes what I was working for," Abby admitted. "I worked at my job with Forestry, I worked here on this farm, I helped Uncle Ronny sometimes with his side business, I went to school in my 'spare time'," she made finger quotes for that one. "It seemed as if I never slowed down for anything. If I wasn't working in one place, there was work waiting for me somewhere else. I enjoyed it, don't get me wrong," she clarified, "but it was something all the time. Always."

"But I am so lucky," she continued, her voice softer now. "Look at how important my home is now. And how fortunate am I to be here and be a part of it? There are people who are starving, or else doing horrible things to keep from starving, and I'm not. True, I'm earning it. I work hard and not even my folks have to give me anything, but I still am blessed to be here." She took a deep breath and released it, almost as if clearing her soul along with her lungs.

"Feel better?" Lainie asked, smiling ever so slightly.

"I really do," Abby told her, a smile blooming across her own face. "I really do."

"Good," Lainie patted the younger woman on the thigh. "Remember, what happened is in the past. Leave it there and look ahead. That's where you're going. Stop looking at where you've been."

"How many times have you said that to the mirror?" Abby asked suddenly, studying the older woman closely.

"I don't know," Lainie admitted. "Lost count when I was about your age, I guess." She got to her feet, dusting herself off, then offered a hand to Abby, who took it after the briefest of hesitations.

"It was nice of you to help me," Abby said softly, looking at the ground. "I wasn't any better to you than to anyone else. Worse even, sometimes. You didn't owe me any kindness."

"Oh, stop that," Lainie punched Abby's shoulder very lightly. "We're family, more or less. I've always heard that family treats one another worse than friends. We do it that way because we always know that family will forgive us, where friends don't. I didn't have much of a family before I came here," Lainie admitted. "Never got to see that in action until I met your uncle."

"He really loves you, you know," Abby said suddenly. "And you are really good for him. Better than Sam would have been. That was somewhere else I butted in when I shouldn't have. Thinking I knew better. I practically pushed Sam at Clay, trying to play match maker."

"Well, I hate to disparage your efforts, but I am glad you failed," Lainie smiled at her.

"Yeah, so is Sam," Abby nodded. "She told me a while back that she didn't think she could handle Clay as well as you seem to be able to. To deal with his issues. She was talking about watching him lash out when you woke him from a nap or where he'd just dozed off for a minute."

"That can be challenging," Lainie admitted. "You just have to have patience to wait it out, and faith that he will recognize you before he does anything."

"I doubt I could do that, either," Abby admitted. "I don't think I'd have the courage."

"Then maybe it was better for you and Jody to end things where you did," Lainie shrugged. "Maybe not the way you did," she clarified, "but where. Jody would be likely to have the same issues that the rest seem to have."

"Yeah," Abby nodded slowly. "Funny. I never once considered that. I should have, shouldn't I?"

"Not necessarily," Lainie shook her head. "You never know, Abby. Sometimes, people fit together regardless of their differences or their individual problems. If you hadn't made the effort, then you'd always wonder if you and Jody could have been an item. Now, you know. It might not be the answer you wanted, or wished for, but you do have an answer. That's more than a lot of people ever get. Examine it, learn from it, and move on. Don't stop moving, or growing, Abby. You owe it to yourself if no one else." She paused for a minute, thinking.

"Would you mind if I came along on this class you're teaching?" she asked finally.

"I haven't decided I'll teach it yet," Abby replied.

"Yeah, you have," Lainie smiled brightly. "I have an Audubon guide to eastern trees, but I've never had much time to study. I'd love to learn, and it sounds like I could learn from you. But I don't want to be a problem for you. Would you mind me tagging along and taking your class?"

"No," Abby conceded the point. "No, I don't mind at all. It might be fun, even."

"It just might be," Lainie smiled again. "I'll see you in the morning!"

CHAPTER FIVE

"-that's why these trees, which we often incorrectly refer to as cedars, are so popular for making bedroom furniture and lining closets," Abby told the class. "In sharp contrast, however, oak and walnut, two hardwoods," she held an example of each one, along with a leaf from each tree, "are preferable for other furniture, such as dining tables and chairs, and entertainment centers. Not only does the wood look beautiful, but it's strong and resistant to damage."

"What are the logs we're building houses out of?" Nathan Caudell asked. "They don't look anything like those," he pointed to the examples Abby was using.

"For the most part, we're using white and yellow pine," Abby replied, pointing to two other examples on the bench in front of her. "Thanks to the twins," she smiled at her cousins, "we have the wilderness sawmills, so we're actually cutting the trees into square beams for building rather than simply using the logs as we find them. It's much easier to seal the houses that way and provides a warmer home in winter."

"What about this one?" Lila asked, pointing to another sample.

"That's a cypress," Abby informed her. "These trees are very rot resistant, and so is the lumber made from them. Part of that is probably because they have to be in standing water at least part of the year in order to grow. The finished wood is also incredibly attractive which is another reason this wood is a popular building medium. It's also popular for siding as well, particular using the board and batten method of siding."

"Why is that?" Anthony Goodrum asked, looking at the wood closely.

"I suspect it's mostly due to the pleasing appearance, to be honest," Abby admitted. "But the fact that cypress is so highly resistant to rot most likely plays a part as well." She paused to see if there were any other questions before continuing.

"Okay, uses for building materials aside, trees are also a source of food," she started into a new area. "We all know that apples, peaches, pears and other fruits come from trees, but did you know…."

-

"Thank you, Miss Sanders, for such a good class," Seth Webb managed not to stammer. His face was fire-engine red as he spoke to Abby, and his sister Lila was laughing at him as quietly as possible. It was clear that Seth had developed a crush on 'Miss Sanders' somewhere along the way, and today's class had merely added fuel to that fire.

"Why, thank you, Mister Webb," Abby smiled at him, sending the teen's face yet another shade deeper. "I'm glad you liked it." Lila drug him away before he could embarrass himself further, laughing at him as she did so.

"Thank you, Miss Sanders," Greg waited until the kids were out of hearing before teasing Abby. "For such a good class. You sure are pretty," he added, batting his eyes rapidly at her, and now it was Abby's turn to blush beet red.

"Stop it," Lainie hit Greg's arm lightly with the back of her hand. "No fair teasing. And it was a good class, Abby. I honestly had no idea about the cedars, what we call cedars, anyway, being moth repellant. I always thought it was used because people like the smell."

"Some do use it for that, I guess," Abby nodded, still blushing from Greg Holloway's teasing.

"Well, are you glad you decided to give this a try?" Greg asked her, turning serious for a moment.

"I guess," Abby managed not to stammer as Greg looked at her directly. "I mean, it wasn't a bad experience. All the kids seem to want to learn, and they asked good questions, too."

"I told you that you'd do fine," Greg said firmly.

"You really did do a good job," Lainie agreed. "And it was apparent that all the kids like you. Some more than others, maybe," she winked, deciding to tease Abby a bit herself over Seth Webb's stammering compliment.

"Thanks," Abby grinned at the light-natured teasing. "And yeah, I did enjoy it, at least a bit," she told Greg. "It was nice to be talking about something I know, and to be sharing it with kids who want and need to learn it."

"So, does that mean you'll keep on being 'Miss Sanders' maybe one or two days a week?" Greg asked her. "It's not just this group of kids, either. There's the younger group of kids, who will need a different lesson plan, and then there are adults who don't know anything about trees and woods, either. Everyone is supposed to be learning."

"I can do that," Abby nodded. "It will make a good break from other work if nothing else. And it will still be contributing to the farm. I can try it and see if it will work. Though I still doubt that anyone over at the Troy Farm will want me teaching their kids after what happened with the baby-sitting thing. For that matter, some of the adults may not be interested in learning from me, either. I don't know."

"Well, it's either learn from you, or do without as far as I'm concerned," Greg told her flatly. "I realize there were issues, but you have more than made up for that and we've all made mistakes and said or done things we wish we hadn't. You didn't hurt anyone, and you weren't trying to hurt anyone, either. Anyone who wants to stay ignorant can feel free to skip it if they want. Their loss."

"Thanks," Abby murmured, once again blushing to the roots of her hair it felt like.

"Well, I have to go," Greg said suddenly. "Sheriff type things to do. Thanks for taking this over, Abby. You've already done a better job than me," he smiled. "See you two later on," he waved, already moving away. Lainie watched him get out of earshot before turning back to Abby.

"You've got it bad for him, don't you?" she said seriously.

"What? No!" Abby spluttered, making a show of gathering her props and displays that she had used for the class. "That's silly."

"I'm sure," Lainie snorted. "I know the signs, girl. How long have you been nursing a crush on him?"

"I can't remember," Abby admitted, not bothering to deny it again. "Seriously," she added when Lainie looked at her with a raised eyebrow. "Seems like forever."

"Well, it's not like he's a great deal older than you," Lainie mentioned. "I mean, Clay's only what? Seven, maybe eight years older than you are?"

"Yeah," Abby sighed. "About that."

"Hm," Lainie hummed. "Well, like I said yesterday. Maybe things blew up between you and Jody because you weren't going to make it. Or," she drew the word out, "because there was something better for you, somewhere."

"He's got a girlfriend, you know," Abby laughed, considering Lainie's words to be teasing. "But thanks for the thought."

"I don't think they're to the point of being a couple, exactly," Lainie tilted her head as she smiled at Abby. "Anyway, I really did like the class," she changed the subject abruptly. "I think I'll keep attending with the teens instead of the adults if that's okay. You might actually need the help at some point."

"Okay," Abby smiled. "I'd like that."

-

It was a week before Halloween, and Clay happened to be lounging out front at the Building Two hang-out when Lake Adcock arrived, leading a small group of vehicles. Two trucks and a MRAP veered away to pull into the new soldier's barracks while Adcock's Hummer pulled up on to the pad in front of Clay. The Captain got out of the vehicle, accompanied by a young woman wearing the yellow bar of a 2nd Lieutenant. The driver got out and leaned against the Hummer, stretching.

"Welcome, Captain," Clay smiled, standing to shake Adcock's hand. "Arriving a little ahead of schedule?"

"We're at a lull for the time being," Adcock nodded. "Things are quiet for the moment, so we decided to get things started early. Clay Sanders, this is 2nd Lieutenant Carla Gaines. Lieutenant, this is Clayton Sanders. He and his family own this farm, and he and his men are all former service. Good people, too."

"Mister Sanders," Gaines extended her hand. "It's a pleasure to meet you, sir. The Captain has nothing but good things to say about you and your group."

"So, the bribe's working, then?" Clay chuckled, taking her hand. She had a firm, business-like handshake.

"Bribe is definitely working," Gaines laughed in return. "There has been a slight change in how things will be laid out, Mister Sanders," she turned straight to business. "Sergeant Gleason will still be assigned here, but the actual number of men billeted here will be twelve rather than sixteen. Three fire teams, plus Gleason."

"Thirteen?" Clay raised an eyebrow. "Unlucky number."

"Just a wives' tale," Gaines shook her head. "Gleason's rank is actually a bit high for a squad command, but I understand that deal was made with the Captain before my arrival. We plan to have twenty men in Jordan, which is where I will have my headquarters, so to speak. Basically, that means me and an RTO, although there's almost no need for his services. He will double as a clerk of sorts for the group, although again, there isn't much clerking to do, either."

"Sounds like a lonely job," Clay smiled. "You guys sit down," he waved to the chairs, taking his seat back as they took seats of their own. "You will be glad to hear that the new Sheriff has established a patrol and sworn in new deputies," he turned his attention to Adcock. "He's also using his patrol as a message board for the area. He knows who has what for sale or trade, and relays that information to interested parties. If it's a large trade, then we'll try to lend a hand with a truck to get things moved. It makes him look good and helps establish a bond between the new Sheriff's Patrol and the people who usually run into hiding when they see him coming."

"Why would they run?" Gaines asked, frowning. "Are they doing something wrong?"

"They've had a hard time here, Lieutenant," Adcock replied before Clay could. "It was in your briefing paper. First with the former department, then with a corrupt civilian authority, and finally with a fake military authority. Those who have survived, and there aren't nearly as many as there should be, are understandably hesitant to go through that again. Re-establishing that trust was one of the many tasks given Sheriff Holloway by Major Whitten."

"I'll need to meet him, and these deputies," Gaines said. "Things like hiring deputies will need to go through me, now."

Clay sighed deeply at that, shaking his head slowly. Adcock's face went red with apparent anger as he turned to face Gaines.

"Lieutenant," he said calmly. "Did you read the briefing material you were provided? About this entire area, but specifically about this area of Calhoun?"

"I skimmed over it as we made the trip out here," Gaines replied. "Sir," she added.

"First of all, Sheriff Holloway was the last surviving member of the former Sheriff's Department," Adcock informed her. "Secondly, he was appointed by the Major himself, and tasked not only with trying to reestablish order here, but also to regain the public's trust. Third, we are rather beholden to Mister

Sanders and his entire group, of which the Sheriff and his new deputies are a part. Finally, Lieutenant, you are not the administrator for this area. I am. Your position here as commander of the detachment and my emergency designee does not make you the authority here."

"You should be aware, having worked in the headquarters area since this began, that the Major is determined to reestablish civilian authority in every possible area as soon as humanly possible. Some areas never lost it while others, like Calhoun, had it fall apart completely. But the goal is for civilian authority to be the norm in every location. So no, hiring deputies, nor any activity for that matter, will not need to go through you in the future. Your primary reason for being here is to command the detachment placed here to assist the Sheriff in maintaining order and protecting the populace, and to help with patrolling the area, should the Sheriff ask or need you to."

"You and your detachment will also help the town of Jordan in training their militia group to a higher standard with joint exercises as well as joint patrols, helping their militia members to gain experience that will make them better able to defend their own and people in the event of another attack by raiders or the like. All of this was spelled out quite clearly in your briefing documents and op order. If you aren't able to decipher them, then I may need to assign you to my own detachment in Lewiston and move Lieutenant Gillis up here to work with the good people of Calhoun. I suggest that you go and get your orders and spend some time reviewing them and perhaps even wander over to observe as Sergeant Gleason organizes the unpacking of his men and their gear. Note that I say observe, not supervise. Sergeant Gleason is more than capable of doing his job without your help. Dismissed."

Gaines, red-faced from the dressing down, got to her feet, came to attention and snapped a salute, which Adcock returned almost lazily. With that, the young woman almost stalked to the Hummer.

"Sorry," Adcock looked as if he wanted to beat his head against the table. "It's not just her," he added before Clay could speak. "All of the younger officers and many of the younger NCOs have a misguided idea of what the martial law declaration has done. I don't know who has been filling them so full, but I imagine when the Major finally discovers who it is, he will fall on them like a ton of bricks. He has no interest whatsoever in establishing any kind of military society or anything else in this area. He wants to see a return to civilian government as soon as possible. That does not include having 2nd Lieutenants with delusions of grandeur deciding who can be civilian law enforcement, either," he snorted, shaking his head.

"It'll work out," Clay shrugged. "She's got to learn, just like the rest of us did. She's just got a lot different classroom than we had. That's all."

"Your patience is appreciated," Adcock assured him. "I really will take her to Lewiston if I have to and send Gillis up here. He's still a 2nd Lieutenant as well, but has his head screwed on straight. The reason I had him with me was because Flores was senior. Now, with Flores gone, I'm short one area commander. Gaines was going to be my new lieutenant, so I'm unlikely to get another. I will likely have to send Gillis over to Moore County and use Maxwell as my second down in Lewiston."

"Well, I don't know Gillis, but I would imagine Maxwell can handle his part just fine," Clay observed. "He strikes me as an excellent Top Soldier."

"He is," Adcock agreed. "Honestly, Gleason is just as competent. He doesn't have the rank simply because he dropped rank to join the Guard after he retired RA. It's usually not done, since retired is retired, but someone, somewhere, made an exception for him. His record is redacted in a lot of places, and even my security wasn't high enough to read it. We're beyond fortunate to have them both."

"Sometimes you get lucky," Clay nodded. "As for redaction, my record probably stops after four years. For all I know I was listed as KIA," he snorted.

"Well, there's redacted, and then there's redacted," Adcock huffed a laugh. "There's a major difference between being on an operation that is still classified and being part of black program that will never be formally acknowledged."

"True that," Clay agreed.

"How did you end up there, anyway?" Adcock asked. "Assuming you can share and don't mind my asking."

"I fit the profile," Clay shrugged. "Didn't visit home often or at all, or else had no home other than the Army. Good skills in the field, weak moral compass, ability to operate with a minimum of instruction or supervision, and dumb enough to say yes," he ended with a laugh.

"So, it was volunteer?"

"I guess," Clay shrugged again, this time with only his left shoulder. "I was visited by a Mister Smith while on leave in Kuwait. You probably met his cousin or brother or something at least once when you were on Iraq, considering you worked in intel," he chuckled and Adcock laughed lightly, nodding his head in agreement.

"They put the team together, made me a 2nd Lieutenant and inserted me as the XO. Six months later, give or take, I was promoted to 1st Lieutenant and placed in command of the team. I expected to stay in Afghanistan or Iraq, but that didn't happen. I've been everywhere *but* there it seemed like. Not that I cared, really. Just surprised us is all."

"How did that work, anyway?" Adcock asked. "Did you get tasked to individual missions or targets, or just get a general order of some kind?"

"Both, depending on where you were and what was happening," Clay replied. "We had the autonomy to check out anything we found suspicious but would occasionally get a frag to look for someone or something. Twice it was to rescue Americans being held hostage in the Philippines. I think the Rangers got credit for the first one and the Philippine Army for the second. We were tasked to a third group, but the hostages were murdered before we could get to the area. After that, our orders changed to hunting down those responsible and eliminating them. Took us about two weeks to get them all."

"Two weeks," Adcock shook his head slowly. "You guys really are something."

"Once the rules don't apply, it's a lot easier to get things done," Clay pointed out. "Speaking of rules, we should probably get Greg over here so you and he can establish what you guys want from each other or can do for each other. I know he said something about finding a moonshine operation that might be good for a fuel additive to stretch your fuel stocks."

"Sounds good," Adcock agreed, recognizing that this was Clay's way of ending the conversation about his past. It didn't offend him or surprise him. He had skipped over one of the most important requirements for an operation like his.

The ability to keep a secret.

-

Amanda Lowery looked down at Zach Willis, holding her rubber training knife to his throat, her eyes shining with victory.

"Got you!" she crowed, positively beaming. "Finally!"

"I suggest you check your abdomen, Miss Lowery," Xavier said softly. Losing her smile, Amanda looked down to see Zach's rubber knife poised to strike her just below her sternum, about where her left lung would be.

"This one would be a draw, I'm afraid," Xavier told her. "It is, however, the first time you have managed even that. I would have to count that as a victory, in your position."

"Me too," Zach nodded. "You did good," he told Amanda as he got to his feet.

"But I still lost," she sighed, slapping her thigh with the training blade. "Damn, I really thought I had you, that time."

"You did," Zach assured her. "I just managed to get where I could get a hit on you, too. But your vest would likely stop a blade from penetrating. Most enemies we face aren't wearing them, though, and don't forget I'm training here, too. So, that's what I would do in that situation. You may get me, but I'm taking you with me," he shrugged. His casual tone almost made her shiver, but she stopped it.

"Exactly correct," Xavier agreed. "We are all training, here, including me. Remember when you first found us, Amanda. What were we doing?"

"Training," Amanda nodded, recalling that day not so long ago when she had asked to join them.

"I must practice my own skills, or risk losing them," Xavier told her. "The same goes for Zach and will likewise apply to both you and Miss Powers. This isn't a degree program. There is no finish line. No matter what skill level you attain, you will have to continue to train in order to keep those skills. You are doing very well, no longer than you have been working. Both of you," he added, looking at Kim Powers. "Now, let us try this again," he smiled.

"Me, this time," Kim said, stepping forward to face Zach. "Let me try."

"Very well," Xavier's smile changed just a bit as he watched the former cheerleader maneuver toward the former ball player. He noted that Amanda's own smile was hooded, but present, nevertheless.

"Begin."

-

"I just don't see any way you can look at this and not say it's my fault."

Tammy Denmark was with Beverly Jackson, the two sitting on the creekbank behind the buildings of the Troy Farm. Of everyone, Tammy was having the most difficulty with Bobby's death.

"I can see a number of ways and reasons where it isn't your fault," Beverly replied calmly. "First and foremost is the fact that had Bobby not been allergic, or else had the venom not found an artery or vein, then he would have gotten sick, but likely not have died. According to Doctor Thatcher and PA Sanders, copperhead bites in the United States resulted in roughly one death for every five thousand, three hundred bites when records were being kept of that sort of thing. With less than one thousand recorded bites per year, those odds are pretty good."

"Bobby still died," Tammy said woodenly. "It could just as easily have been Diane," she added suddenly, showing Beverly what the problem was all along. Beverly had already suspected it, being very good at her trade, but she had finally gotten Tammy to admit that her fear was that her own daughter would have been bitten but for luck of the draw.

"It could," Beverly said carefully. "Could also have been JJ," she mentioned her own son. "Snakes don't just bite children. After the attack that happened just after you got here, they pulled a body out of the culvert in front of the pad once the battle was over. Did you know that?"

"No," Tammy said flatly, staring at the water.

"There were some unkind things said about the man by those who knew him before the lights went out," Beverly recalled. "But the point is that he crawled into that culvert to hide, and crawled right up onto a rattlesnake, apparently. I say apparently because the snake was already gone, and he was dead. He disturbed the snake, and the snake didn't hesitate to show his displeasure. Snakes don't just bite children, Tammy, and sometimes the adults die as well."

"How does that make it not be my fault?" Tammy demanded.

"How many children were you and Callie supervising?" Beverly replied with a question of her own.

"What difference does-,"

"How many?" Beverly all but demanded.

"Nine," Tammy finally said. "There were some other children who had joined them, but we had nine from the orphanage. Trudy had kept the rest because they were too small to be outside like that. Four others who are probably less than two, still, and are still in diapers."

"Were you keeping the children all in one area?" Beverly asked.

"What?" Tammy finally looked up. "What would be the point of being outside in the playground if we did that?"

"Indeed," Beverly smiled. "What would be the point? Children were playing and one got injured. Could Bobby have fallen from say, the slide, and hurt himself so badly that he died?"

"I-," Tammy started to answer, but stopped short as the question settled on her.

"Well?" Beverly pressed, not wanting to give up her advantage.

"Sure," Tammy nodded. "Of course, he could. Any of them could do that."

"Would it be your fault if a child lost their footing and fell?" Beverly asked her.

"I should have been there," Tammy argued.

"And while you were catching the child that fell from the slide, another child might have fallen from the swing and died from that fall as well," Beverly said. "What then? Do you drop the child from the slide to run to the swing?"

"No!" Tammy exclaimed.

"No," Beverly nodded. "There were two of you and nine children. Two people can't possibly be where they can simply reach out and grab any of those nine children at any second. It isn't physically possible. Nature will do what nature does, Tammy, and in this case an annoyed snake bit a child. It happens. It's what they do. Bobby's death is tragic, there's no doubt, but it isn't your fault. You need to accept that, and you need to deal with the fact that you can't control everything that goes on around you, no matter how hard you try. Bobby, sadly, will probably not be the last child we lose, Tammy."

"How can you say that!?" Tammy demanded.

"Because it's true," Beverly replied evenly. "And I say that as a mother who fears for her child the same way you do. Winter is coming, and with it comes flu, pneumonia and who knows what else. We no longer have all the awesome drugs we once did to battle those illnesses. What happens when a two or three-year-old develops pneumonia from a respiratory infection and we don't have a modern hospital with a pediatrician and a pulmonary specialist to deal with it?"

"I-, I don't...."

"Neither do I," Beverly sighed. "But I do know that the odds are that it will happen. Maybe not this year, but the further along we go, the more likely it will become. If you haven't read any early American history, I suggest you see if the twins have anything on it you can look at," she got to her feet, then offered a hand to the other woman. Brushing herself off, Beverly looked at Tammy.

"You'll be surprised what you learn about early American families, I think. I've read of families where they had nine children and only two survived to adulthood. Fevers, injuries, and yes, snakebites, took the other seven children. Unfortunately, we're heading back into those days, I think. I say that, again, as a mother who fears for her child with almost every breath. I know you do as well. But all we can do is still all we can do, Tammy. That snake could have been anywhere on that playground. Could have been where the older kids were having school. Could have been wherever it wanted, because it's a snake, and nature is his living room."

"It isn't your fault," Beverly's voice was firm. "Let Bobby rest peacefully. There are still a dozen children, your own being one of them, who need you. You have to be there for them. There is no one else."

"Okay," Tammy spoke so softly that Beverly wasn't sure she heard her.

"I will," Tammy spoke louder this time. "Thank you," she smiled slightly, probably the first time she had since Bobby had died.

"You're welcome."

-

"We'll be leaving one truck here with Sergeant Gleason," Adcock noted. "They'll need it for transport if they have to go anywhere."

"That's a rough way to ride into trouble," Clay mused, looking at the modern equivalent of the two-and-a-half ton trucks his men had captured from the phony military unit.

"It's armored, and enclosed," Adcock noted. "Also has a gun emplacement above the cab," he pointed to the slight rise on the top of the truck. "We're working on freeing up some other vehicles, but it takes time to get things running again, and we have a limited amount of personnel who know how to do it. Once we manage to do that, we may be able to eliminate using trucks as transports other than moving them from one station to another. Until then, this is what we have," he shrugged.

"Well," Clay made a snap decision, "if they need to go somewhere as a patrol, we'll see if we can't fix them up with something a little better than a deuce-and-a-half. No promises, but that truck just doesn't seem like a good idea, except as a supplement to a heavier column."

"I won't argue that point, and will gladly accept any assistance you can render," Adcock said at once.

"Just make sure Gaines knows that it's a loaner car," Clay snorted in amusement, and Adcock laughed outright.

"She finished reading her op order a little while ago," he mentioned. "Her attitude seems to have changed since then. I really do believe that someone in the headquarters company is filling the younger crowd full of BS ideas on how we're supposed to be operating. That may have been what happened with Flores, I don't know. I do know that Whitten is working to straighten that out and has the support of a lot of others. It may take time, but he'll get it done."

"Meanwhile, though, Gaines and I had a very pointed conversation after she finished reading in. She is completely aware, now, of the situation here, as well as what happened to Flores. I believe you can expect a different attitude from her in the future. She had been convinced that she would somehow be the authority wherever she was posted and brought that with her on this posting. I have disabused her of that notion a bit further than I did at your table. She has two good NCOs which I encouraged her to lean upon for support in getting her job done. In her defense, she's never been in a situation like this so it's on-the-job training, in a manner of speaking. But I trust Gleason and Deering to take care of her and get the job done."

"I need to go and meet Deering, sometime," Clay nodded as Adcock finished. "Sounds like he's a solid troop as well."

"He's not as sharp as Gleason or Maxwell, but he doesn't have their experience either," Adcock informed him. "But he does know his job and does it well. He is also clued in on how much you and your team have contributed to our operations, and he was the beneficiary of the cookout you gave us the first time we were here. You can count on him to be solid."

"Outstanding," Clay commented. "So, what else is on the agenda?"

"Now I take Gaines and head back to Jordan," Adcock said, moving toward his Hummer. "We left Deering there with the rest of the detachment and their vehicles. He should about have the post established by now, I think."

"Well, don't be a stranger," Clay shook hands with the officer. "As the old commercial used to say, we'll leave the light on for ya."

"Appreciate it," Adcock laughed. "I won't be around much through the winter, I figure, but I will try to get by here when I can. We'll be doing our best to save our resources and stretch our fuel as far as we can. I do intend to take Greg's advice about using things like that shine as a fuel additive. We may can establish a good operation for that next year."

"If we can lend technical support, let us know," Clay nodded. "Drive safe!" he added to Adcock's back, laughing again. Adcock waved over his shoulder before climbing into the Hummer. Watching them head out, Clay turned and headed back toward the barracks to see Gleason.

He wondered idly what effect the arrival of the military contingent was going to have on the farm. They had discussed it, of course, before agreeing to the plan, but discussion was one thing and actual application was another.

He decided it would be an interesting winter, for sure.

CHAPTER SIX

"So, what are we doing for Halloween?" Lainie asked as she and Clay walked from their home down to Angela Sanders' outdoor kitchen for dinner. Eating there had become a regular occurrence again with Clay and his mother having been able to start patching up their relationship.

"I don't know," Clay looked at her in surprise. "That's not my department, is it?"

"Well, you *are* the one in charge," she teased, kissing his ear lightly as she propped an arm on his shoulder. "I figured you would have something going."

"We can have a bonfire, I guess," he shrugged. "That's what we always did. Have a bonfire and drink beer until we passed out or run out of beer," he chuckled.

"I can't imagine you did that here," Lainie scoffed.

"I didn't say it was here," Clay pointed out. "But to your original question, what do you want to do? I would imagine, based on past precedents, that you and several of the others have already discussed this?"

"We have," she nodded, smiling. "And we were thinking of a bonfire as well, along with homemade candy for the kiddies and some simple costumes. The twins have a machine that makes hot dogs, so we can roast them over the fire. No one has mentioned drinking our way into unconsciousness yet, though," she added with a near giggle.

"Sounds like a plan," Clay shrugged, smiling. "Tell me what you need done and I'll have it done. Where did you want to do all this?"

"I'd like to have the bonfire behind the Troy buildings," Lainie suggested. "We can light the way there and back with torches, like the old days. We'll let the kids visit each house to trick-or-treat, and then gather to roast the hotdogs. Sound good?"

"It does, actually," Clay nodded. "Do you want to invite the soldiers?" he asked, looking at her closely. She paused, her face taking on a look of surprise.

"I had forgotten they were here," she admitted. "I don't know. I'm not really in charge so much as we're all contributing, so I don't think I can say one way or another on my own."

"Well, you need to make a decision about it, soon," he told her as they neared his mother's dining area. "There are thirteen of them counting Gleason. They seem like a good crowd, and Gleason has them firmly in hand. My only concern would be how it might affect some of the others. You might talk to Beverly about it, and then the two of you talk to the women that were found in Peabody. Just a suggestion."

"It is a good idea," Beverly noted, once Lainie had explained. "The girls who still have those issues are going to have to get past them some way or another. Limited exposure to such a small, well controlled group is a much better way than just tossing them into the mix, so to speak. They all did well at the street market, so crowds don't seem to be a problem." She paused, clearly weighing benefits against potential problems.

"I'd say invite them," she said finally. "Extend the invitation to Gleason and let him make the decision on who can or can't go and how long they can stay and what have you. That puts him firmly in control rather than having us make the decision for him. Don't do anything that undermines his authority."

"Sounds like a plan," Lainie nodded.

"Agreed," Martina Sanchez agreed.

-

"Oh, me!" Angela Sanders made a big deal of the tiny terrors who knocked at her front door. "What do we have here?"

"Trick-or-treat!" a dozen small voices yelled a ragged chorus out.

"Well, I can't stand any tricks, so treats it is!" Angela declared and began passing out homemade rock candy to each little bucket. Also included were three cookies each that she had baked just an hour before.

"Thank you!" another tiny chorus hit her as she finished delivering their plunder.

"You're welcome!" she smiled. "Happy Halloween!"

"Thank you!"

"Almost seems normal, doesn't it?" Gordon said quietly from behind her. She nodded without turning.

"It really does," she agreed happily. "It probably won't last, but even so, it's a tiny piece of normal for small children. I'll take it, gladly."

-

Sergeant First Class Shaun Gleason studied the dozen men arrayed before him carefully, walking down their line as he inspected the squad.

"We *will* be on our best behavior this evening," he told the assembled soldiers in front of him. "You no doubt are going to feel the urge to talk to the young ladies in attendance. I have been assured by the inviting party that such actions are allowed but will *only* be tolerated within the bounds of societal politeness. For those of you who lack a proper education, that means you *will* speak respectfully *at all times* and will keep your suggestions of what constitutes a good time to yourselves. I *trust* I make myself clear on this?"

"Yes, Sergeant!" a much cleaner chorus than the one at Angela Sanders' home replied.

"If the need arises for me to remind any of you of these simple rules, you will regret it," he finished, his voice so quiet that some had to strain to hear it. "There will be no second chances. Let's head out."

-

“I heard them soldiers are gonna be there,” Petra Shannon remarked as she, Amanda Lowery, Kim Powers and seven others made their way down the hill in a group, headed for the bonfire.

“I heard the same thing,” Amanda nodded. “I also heard that their sergeant was going to squat on them hard, and that they’re pretty good people. If they weren’t, Clay wouldn’t allow them to be here to start with.”

“I don’t know,” Gail Knight sounded unconvinced. “I’d like to believe it, though.”

“Look,” Amanda stopped at the front of the group, forcing the others to stop as well.

“This has to stop,” Amanda told them flatly. “It has to. We can’t keep living like this, afraid of every uniform we see or every man who happens by that we don’t know. We are not the same people we were just a few months ago. We are not helpless maidens and we can’t keep acting like we are. We’ve been through some of the harshest training these guys could throw at us, and we beat it! It’s okay to be cautious, or even scared. But we can’t let that dictate how we live! If none of that gives you any confidence at all, then consider that we’ll be surrounded by people like Xavier, Kevin, Tandi and Zach among all the others. There is nothing that a dozen soldiers are going to do that those guys can’t handle. For that matter, *we* should be able to handle it,” she added firmly.

“She’s right,” Kim was nodding her agreement. “We have to get over this, and tonight is a good place to start. I, for one, am going down there and have a damn good time and not worry about who’s there and who isn’t.”

“Other than Zach Willis?” Petra Shannon snickered, causing the former cheerleader to blush a deep red.

“Back on the subject,” Amanda snapped her fingers to get everyone’s attention. “No fear from here on out. We are badass women who can handle whatever gets tossed our way. Right?” A quiet, ragged reply came from the group.

“I *said* we are badass women who can handle *whatever* gets tossed our way!” Amanda said again, much louder. “Right?”

“Right!” The reply was clearer this time. Stronger.

“Let me hear you say it!” Amanda insisted, looking at the group.

“We are badass women who can handle whatever gets tossed our way,” the young women repeated, though again it was ragged and not nearly as firm as Amanda wanted.

“Again!” she all but shouted. “Like you mean it!”

“We are badass women who can handle whatever gets tossed our way!” she led the chant, looking from one woman to the next as they spoke.

"Again!" she walked up and down the line that had formed as the women now shouted the mantra in near unison.

"Better," Amanda nodded firmly. "Now. Heads up and backs straight! We walk in there like we own the place! Like we're the people who are supposed to be there and they are the visitors, because that's how it is! Any questions?"

"When did you make Sergeant?" Petra Shannon asked, amusement clear in her voice.

-

"Thank you for inviting us, tonight," Gleason said as his men made their way carefully to where the food was arrayed on tables.

"I'm glad you decided to join us, Sergeant Gleason," Lainie smiled. "You're going to be here all winter and working often with people here on the farm. It makes sense for us to get to know one another in an easier setting than doing farm work."

"That does make sense," he returned her smile. "My men are to be on their best behavior. Should you see or hear of anything otherwise, please let me know at once. Though I will be watching as well," he added firmly.

"I'm sure it will be fine, Sergeant," Lainie nodded, trying to sound confident. This was a large gamble in some ways, but she hoped it would pay off.

-

"They don't seem so bad," Petra Shannon noted as she and the others settled in on hay bales, across the fire from the soldiers.

"Not from here, anyway," Heather Patton agreed. "At least they aren't staring," she added.

"But we are," Amanda noted. "Stop it. You look like antelope watching a lion in the distance. That's not how we're going to act. If anything, we're the lioness, now. So, act like it!"

"I'm still wondering when you became Sergeant Lowery," Petra shot back, smirking.

"When no one else was willing to step up," Amanda shrugged. "And I'm not trying to be anything other than me. I just don't want us to sit here, petrified, just because there are strangers around. Hell, lots of the people we trust with our lives now were strangers when we got here. More than one of the guys who rescued us were strangers, for that matter. Remember that those guys," she nodded slightly in the direction of the soldiers across the way, "have stayed through thick and thin, and are working for what is basically room and board. They're doing that to try and make a difference, no matter how small. They're not that much different from us, really."

"I doubt anyone kept them in cages," Jenna Waller muttered, and a few others nodded their agreement.

"I doubt anyone will ever keep us in one again," Amanda's rebuttal was quick and pointed. "You may as well accept the fact that we're going to be targets in the kind of world we live in now. I hate it, all of you hate it, the men who trained us hate it. None of that matters. It is what it is. That means we must be extra careful, and it means we have to show no mercy to our enemies. A lioness doesn't show mercy, does she?"

"You're really stuck on that lioness thing tonight, aren't you?" Janessa Haynes smiled.

"It just struck me as accurate, earlier," Amanda shrugged. "We can be leopards if you want. Or cheetahs," she laughed.

"Well, I kind of like lioness, though lions work in prides," Gail Knight noted. "That means-,"

"Yeah, I know what it means," Amanda snorted as she rolled her eyes. "I wasn't planning to take it that far, thank you."

"Just how far were you planning to take it?" Petra asked her, a small smirk on her face.

"Right up to the kill," Amanda surprised her with a near growl that wiped the smirk from her face.

"Well, if we're lionesses," Kim Powers stood up suddenly, "I'll be damned if I sit here in my own territory, afraid. I'm getting something to eat and walk around."

"Me too," Petra agreed, getting to her feet.

"Same here," Amanda nodded. "Mix and mingle, ladies," Amanda practically ordered. "There are a lot of people living on this farm that we barely know, and that's not counting the soldiers who just moved in. Tonight is an excellent time to get to know them."

"Yes, ma'am!" several snapped, laughing. Amanda flipped them the bird as she headed for the food table herself.

-

"I think it's working," Lainie murmured to Beverly as the two watched the interaction among the young women. "Looks like the Lowery girl is emerging as a leader among them, as well," she noted.

"I was just thinking that," Beverly agreed. "It seems to me that she has been the one who built them up for tonight. She inspires them to put their fear away, or at least to suppress it enough to live and work around it. She's a strong one, she is. She would bear watching as a future leader, I think."

"It would be good for them to have one of their own be their leader, wouldn't it?" Lainie asked.

"Possibly," Beverly was more cautious than her friend. "But only if she does a good job. So long as they keep confidence in her, then yes, she might very well make an excellent leader, and that in turn would be good for them as a group."

"Hm," Lainie hummed.

"What are you thinking about?" Beverly asked, seeing the look of near mischief in Lainie's eyes.

"Me?" Lainie feigned shock and innocence, laying an open hand to her throat. "Why, whatever do you mean, Miss Jackson?"

"Oh, God, don't call me Miss Jackson," Beverly groaned. "It took me years to leave that damned song behind!"

-

"Have you been observing the young women tonight?" Xavier's voice came from nowhere and Clay forced himself to turn his head slightly to see his friend standing in the shadows.

"Yeah," he replied calmly.

"I admit that I had already thought that Amanda might make a decent leader of sorts, certainly for a fire team once she had a bit more training and experience, but tonight has shown an entirely new side of her abilities, I do believe. In fact, it was her encouragement that got most of them to attend this evening." Xavier's voice betrayed true respect for Amanda's accomplishment, which was rare for him.

"I agree," Clay told him. "While I'm not ready to jump on the 'Sergeant Lowery' band wagon, I might be convinced to try a 'Corporal Lowery' as a fire team leader, though, as you said, when she has a bit more experience and training."

"We should alter her training slightly to prepare her for that," Xavier suggested. "It is a much larger responsibility than simply training as an infantry man. Woman. Person," Xavier kept searching until he hit a word he liked.

"Get with Pancho tomorrow and talk it over with him," Clay nodded. "He's taken the lead on that kind of thing."

"Very well."

-

"Looks like your guys are starting to mingle, finally," Jose Juarez said as he and Gleason stood watching the crowd.

"They should be on their best behavior," Gleason promised.

"I'm sure they will be," Jose nodded. "They seem like a good bunch. I note that most of them are on the younger side," he added.

"Too many, I guess," Gleason nodded slowly. "Too many of them are young enough to have missed out on deployments that might have firmed them up a bit. Of course, no one expected to have the States become a combat zone, either. They have, unfortunately, gotten a good bit of experience since then," his voice turned grim.

"We heard from Adcock that Nashville and the other larger cities were quite the mess," Jose mentioned.

"That's putting it mildly," Gleason agreed.

"I'm surprised that people haven't streamed out of places like that, looking for places like this," said Jose, wondering if Gleason knew why that had not materialized.

"In the case of Nashville, they invaded the suburbs and small towns around them," Gleason answered readily. "The problem is that most of the people who managed to come out on top in the struggles within the cities, they have no desire to migrate into the countryside. They want to maintain their power, where they are, and are willing to go to great extremes to do so. *Great*, extremes," he stressed, looking Jose dead in the eye.

"We've seen a little bit of that here, as well," Jose sighed. "I don't understand it, either," he added. "While it's true that farms such as this one can only produce so much, and that they only harvest once in a year, there is food in abundance in the wilds. Fruits, vegetables and meat all there for the taking. I can't imagine taking another route, especially that one, when there is food laying there, waiting for me to come and get it."

"Do you know which foods you find in the woods are safe to eat?" Gleason asked him, looking at the group once more, watching their interactions. "Do you know how to hunt or trap or fish, and then clean and cook what you manage to kill?"

"For the most part, yes," Jose nodded slowly. "I will admit there are some berries and mushrooms around here that I am not familiar with, but I am actually learning all that now, thanks to a change in our training and education programs."

"Yeah, well, most of the people who survived the riots and purges in places like Nashville and Memphis don't know dick all about living off the land. If they can't get it from a can or a sack, they can't deal with it. That will always lead to trouble, and it has. God help us," he added in a mutter.

"That bad?" Jose dared to ask.

"The Captain told you the cities were no-go zones, right?" Gleason finally looked at Jose.

"He did."

"Well, that's because we lost," Gleason said flatly, returning his gaze once more to the group at large. "We fought the uprisings and we lost. Everywhere. We weren't allowed to go active in time to gather our strength and matter, and we lost. We worked with the police and fire forces that stayed, but it wasn't enough. There were too many hungry, angry people who were looking to strike out at anyone they could possibly lay blame on for their misfortune. You noted that most of my squad here is too young? Well, a lot of the more experienced hands are dead. Along with hundreds of law enforcement officers all over the country, let alone just here at home in Tennessee."

"They're young because they're what's left," Gleason finished. "Tank driver," he pointed to one young man who was smiling. "Cannon-cocker," he pointed to another. "Mortar monkey," he moved to the next. "Everything we need to run an Armored Cavalry Regiment," he snorted. "A brigade in all but name, really. Everything we need except equipment," he turned once more to Jose.

"Equipment left in the desert for the next combat team, with promises of replacement gear when we got home. Most of which we didn't get, and none of which would have really helped. No one is going to turn an M-1 or a Bradley lose on civilians. No one I serve with, anyway," he shrugged. "We taught them to fight from a tank, from an APC or MRAP, from a Hummer, even from a helicopter. We never taught them to fight in their own cities, on the ground, fighting building to building. Some of them hadn't handled a rifle since basic except to requalify each year."

"We trained them to support the guys who did that kind of door-to-door fighting. Guys we didn't have. We tried to support the cops as best we could, but there were too few of them, and a lot of them took their own families and ran. Not that I blame them one bit. If I had a family, I'd have done the same thing in their shoes." He paused, as if realizing what all he had said.

"So, yeah," he finally continued. "The cities are no-go zones. But I warned the Major and I'll warn you guys now. The groups in those cities are not going to stay there forever. Sooner or later they will have to start moving further out in search of food. And a lot of them will have turned stone cannibal by now. We may not have problems now, but you can bet they're coming." He looked back at the crowd, which was finally loosening up and beginning to have fun.

"Trick or treat."

-

"You shouldn't stray too far from the fire alone," the voice almost whispered in Kim Powers' ear.

"Holy shit!" she screeched, jumping a foot off the ground. "Where the hell did you come from!" she demanded as Zach Willis drifted into view from the dark.

"I've been here the whole time," he told her. She noted he was in his full gear, including what she assumed were night vision glasses attached to his helmet.

"What for?" she asked, her fright at least momentarily forgotten.

"Someone is always on watch here," he told her simply. "You should know that by now," he chided gently. Not really scolding so much as reminding her she should be aware of the fact.

"I knew that," she replied, because she had. "Why you?" she asked him.

"Why me, what?" Zach asked, frowning.

"Why you on watch?" she clarified. "Why aren't you having a good time with the rest?" she waved toward the bonfire.

"Someone has to take the duty," Zach shrugged. "It was better and easier on the rest if it was me, so I just volunteered."

"Why is it easier for you?" she wanted to know next.

"I don't have children, or a girlfriend," he shrugged. "The others have one or the other, or both. They don't get much time like this anymore, so I volunteered to take the whole watch so they could have this. Jody and Kurtis did the same thing. Jody's in the tower and Kurtis is prowling somewhere just like I am. Virgil Wilcox is on watch up on the Hill. We got it covered."

"Do you really think all that is necessary?" her voice was quieter now, and less demanding.

"Yes," his reply was instantaneous. "We've been attacked too many times not to be on watch and be careful. It may sound paranoid, but there are enemies everywhere out there. The past events have proven that if nothing else."

"Yeah, that's true, I guess," she nodded.

"What were you doing out here?" he asked her for a change.

"Oh," she suddenly fidgeted a bit. "I was going to the bathroom," she admitted, glad he couldn't see her blushing.

"Head for Building One," Zach pointed. "There's a bathroom just inside the back door."

"I knew that," she said once again. She had just forgotten. "Will you be here when I get back?"

"No," he replied simply. "I have to move on." He was already doing just that.

"Okay," she almost sighed but caught herself, heading toward the bathroom in Building One.

-

"I have to admit it. I'm a little surprised that things went so well."

Clay and Jose were watching as two of Gleason's men helped Titus and Gordy police the area that had been used for the bonfire. Off to one side, Samantha Walters and Marcy George waited for the latter two to finish.

"I figured it would be okay," Clay replied. "There was no alcohol allowed and Gleason sat on his guys while we sat on our own. The civies were all in good spirits and didn't bother making time to cause problems, either. It was a good time."

"Maybe we should do this kind of thing more often?" Jose stated/asked.

"I'm for it," Clay shrugged. "Remember, other than having the bonfire built, I had nothing to do with this luau. Far as I'm concerned, anytime the ladies want to have a shindig like this, all they need to do is tell us what they want done."

"Interesting you should say that," Jose grinned. "Martina and Cristina both mentioned this would be an excellent way to have that very thing. A luau, I mean. Cook the fattened pig and maybe some potatoes. Make a day of it."

"Have to do it soon," Clay noted. "Tomorrow is November One. It will soon be a little cold for that kind of thing."

"I mentioned that, but they want to at least look at the idea," Jose agreed. "I did suggest that they incorporate that into a get together maybe for Thanksgiving. Maybe make a two or even three-day affair of it? Games, food, some friendly competitions, that kind of thing?"

"Again, sounds good," Clay nodded.

"Did you talk to Gleason any?" Jose changed the subject suddenly.

"I did," Clay replied, his voice grim. "I take it he had the same warning for you?"

"Trick or treat," Jose nodded slowly.

"Yeah," Clay sighed, deciding to head home.

"Happy Halloween."

CHAPTER SEVEN

"Hey! You guys realize that nothing bad has hap-,"

Titus Terry's words were lost as friends old and new alike dog piled him to shut him up.

"Hey, hey, hey, now!" he cried from the bottom of the pile. "I'm delicate, remember!"

"Stop jinxing us with crap like that!" Corey demanded. "Let us enjoy what we got while we can!"

"I was just saying," Titus accepted a hand from Kurtis to help him up. "I was happy, that's all."

"Well, next time just clap your hands or something," Gordy told him. "Seriously, man. Let's don't take the chance that something can jinx it. Especially not with a patrol going out."

-

"Another burned out house," Greg sighed, marking his map and making a note of the address. "This is the Tatum place." He didn't always know who lived in the homes he had found destroyed, but this time he did. "Was, anyway. I wonder where they got to. Or if they were even home?"

"Sorry," Petra Shannon was behind the wheel today as Heath Kelly and Devon Knowles sat in the back. Greg was trying to make sure everyone got the opportunity to operate the vehicles.

"We weren't friends or anything," Greg shrugged ever so slightly. "But they were good folks, so far as I knew."

The number of burned out homes had surprised many, but when Greg had mentioned it, Abigail Sanders had been the one who had clued the rest of them in.

"No heat," she told them flatly. "No lights, either. People are burning candles, and wood, in houses that aren't designed for it. The candles are no problem so long as you're safe with them, but it is still an open flame. The fires, though, that's different. A lot of people will likely be trying to burn wood in places meant for gas or propane, since both are probably gone by now. Others might even try to set up a chimenea or something similar inside their home. All it takes is a spark or two, especially on carpet, and that's it. I suspect a great many of what you've seen are either newer homes with wood or vinyl siding, or else modular constructs?"

They had been.

"Both are highly susceptible to fire," Abby had told him. "If you're lucky, most of the worst of it is over."

"Yeah, if we're lucky," Greg muttered, looking out the window as he recalled Abby's words.

"What's that?" Petra asked, never taking her eyes from the road. She was a good driver but handling something like the Hummer was a new experience for her.

"Just thinking about what Abby told us," Greg mentally chewed himself out for drifting off like that while they were on patrol. "If we're lucky, we won't keep seeing this kind of thing."

"Hopefully not," Petra agreed. "I didn't know many people up this way. Those I did were people I went to school with." They were in the far northwestern part of the county today, an area they hadn't yet been to since the formation of the 'new' Sheriff's Department.

"Once you leave the highway, this is pretty isolated, up here," Greg agreed. "Hard to find addresses when you're on a call."

"How are we ever going to have a system where people can call for help when they need it?" Devon Knowles asked from the back seat.

"That's a great question," Greg admitted. "Wish I had an answer."

-

"I didn't say it wouldn't work. I said it would be difficult at best to make it work."

Leon and Leanne Tillman rarely argued, or disagreed as they preferred to call it, but today was apparently going to be one where they did.

"The lines are already there," Leanne replied to her brother's observation. "We can use them to have stations in different places around the county."

"Have you thought about how difficult it will be to trace that wiring?" Leon demanded. "And a lot of it is underground at that," he reminded her.

"That is true," Leanne chewed on her bottom lip. "But the idea is sound," she rallied.

"Never said it wasn't," Leon reminded her. "It just won't work in its present form."

"What if we could salvage the wire from underground?" JJ dared weigh in between them. "Then we could use utility poles and run the wire where we needed it, right?"

"That isn't a bad plan," Leanne mused, mind racing over the problem.

"It would limit the connections until we could get some kind of switchboard going," Leon murmured, also running over the issue.

"That is a lot of wire, guys," Millie decided to put her oar in the water. "It's fifteen miles from here to Jordan, if I remember you guys right. And that's a lot of poles someone will have to climb to run that wire, too. I think you're over complicating things, at least where a simple reporting system is concerned."

"How so?" the two demanded in unison, causing JJ to duck down in his seat.

"Radios," Millie said simply. "We're still picking up radio signals on ham and citizen's band frequencies," she pointed to the bank of radio receivers used in the Operations room. "Those radios can reach a long way without any kind of aid. While the ham repeaters are probably toast, batteries will be dead even if they survived the CME, a lot of the radios will still work just fine. Maybe most of them in fact. A great many radio enthusiasts are also preparedness enthusiasts and will have had the time to place their electronics into a simple Faraday cage, like what you did. Some even store them that way when they aren't using them in order to protect their more expensive equipment. Which means all they need is power. You can place those radios in the same places you would have placed a community telephone and they can be used to report in. All they need is a power source."

"Generators and car batteries would work for a bit," Leon said. "Those batteries, the good ones anyway, haven't been down long enough to keep them from holding a charge."

"We can use hand cranked generators like they originally used during World War Two," JJ offered. "Even bicycle gears will work, though most people will be wanting to hang on to those, now. Just rig up pedals to crank the generator by hand."

"There is no telling how many generators and alternators are sitting on cars all over the highway, along with the batteries," Leon was getting excited again.

"With a homemade water wheel like yours, you could charge an entire bank of car batteries that are linked together," Leanne was grinning now. "We need the radios, coax, and antennas of course. Cables for the batteries, too."

"Jumper cables would work for that if nothing else," Leon mentioned.

"Just take the wires from the dead cars," JJ suggested. "There's nothing wrong with them."

"Great idea!" Leanne almost clapped. "Why didn't we think of this before!"

"We did, sort of," Leon reminded her. "But we weren't allowed to say anything about it. We bought several radios that we assumed would work, but we've never unpacked them because we haven't needed them. And we have been busy with other things, in our defense."

"I would look for other radios first," Millie cautioned. "Save what you have as a last resort. Once you start pulling things like that out of storage somewhere, you make yourselves a target for people who will expect you to have other things. Which in this case, you do."

"True," Leon nodded, wrapping an arm around her waist. "You're so smart," he grinned at her, making her blush. She both loved and hated that at the same time.

"Well then," Leanne ignored their by-play. "I guess we can present this to Greg, and he can start looking!"

-

"I know one or two people who had serious setups before the Storm," Greg nodded his agreement. "I have a handheld programable myself. No idea where it is, or why I didn't think of it myself," he admitted.

"Who would you have talked to," Leon shrugged. "Besides, we were trying to stay quiet, remember? Not call attention to us and all that stuff? Being on the air is the exact opposite of that."

"That is true," Greg allowed. "Well, I can start looking for others as I move around. People with antenna farms and what have you. And you think CBs will still work, too?"

"Probably," Leanne nodded. "Some of them, anyway. The problem will be getting them power. We need to get Jake and Uncle Clay to make a deal with someone to start stripping batteries from all those cars on the interstate if they haven't already. Some of them will almost certainly still hold a charge, and even if they won't hold much will work just fine as a conduit for a hand turned generator."

"Then it's just a matter of finding people willing to serve as conduits for messages," Greg winked at her. "Great idea, kids."

"Don't call us kids," the two objected in unison.

"And we had help," Leon added. "Millie and JJ both contributed as much as we did. We overlooked this idea, looking to try and use the old system somehow. We really were making it way more complicated than it had to be," he admitted, a bit shamefaced.

"We were," Leanne agreed. "Always looking for the science and never the application, I guess," she shrugged just a little. "The simplest answers are usually the ones we ignore, and we proved that today, I'm afraid."

"As much as you two have contributed on your own, I think this is a freebie, though," Greg assured them. "If you really want to do something new, now, get the Ten Codes card from my old patrol car. There are also what we called Signal Codes as well. Review them and see what we can do about simplifying them, making them fit our new reality."

"What's wrong with them now?" Leanne asked, frowning slightly.

"Well, I doubt I'll get many calls about speeding, now," Greg laughed. "And I'm not going to spend the fuel to go investigate public intoxication if there's no threat to anyone else. Doubt I get many calls for loud music, either. Besides, most people aren't going to take the time to memorize all that, and if they do use them all it will just end up sounding like a verbal Morse code. We can do without that."

"All true," Leanne sighed, reminded yet again that the world around them was vastly different than it had been just a year ago.

"Thanks again, guys," Greg said seriously. "All of you."

-

"So how are you planning on dealing with nuisance calls?" Clay asked as he watched three radios and the associate equipment into the back of the MRAP that was now part of the Sheriff's Patrol.

"I'm not," Greg admitted. "I intend to explain that to everyone who agrees to operate a station. There's just no way we can."

"So, what happens when those nuisance calls escalate?" Clay wondered. "What then?"

"Depends on how far and how hard it escalates," Greg admitted. "I'm thinking about trying to find some people in each community that's still working to serve as a constable. More of a peace maker to help solve smaller problems like that rather than a police officer. I don't want them getting hurt, just hoping they can help others get along."

"Not a bad idea," Clay nodded. "Might really help pull the communities together, too."

"I hope so," Greg sounded less enthused than he usually did. "It's pretty bad in some places, man," he said quietly. "Everything is overgrown now, and there are a lot of burned out homes. And a lot of fresh dug graves, mostly in people's yards. I mean, knowing it is one thing, but seeing it is something else again. It's depressing."

"I imagine so," Clay said gently. "Dude, maybe you should think about seeing Beverly. Talking to her might help you deal with all that."

"Are you talking to her?" Greg asked.

"No," Clay admitted.

"When you go, let me know," he walked to the passenger door of the Hummer. "So will I." He stepped up into the vehicle and closed the door before Clay could reply.

-

McCauley's Country Grocery was the first place Greg stopped. He had already been there once, finding the small country store still operating, though in a completely different manner than before the Storm. It had become a trading post of sorts, and a clearing house for information. Being on the eastern side of the interstate had spared that are from the wildfire and things were not nearly so desperate as people accustomed to country living managed quite well. Tom McCauley was looking the setup over as Gordy finished hooking it up.

"And that itty-bitty antenna will let me talk to you in Jordan?" the storekeeper's doubts were clear.

"It will," Gordy answered for Greg. "The magnet will hold it to your old air conditioner casing, which will put it up more than high enough to get your message out. Just remember, though, that the batteries may or may not hold a charge for long. It's possible, but not promised. You may need someone to crank the generator while you talk."

"Looks like those rigs on the old World War Two movies," McCauley nodded.

"That's where the idea came from," Gordy nodded. "The battery will work, even if it won't hold a charge. The power from the generator will run through the battery bank and power the radio, no problem. I need to run the line and get it hooked up," he told them, getting back to work.

"Now, how am I supposed to make any money, or what passes for money anymore, out of this rig?" McCauley asked.

"You're not," Greg all but growled, angry at even the suggestion. "I chose you because you're practically the center of this whole community and know everyone. Plus, this puts you in a position to hear what else is going on, so long as you've got the radio powered."

"Seems like I ought to be getting something out of it," McCauley hinted.

"Seems like I ought to be busting that still out back into about a dozen pieces and hauling your ass before the magistrate too, but here we are," Greg replied calmly.

"Alright, alright," McCauley held up a hand. "I get it. No need to get personal."

"It is personal," Greg didn't let up. "If you don't want to be the one people come to when they need help, tell me now and I'll take it down. Someone else around here will probably be glad to do the job just so they can know the news from elsewhere."

"I said I'd do it, and I will," the other man promised. "Man has to make a living somehow, though. Not all of us still have a real job," he took a cheap shot at Greg.

"I got a job, as you call it, but for nothing," Greg told him. "Still have to work just like you do, digging my food out of the ground or killing it myself. Tom, I'm not playing about this at all. If I hear even a hint of you holding out on this, to anyone, I will cloud up and rain all over you. I thought you were a better man than that when I asked you about this."

"That was a low blow, Deputy," McCauley shot back.

"It's Sheriff now," Greg reminded him. "Not Deputy. And it's no lower than you were suggesting that you get money for being allowed to have the only lifeline in your entire community, now is it?"

That brought McCauley up short as Greg's words hit home.

"You're right," he admitted softly. "I shouldn't have even thought it, let alone said it. Was just thinking how to turn things to my advantage. Had to start thinking that way after what happened. Gotten to be a habit, now."

"I can well understand that," Greg promised. "And it may be that one day I can offer you something for the trouble," he extended an olive branch of sorts. "I just don't have anything or anyway to do that right now. You're doing your community a service, though, and I'm sure they'll appreciate it. So do I.

I'll do what I can to make it worth your while, whenever I can. That's all I can promise, though. I don't have anything to offer right now."

"I understand," McCauley nodded as Gordy came back inside to complete the installation. "Like I said, I was out of line. Sorry."

"We're all wore down, Tom," Greg shook his head, accepting the apology. "We just need to try and pull together. Hopefully this," he pointed to the radio, "is the start of it."

"Hopefully."

-

"-and here," Greg spotted the final station he had established on the map the twins kept in the Operations room. "That's seven in all. I don't have anything in this area," he pointed to the area north of the farm where the wildfire had ravaged. "There's just nothing much there right now. Maybe next year, when stuff starts to grow back from the fire."

"We've been thinking," Leon said.

"Now what?" Greg faked a groan before smiling.

"We were thinking about trying to establish a news broadcast over the radio system," Leanne told him. "Make it at a prearranged time each day, or maybe every other day or something. Announcements can be made like the street market in Jordan, or threats known to be in the area, that kind of thing. We can also use that time to transmit message like they did back during World War Two. They used radio shows to send messages to resistance fighters behind German lines."

"Yeah, I can see how that would work," Greg was slowly nodding. "I kind of like that idea. Maybe even set up a daily time to send and receive messages. Not silly stuff, but important messages. Even advertise important trades like livestock or equipment. That could work just fine."

"We'll try and work out a proposal for it," Leon promised. "Keeping those limits on it and trying to establish the best times."

"I'm going to deputize the both of you," Greg told them, smiling.

"Thanks!" the twins replied in unison, beaming at him.

"Raise your right hands," he told them. Both looked stunned.

"Wait, you were serious?" Leon almost goggled while his sister just looked stunned.

"Serious as a heart attack," Greg nodded. "You're essentially my dispatchers now. All of you are for that matter. Might as well get the title for it. There's no pay, though," he added with an apologetic shrug. "Sorry."

"Do we get a badge?" Leanne almost whispered the question.

"I can get you a badge," Greg nodded. "I don't have a way to make an ID for you, though."

"We do," the two replied together as they raised their right hands.

"Repeat after me."

-

"No, mounting from the left is just a tradition," Charley Wilmeth shook her head. "The reason we continue to do it now is one of convenience as well as habit. Since most horses are trained that way, we still train to mount from the left."

"Why was it that way to start?" one soldier asked, respectfully. They had all been threatened with immense bodily harm if they even looked at the female instructors wrong, let alone said anything untoward.

"In ancient times, and right up through probably World War One, cavalrymen would have their swords on their left hip," Charley placed her own hand to her side. "They mounted from the left to prevent the sword injuring their horse."

"Wow," another solider farther down commented. "I would never have considered that being a problem."

"You never carried a sword before, either," the man next to him noted. "We all base our presumptions on what we know. There's no reason for any of us to have considered a sword."

"True," Charley smiled. "Okay, it's time to mount up. I know a few of you have apparently rode a time or two, but for all our sake, please forget everything you think you know and let me go through the steps for everyone else. Take a firm hold on the saddle horn, holding both the reins...."

"Your guys are pretty smart for grunts, Sergeant Gleason," Clay mentioned softly as the two watched the training.

"Most joined the Guard to get help with college," Gleason nodded. "They're all good kids." Anyone less than thirty years of age was a kid to Gleason, who was in his mid-fifties.

"They seem to be good students, too," Clay added. "Asking good questions and following instructions carefully."

"You seem surprised at that, sir," Gleason looked at him.

"No, it's jealousy," Clay snorted. "We had to teach some of our own how to handle a horse, and most of them are still learning the finer points. Had they been more like your men, we might be done with them," he chuckled.

"I appreciate you saying that sir," Gleason said, mollified now that he knew his men weren't being maligned.

"You don't have to sir me, Sergeant," Clay told him. "I haven't been a 'sir' in a long time, and I lost the right to be called that anyway."

"It's Shaun, then," Gleason nodded his acceptance.

"Clay," Clay extended a hand and the older man took it.

"How did you lose the right to be properly addressed as an officer?" Gleason asked, curious.

"Ah, I did something I wasn't supposed to," Clay sort of waved the whole thing to the side. "I accepted an 'Other Than Honorable' to keep my men out of trouble. It was neck-and-neck to see if I got that much. I had to resort to blackmail to do it."

"Blackmail?" Gleason looked shocked.

"Oh, it wasn't personal," Clay assured him. "I threatened to rat out a black program to the hacks in Congress," he snorted. "Suddenly I found myself out of the Army with a pat on the back and don't come back. Which was fine," he shrugged. "It was probably better than I deserved. And again, it kept my men out of trouble."

"Takes a good officer to fall on his sword for his men," Gleason observed.

"They wouldn't have been in trouble if not for me," Clay told him. "Seemed only fair I get them out."

"Most officers, especially junior officers, don't share that opinion, if you'll pardon me," Gleason noted carefully.

"I was a Mustang," Clay grinned. "Didn't even get the full ninety days. It was just a convenience."

"That explains it then," the two men shared a laugh.

-

"You boys look a little rough," Titus Terry said as he watched the soldiers moving stiffly about their day.

"Never imagined just sitting could hurt so bad," one nodded. "I'm sure you think this is hilarious," he told Titus and the others around him, one of whom was Corey Reynard.

"Oh, hell no," Corey shook his head. "We been there, dude. We literally feel your pain. Some of us are still feeling it. You won't get no laughter from anybody around here for being saddle sore."

"How do you get rid of it?" the young soldier asked.

"Just what you're doing," Titus told him. "Walk it out. I never wanted a hot tub so bad in my life, man. No such a thing anymore. Just had to suck it up."

"It sucks right enough," the soldier agreed. "See you guys later."

"Later."

CHAPTER EIGHT

The newly established limited communications systems, (the Duo and their Minions were still working on a better name for it) came into play two weeks to the day after completion.

JJ Jackson was sitting in Operations reading when the radio began to squawk.

"*Uh…Dinner Plate…no, no, Home Plate, yeah, Home Plate this is Garrett's Grocery, come in?*"

Looking at the map, JJ realized that Garrett's was in the extreme southeastern area of the county, near the Alabama line and in a very rural area. It also wasn't far from Lewiston, as the crow might fly. By road was another matter.

"This is Home Plate, Garrett's, please go ahead," JJ replied.

"*We've had a robbery up here, Home Plate. Five men in a working four-by-four have shot two people and taken everything they had on them. One man is dead, and another is in rough shape. We could really use some help up here. Over.*"

"Understood, Garrett's," JJ was scratching out notes. "Can you describe the vehicle? And any of the men involved?"

The man did his best to relay that information while JJ summoned Greg. He arrived just in time to hear the last bit of the message.

"*-just told me they think Chester is dead as well,*" the voice on the radio relayed sadly. JJ tore the notes he had made from his book and handed them to Greg.

"Lewis County tags," Greg mused. "Tell them I'm on my way, but it will take a bit. If they get you any more information on the guys in the truck, I want it."

"Yes sir," JJ replied and turned back to the radio. JJ had done his job well, Greg realized, when he stepped outside to find the Hummer and MRAP sitting on the pad, ready to go. Amanda Lowery was behind the wheel of the Hummer, with Titus Terry and Kevin Bodee in the back, an M240 mounted on the top. Behind them sat the MRAP, with Corey Reynard at the wheel, Zach behind another M240 mounted in the turret, with Devon Knowles and Petra Shannon in the troop area.

"We're ready to roll, Sheriff," Amanda informed him, her usual humor and sass nowhere in sight.

"Good deal," Greg told her appreciatively. "Head out the back way. We're going a long way and most of it is backroads."

"Got it."

-

There was, of course, no way at all for Greg and his team to get to Garrett's in time to be of any help to the victims. Still, thirty minutes after they had received the call, the two vehicles rolled into the parking lot of Garrett's small country store, where a group of men stood in a circle around two shroud covered bodies. Greg got down from the Hummer with Amanda and Titus, while Kevin stayed behind on the gun.

Behind them, Zach turned his own gun to their rear to cover that angle, while Corey, Devon and Petra all dismounted, spreading out around the vehicles but not following the others up to the scene.

"Bit late on timing, there, Holloway," one man said before Greg could even open his mouth.

"We're a bit late on everything these days, Harley," Greg replied evenly, refusing to take the bait. "We're a long way from you even when we're at the station. Who was it?" he nodded to the bodies. Ransom Garrett pulled the sheets back to expose the faces of the two men on the ground.

"Chester Parks and Freddie Perkins," Garrett told him, pointing to each man in turn.

"I knew Chester," Greg said gently. "Used to haul hay for him some when I was a kid. Who saw the truck and the men who did it?"

"The truck just pulled in, shot both, grabbed everything they could get and then took off," 'Harley' told him. "Five guys in all. Three white, two black. The truck was blue, an older model Chevy. Looked like an old K5 Blazer with the top off. Two had them black rifles and the rest had shotguns. One of the white guys had a long beard," he motioned on himself down to his chest, just below his chin.

"They hit the Old Stage Road and took out like a scalded dog," another man who Greg didn't know pointed to the road in question. The area around Garrett's was a crossroad of sorts for backroads, with a total of five different roads meeting within a half-mile.

"Was anyone else hurt?" Greg began asking questions. No one else had been hurt.

"Have you seen the men or the truck here before?" No one had. "Has anyone been missing anything of late? I'm talking about things probably being stolen?" Three men had and Greg listened as they described the missing items, all of which were easily moved and would be valuable with modern amenities gone.

"And no one knew or recognized any of them," he checked once more. No one had.

"Okay," Greg sighed. "We're going to follow down the road and see if we can find the truck. If I do find them, do you think you'll know the men if you see them again?"

"I will," 'Harley' promised. Two others agreed that they would as well.

"What do we do with Chester and Freddie?" Ransom Garrett asked, covering them back up.

"Same thing we have to do with our dead," Greg told him bluntly. "Bury them."

"Ain't that up to you to do?" Harley demanded.

"No, it ain't," Greg was moving toward the Hummer, the others already mounting up. "My job is to go after the men who did this. Which is what I'm doing. If we can catch them, we'll bring them by for you to ID."

Before any of the rest could object, Greg was on board and Amanda was moving them toward the road they needed to follow.

"Rough business, this stuff," she noted quietly.

"It always is," Greg told her.

-

"Hold up, hold up," Kevin Bodee called from the Hummer's turret. They had been slowly following the Old Stage Road for twenty minutes, having gone about nine miles.

"What is it?" Greg asked.

"Did he say that truck was blue?" Kevin asked.

"Yeah," Greg replied. "He did. Said it looked like an old Blazer with a lift-off top."

"Then I think we got a winner," Kevin told him. "Ahead on the left. Looks like they tried to hide it, but the cover has come part way off. I can see the side of it from here."

"What does the place look like?" Greg asked.

"Got a chain link fence around the front yard and another around the back," Bodee reported. "I can't see any dogs from here. I imagine if they have any, they'll swarm us when we get there."

"Yeah, that's a safe bet," Greg agreed. "Okay. I can't just go storming in there, even under these circumstances. Which means we're going to have to go up there and actually try to talk to whoever is there." He keyed his radio.

"Corey, you guys been listening in?" he asked.

"*Got it all, Sheriff,*" Corey promised.

"We're going to pull into the drive when we get up there," Greg told him. "I want you to continue just far enough down the road to clear the front of the Hummer and put Zach where he can cover us. Petra and Devon can dismount and cover the opposite flank from the front and rear of the vehicle but using the vehicle to shield them from the house. Copy that?"

"*Copy all. We're good to go.*"

"Zach, remember that we need to talk to them, first," Greg added after a moment to think.

"*Why does everybody always remind just me of that stuff?*" Zach asked, his voice light. "*Why is it no one ever reminds Gordy or Corey or Titus about that crap? Is it personal? Cause it sounds personal. I haven't done anything to you, have I?"*

"I get it, Zach," Greg had to fight not to laugh despite the situation. "From here on we're radio silent other than for urgent business. Let's go," he added to Amanda, who put them in motion once more, much slower this time.

"Is this thing going to stop a bullet?" Amanda asked as she neared the drive.

"Funny time to bring that up, isn't it?" Greg looked at her in surprise.

"I honestly just thought of it," she admitted. "So, is it?"

"The vehicle itself will," Greg promised. "Supposed to stop anything up to a fifty, or so I've read. The glass, I don't know. Might not stop a deer rifle, but I'd imagine it would stop a shotgun or handgun."

"You imagine?" Amanda risked a glance at him. "That doesn't sound like warranty information, Sheriff."

"This thing was made by the lowest bidder, Deputy," Greg reminded her. "Always remember the lowest bidder rule."

"Lowest bidder," Amanda repeated. "Yeah. I don't think I like that," she added as she pulled into the gravel driveway.

"I never did either," Greg admitted. "Still better than a cruiser. Angle the front to the right a bit," he ordered. "That will afford us some cover as we dismount." She placed the Hummer where he wanted it, then pulled to a stop.

"Well, I'm going to have to get out and go see if they're home," Greg sighed.

"Not by yourself you ain't," Titus Terry said at once, his door already open.

Greg was on the verge of ordering him to stay behind when he thought better of it. Titus was essentially a soldier now, and a sworn deputy at that. He was adult enough to make those choices on his own.

"I got you," Kevin Bodee said softly, the sound of a round being racked into the M240 above them giving proof to the promise. Greg looked at Amanda, who was tense, but appeared to be handling it well.

"If you have to dismount, climb over the console and exit over here," he told her.

"Oh, I was gonna do that, anyway," she assured him, her face so serious that Greg had to stifle a laugh. Looking over his shoulder, he found Titus Terry watching him.

"Well, Titus, let's go see if they're home."

"Works for me," Titus said, opening his door just as the first bullet hit the driver's side of the Hummer.

"Hey, looks like they're home!" Titus said as he dove for the ground. Above him, Kevin Bodee began to methodically hose down the window the shot had come from, along with any other opening where he saw movement. Or what might be movement.

Scrambling over the console between the front seats, Amanda Lowery dove headfirst out of the Hummer and onto the ground, her rifle still in hand. Greg reached around her for the microphone and keyed the PA system.

"This is the Calhoun County Sheriff's Department!" his loud announcement booming through the amplified system. "Come out of the house, unarmed and with your hand visible! I repeat, come out unarmed, with your hands-,"

His orders were cut off by a fusillade of fire coming from the house. Behind him, Greg could hear Zach open fire with his gun, helping Kevin keep the people inside pinned down.

"Well, this is turning out to be a fine day, ain't it?" Greg said to himself.

"I'm gonna go out on a limb here and say they aren't going to surrender," Amanda told him, moving to place herself behind a tire.

"Pretty sure she's right," Titus agreed. He was behind the rear tire, watching the house window in front of him for movement. He had reserved fire for now, waiting for his shot.

"We can't see what they're doing around back," Greg noted. "They could be out there right now, either preparing for a flanking move or else escaping while their buddies are still firing."

"I can probably get around to where I can cover the back," Titus told him.

"No," Greg shook his head. "I won't risk losing anyone to these thugs. We'll take what we can and be satisfied. Kevin, which window do you think would be best for a 1060?" He was pulling a short, stubby looking weapon from the area behind the front seat.

"A thermo?" Kevin sounded incredulous. "Really?"

"I meant what I said, man," Greg replied, breaking open what looked like a large shotgun and slipping a canister inside. "I'm not losing anyone to these guys. I hate to waste the round on them, but whatever they're using, they've got a lot of it."

"Second window from the left has the most action," Kevin informed him. "It and the third window are likely the living room windows, but that's a guess. I estimate there are three shooters using those two windows."

"Copy that," Greg replied. "All units stand by for forty mil fire. Repeat, stand by for forty mil round. As soon as the round cooks off, Titus and I will hit the carport and try the door there, so watch for us to move. All units acknowledge." He waited for everyone to inform him they had heard his warning. Slipping around the front tire, he aimed for the window Kevin had told him to use and fired. He jerked back behind the tire at once, calling out.

"Round out! Round out!"

Almost as soon as he finished talking, the windows on the house seemed to belch smoke and flame. Greg had moved to the rear of the Hummer by then and tapped Titus on the shoulder to let him know it was time to move, while the people inside still had their heads spinning. Amanda began to fire single shots from behind the front tire in an effort to throw off anyone who was still conscious inside the house. Kevin Bodee also returned to firing the M240 in short, controlled bursts at each window to force the people inside to keep their heads down or get them shot off.

Greg raced for the carport, Titus hot on his heels. As he hit the carport's concrete floor, he heard Titus grunt behind him. Turning, he saw the teen holding his right arm, blood seeping through the sleeve.

"Ain't this some shit?" Titus complained. He pulled a compression bandage from his gear and Greg quickly wrapped it around the wound and tied it off.

"You good?" Greg asked him, looking him in the eyes to check him.

"It's okay," Titus promised. "I'm good to go." Patting his shoulder, Greg nodded and turned toward the carport door. A solid kick from his boot splintered the cheaply made door, busting the bolt and lock completely free. Titus saw the spoon of a fragmentation grenade go flying just before Greg called "Frag out!" and ducked against the wall as the grenade bounced around the corner and into the house.

Once more flame and smoke erupted from the house, though not nearly as much as the first round had caused. This round had produced a good deal more shrapnel, however, and Titus could hear someone crying out in pain. *Served the fucker right*, Titus decided.

"All units, hold fire," Greg called. "Moving in. Say again, all units hold fire!" He waited for the firing from outside to halt and to hear acknowledgments from everyone on the team before moving in.

Greg moved cautiously through the door, sweeping the room with his rifle before moving on. Titus trailed him, watching their back as he followed Greg through the house.

The house was a mess, and clearly had been even before the two grenades had made their impact. Whoever was making their home here clearly had no qualms about living in filth. The kitchen had a small bar but was otherwise open into a dining area. From there, a hallway stretched out of sight to other rooms, while a single door led to a front room of the house.

A figure holding a shotgun appeared out of the smoke in that door and earned a three-round burst from Greg's rifle for his troubles. Titus could see the body of another man lying in the dining room floor, clearly having caught the brunt of the frag Greg had lobbed inside. Just as Greg turned the corner of the doorway to check the front room, another man came running toward them down the hallway. Titus didn't hesitate, firing a pair of three-round bursts into the man before the rifle he carried could be brought to bear.

"That's three," Titus said, watching the hallway and the sliding patio door at the same time.

"Two more down in here," Greg informed him. Titus covered them while Greg checked the two figures. Neither was breathing.

"They're gone," he said, returning to the door. "You good to sweep and clear the house?"

"Right as rain," Titus promised. Greg nodded and moved down the hallway, stopping to check the man Titus had downed more from training than need. Six rounds had stitched him good and he was no longer a threat to society.

The rest of the rooms proved to be empty of any combatants, though they were full of plunder stolen from who knew where.

"House is clear," Greg keyed his radio. "Say again, house is clear. Gunner and Arrow remain on cover. Everyone else move into the house." He looked over at Titus, who was leaning against a wall, blood clearly soaking through his bandage.

"We need to get you home, man," Greg told the teen.

"Yeah, I think that might be a plan," Titus admitted, sliding down the wall. "I don't feel so good."

-

"Get him back as fast as you can," Greg ordered Amanda. Petra Shannon was in back with Titus, trying to administer what first aid she could. Kevin would go with them and inform Clay of their needs on the site.

"Go!" Greg slapped the door of the Hummer and Amanda took off. Greg watched them go before walking over to the MRAP and leaning against it.

"He okay?" Corey asked, having dismounted when the all clear was given. Zach remained in the turret for the time being.

"I think so," Greg replied. "It's a bleeder is the only thing that worries me. If they get him home fast enough it shouldn't be a problem."

"Okay." There wasn't much else to say to that.

"What do we do now?" Devon Knowles asked, still a little shell shocked. This had been her first time in any kind of actual combat.

"We'll wait for some help from the farm," Greg told her. "I asked for a truck and some muscle to haul this stuff out of here. We'll take the Blazer with us, or they will, while I head back to Garrett's to let them know we took care of it. After that, I'll need to check on Titus, and if he's okay, I imagine I'll take a shower and get a nap."

"That's it?" she asked, though not challenging. She was genuinely curious.

"That is it," Greg assured her. "We've answered the complaint, solved the problem and eliminated a threat to the community. A good day's work for any department. So long as Titus is okay, then it was a good day at work."

-

Amanda Lowery drove much faster going home than she had getting to the original call. Petra was doing her best to stop the bleeding, but she wasn't Tandi Maseo and it showed. Once they were moving and out of the immediate area, Kevin Bodee had dropped into the compartment and began assisting her.

"Tee, are you a bleeder?" Kevin asked.

"I seem to be bleeding right now," Titus replied with a chuckle. "But if you're asking if I make a habit of it, well, I try not to."

"Are you a free bleeder, you little ass wipe?" Kevin laughed as he slipped another bundle of gauze beneath the compression bandage and then tightened the bandage down.

"Not that I've ever been made aware of," Titus replied more seriously. "Maybe it was just a really big bullet?" He couldn't stay serious for long.

"Or maybe it hit a vein," Petra told him. "I need you to stop moving around so much, Titus. Every time you move that arm, the bleeding starts again."

"A vein?" Titus sounded alarmed. "Damn, that can't be good. I mean, it doesn't *sound* good."

"It's not good," she assured him. "But it's not the end of the world, or of you, so long as you *stop moving around*!" she hissed the last few words, trying to get through to him.

"Okay, okay," Titus held up his good arm in a placating manner. "This is me, not moving around. Sorry. See? Here I am, just a knot on an old log, laying here in the-."

"Does he ever shut up?" Petra asked Kevin, who was trying not to laugh despite the seriousness of the problem.

"Only rarely, and never for long," he assured her.

"I'm right here, you know," Titus reminded them.

"Yes, we know."

-

Amanda had warned JJ, who in turn had warned the clinic that there was a gunshot wound inbound, and that it wouldn't stop bleeding. By the time the Hummer screeched to a halt in front of Building Two, three men with a stretcher were waiting to unload Titus and carry him inside, where Jaylyn, Patricia and Kaitlin all three were waiting.

"Talk to us," Jaylyn ordered as Kevin came through the door.

"Well, I'm a Pisces," Titus muttered. "I like picnics, pretty sunsets and big-,"

"Not you, stupid," Patricia told him with a laugh, covering his face with the nitrous mask as she patted his cheek fondly.

"He took a round to the arm in a house assault," Kevin reported. "Wrapped the wound and continued to clear the house before stopping to rest, at which point he didn't exactly collapse but was pretty weak. We've worked all the way back trying to stanch the bleeding, but we couldn't quite get it to stop. He's lost enough blood that he's punch-drunk, but I don't think it's enough to be threatening just yet. We saved all the bandage material so you could judge for yourself, as much as possible, anyway." He held out the bloody bundle and Jaylyn quickly and efficiently looked through it.

"He's close, though," she murmured. "Thank you," she told Kevin without looking at him. "We need an IV started with fluids to help him build back his blood volume. We're also going to have to dig around in there," she pointed to the wound. "I think it's likely that the bullet is still there since it's a deep wound and there's no exit. Whatever it hit, that is likely what makes the bleeding want to continue. I don't think it's arterial since it's on the outside of the arm, nor a vein, but it could be a nick of some kind in the vein if it's deep enough. Which means we'll have to take a look and see." She glanced at Titus.

"Is he under?" she asked Patricia, who nodded.

"Oh yes," she replied. "Took about ten seconds and he was gone."

"Good," Jaylyn nodded. "Let's get this show on the road while he's out. This will hurt like a bitch."

-

Gordy was in the small 'waiting room' area in front of the clinic when Marcy George came busting inside, sliding to a halt at the clinic door. He had expected this, and before she could continue her bursting into the clinic itself, Gordy had grabbed her arms from behind and pulled her away from the door.

"Let me go!" she shouted, and he did, but quickly enveloped her in a hug instead, continuing to pull her away from the doorway.

"Dammit, Gordy Sanders, *let me go*!" she yelled, fighting him every step.

"Stop it, Marcy," he said gently. "He's in surgery now, so you can't see him or talk to him, and we would just expose him to germs he doesn't need. Just wait until they get done and I'll make sure you can see him even if he's out cold."

"I need to see him *now*!" she insisted. "What happened to him? Who let him get shot? How bad is it? Are you gonna tell me or not?"

"I will if you let me get a word in edgewise," Gordy promised. "As to what happened, you already know that. He did indeed get shot, in the arm. He was helping go after some men who had murdered two people in cold blood up in front of Garrett's Store. He caught the round as he made for the house. He and Greg wrapped it in a bandage and cleared the house, but Titus was still bleeding so Greg put him in his Hummer and sent him back right then. Now he's in surgery and you know everything there is to know until they finish."

He concluded. He loosened his grip but tightened it again as she moved against him in an instant.

"Marcy, promise me you'll stay here and behave, and I'll let you go," Gordy told her gently. "I'll stay here with you the whole time, I promise. But you can't go busting down the door while they're in there digging around for a bullet and sewing him up like that. Let them do their work and then you can see him. I'll make sure of it."

"Fine," the answer came out sharp, as if it were a cross between surly and a sob. "Is he gonna be okay?" she asked softly.

"I think so," Gordy told her, carefully releasing her. "The only thing they were concerned about was the blood loss, and from what I was told, it wasn't quite enough to worry them based on the bandages. He was still talking and cracking jokes when they put him under."

Marcy turned suddenly and buried her face in Gordy's chest, sobbing so hard that her entire body shook. Gordy hugged her close and let her cry. Marcy had held fast to Titus since her family had gone to Jordan. She had refused to go and been effectively disowned because of it. While she had friends and people who were as close as family all around her, it wasn't the same as having your actual family about you. Gordy could understand that even though he had no way to empathize, since he had always been surrounded by his own family.

But that didn't keep him from realizing and recognizing the importance that Titus Terry played in her life. Sam was in a similar position, though her close friendship with his sister Abigail and her relationship with his parents through that friendship meant that Sam was not quite so isolated as Marcy felt.

Gordy wondered if race played a part in her feelings of isolation. There were but seven black people on the farm aside from two of the orphans. Titus and Marcy were two of them, then there was Beverly Jackson and her son JJ, Moses Brown, Stacey Pryor, and now Janessa Haynes. So far as Gordy knew, there wasn't a single person on the farm anywhere that had any kind of racial prejudice whatsoever, at least not in their group, but that did not lessen the impact that Marcy might be feeling despite that fact. Titus didn't seem to feel it, but Titus had been friends with Gordy and the others for so long that they were more like brothers. Titus had spent many a weekend at the Sanders' home, and even weeks at a time during the summer. They had played ball together, chased girls together, fished and drank beer together. Had anyone ever said anything remotely racial to Titus over the years, that someone would have found themselves surrounded by his friends, all looking for a piece of the offending party. They never had to bother declaring themselves as equals because it had always been so.

Gordy didn't know how Beverly and JJ felt about it, but neither seemed to notice the disparity. They were from a large city, however, where such things might not be as prevalent as they were in rural America. Moses Brown was an older man than any of the others, and had no doubt suffered that kind of isolation and discrimination through the years of his own life. Mister Brown was also possessed of a confidence and character that showed he had long ago mastered how to deal with the concerns he might face due to race. Gordy liked and respected Mister Brown a great deal.

Janessa was a local and had obviously known some of the others in her group before the Storm had hit. She had bonded with the remainder of the group during training, seeming to get along well with all the others, including Abby and Sam. While Janessa had also lost her family, albeit to violence rather than a bitter falling out, she was probably six or maybe seven years older than Marcy, years that meant a great deal in terms of maturity. Maturity that might well help Janessa better deal with current events than Marcy could. Not necessarily easier, just better.

Stacey Pryor had men around him that were as good as family and had no difficulty fitting in. Neither had John Barnes, for that matter. Gordy assumed that his Uncle Clay and the others paid about as much attention to their racial differences as Gordy and his own friends did, which was not at all.

Marcy was literally the odd woman out without Titus in the picture. No one on the farm would ever treat her poorly or less than equal with everyone else, but she had clung to Titus when her family situation had come apart and he had become very important to her in more ways than one. He had become a lifeline for her when the world seemed to be crumbling around her yet again. The idea that she might lose him now had to be terrifying to her in a way that Gordy doubted he could fully understand.

But he could lend her his shoulder to cry on, and he did, holding her as she bawled her eyes out against him while they waited to hear from the medical team about Titus' condition.

"It's okay, Marcy," he soothed as best he could. "You know you're not alone, right? All of us here consider you family. Titus is going to be okay, and we're going to be right here with you. He'll be using this for months to get out of working. Probably lay up all winter long, whining and complaining."

He kept talking to her, low and gentle, until she finally seemed to cry herself out. She tried to pull away from him, but he refused to let her, guiding her instead to a group of chairs along the wall.

"Rest," he ordered her, placing her on an office sofa, something you would find in an actual waiting room. "Rest and get your calm back, okay? I'm going to get a blanket for you and will be right back. You better be here when I do, too."

"Or what?" she challenged, a hint of her normal personality shining through.

"You're not too big to go over my knee, young lady," he threatened, then grinned at her. She managed a small laugh and stuck her tongue out at him.

Shaking his head, he went to a cabinet for a blanket for her and returned only to find her curled into a ball on the sofa, sound asleep. Smiling, he put the blanket over her and then took a seat next to the sofa, keeping his promise to stay with her until they knew anything.

-

It was Patricia who brought the news out to the small waiting area. Clay had joined them after dispatching a truck and more help for Greg, concern showing on his face as Gordy relayed what he knew of the situation.

"Got to expect more of that I guess," Clay sighed. "Been going on all this time I'm sure. It's just that now we got the radio system working, so we hear about it."

"That and Greg has to go check on it," Gordy nodded. He stopped talking as the door to the clinic opened and his mother stepped out. He carefully shook Marcy's sleeping form and the girl shot straight up, blanket falling away as she rubbed sleep from her eyes.

"How is he?" she demanded at once. "Is he gonna be okay? Where is he? Can I see him?"

"Easy there," Patricia smiled, holding a hand up. "He's still asleep, but yes, he's going to be fine. He had a bullet lodged in his arm and that was what kept the wound bleeding. Weeping, we call it. It was only a trickle of blood, but it was enough to make the others concerned, and rightly so. But he's going to be fine. Probably be milking this for all it's worth for the next month or so, but truthfully he should be okay in no more than two weeks."

"When can I see him?" Marcy was on her feet.

"You can go in now if you stay quiet," Patricia told her. "You can sit with him until he wakes up. I'm sure he'd love to see you when he opens his eyes. Just don't try to wake him. Let him come to on his own. Okay?"

"I will!" Marcy stage whispered as she ran for the clinic door. "Thank you!"

"You're welcome, dear," Patricia couldn't help but laugh. Shaking her head, she turned to her son and brother-in-law.

"I assume you kept her from running in during his treatment?" she asked Gordy.

"Yeah," he nodded. "I knew as soon as she heard she'd come barreling in here, and she did."

"Good job," she patted her son on the shoulder fondly. "When did you grow up on me?" she smiled, kissing his forehead. She turned to Clay.

"He's okay," she assured him. "His arm will be sore for a while, and he's now got a nice bullet to make a necklace out of, but he's okay."

"Good to hear," Clay sighed. "Too much excitement around here lately."

"Things are a lot quieter than they used to be," Gordy mentioned. "If what we had before is the alternative, I'll take this and be just fine, thanks."

CHAPTER NINE

"Do you know any of these guys?" Kevin Bodee asked as the fifth and final body was brought from the house and settled on the ground.

"That one is Neil Bonney," Greg pointed to a dark haired, bearded body at the end of the line. "He was a suspect in several robberies, but we could never prove anything. He was always careful. This one," he kicked the foot of the last body out, "is Kiefer Bone. Never knew the two of them to run together, but I guess stranger stuff has happened of late."

"Kiefer Bone?" Kevin repeated. "Please tell me that's not his real name."

"That is his real name," Greg confirmed. "His mother was a fan and named him after the actor. Bone was his daddy's real last name. His mom died when he was maybe seven or so, I think. Raised by his dad's people after that, and they are complete losers. If any of them are still alive then once this gets out, they'll paint for war as the saying goes. They're a big outfit, too. It'll cause some issues, probably."

"You don't think they'll consider it better to cut their losses, considering?" Kevin motioned to the MRAP behind him.

"Not that bunch," Greg shook his head. "They-, do you hear that?" he stopped short, tilting his head.

"*Vehicle sounds from the south*," Zach reported just then, still in the MRAP they had originally been in. When Greg had sent Titus to the farm for medical attention, he had asked Clay for more help. That help had included Stacey Pryor, Shane Golden, Cliff Laramie and Janessa Haynes, as well as the return of Kevin Bodee, Amanda Lowery and Petra Shannon. They had arrived with the six-wheel MRAP nicknamed Gray Ghost, as well as a pickup truck with a trailer suitable to pull a car if necessary. The Blazer had already been loaded onto the trailer as soon as the top had been replaced. Now people were streaming in and out of the house carrying stolen goods and placing them either in the back of the truck or into the Blazer, depending on what they had found.

"Okay, let's get deployed!" Greg called. "Vehicles inbound from the wrong direction to be ours! Shane, Stacey, Amanda, Petra, inside the house and on the windows. Be sure and watch the back, Shane. Cliff, you're inside as well," he told the sole noncombatant. "Everyone else spread out and be ready to take cover. Kevin, get the gun in the other MRAP manned."

"On it!" Kevin was already moving. Greg watched as Corey moved to stand by the fender of the Sheriff's MRAP while Janessa stayed close to the Ghost. He motioned for her to move behind the armored fender of the vehicle and she complied with a nod.

"*We're set*," Shane Golden's voice sounded in his ear.

"Roger that," Greg replied. "We'll just have to see who this is."

"*It's an MRAP,*" Zach said quietly from his vantage point in the turret. "*Like this one. There's a fifty mounted on it, and it's manned.*"

"Good eye, Zach," Greg replied. "Kevin, that's going to be on you," he added. The Ghost also had a fifty.

"*I am good to go,*" Kevin assured him.

Greg waited as the vehicle came into sight. Behind the small MRAP were two Hummers, also with guns in the turrets. All were flying the flag, but these days they didn't mean as much as it once had. The three vehicles slowed as they saw the collected vehicles near the house, coming to a stop about twenty-five yards away from the nearest Sheriff's vehicle. Greg didn't miss how the big fifty on the MRAP swung around to cover his people, but he stayed still for the moment.

Two people got down from the MRAP. Greg would once have thought the two were clearly soldiers, probably Guardsmen, based on their dress and equipment, but those days were long gone. Now they were heavily armed potential enemies. As they drew closer, Greg could see a bar on the younger man's collar, and stripes of a Staff Sergeant on the older man.

"Who are you?" the younger man demanded. No hello, nice to meet you, how's it going, nothing.

"Greg Holloway, Calhoun County Sheriff," Greg replied amiably. "Who are you?"

"What's going on here?" the man demanded without answering.

"I'm finishing a murder investigation at the moment," Greg replied. "I asked who you were."

"What authority do you-,"

"Oh, for fuck's sake, I'm not doing this," Greg interrupted. "Who the hell are you and why are you in my county in military vehicles and carrying military gear?"

The young man's head rocked back as if he'd been physically slapped.

"I'm Lieutenant Faron Gillis," the man replied.

"Ah," Greg nodded. "You're Adcock's second down in Lewis, then. What are you guys doing up here? Not enough to keep you busy around Lewiston?"

"How do you know Captain Adcock?" Gillis asked, now looking a little nervous.

"Met him when he visited the Sanders' Farm," Greg replied. "He said you'd be handling things for him out of Lewiston while he commanded the area overall. Still, you're off the beaten path from Lewiston, a bit."

"We heard shooting and came to investigate," Gillis told him.

"Well, we appreciate that, but in this case the fun's already over," Greg shrugged. "These misguided individuals robbed and killed two men in broad daylight earlier today back up the road in front of a country store full of witnesses. We tracked them to here and they refused to surrender by opening fire on us, wounding one of my men. Now we're just cleaning up."

"What are you loading up in that truck?" Gillis asked.

"We call that evidence," Greg was getting tired of attitude. "I'm hoping to find the owners of said evidence still living but based on the way these miscreants acted this morning, I'm not overly hopeful. Still, a man can hope. Otherwise, I'm hoping that recovery of this stuff will close other open cases such as theft of property in this immediate area. Several members of the community reported they had been missing items recently. With any luck, some of it will be in here, and I can return it to the rightful owners."

"And if you can't?" Gillis demanded.

"Goes into lockup until the time runs out, then probably gets sold by the county. That was the old way, anyhow. No idea what the new way will be, assuming there is one. Like I said, I hope most of it can be returned to its owners. If not the actual owners, then at least their next of kin. Try to at least get it back home."

"I don't remember seeing you at the Sanders' Farm when I was there," Gillis said, eyes narrowed.

"I don't recall seeing you there, either," Greg shrugged. "Just remember Adcock talking about you."

"That's *Captain* Adcock," Gillis corrected.

"To you," Greg nodded. "He's not my Captain. Look, I hate to be rude, but we still got a lot of work to do, so what else can I do for you?"

"I think I'll have to detain you until I can clear your story with the Captain," Gillis was shaking his head even as his sergeant was trying to whisper in his ear. Greg's laugh cut the quiet conversation off as Gillis' head jerked up sharply.

"How did Adcock get stuck with all these asshole Lieutenants?" Greg asked. "I mean, he seems like a good guy, and Sergeants Maxwell and Gleason seem to have their shit wired straight, but man, he was three up and three down with you clowns. Flores, then Gaines, and now you."

"Let me tell you something, kid," he continued. "You ain't detaining shit. Got that? I am the senior law enforcement official for the entire county of Calhoun, appointed to that post by Major Whitten, by virtue of being the sole surviving member of my department. I'm fairly certain that your sergeant there," Greg pointed, "is doing his best to keep you from screwing up, so if he is, I'd listen to him. You are not only out of your assigned patrol area, you're interfering in a civilian law enforcement investigation, which you lack the authority to be doing."

"Now I don't have a problem with you all moving through Calhoun, so long as you don't cause trouble, but don't think for a damn minute you're going to come in here on top of me and my men and act like you're in charge and taking over. I assure you, you ain't."

The young lieutenant and his sergeant conferred for a second.

"I think he's the right guy," Gillis said finally, allowing his rifle to hang on his sling.

"Yes, sir," The sergeant turned to the vehicles behind them and made a series of hand motions. The men in the turrets visibly relaxed and their weapons turned away from Greg's vehicles.

"*Did I miss something*?" Kevin asked softly. No one replied as Gillis and his sergeant walked forward.

"Hi, I'm Faron Gillis," the officer smiled, extending his hand. "This is Staff Sergeant Lowell Martinson. Sorry about the asshole bit," he apologized sheepishly. "Our briefing was that this area had been hit hard by a phony military unit. We were just making sure that wasn't making a comeback."

"Greg Holloway," Greg took the hand. "I understand." He turned his head. "I appreciate it, actually. Okay, we can get back to work!" he called back toward the house. Gillis' eyes widened slightly as five people exited the house, four of them obviously trained and equipped to take on trouble.

"Yeah, you were about to get whipsawed," Greg nodded. "Good move to stop so far back, though. Most people would have just rode right on up on us."

"Ole Lowe here would kick my ass if I did that," Gillis laughed, jerking a thumb at Sergeant Martinson. "He trained me better than to completely screw up."

"That don't mean he doesn't partly screw up, however," Martinson chuckled. "Nice to meet you, Sheriff," he shook Greg's hand. "Was pretty sure I heard a couple of grenades," he added, looking at the bodies on the ground.

"You did," Greg nodded. "I'm not going to lose any of my men trying to take murderers alive if they won't surrender. They were holed up in the house and hosing us down pretty good. I fixed that."

"Looks that way," Gillis agreed. "Was this all of them?"

"According to witnesses there were five in the attack this morning, and in a vehicle just like that one," he jerked his head toward the Blazer. "If there are more of them in the group? No idea, and no one this morning reported anything of the sort. You been having problems, too?"

"Not us, per se," Gillis shook his head. "We've been trying to support the LEOs out of Lewiston and they've had some serious issues, but so far as I know they don't even have a description of the attackers. Whoever it is, they choose their targets carefully, hitting isolated areas where there aren't many people. And they don't leave anyone alive behind them," he added grimly.

"I can't honestly say what this crew was doing other than their attack this morning," Greg admitted. "They pulled up, shot two men down, took whatever they had, and ran. There were plenty of others around, but they didn't move on them at all."

"Probably not connected then," Gillis mused. "Doesn't pay to assume that, of course, but it's likely. Well, we need to finish our sweep, Sheriff," Gillis extended his hand once more. "We cut off to come investigate the gunfire. Have to finish up so I can report in that I have done my duty."

"Been there, done that," Greg nodded. "It was good to meet you guys. Adcock had good things to say about you, by the way. Just so you know," he winked, and Martinson chuckled as Gillis turned red.

"I'm sure," he muttered to himself.

"I'm serious," Greg promised. "Said 'he's young, but his head is on straight'. In the Corps, that was a compliment. Don't know about the Army."

"Well, I appreciate his confidence," Gillis finally mumbled. "Good luck, Sheriff. Maybe we'll meet again under more pleasant circumstances."

"Maybe we will," Greg agreed. "I'd like that. You guys ride safe."

"Well, Clay did mention that Adcock said he had at least one officer with the sense God gave a piss ant," Shane noted as they watched the three-vehicle group turn around and depart.

"Yep," Greg nodded. "Seems like he's right. Where are we on getting this stuff loaded?"

-

"That's them," one of the men at the grocery said firmly. "And that is definitely the truck," he added, pointing to the Blazer.

"Hey, that's looks like my hand augur!" another man exclaimed, looking in the bed of the truck.

"Probably is, if yours is missing," Greg told him. "If you think it's yours, take it." He looked at the group around him.

"Any of the rest of you missing anything? Or know anyone this stuff belongs to? Unfortunately, it may have to go to next of kin, depending on how this bunch was operating. Gather around and help me figure it out if you can."

-

"Everyone makes it up here once a week or so," Garrett promised. "It's how we can keep up with who's okay or not. Anyone who comes in can claim whatever belongs to them or their folks. I honestly don't know who any of it goes to, myself. Still, I can leave it in the glass case and folks can look."

"Appreciate you doing that, Ransom," Greg assured him. "I'll do something to make it up to you, soon as I get the chance."

"Could leave me that Blazer," Garrett joked.

"Can't do that, but I may can get you something else," Greg surprised him. "You still got gas?"

"About three hundred, three hundred fifty gallons, give or take," Garrett nodded. "Hadn't been long past a top off when the lights went out. Got a five-hundred-gallon tank. Lost some to evaporation I'm sure, and it's gone a bit stale by now, but a gallon or two of creek water will perk it right up," he winked. 'Creek water' had long been a euphemism for moonshine.

"That it will," Greg laughed. "Okay then. I'll see if I can't round you up a truck of some kind for the store. My only condition is that you have to help the community with it when it's something really important. Maybe organize trips into Jordan or Lewiston at some point when things start picking up."

"I can do that," Garrett nodded. "Thanks for thinking of us like that, Greg. And for taking care of this," he indicated the bodies on the trailer.

"That's my job," Greg slapped the older man's shoulder. "What they pay me for," he added with a grin.

"They're paying you?" Garrett asked, eyebrows raised.

"Lord, no," Greg scoffed. "That was a joke. What would they pay me with? See you around, Ransom."

"Be safe, Sheriff."

-

"Sounds like you had a full day," Clay observed after Greg had summarized the day's action.

"That and then some," Greg agreed. "Thanks for the help, by the way. Titus awake?"

"He is, and got Marcy George chewing his ears off," Clay grinned. "She's waiting for you to get there, too."

"Perfect," Greg snorted. "Well, I don't blame her. But for him I guess she feels all alone up here, nowadays."

"I would imagine she does," Clay turned serious. "We've got to fix that, somehow."

"Got any ideas about how to do it?" Greg asked over his shoulder as he started to the clinic.

"No," Clay admitted. "I don't. I think I'm going to turn it over to the ladies and see what they can do. I feel certain they can do a better job of it than me."

-

"I have thought about that," Lainie said later that evening. "It's not just her family being gone, either. It's also a racial divide, you know."

"No, I didn't know," Clay frowned. "Is someone causing problems along that line?"

"No one has to, Clay," Lainie shook her head, hair swishing behind her. "It's just a natural fact. There are just seven black people on this entire place aside from I think two children in the orphanage. Jose, Martina and her children are the only Latinos here as well. Tandi is the sole Asian. Jody the lone Native. I mean, technically it's as diverse a group as you could ask for in the rural south I should think, but that doesn't mean anything to the individuals in the group who are facing it."

"While no one on this farm that I'm aware of has uttered a single racial remark at all, and I mean since the start of things, that does not eliminate the feeling of isolation that they may well be feeling because of the disparity. I've thought of this more than once, but I honestly don't know what we can do that we aren't already doing."

"Stacey and John never seemed to have any trouble," Clay frowned, searching his memory. "Tandi and Jose don't either, at least not that I know of. Nor Jody neither, since you mentioned him."

"All of them were part of your unit, Clay," Lainie explained patiently. "All of you are as close, or closer than brothers and have been for some time. So no, they aren't going to experience that kind of isolation in the same way civilians are likely to. That doesn't mean they won't feel it, or experience it, just that it will be unlikely to have the same impact on them."

"Huh," Clay sat heavily into his recliner, staring at the wall in front of him. Of all the things he had worried over and planned for, this had not been one of them. Clay didn't think in terms of race himself, and apparently had decided that meant no one else did, either.

What else had he missed that might be having a negative effect on someone that was at least nominally under his care?

"Stop that," Lainie knew the signs that were playing across Clay's features. "We've already covered this ground, Cowboy. You can't think of everything, and the rest can think about these problems as well as you can. Let them deal with some of that. You've got enough on your plate as it is. I loved Leon like my own family, but he handed you a mess when he died. You have done a remarkable job dealing with it, but it has taken its toll, too."

"Still, I should have at least been-,"

"Stop it, I said," Lainie cut his protest off cleanly. "I'll gather some of the others together and see if we can have a real discussion about this. For all we know, no one is suffering from it at all, other than possibly Marcy, and we don't know for sure about her. She has the added trauma of what happened with her and her family to deal with as well. There may not be a problem at all, even for her, so don't borrow trouble. If there is a problem, we'll figure it out."

"Sure," he didn't sound convinced, his confidence shaken by having overlooked something so basic. Of late he had felt more confident, really, having thought he was dealing with things much better than he had early on. Now, he had to go back and reevaluate his job performance. Lainie was right in that Leon had left a bit of a mess behind, but it was more than that. With Leon gone, there was no one to warn him about things just like this.

"Hey," Lainie was suddenly standing over him, and he honestly hadn't even seen her moving. "Enough," she ordered, leaning down to put herself face-to-face with him. "No more of this tonight. Understand?"

"I'll try," he promised, mustering a weak smile. "Best I can promise."

"I bet I can distract you," she smiled softly.

-

"You know, it ain't like I did it on purpose," Titus said wearily to an irate Marcy George. "And Greg, he made me do it!" he added as the latter walked in.

"What?" Greg almost yelled. "You were the first one out of the truck, Titus Terry!" the offended Sheriff of Calhoun County bellowed back. "Don't try to foist your failures off on me!"

"Foist?" Jaylyn Thatcher chimed in from across the room. "Awful big word for a Marine, ain't it?"

"And no commenting from the peanut gallery, either!" Greg shot back, laughing. "They tell me he'll live," he added.

"I had thought so until she got here," Jaylyn nodded toward Marcy as she continued working. "Now? Not so sure."

"Well, I guess I'll just be going, then," Greg snorted. "If he ain't gonna make it anyway, there's no reason for me to waste the time and effort talking to him."

"See?" Titus exclaimed to Marcy, as if that exchange proved his point. "Absolutely no regard at all for my well-being!"

"If I didn't know you like I do, I might be more inclined to believe that," Marcy replied somewhat flatly. "Since I do, however, I'm forced to give the county official the benefit of the doubt in this case."

"Guess that told you," Greg said firmly, smirking at Titus. His look grew more serious after that, as he looked down at Titus.

"You look like you're going to be in good hands but is there anything you need?" he asked.

"Nah, I'm okay," Titus promised. "Shouldn't be laid up more than three months or so-,"

"Two weeks," Jaylyn corrected without bothering to look up. "Two weeks and he'll be more than able to do at least light duty."

"But another three months or so before I can-," Titus kept trying.

"A month at best before he's back to full battery," the doctor had heard all of this once already. "He's fine. Honestly, he'll need more time to build his blood back than for the wound to heal."

"So, I'll be too weak to do any-," Titus tried one more time.

"Give it a rest, you goldbrick," Marcy was the one to cut him off this time. "Here I was scared half to death, and you had basically cut yourself shaving."

"He shaves?" Greg feigned surprise. "I had no idea!"

"Har, har," Titus affected a hurt look. "Just go ahead and kick a man while he's down, why don't you?"

"Well since you seem to be doing fine," Greg snorted, "I'm going to get cleaned up and turn in. I've had a long day myself. Get some rest, since you're all crippled and what not," he took one last jab at Titus.

"He will, as soon as I'm done talking to him," Marcy promised.

"I'm awful sleepy…," was the last thing Greg heard Titus saying as he left.

-

Greg's swift action in dealing with the murder and robbery at Garrett's spread along the radio circuit, and more importantly, through the gossip grapevine. People who had avoided his patrols up to that point began to remain in the open when the Sheriff's Patrol came through, often waving Greg down to report on something or other, or else just to ask what was happening around the area.

It had taken the twins less than a week to decide how to handle their idea for a radio news show. Using the amateur bands as well as the citizen's bands, they would be able to broadcast what news there was to everyone within hearing distance but focused primarily on the people of Calhoun County. They were careful to prepare ahead of time to ensure that they weren't putting anything over the air that might give criminals any more information than they already had access to. They chose Friday evenings at six o'clock to make their broadcast, and Greg began spreading the news to anyone he encountered in his travels, as well as warning all those with radios to be listening in.

The first show lasted only eight minutes by Leon's watch. There was not a great deal of information to share so early on, and most of that was limited to announcing that yes, the National Guard was present in the area, and yes, it was the real National Guard this time, and that they were trying to help restore order as much as possible. They had also announced that Greg had been made Sheriff, and that the patrols that had been seen were also real and could be flagged down for help or for information.

Leanne had already spoken to Doctor Thatcher and to their Aunt Patricia about the possibility of doing short talks on how to maintain better health and what could be used as alternatives for various medicines and hygiene products. The idea was to gradually add as many types of helpful tips and tidbits as they could, hoping to help as many people as possible.

After the first week, Leon had hit upon the idea to allow each of the stations to have five minutes of time following the initial news show to send messages for family members separated by long distances, to advertise community get-togethers and also goods and services that were available. Anything that would serve as a morale booster and also help return life to at least some small semblance of normal. Doing that had extended the show to a half-hour more, depending on what each 'station' had to say.

By the time Thanksgiving was approaching, the radio 'shows' had become a big hit, with everyone gathering around the nearest radio to hear what was being said, even if they already knew whatever it was. The simple act of hearing someone talking over a radio helped isolated families and communities feel less cutoff from the rest of the area. It wasn't a true replacement for what had been lost the year before, but it was something.

It was a start.

CHAPTER TEN

It was the day before Thanksgiving and the weather had turned colder, with what appeared to be rain on the horizon. 'Perfect pneumonia weather', the older folks called it.

Greg had decided to make a long patrol on both Tuesday and Wednesday before Thanksgiving trying to cover as much of the county as possible before the holiday. Tuesday had gone by without a hitch and Wednesday was well on the way to doing the same.

"I'm not complaining about anything being boring," Amanda said as the Hummer sped along, "but-,"

"Shut up!" Gordy, Greg and Shane all said at once, startling her.

"Sorry," she shrank down a bit in the rear passenger side seat. "Just saying."

"When you say it, it screws everything up," Gordy said from behind the wheel. "It's uncanny."

"But still true," Shane nodded.

"How you guys making it back there?" Greg smiled at the antics around him as he checked on the MRAP following them. Stacey Pryor, Tandi Maseo, Heath Kelly, Janessa Haynes and Devon Knowles were riding there, Janessa taking a turn behind the wheel.

"*We're chopping in tall cotton as my grandma used to say*," Stacey replied with a chuckle. "*Had to bust up a card game earlier, though.*"

"I'd rather we play cards than have trouble," Greg laughed. "At this rate, we may make it home in-,"

Whatever Greg hoped to make it home for would remain forever unsaid as the windshield of the Hummer stared in six different places within the space of two seconds as bullets impacted all over the vehicle.

"We're taking fire!" Greg yelled into the radio as Gordy fought to get control of the vehicle, having momentarily lost it when he had been startled by the gunfire.

"Fire flashes coming from that barn ahead to the east of the road," Heath Kelly informed him from the turret of the MRAP. "Range, two hundred twenty yards."

"Stop or go?" Gordy shouted, finally having the Hummer back in hand. He was now weaving from one side of the road to the other, reminiscent of how stock car drivers would drive when trying to save their brakes while following a pace car.

"Anyone hurt?" Greg asked rather than answer.

"Does my underwear count?" Shane tried to joke.

"I don't actually feel so good," Amanda said from beside him. She brought her hands away from her abdomen with blood on them.

"Amanda's hit!" Shane called, moving to pull her vest and blouse away from the wound. "She took a round on the lower left side, above the belt line!"

"Find us a place where we can cover long enough to get Tandi in here or else get her in the MRAP!" Greg told Gordy.

"Doc, we got a casualty up here," he then called back to the MRAP. "We're hunting cover so we can do a transfer. Heath, can you still see gunfire from that barn?"

"*Nothing since the original flashes*," Heath replied.

"Can you-," Greg's request was cut short by a booming rifle from behind them as Heath Kelly opened fire on someone in the distance.

"Okay, here's what we're going to do," Greg said as Gordy began to slow as he pulled behind a heavy stand of trees. "Shane and I are going to move to the Cougar while Doc, Devon and Janessa move up here. Gordy, you stick here and as soon as they're on board, you take out for home and don't spare the horses. We'll take the Cougar and move up on the barn, throwing suppressing fire on them as we go. Everybody got that?"

"No one to work the gun in here," Gordy reminded him. Greg thought about that for all of five seconds.

"You take it and put Janessa behind the wheel," he ordered a quick solution. "Okay, let's move!" he ordered as the vehicle pulled to a halt.

Behind them, Doc, Janessa and Devon were already moving forward. Greg and Shane both bailed out of the passenger side and ran for the Cougar as Doc crammed into the back seat with Devon Knowles, while Janessa Haynes slid behind the wheel even as Gordy made his way into the turret.

"We're good, let's go!" Doc yelled as he tore his bag from his back and dropped it in the floor below him. "Let me see," he told a trembling Amanda. "Move your hands, Amanda, and let me see," he repeated as she continued to hold her hands to her side.

"Dammit, Mavis, *move your fucking hands*!" Devon screamed, fear and anger giving her voice strength. That got a reaction as Amanda's eyes narrowed.

"I have asked you, *repeatedly*, not to call me *Mavis*!" she ground out through clenched teeth, allowing Doc to pull her hands away. Shane had already unclasped Amanda's harness and vest, so all that remained to do was pull it over her head. Devon took care of that, fighting for balance as Janessa whirled the vehicle around in the road and began speeding back the way they had come, weaving the vehicle from white line to white line just as Gordy had done. Gordy rotated the turret around so that he was facing back toward the barn, though the odds of his hitting anything with the M240 with them maneuvering like this were limited.

Tandi tore Amanda's blouse open, exposing her torso and learning that Amanda had not deigned to wear a bra or shirt beneath her uniform today.

"Laundry day," the red-faced Amanda explained. Tandi had ignored her bare chest anyway in favor of looking at her wounded abdomen. Rinsing the blood away with distilled water, he managed to get a look at the wound. He felt carefully behind her for an exit wound and breathed a slight sigh of relief when he didn't find one. Anything strong enough to go through her vest would have destroyed her back on the way out. As it was, her vest had apparently slowed the round enough that it could not do near the damage it might have.

"Okay then," Tandi muttered to himself. "Devon, check the plates on her rig. I need to know if any of the material is missing. It could have fragmented into the wound and-,"

"It didn't," Amanda didn't look at him as she spoke.

"How do you know?" Tandi demanded.

"I wasn't wearing them," she admitted, her voice subdued.

"You what?" Tandi asked, as if he hadn't quite heard her.

"I wasn't wearing the plates, okay!" Amanda gasped as Tandi's hands probed her wound. "I…it's really uncomfortable on the girls when I'm not wearing a bra, and it's a damn holiday and, well…." She didn't bother finishing, seeing the look on the medic's face.

"It's uncomfortable," he repeated. "You left the ceramic out of your vest, the same ceramic that would likely have prevented this wound from being more than a bruise, *because it made your tits uncomfortable?*!" He was screaming by the time he finished. "Are you fucking *kidding me*?!"

"Easy, Doc," Gordy said from above. "Plenty of time to chew her ass out later. Assuming you make sure there is a later."

"Unbelievable," Tandi was shaking his head. "Bear wore his vest and caught the unluckiest round ever. Shane wore his and was almost hollowed out from the inside. And you," he glared, "you wanted to be more comfortable."

"S-s-sorry," Amanda stammered, pain hitting her now that the shock was wearing off. "I really thought t-t-today it would be okay, Doc. I've never not worn them before, I s-s-swear. I just didn't have anything to wear underneath."

Tandi ignored her as he set about trying to save her from her own lack of forethought.

Meanwhile, Shane had taken the wheel in the Cougar and was now charging hard straight for the barn where the fire had come from.

"Whatever they're using it had to be strong enough to go through her vest at two hundred plus," Greg was saying. "Got to be a hunting rifle, and we need to be damned careful. This is the same round that punched through a Hummer windscreen before penetrating a vest."

"She didn't have her plates in," Shane informed him calmly.

"What?" three different voices said in unison.

"She wasn't wearing her plates," Shane repeated.

"How do you know?" Stacey asked.

"I would have felt them when I unfastened her harness and vest to get to her wound," Shane replied. "I didn't. For whatever reason, she wasn't wearing them."

"For fu-," Greg cut himself off. Cursing her decision would do no good right now. Not with six or more rifles aimed at them.

"Heath, anything?" he asked instead.

"Not since the one," Heath replied, still searching the area around the barn as they drew close.

"Have you seen anyone leaving the barn?"

"No, but you can't use that," Heath told him. "We were out of sight while we played musical vehicles. I couldn't see anything going on then. The one I got was still in the loft, but for all I know he was alone."

"Okay then, we'll play it hard and fast," Greg decided. "Shane, if the barn door is open, drive us right up inside. If it's closed, bust it down and drive us right up inside. Heath, you get the gun up and cover for us. If we start taking fire, then we back out and come at them on foot under cover from Heath on the MG. If we don't take fire then the three of us dismount with Heath providing cover and search the barn to see if we can find out who hit us, and maybe why. Questions?"

There were none.

"Then let's get to it."

Shane had slowed ever so slightly to make the turn off the road, but as soon as he was straightened out, he floored the Cougar. While it didn't have all that much top speed, it had plenty of raw power to spare. Shane saw that the door was open wide enough to squeeze through and jammed the vehicle through the sliding doors, sliding to a stop inside.

No fire hit the Cougar. For a few seconds there was just the sound of the idling engine and the whine of the turret. Finally, Heath called out.

"I think we're clear," his voice sounded far too loud for him in the silence following the action they'd just seen.

"Heath, cover," Greg reminded. "Take the ground first, then the loft. Here we go."

It was a textbook sweep and clear, in as much as something like that could be called textbook. The three men on the ground moved quickly and cleanly through the barn while Heath provided cover, first of the upper floor and then of the ground as the three moved up.

"One down," Shane called a minute after they hit the loft. "Solid hit to the chest, Heath. Just outside the triangle."

"Roger that," Heath's quiet reply was the most normal sound they'd heard in what seemed like hours.

"Son-of-a-bitch," Greg cursed as he moved over to look.

"Know him?" Stacey asked.

"Landon Bone," Greg scrubbed at his face with one hand. "How the hell did they know we would be coming this way?"

"You think he was laying for us?" Shane asked. "Wait. Bone, like the guy at the store robbery, Bone?"

"Just like it," Greg nodded. "Cousin. I said then that we probably hadn't hear the last of it. This will just make it worse."

"Looks to me like they'd write this one off as a loss and move on to something else," Stacey mused. "Oh-for-two and what not."

"We don't know yet if it's a zero for them," Greg reminded him. "Depends on how Amanda is. Why in the hell would she not be wearing the plates in her vest?"

"Don't know, man," Shane shrugged. "What do you want to do here?" he nudged the body with his boot.

"We'll drag him outside," Greg decreed. "It's a mile or more to the nearest house that I can remember. We'll drag him across the road into the open field and then head for home. No," he paused. "We'll drag him across the road, go check that nearest house, and then head for home. I don't want to miss anything while we're up here."

"Sounds good," Shane nodded, grabbing one leg of the late and unlamented Mister Bone.

-

"What's going on?" Jose asked as he stepped into Building Two and head long into organized chaos. People were running back and forth, some yelling questions, some yelling orders and others replying to both.

"Greg's patrol got hit," Clay told him, face tight. "Hummer's on the way in with Amanda Lowery hit hard. Somewhere around her appendix, it sounds like. The Cougar was covering and then going to try and see who was shooting at them."

"How long until they get here?" Jose asked, but before he could answer they could hear a large vehicle roaring to a stop at the front of the building. Seeing Patricia moving with a stretcher, Clay and Jose grabbed it for her, following her outside.

There was blood everywhere in the back of the Hummer as Tandi worked over Amanda's prone form. She had lost consciousness at some point, though from pain or blood loss there was no telling at first glance. If anyone was surprised to see her topless, they didn't say so.

"She's at least part way into shock," Tandi said as he helped move her out of the Hummer and onto the stretcher. "I've got an IV going to pump her blood volume up, but she has lost a lot of blood. The round entered the lower left torso, right about the area of the appendix. I don't know if she still has an appendix or not."

"She doesn't," Patricia supplied. "It was part of the medical history we took on everyone a while back. To help in times like these. She had it removed when she was a teen."

"Then I don't know where the blood is coming from unless it hit a tied off artery or something," Tandi shook his head as the group hurried inside. Clay and Jose carried the stretcher into the clinic where Jaylyn Thatcher and Kaitlin Caudell were already prepared to receive her.

"Single gunshot wound, lower left side," Tandi reported. "Blood pressure is one hundred over sixty but steady, respiration has bounced up and down between eleven and nineteen before she lost consciousness, then steadied at thirteen after that. Pulse is eighty-five, but also slightly erratic, again while she was still conscious. After she passed out, her pulse rose to ninety but stayed there. It has been spotty at times, but that could have been our working conditions. Her pupils are reactive to light, and she was oriented times three before she passed out."

"Where is her vest?" Jaylyn asked. "We need to see if-,"

"There won't be any shrapnel from the plates, because she wasn't wearing them," Tandi almost spat. "There is a hole in her blouse, and a chunk missing from her web gear. You'll need to be on the lookout for those."

"Why wasn't she wearing her plates?" several voices asked at once.

"I'll let her tell you, assuming she gets the chance," Tandi shook his head rather than say. Devon Knowles had no such hesitation.

"She didn't have a bra to wear, and if you're not flat-chested then the plates rub you the wrong way without one," she replied to all at once. "That simple."

"That isn't simple," Clay looked toward the ceiling. "Of all the things…."

"Worry about that later," Jaylyn order brusquely. "Right now, everyone who doesn't need to be here, by which I mean everyone I don't need to help me, clear out. Now!"

Everyone she didn't need cleared out.

-

"I understand that Amanda Lowery was wounded?"

Clay looked up to see Xavier Adair standing over him. He did a double take since it almost looked as if Xavier was concerned. Clay shook it off as a figment of his imagination.

"She was," Clay nodded.

"And who might we have to thank for that?" Xavier asked, polite as always.

"Technically, her," Clay informed him. "She had taken the plates out of her vest because they were uncomfortable to wear without a bra on, and she didn't have one."

"I see," Xavier didn't react otherwise. "I was actually more interested in who might have pulled the trigger," he clarified. To those who knew him, that overly polite and precise manner hinted that he was angry. Something rare indeed for Xavier Adair.

"I don't know," Clay admitted. "Greg hasn't returned yet, and they haven't called anything in. I'm hoping-," he stopped, cocking his head to one side and listening. Both men turned to see the Sheriff's Cougar coming up the road much faster than normal.

"Maybe we can find out now," Clay said, getting to his feet. The Cougar didn't slide to a stop the same way the Hummer had, instead pulling in at a more sedate speed to drop Greg off before continuing on the way to be cleaned and fueled. Greg looked exhausted as he walked toward the two men waiting for him.

"Any word?" he asked simply.

"She's in surgery," Clay told him. "All we know at the moment. What happened?"

"The Bone family somehow either knew what route we were taking, or else made a lucky guess," Greg sighed. "Laid an ambush for us up on Low Gap Road, in that isolation barn that Mister Jacobs used to use for hay and to hold stock in once in a while."

"Bone family?" Xavier asked. "Is that some sort of gang affiliation?"

"Oddly enough, it is if you were in Memphis," Greg nodded. "Here it's just ordinary riffraff. Mean and vengeful riffraff, mind you, but riffraff, nevertheless. This has to be them striking back at us for Kiefer. Heath killed one of the shooters and it was Landon Bone, a cousin of Kiefer's. We think there were at least five more, but they managed to get away clean while we stopped to let Doc take over the Hummer to get Amanda back here ASAP."

"I mean this in no way to be critical," Xavier said gently. "But did you not do a gear check before heading out?"

"I did, but it was visual," Greg shrugged. "Everyone was kitted up and ready for action. There was no way to know she wasn't wearing her plates. It never even occurred to me, as often as we preached about safety, that she wouldn't have them in."

"Nor would it have to me," Xavier admitted. "At some point we must all be responsible for our own well-being."

"I'm going to check on everyone else and then try and clean up and get some chow," Greg said. "I want to try and be down here when they bring us the word."

Clay hadn't even noticed that Xavier had left until he went to tell him something.

-

"Heard Amanda got shot," Zach mentioned as soon as Xavier approached him. "That right?"

"I'm afraid it is," Xavier nodded. "I suppose the proper thing to do in this instance is to await the Sheriff's handling of this situation," he said idly, looking off into the distance.

"Probably," Zach agreed.

"Are you familiar with these Bone people?" Xavier asked, turning to look at him.

"I am," Zach nodded. "Wonderful folks," his sarcasm had the usual bite to it.

"I should like to pay these people a visit, I believe," Xavier remarked almost serenely.

"I just happen to know where they live," Zach assured him.

"How many of them are there?" Xavier asked, settling down to business.

-

Greg was standing before he even realized he was getting on his feet, Clay about two seconds behind him, and Jose about one behind that.

"She'll recover," Jaylyn didn't keep them in suspense. "The blood was from a tear where her appendix was removed some years ago. It's a simple procedure that rarely if ever needs any sort of follow-up. It wouldn't have this time had she not been shot."

"Fortunately, the tear was small. The bullet caught the very edge of the area where the ligature was placed for her appendectomy. A one-in-a-million shot, probably. Otherwise, it would have been messy but not likely a problem otherwise. As it is, the damage is minimal considering the bullet," she held up the offending metal. "Thankfully, it was a full jacket, a thirty caliber of some type it looks like, and didn't splinter. Had it been a soft nose…well," she left the rest unsaid.

"She's still under the influence of the drugs and will be for some time," she continued. "We really need someone to sit with her, preferably one of the other young women since they seem to stick together. It would be better for her to see a friendly face when she wakes."

"When do you think that will be?" Greg asked her.

"Early tomorrow, barring unforeseen complications," Jaylyn promised.

"You expect her to recover fully?" Clay asked. "She's the type to want to know if she'll be able to keep going out," he explained. "I don't want to lie to her about it."

"No, don't ever lie to a patient about their recovery," she agreed at once. "And yes, barring as I said any unforeseen complications, she will recover fully. And once cleared for duty, should she desire to continue to go out on patrol, she will be able to do so. Now, if that's all, I really do need to rest a bit," she smiled.

"Of course," all three said in unison. "Sorry to keep you, Doctor," Greg added.

"That's quite alright," she smiled a bit brighter as she made for the stairs. Once she was gone, Greg let out a long breath he didn't know he'd been holding and collapsed into his chair.

"Thank God."

CHAPTER ELEVEN

"It's a problem for more than just her," Lainie informed Clay once he had let her know what had happened to Amanda and why.

"What do you mean?" Clay frowned. "It wouldn't be a problem if she hadn't taken the plates out of the carrier. That's what they're there for!"

"You said Devon told you that Amanda didn't have a bra to wear, and that was what made her uncomfortable," Lainie reminded him. "That-,"

"That's no reason to remove something that might save your life," Clay muttered. "How bad can that even be?"

"For some of us," she raised an eyebrow at him, "it can be very bad. Painful, even. And yes, the plates do make it worse. When I said it was a problem for more than just her, I was referring to the fact that more than one of them has only limited undergarments suitable for that kind of work. A woman with much in the way of build really needs an athletic or sports bra for something like that, and unfortunately, several of them don't have even one, let alone two or three. So, they're doing the best they can with what they have. We're trying to make more for them, but there are always a dozen other things that need our attention at the same time."

"I still don't see-,"

"Imagine one of your balls," Lainie said, deliberately using crude language to get his attention, "caught outside an athletic supporter while the other is still inside and you're riding your horse at a gallop. How bad is that?"

Clay had no immediate response.

"Why didn't she say something?" he finally murmured, sighing in mild exasperation.

"How often do you let others know when you aren't wearing underwear?" Lainie replied at once.

"I meant about the plates," Clay rolled his eyes. "She could have told Greg she was having trouble, and he could-,"

"A woman tells you, a man, she's 'having trouble'," she used air quotes, "and what's the first thing that pops into your head?"

"Well," Clay hesitated, thinking.

"Exactly," Lainie nodded firmly. "Those girls are doing their best to hold up their part of the bargain they made with you. Having one of you give her hell for missing a patrol due to 'issues'," she again used air quotes, "puts her in an awkward position where she gets ribbed about it later. No woman wants or needs that kind of shit, especially from a man."

"Okay, alright, I get it," Clay held up his hands in a gesture of surrender.

"I doubt it," Lainie gave a very unladylike snort of derision. "Every one of you would be on about having to make adjustments for the 'girls in the crew'. And again, the situation is awkward enough without having some asshole assume she meant 'female issues' and not bothering to check and see what was actually wrong. Because God forbid one of you has to actually consider how easy things are for women in these new and exciting times we live in!"

"How did I become the bad guy, here?" Clay demanded, though not harshly. "None of this is my fault, Lainie! And since when have you ever heard me giving someone a hard time like that for something they have no control over? For that matter what have you learned about any of my guys, either from the unit or from Gordy and his friends, that gives you the idea that a single one of them would do something like you're describing? Not a one of them are that kind of men, and you know that, or should."

Clay fought to control his breathing after his almost tirade. Those accusations had come from left field and caught him completely by surprise, provoking a stronger response than they normally would have. On the other hand, Lainie had no right whatever to assume that he or any of the others would be so crass.

For her part, Lainie recognized that she had gone too far with that last statement. She had all but accused Clay and the others of being exactly the kind of men who would treat women so badly.

"I have done all that I could to make things easier on you, and by extension every other woman on this place," Clay broke the silence between them first. "To make a safe home for all of you, a safe place to call home, to allow you all to live as freely as possible and without fear. Carried crews to gather private belongings and to strip abandoned homes of goods and killed I don't know how many men in order to keep this place and the people on it, including the women, safe."

"We've been together over a year now. You've known the others, the initial guys anyway, almost as long, and the women with them, assuming they have one. Name one time that you've seen or heard a single one of us do something so disrespectful to any woman living on this farm. Just one. And if you can't do it, then I suggest you think long and hard about what you say next."

The harsh words caught Lainie by surprise this time and she realized that she had struck a nerve with her tirade. One that she maybe shouldn't have, in this case. Had she been speaking in general terms it would likely have been fine, but she had specifically accused Clay and his men.

Atop that, Clay was correct in saying that she had not heard, or heard of, a single instance of any of them, from the youngest to the oldest, acting with anything other than respect to any woman on the farm. Her face burned as she realized what she had implied, having given her exact words no thought.

"I'm sorry," she said quietly, at long last. "You're right. There isn't a single time any of them have behaved in such a manner and I had no right at all to even insinuate it. I was trying to defend her decision, her actions, and let my emotions get the better of me. For that, I apologize."

Clay said nothing for the moment, still working on regaining his calm, which had been severely damaged by a careless accusation.

"If it's such a problem," he said finally, moving toward the door, "then I would suggest that you and the others responsible for making clothing or alterations start spending more time to remedy it. Amanda could have died today. We were extraordinarily fortunate that she didn't. If Jaylyn Thatcher wasn't here, Amanda might have died anyway. As it is, she should be nursing a bad bruise and nothing more. Instead, she's out of action for no telling how long, in pain, and likely reconsidering her decision to help out. No one can blame her for that. Being shot takes the glory out of anything like this."

"We also used valuable medical resources to treat her that we can't replace," he finished. "Resources that we would not have had to use had she been wearing her plates in the carrier we gave her for that specific purpose. She knew that her safety depended on it and knew that she was always supposed to be wearing it if she was working. And for your general information, it's not very comfortable for men, either. It may not be as bad as it is for a woman, but it's still bulky, heavy, and gets in the way of everything. We wear it anyway because we want to go home at the end of the day."

"I'm going back to work," he opened the door. "You know, I was talking to you about this because I didn't understand. I needed to understand how I almost lost a trooper today when I shouldn't have. But you've cleared that right up for me. It's my fault, or else the fault of the men I work with, because of something we might have said if we'd known. Somehow, we're to blame, and not the woman who disobeyed orders by not wearing her safety equipment, or the guy who actually shot her. Got it."

He was out the door and gone before Lainie could frame a reply, leaving her red-faced in the middle of the living room.

Outside, Clay stalked down the driveway, heading back to his office. He had meant to be home for the evening, but now he had to get out. Clay knew that his temper was a weakness and did all he could to avoid situations where it might get the better of him, even if that meant having to walk away from something or someone. The very last person in the entire world he wanted to be guilty of lashing out at was Lainie Harper. It didn't matter that she had provoked him, even unknowingly. That meant he had to go for a while and let that anger burn out of him. Walking would help, and he might even run for a while. It was something he did when he was worked up.

Anything would be better than staying there with her and possibly saying something that he could never take back. She was far too important to him for that. He was not the bad guy here and was not going to turn into the bad guy because he threw a temper tantrum over her own baseless allegations and accusations.

He started mentally reviewing the specs of the rifle he was carrying as he picked up the pace. It would keep him occupied, which would keep him from making an ass of himself.

-

"You know we're going to get into forty-seven kinds of trouble for this, right?"

Zach was pushing a ragged but working pickup truck away from the farm, leaning against the tailgate. Xavier was pushing from the open driver's door, steering them down the road.

"That is an oddly specific number, Zachary," Xavier replied. "Any particular reason for choosing it?"

"My jersey number," Zach chuckled. "Coach always said it was the perfect number for me, since I was forty-seven kinds of trouble."

"A bit late to tell me that at this point, wouldn't you say?" Xavier laughed.

"Figured you had worked it out by now," Zach chuckled. They had pushed the truck since just before dark, and were now, finally, to the interstate.

"I believe we are far enough away at this point that we can start the engine," Xavier said, sliding behind the wheel.

"Cool," Zach ran to the passenger door and jumped in. Xavier adjusted his night vision gear before turning toward Zach, who was doing the same.

"Which way?"

-

"Penny for your thoughts, Sheriff."

Greg looked up from his ruminations to find Talia Gray looking down at him. He was sitting at the table before Building Two, alone for the moment.

"Long day," he shrugged. "Just reviewing."

"It's not your fault, you know," she sat down across from him.

"Yeah, it is," Greg replied, his tone conversational. "I was in charge; therefore, I am responsible. I ran a gear check, but I did it visual and didn't ask for verbal acknowledgement. If I had, then she would have had to admit she wasn't wearing the plates."

"Or had to lie about it to stay out of trouble," Gray suggested, but Greg shook his head.

"No. I've worked with Amanda long enough to know she wouldn't lie in reply to a question. She might not tell me something, but that's not the same thing."

"A lie by omission-," Gray started.

"A failure to plan," Greg riposted. "I should have checked. I didn't. Is she responsible for doing something she shouldn't have? Yes. Am I responsible for not catching her at it? Yes. Enough blame to go around." His eye caught movement and he looked to see Clay coming toward them. Stalking toward them might have been a better statement.

"What's up?" Greg asked, surprised to see him. "Thought you were headed home."

"Forgot something I needed to do," Clay replied evenly, and Greg almost frowned at his friend's tone. He was clearly angry.

"Well, I have to go inside," Talia got to her feet. "It's my turn with Amanda. We're taking it in two-hour shifts." She entered the building, leaving Greg and Clay in private, at least for the time being.

"Problem?" Greg asked carefully.

"Just the usual," Clay shook his head. "Everything okay with you? I figured you'd be racked out by now."

"Could say the same for you," Greg countered. "But yeah, I should be. Just can't sleep. I've been sitting here, alternating between thinking about what went wrong today and what to do about the Bones. What really bothers me is how they set up that ambush. No one knew where we were going or when. I just chose it at random. And that means they had to be set and just waiting, knowing we'd be that way sooner or later."

"Probably," Clay agreed, finally taking a seat and laying his rifle on the table. "They have the advantage because they know you have to patrol to do your job. They can pick a good spot and then lie in wait because they know that sooner or later, you'll be by. And you can't not go, because it's part of your job and has to be done. I think that's an advantage that you won't be able to overcome with tactics, man. Everything is on their side. Kinda like Afghanistan, really," he murmured.

"I thought about that earlier," Greg nodded absently, clearly thinking of his own experiences. "Today was exactly like that. Man down, trying to get help for them, trying to suppress enemy fire and find cover, then finally moving to take down the ambush. It was all exactly the same."

"Never imagined it here, though," Clay smiled wanly. He levered himself out of the chair and stretched, then picked up his rifle.

"I need to get to my cubbyhole and get some work done," he said tiredly. "You look like a man who needs a stiff drink and a good night of sleep."

"Yeah," Greg took a deep breath and exhaled sharply. "Yeah, I think that might help. I would appreciate it if you'd have someone holler at me if Amanda wakes up and I'm not here."

"I'll leave instructions in the clinic and Operations to call you," Clay promised. "It wasn't your fault, man. You gave her the gear and told her how important it was. She's already been in one firefight. She knew she was supposed to be wearing them."

"Yeah," Greg didn't sound convinced. "Thanks, man. Night."

"Night."

-

"Well, it's a nice night for a walk, anyway," Zach sighed as he pulled his gear on.

"Indeed," Xavier smiled, though no one could have seen it. "I think we have hidden our ride well enough, don't you?" The truck was now sitting behind the remains of a tractor trailer that had been abandoned on the highway. It looked as if it had been wrecked and left where it was.

"Probably," Zach agreed. "Unless someone saw us bring it in here, no one will know it's there anyway."

"Where to from here?" Xavier asked, walking out onto the black top.

"This way," Zach pointed and started walking west on the side road. "We're about five miles or so from their little village. You'll need to watch for trip wires and tangle foot as we get closer. They cook meth and make moonshine both up here, along with no telling what else these days. The road will probably be clear for customers, but it's also likely to be guarded. I figured we'd head into the woods a mile or so from there."

"Sounds like a plan," Xavier agreed. "You estimate there are twenty-three of them?"

"I'd be really careful with that number, but yeah," Zach sounded less than confident. "Their number was always fluid anyway, and since the Storm there is no telling what they've been about. They could have added to their number, and we know they've lost at least two, since we killed them." He stopped, looking at his mentor in the eerie light of the NVD.

"You know that if we don't kill them all, it will mean war, right?" he asked quietly. "This is one of those families that will fight to the death over one of their own, even when that one is in the wrong. If they were better people, it might be worthy of admiration, I guess."

"But they are not better people, are they," Xavier stated rather than asked. "We have established already that the world in general and this county in particular would be a much better place without them, have we not?"

"Oh, absolutely," Zach nodded. "I got no problem going after them. Just wanted to make sure you knew what kind of people they are."

"Noted," Xavier confirmed. "Now, let's be about it. We've a long night ahead of us, no doubt."

"No doubt," Zach echoed, smiling into the dark. "No doubt."

-

"Have you seen Zach this evening?" Kim Powers asked as Clay walked outside to get some fresh air.

"Sorry," he shook his head. "You can check in operations and see if he's on watch."

"I already did, and they said he wasn't," she informed him. "I guess he's just out doing other stuff. Probably off learning a new way to kill someone from Xavier," she snorted. "Good night," she waved as she started up the hill.

Clay watcher her go, wondering why that conversation bothered him so much. Why should it matter that Zach and Xavier were training together out in the night? Xavier and Brick both had been teaching Zach everything they could, and the teen just seemed to soak the knowledge up like a sponge.

Perhaps more importantly, both had been helping Zach deal with the issues he faced that might lead him down another rampage such as the one he had gone on when Kaden Ramsey was killed. While that particular episode had done no lasting damage, that did not mean another one wouldn't. It was better for everyone if Zach was able to control those overwhelming urges, and the two estranged brothers were perfect for that.

"Have you seen X?" Jose asked, jarring Clay out of his thoughts as he looked around.

"What?" Alarm bells were ringing in Clay's head, though he hadn't made the connection just yet.

"Have you seen Red anywhere?" Jose repeated. "I walked out to the motorhome he's staying in to tell him he had the early duty tomorrow and he isn't there. I've looked everywhere he might normally hang out, and nothing. No one has seen him for hours."

"You didn't happen to see Zach during that search, did you?" Clay asked carefully, an idea finally taking shape in his mind.

"No, but I wasn't looking for him," Jose shrugged. "Why?"

"Because no one has seen either of them for hours," Clay sighed, sitting heavily into a chair. "Amanda Lowery is a favorite of Red's. He's been teaching her for two months or better. I don't really know how long now that I honestly think on it."

"Aw, shit," Jose muttered. "They've gone off the reservation."

"I'd say that is a safe bet," Clay nodded, standing once more. "I need to find Greg. Very quietly put a three-man team together, including me. One small Cougar with a Deuce, and standard field loadout."

"Going after them?" Jose asked.

"I don't know where they've gone," Clay admitted. "But I assume they're going after this Bone family. To retaliate for Amanda."

"You don't seriously think they need help with that," Jose stated, disbelief showing on his face. "X and Zach both versus a bunch of inbred hillbilly trash? No offence," he added when Clay raised an eyebrow.

"None taken," he chuckled. "I don't know a one of them, but I'm assuming from Greg's description you are spot on the money with that one. I need to go find the Sheriff. You put that package together for me."

"Yes, sir."

-

"What a quaint little village," Xavier whispered as they overlooked the home of the Bone family.

Just as Zach had said, it was more of a small village or settlement than a neighborhood. There was even one rather old two-story building that looked as if it might have once been a hotel of some kind.

"See that line there?" Zach whispered, slowly pointing to an area of grass that was much different than the rest. It ran in a straight line just west of the large hotel type building, and right between the two more or less halves of the 'village'.

"Railroad?" Xavier asked, and Zach nodded.

"They took the railroad up years ago," Zach informed him. "Little places like this that had been a sort of whistle stop, they just sort of died out for the most part. Or turned out like this."

"How charming," Xavier replied, examining the area through a pair of night vision binoculars. "What was once a hotel is now apparently a house of ill-repute?"

"If you mean whore house, then prob'ly," Zach agreed. "That was a rumor running all through school. None of us bothered to come out here, though. Figured we'd catch something even bleach wouldn't get rid of." Xavier made a choking sound and it took Zach a second to realize that he was trying to smother a laugh.

"Oh, me, Zachary," Xavier finally managed to speak. "You really do have a way with words, sometimes."

"It's a gift," Zach shrugged. "Anyway, back before the Storm, this was the place to get bad shine, bootleg store whiskey, weed, meth or laid. Not necessarily in that order. Been a many a fella come out here and mess his life up but good."

"And the law did nothing about this?" Xavier asked.

"Pepper was the law back then," Zach snorted. "Long as Old Man Sanders was running things, they kept the whiskey where it wasn't poison, but even he couldn't stop the meth trade. I doubt anyone can, even now. Long as they can find what they need to cook, they'll keep cooking."

"Sounds rather like the poppy trade," Xavier murmured to himself. "Well, this Pepper gentleman aside, I believe we'll be putting this place out of business this evening. I feel we have somewhat of a large score to settle. I am also quite angry, to be honest. I rather like Amanda Lowery."

It was all Zach could do to keep the surprise off his face. He had known that, but he'd never expected to hear Xavier admit to it. Hearing it made it more than real.

"We shall move in from the north, I believe," Xavier quickly sketched out a plan. "One to each side of their little slice of heaven. We shall use blades for as long as we can, then suppressed handguns. With subsonic ammunition they should be quiet enough, considering the noise level. I have seen nothing that even remotely resembles a guard, but you feel there will be one, somewhere?"

"I can't say," Zach shrugged. "Never been here other than out riding and drinking beer, and we never stopped. Always was told to stay away from out here, and we mostly did. Didn't want any trouble with this bunch."

"Well, they have trouble this evening," Xavier's voice was grim. "Be watchful for a guard, then. We will move further north before moving in. Perhaps that will reveal any observation posts to us before we attack. Any questions?"

"Some of them girls likely ain't here by choice," Zach noted, letting the comment hang.

"If she isn't trying to kill us, I see no reason to kill her," Xavier agreed. "Our bone of contention, so to speak, is solely with this Bone family. Which still sounds like some sort of voodoo cult every time I say it."

"I know," Zach snorted. "There is, or was anyway, a big gang in Memphis called the Bone Family, long time ago. Rumor had it they even sent someone up here to 'suggest' the Bones stop using the name."

"What became of that envoy?" Xavier asked as he refitted his NVD to his face.

"Ever hear the song 'Rocky Top'?" Zach snickered.

"Ah, I see," Xavier chuckled. "'Strangers haven't come down, so assume they never shall?' Something of that sort?"

"Close enough for someone of your social standing," Zach smothered his own laugh.

"Thank you," Xavier's voice was dry. "Are you ready?"

"I am indeed," Zach promised. "Lead the way."

-

"What makes you think they'd go after them?" Greg asked, still blinking sleep from his eyes. He had been asleep less than an hour when Clay had shaken him awake.

"What else would they be doing?" Clay asked, clearly exasperated by the entire situation. "They're both close to Amanda, and she was almost killed today. And you've already said that this will be a feud situation that will last until they feel they've gotten even. What kind of challenge would that sound like to the two of them?"

"A rather strong one I can assure you," Brick's deep voice startled them both. They turned to see him standing in the doorway, filling the doorway might be a better way of putting it, leaning on the frame.

"Exactly," Clay recovered quickly. "My official estimate is that they've gone after the Bones to make sure what happened today doesn't happen again."

"And you're unhappy with this, why?" Greg asked, confused.

"I really don't want to lose those two," Clay told him. "Or any other two, for that matter."

"Dude, there ain't no way that bunch can take down those two without Zeus himself coming down with a lightning bolt on both of them," Greg scoffed. "In the dark? With those two slipping through their tiny hamlet, going from hovel-to-hovel? If they really have gone after them, I'd say the odds are that the Bones are as good as dead. If I was you, I'd be more worried about what Adcock, or worse, Gaines might say when they find out."

"I find myself agreeing with the Sheriff in this matter, Clayton," Brick said quietly. "The two of them are a formidable team, and they will not allow anything remotely resembling a fair fight. There is little chance that this family will be able to stop them."

"But there is a chance, small though it may be," Clay nodded as if Brick had just made his point for him.

"Fine," Greg got tiredly to his feet. "Let me get my gear and we can go. But if you're wrong," he told Clay, "and they aren't there, then we're going to start a great big firefight that they will definitely hear in Lewiston. So be prepared for that."

"I'll worry about that if it happens," Clay promised. "Right now, I'm more worried about my men."

"It's a wasted worry, man, I'm telling ya," Greg said over his shoulder, already on his way to gear up.

"It won't cost me anything," Clay insisted. "You want to go along?" he asked Brick, thinking he would need a bigger MRAP if so.

"I do not believe this requires my attention," Brick shook his head. "I honestly don't believe it warrants yours, either, but then you are in command and have the responsibility none of the rest of us have. Good luck," he added as he turned to go.

"Thanks."

CHAPTER TWELVE

Elmer Bone walked out of the small house his family used as a bar and stood on the porch, stretching. He had been sitting in the same chair for hours, playing cards with his brother and cousins. He belched suddenly, tasting the shine he had been downing since before the sun had set.

He chuckled to himself as he staggered down the four steps at the end of the porch, intending to head for the hotel. His own house was in the other direction but there was no one else there. The hotel, on the other hand, well, it had-,

Elmer Bone felt something wrapping around his forehead and then a cold sensation along his neck. He screamed for help, expecting his family to come running, but his vocal cords had already been severed even as his life's blood poured from his ruptured jugular.

Behind him, Zach Willis drug the much heavier Bone into the shadows between the 'bar' and the next building, taking the time to settle the body on the ground. A casual glance would show someone sleeping off a drunk that had gotten out of hand.

Wiping his knife on the pants leg of his victim, Zach paused to listen. He heard no sound of alarm, no one crying out. Good. This was number four for him. With this one done, he circled around the bar, ignoring it for now. The plan was to eliminate everyone they could find alone first. Then they would team up to go after the rest.

Across the narrow lane between the rows of houses, Xavier Adair had entered a third home, finding a fat man in a soiled wife beater and boxer shorts sitting in a recliner, snoring. Covering the man's mouth with his free hand, Xavier slipped his blade between the man's ribs, piercing his heart the man's eyes had flared open but only for an instant before closing again, this time for good. Xavier waited fifteen seconds before removing his hand. He looked at the soiled clothing in disgust before cleaning his knife on the only slightly cleaner chair. As he moved the blade across the chair, he heard a whimper from the back of the house. He closed his eyes for just a few seconds, knowing in his heart what that sound meant.

Moving quietly to the back of the house, he opened a door that he assumed led to a bedroom. Peeping inside, he found exactly what he feared, though slightly worse than he'd expected.

A girl who could not have been more than twelve or thirteen years old sat huddled on a filthy bed, a chain around her neck holding her to the headboard. As far as Xavier could tell, the child was stark naked.

Promising himself he would return, he slipped away without the girl ever knowing he was there. As he passed her now very dead tormentor, Xavier wished he had killed the man more slowly, and much more painfully.

This would complicate matters.

-

"Why is this taking so long?" Clay demanded.

"Dude, we are literally waking people up who have been asleep for maybe an hour," Jose rolled his eyes. "They need a minute to get straight."

"What if we were being attacked right now?" Clay asked him, borderline angry.

"Then I would imagine they'd be doing better," Jose shrugged. "We're not, though. So, they're working on it."

Clay stalked away, his anger having nothing to do with Jose, how slow everyone seemed to be moving, or even X and Zach.

Not that it mattered.

-

Xavier knew as soon as he saw Zach exit the last house on his side of the street that the teen had found something similar to his own discovery. Moving in shadows, the two met up one house down from their remaining targets.

"Dude, I-," Zach began, but Xavier cut him off.

"I know," the older man assured him. "I discovered the same. One thing at a time, remember. Count?"

"Six," Zach reported. "You?"

"Seven," Xavier smiled despite the situation. "You lag behind, young apprentice," he joked as he pulled his pistol and checked the magazine and the suppressor.

"Well, a man your age should know more than me, anyway," Zach shot back, though clearly not in a joking mood.

"Estimate for their recreation lodge?" Xavier nodded to the little bar.

"At least five, counting the guy acting as a bartender," Zach told him. "What about the hotel?"

"No way to know for sure," Xavier shook his head. "There are ten rooms, five upstairs and five down. All are closed. For all we know they are all empty, though I seriously doubt it. Suggestions?" Even in such a time as this, Xavier was teaching.

"Take the bar together and then move on the hotel," Zach said at once. "Once we start making noise, we need to stick together. We can't afford to get pinned down here. The ones in the bar only make it eighteen, total. There has to be more than that."

"We'll know for sure very shortly," Xavier informed him. "Your plan is a good one, so we'll go with it. I will take the right; you shall take the left. Once we clear the building, we go immediately to the hotel. We will eliminate any upper floor opposition first, then move to the ground floor. I should expect the lower rooms are the most likely to be occupied if the establishment isn't full."

"Works for me."

-

"Can we go now?" Clay was getting testier by the minute. He knew that he was, knew why and was trying his best not to. It wasn't working very well, but he was making the effort.

"Yes, *bwana*, we go now," Greg told him, rolling his eyes. "Mount up," he ordered. Shane Golden was behind the wheel with Greg taking the passenger seat. Behind them sat Clay, Mitchell Nolan and Stacey Pryor.

"Which way?" Shane asked as they approached the highway.

"South, I think," Greg replied, frowning.

"You think?" Clay repeated.

"I know roughly where we're going," he promised. "Just never been there at night is all. I don't know the exact exit I need to take using the interstate, so I'll have to wing it."

"Of course, you will," Clay groaned and sat back, shaking his head.

"We'll be there soon enough," Greg assured him.

-

One minute everyone was having a good time, two men shooting pool while the other three played darts, then the next, blood and brains were flying everywhere as what sounded like firecrackers exploding rolled through the room.

Xavier and Zachary both exchanged magazines in their pistols before moving. The next move was for Xavier to check the bodies to make sure they were, indeed, dead, while Zach watched the door. That completed, it was the work of less than a minute to clear the rest of the ramshackle building.

"Now on to the main event," Xavier whispered as the two moved out a side door into the shadows. The examined the windows for any sign of light or life but found none. Hopeful, the two found a rickety fire escape ladder and carefully climbed their way to the top floor, stopping twice along the way as the ladder groaned painfully and swayed dangerously. Finally, they stepped over the railing and onto the top floor runway.

Xavier walked to the first door and simply turned the doorknob. It opened without resistance and Xavier stuck his head inside as Zach covered him. A lone man sat up from the bed, sleep still clouding his vision.

"Pete? Is that-,"

His question died with him as Xavier put a round in his head. Before he could so much as speak, the woman next to the now dead man came screeching to her feet, hands curled like claws as she rushed at Xavier. Surprised, Xavier reacted as he would have to any threat and shot her in the head.

"I would never have imagined a woman being here willingly," he whispered to Zach. Zach merely shrugged. There was no accounting for taste.

The next two rooms were empty, but the fourth room found two male members of the Bone outfit and a very helpless woman tied to a metal bed frame. This time it was Zach who was first in, killing both men before they could react. The woman looked up at him, desperate pleading visible on her face. Zach put a finger to his lips and held up a finger, and the gagged woman nodded frantically.

The fifth room on the top floor held two women, both of whom attacked them at once, and died just as quickly.

"I do not understand how any woman would live in such conditions," Xavier said, shaking his head. The two returned to release the woman in the fourth room, warning her to stay quiet, then asking her if she knew how many men might be downstairs. She didn't know, but instantly began pleading with them to take her with them.

"Quiet," Xavier told her. "We shall, but we aren't leaving just yet. This is the safest place for you until we have completed our business here. Remain in this room, lock the door and say quiet. We'll knock when we return so you know it's us."

The woman tried to argue but a warning look from Xavier shut her down and she moved to a corner behind a cheap dresser and hid.

"She is soon to go into shock, I would think," Xavier noted as they made their way to the stairs.

"Nothing we can do about that," Zach replied. "We have to finish now that we started."

"Just so," Xavier nodded. "Reverse order, this time," he said, moving to the room on the far right to start, but finding it empty. The next two rooms were likewise empty, but the middle door had made a loud screeching noise when opened and the two sighed at the jarring sound. Sure enough, the fourth door flew open and a man naked but for the jockey shorts he wore stomped out, already cursing a blue streak at 'whichever of you dumb sons-a-bitches woke me'.

Zach shot the man between the eyes before he ever realized he wasn't cursing at someone he knew. He tried to catch the man's body before it hit the porch, but the man fell backwards, out of reach.

"Hurry," Xavier warned, patting Zach's shoulder. The two moved immediately to the final door, which Zach busted open with one sharp kick, ducking as he did so.

Xavier stayed high, his pistol shooting the single occupant of the room as he tried to grab a shotgun from beside his bed. In the movies, the man would have been flung backwards into the headboard or the window behind him, but in real life he simple crumpled off the bed onto the floor as his head snapped back on his shoulders.

"I would love to say we are finished, but we are not," Xavier sighed.

"No," Zach agreed. "You get the woman upstairs. I'll start on the houses. We need to drag all these cretins out to the track bed and burn them, I guess. These houses aren't really suitable for anyone to live in though," he mused, thinking.

"We need to ensure the safety of those children before we concern ourselves any further with this riffraff," Xavier interrupted his planning. "Let us be about it."

-

"Turn here," Greg ordered. Shane dutifully took the small ramp that led to an equally small back road.

"I think this is it," Greg said firmly.

"You said that last time," Clay noted. "And the time before that, too."

"Yeah, but I'm sure, this time," Greg sounded confident.

"Why?"

"Because that truck sitting back there came from the farm," Greg jabbed a thumb over his shoulder toward the interstate.

"What truck?"

"The one they took to get here, man," Greg was shaking his head. "It's a good thing you've got me around, dude."

"Yeah," Clay muttered. "Great thing."

"Look," Shane pointed toward the horizon. "Up there," he was pointing south-east of them.

"Well, that's a fire," Greg stated matter-of-factly. "You need any more proof this is where your boys are?"

-

Once the four entirely too young girls and one severely abused woman were secured in a pickup truck that had been in use by their captors, Xavier and Zach had decided it was best to drag the bodies out rather than burn the buildings. This was more in the interest of safety than any desire to preserve the filthy hovels the group had been living in. No one wanted another brush fire of any size.

Zach had upended ten full gallons of moonshine onto the pile of bodies before setting them aflame, ensuring that there would be nothing left once the fire was finished. The two were in the process of gathering any plunder within the houses, especially weapons and ammunition, when they heard a vehicle approaching. Moving into the shadows, they waited.

"Perhaps a few of them were out pillaging somewhere," Xavier said calmly as he attacked a suppressor to his rifle. Zach nodded while doing the same.

"That did occur to me," the teen admitted. "No way to know if we got them all. Had we thought of it we might have asked the woman, but I wouldn't put her through that if I could help it."

"Indeed," Xavier agreed. "Better to chance running up on one of them somewhere else. At any rate, whoever might remain will have little to work with once we're finished here."

The two fell silent at that as headlights popped into view, flickering as they ran behind a line of trees before turning into the lane that served as a drive for the former home of the Bone family.

"Well, shit," Zach sighed, seeing the light bar on the Cougar and the star on the hood.

"Succinctly put," Xavier nodded. "We are, as they say, busted." Neither seemed overly concerned about it. Shutting off their night vision, the two moved into the open where the lights of the Cougar would illuminate them. Greg Holloway was the first out of the vehicle, slouching forward with a smirk on his face.

"Fancy meeting you two here," was all he said. Before anyone else could speak, Clay arrived.

"What in the hell do you two think you're doing?" he demanded.

"We're killing people and breaking shit," Zach replied evenly.

"How many people?" Greg asked, frowning.

"Twenty-six," the two said in unison. "Twenty-three men and three women," Xavier clarified.

"Women?" Greg started at that.

"Attacked us directly and defended the men in question," Xavier confirmed.

"We also rescued one grown woman and four…four teen girls that might be in puberty at best," Zach nearly choked on the sudden rage that enveloped him over that, but he calmed almost immediately. "They are all in that truck over there," he pointed to an old light green four-door truck that had likely come from a surplus auction for the national forestry service. Greg headed that way with Shane behind him, while Clay stayed, staring at Xavier and Zach for some time before speaking.

"How many times do I have to talk about this?" he asked finally.

"Probably best if you just stopped," Zach surprised both Clay and Xavier. "If you think I'll sit on my ass and let something like this go by me, then you don't know me like you thought you did. The shit I seen tonight?" he shook his head. "No. Anytime from now on that I think or hear that something like this is happening, you can bet I'm gonna be right there, checking to see. And if it is happening, then I'm gonna do the same thing I did here. If that don't work for you, I understand, and I'll leave rather than make it hard on you. But

I ain't letting this shit go on around me. No sir." The final two words were flat and final.

Clay was initially taken aback, as Zach had never openly defied or challenged anyone over anything. Tonight, however, seemed to have struck a nerve.

"Either of you hurt?" he asked finally, to which both snorted.

"Please," Xavier scoffed. "By the animals in this pigsty? Let's not devolve into insults, here."

"Just checking," Clay promised. "We may as well keep gathering whatever you've found here, I guess," he sighed. "What made you think of this?"

"Somewhat of a get well present," Xavier smiled slightly.

"I was just bored," Zach admitted.

"Figures," Clay snorted. "C'mon then. I'll help finish."

Meanwhile, Greg Holloway had approached the truck the women had been placed in, making sure his badge could be clearly seen.

"Ladies," he said calmly. "I'm Sheriff Greg Holloway, Calhoun County Sheriff's office. Can you all tell me who you are, where you're from and how you came to be here?"

No one spoke. All of them just looked at him dully. Even the grown up.

"Ladies, I can't help you get home if I don't even know who you are," Greg said gently. "You don't have to talk to me about what you've been through, okay? All I need to know is how I can find your people. To take you home."

Nothing. Eyes blinked at him but that was it.

"Okay," Greg sighed. "I can take you to Jordan, but I don't know what services they can render to you. I can also take you to Lewiston, but again, I don't know what they can do for you. I don't have any resources at the moment to help you with. All I can do is try to get you home if you tell me where that is."

"I'm from Peabody," the grown woman snorted. "How much of it is left?"

"There's a good bit of it left, but no one stayed behind, it looks like," Greg admitted. "You have family anywhere else we can search for?"

"I have a sister in Lewiston," the woman nodded. "I did, anyway. No idea if she's still there."

"Then I'll take you there for a start," Greg promised. "Have any of the young ladies said anything about where they hail from?"

"No, and I doubt they will," the woman shook her head. "They haven't spoken at all. None of them."

"I see," Greg had been afraid of that. "We'll do whatever we can for them. I know this was bad, and I'm sorry it happened. It won't mean much, I imagine, but you've already seen that this bunch, at least, will never do it again."

"You're right," the woman assured him. "It don't mean shit."

"Sorry," Greg apologized. "We'll get on the road as soon as we can. I'll leave my deputy here to watch over you, and if you need anything, he can call me." Greg turned away and started to speak to Shane, but the soldier just nodded.

"I got it."

Greg nodded and headed back the way he had come, watching as Clay and the others continued to pull loot from the houses and other buildings.

"Ought to burn the whole damn place to the ground," he muttered to himself, but not as quietly as he thought he had.

"Thought about it," Zach assured him. "Afraid it would get out and cause another fire. Decided to just burn those assholes instead. Ten gallons of rotgut should have'em down to ashes before it's through. Better than they deserve, really, but I didn't want to risk ruining the water by leaving 'em laying, either."

Sometimes Greg forgot just how differently Zach's mind worked from most of the rest of the people at the farm. Perhaps one reason he got along so well with Xavier and Brick.

"Good plan," he decided to say. "And yeah, I got no desire to see another wildfire ever," he agreed.

It took another twenty-five minutes to finish checking everything and gather all the firearms, ammunition and stolen goods. Greg took the time to take the copper worm from the still, knowing someone he could trade it to and possibly save a life or two in the process. He also noted there was over three hundred gallons of capped whiskey here that could be used as a fuel supplement, and decided he might offer it to Adcock if need be to get him to forget how this had all come to pass. But only if need be.

At last it was determined there was nothing of value left at the place, and the fire had burned so hot that there was little more than bone remaining. Greg snorted at that thought, thinking how appropriate it was.

The woman drove the truck herself, refusing to trust even Zach or Xavier to do so despite their having saved her. Neither took offense nor even acted as if it mattered. They had the truck they had taken from the farm full of everything taken from their target and headed for home, satisfied they had done the world at large a great favor.

The Sheriff's MRAP led the truck with the surviving women in it straight to Lewiston, where Adcock was roused from his sleep to find a woman driving a truck with four teen girls who had been missing since long before he had arrived. Van Bronson arrived a short time later, confirming that the four teens were indeed missing from Lewiston and had family still in town.

The woman, whose name Greg hadn't bothered to try to learn, had been recognized by Bronson as well, and was taken to her sister's home with the promise that the doctor would be over shortly to see her.

"Really appreciate this, Holloway," Bronson said quietly as family members arrived to take charge of the near catatonic teens. "They look to have been treated rough."

"Very," Greg nodded. "They were enjoying the hospitality of the Bone family," he added. "All of them treated worse than dogs."

"Ought to kill every one of them," Bronson muttered.

"They did," Greg told him. "Two of our men killed them all, stacked their bodies along the old rail bed, and burned them to ash. They won't be taking women from here or anywhere else again. We recovered some stolen property. If we can't find someone who can identify it, I'll bring it down here. Might be some of it came from here, I don't know."

"How many of them were there?" Bronson asked, somewhat respectfully.

"Two, like I said," Greg replied.

"No, I mean of the Bone outfit," Bronson clarified.

"Twenty-six," Greg forced himself not to smile at Bronson's reaction.

"Damn," Bronson removed his hat and rubbed his head. "You boys don't play, do you?"

"It ain't a game," Greg shrugged. "They took the first shot, anyway. This looks like it's under control and no longer our business, so we're headed home. You guys stay safe."

"You too, man," Bronson waved. Greg stepped back onto the Cougar, as Shane climbed behind the wheel. No one else had gotten down.

"Find homes for them?" Clay asked. He had worried about the girls all the way to Lewiston. He had already decided if there was no one in Lewiston to care for them, he was going to break his own rule and carry them to the farm for treatment.

"All with family," Greg assured him. "Even let Bron know that two of your guys were all it took to wipe the Bone family off the map. He was suitably impressed, by the way," he smirked.

"Great," Clay's sarcasm floated up from the back. "I came down here hoping to impress Van Bronson most of all."

"Well, mission accomplished then!"

CHAPTER THIRTEEN

Jose Juarez was sitting in front of Building Two, feet propped up on the table, when the ragged truck he recognized as one the farm had captured months ago pulled into the drive. Mitchell Nolan had warned him from The Roof that the truck was inbound, so it wasn't a surprise. Nor was it a surprise when Xavier and Zachary got out, each carrying a bundle of gear.

"You boys been out on the town?" he asked, a faint smile playing across his features.

"Just taking a moonlight drive," Xavier replied. "Is there any way you could have this washed and waxed while we dine?" he added, his dry humor coming to the fore.

"Not by me," Jose snorted. "What do you really need?" he asked.

"If anyone is available to unload the goods in the back, we really need to clean up," Xavier replied. "We have been in some disgusting places this evening. I wouldn't bother but there are some things in the truck that weather will affect."

"Why not pull it into Building Three for the night, then," Jose ordered. "Just leave it there, loaded. We'll go through it in the daylight. Better that way, anyway."

"Excellent suggestion, my good fellow," Xavier joked. "I shall add a tip to your usual fee." He looked at Zach.

"I'll take it," the teen took the hint. "Will you hang on to this?" he handled the bundle of his gear over before getting behind the wheel and taking the truck to park it inside.

"You guys weren't gone long," Jose noted as Zach left. "You run into Clay while you were out?"

"Indeed," Xavier nodded. "He seemed less worked up over our little jaunt and yet, still angry, somehow," he sounded puzzled. "Odd, really."

"He was like that when he came back down here probably three hours ago now," Jose nodded. "I suspect he and Lainie had a dispute and she said something that set him off, so he had to leave for a while. He'll probably be fine by the time he gets in. Speaking of which?" he hinted.

"There was a woman and four girls being held by the esteemed Bone family," Xavier informed him. "The others have taken them to Lewiston to look for their family members. I'm sure they will be along presently. Have you any word on Amanda?"

"She's doing fine," Jose assured him. "Is expected to recover fully, though it will take some time. She's still under but expected to wake in the morning. Jaylyn prefers to let her wake on her own, so she can rest."

"Very good," Xavier almost sounded relieved. "Well, I believe I shall avail myself of the shower and then get some sleep."

"You were scheduled for early watch, by the way," Jose told him.

"I'll be there," Xavier didn't even wince.

"I've covered it. You have ground watch from twelve-to-four, instead. Both of you," he added as Zach walked up, taking his gear back from Xavier.

"Cool," the teen shrugged before starting up the hill. "I'm taking a shower and hitting the hay myself. Night."

"I as well," Xavier agreed. "Good evening, Pancho."

"Night, X."

-

Clay didn't say much as the Cougar made its way home. Everyone on board was tired, so the ride was made in mostly silence anyway.

Once they were home, Clay went to his office without much more than a goodnight to everyone around him, dropping his gear behind the small table he used as a desk. Along the far wall was a folding cot with a single blanket for a covering and another rolled into a makeshift pillow. Normally, he used it to catch catnaps when things were busy, but tonight he decided to sleep there rather than walk home.

He knew that part of that decision was because he was still angry over the things that Lainie had accused him and the others of and didn't trust himself not to return her verbal assault, even if it were justified. He would rather avoid the matter altogether until he was certain he had a rein on his anger. Avoiding the problem would not make it go away, but trying to face it angry, and exhausted, would be more likely to make the problem worse rather than better.

As he stretched out on the narrow frame cot, he wondered if his reluctance to face the problem, even with the reasons he had for doing so, was a weakness of some kind. He knew that his anger was a weakness, and it was one he had fought against most of his adult life. In fact, he would have sworn it was firmly in hand until he had been blindsided tonight by accusations that had no basis in fact and hit more nerves than a blow to the nose would have.

Still angry, he pulled the rolled blanket beneath his neck and closed his eyes. He was asleep before he could think of the problem, or any other problems, again.

-

Lainie had waited for Clay to return, unaware that he had left due to the discovery that Xavier and Zach had gone temporarily rogue. The more time she spent waiting, replaying her words over and over in her mind, the more embarrassed and guilty she felt. She had allowed her own past problems to influence her thinking, which in turn influenced what she said. She had not meant to directly accuse Clay or any of the others of having committed such offenses, and yet her accusations had been intended as an indictment of men in general. Had she stopped there, she could have felt justified in being angry at Clay's reaction to what she had said, and even pointed to it as another reason for Amanda's reluctance to 'say anything'.

But of course, she hadn't stopped there, had she? Instead she had flat out accused them all of being ready in an instant to ridicule a woman who was having any sort of 'female issue' and using that to make life more difficult for her. She had nothing to base that on, no evidence of any kind really that it would happen. She had simply jumped to the conclusion that it would. In doing so, she had all but accused Clay and the others by name of being guilty of something that hadn't even happened.

'How did I become the bad guy, here?', Clay had asked her. As she thought that over, she came to the conclusion that this was exactly what it had looked like to him, while to her it simply looked like she was defending a young woman who had made what seemed like the best choice she could.

Of course, it hadn't been a good choice, as events had proven. In reflection, Lainie could see the source of Clay's frustration. Amanda had made a mistake and as a result was lying in the clinic now, with a gunshot wound that didn't have to happen. Should not have happened. It dawned on her that this was what Clay had been most upset over when he had tried to speak with her, Lainie, earlier in the evening. The fact that someone he felt responsible for was laying in the clinic with a gunshot wound.

Looking at the clock, she realized it was well after midnight. Either Clay had gotten busy with something, or else he wasn't coming home. She didn't know which it might be. Suddenly, she very much wanted to know.

Getting to her feet, she dressed quickly and headed for the Troy Farm.

-

Jose Juarez had stayed behind at the hangout before Building Two when all the others had dispersed. While he was not on duty himself, he had found the cool air and the quiet to be inviting and decided to enjoy it for a bit before turning in.

He had been sitting alone for several minutes when he heard footsteps from the direction of the Sanders' farm and turned his gaze that way, expecting to see one of the watch standers moving his way. To his surprise, he instead saw a rather determined looking Lainie Harper moving toward him, jacket wrapped around her against the chill.

"Evening, Miss Harper," Jose smiled. "How are you?"

"I'm fine, thanks," Lainie's smile didn't reach her eyes, or her voice either, Jose noted. Suddenly he had an epiphany of why Clay had seemed angry earlier in the evening.

"Can I help you with anything?" he asked, doing his best to keep his voice casual. Willing to help, but not nosy.

"I'm just looking for Clay," Lainie shook her head. "I assumed he was down here into something and wasn't looking at the time."

"Well, that's partly accurate," Jose nodded. "He went with Greg a little earlier to check on something, but they're all back now, safe and sound. Last I saw Clay he was headed inside," he pointed over his shoulder with a thumb. "Said he had some work to do but didn't elaborate."

"Thank you," Lainie smiled again, headed for the door. "Have a good evening," she added as she pulled the door open and disappeared inside.

"And with that, I believe I will go home," Jose said aloud to himself, rising from his seat. Affairs of others were none of his.

-

Lainie noted that Clay's office light was out, but went there anyway, flipping the light on as she walked inside. She heard a groan from her left and turned to see Clay shading his eyes from the light as he either tried to wake up, or else go back to sleep. Surprised, she didn't say anything as he levered himself up to a sitting position with his feet on the floor.

"What is it now?" he asked, still looking at the floor. "I thought everyone was back."

"Why are you sleeping down here, Cowboy?" she asked rather than demanded. Hearing her voice, Clay's head came up.

"Figured you'd be asleep by now," he said before scrubbing his face with his hands, trying to get awake. "What time is it?" he asked, looking for the cheap clock on his wall. "Great," he muttered, seeing the time. "Not even an hour."

"Sorry for waking you," Lainie's voice didn't quite convey the idea of sorrow or apology. "What made you curl up on that cot rather than come home?"

"I got in a little while ago and figured you were either asleep already, or else waiting to continue our little discussion. I didn't want to wake you if you were asleep, and I definitely didn't need another lecture on how crass and classless I and my men are, so I chose the cot. In the interest of full disclosure, I will admit that the fact that I was exhausted also played a part in that decision." He reached for a cannister he normally kept water in and shook it. Hearing a very slight sloshing sound, he removed the top and drank the water, swishing it around his mouth before swallowing.

Red-faced, Lainie waited for him to get a drink before replying.

"I apologized to you for that," her voice was quiet.

"Which did nothing to calm my anger at that point," Clay nodded. "Rather than stay and maybe say something I'd regret, I left. Same reason I stayed here. Still angry, still didn't want to risk the possibility that I'd say something I couldn't take back or make up for. Isn't worth it."

"What isn't worth it?" Lainie felt a flutter in her stomach suddenly.

"The risk of saying something to you that I would regret," he replied, missing any indication of how his former statement had shaken her. "I'd rather just sleep on this cot than say something ugly to you in anger. And I was very angry. I don't think I'd have said anything bad, but better to remove the risk, I figured. And the cot ain't too bad," he shrugged. "I've definitely slept in worse places."

Lainie felt the urge to cry at that but fought it down. Despite his anger, despite her careless words, he would rather be uncomfortable than risk saying something equally bad to her in return.

"I really don't deserve you," she all but whispered.

"What?" he frowned, looking at her as he placed the water bottle back on his table. "I couldn't hear you, sorry."

"Nothing," she shook her head. "If you think you're over your mad now, why don't you come home?" she asked him gently. "That's where you belong."

"Okay," he shrugged, getting to his feet. He walked behind the table and picked up his gear before moving to her side.

"Let's go before I fall asleep again," he almost smiled, his mouth twitching at the corners.

"Okay."

-

Amanda felt as if she was fighting against some unseen force that was trying to hold her down by standing on her stomach. She tried to get up, but no matter how hard she struggled, the foot, or whatever, on her torso would not move at all. She grabbed for the knife she carried on her harness, but found that she had left it behind, somewhere. In fact, all her gear was missing. She was wearing her harness, even her vest, but there was nothing there. Every pouch, every pocket, every sling was empty.

She tried to cry out by all she could manage was a wordless bellow that sounded more like a moan than anything. Try as she might, she could not form any words, even though she could think them. She tried to use her hands to get the weight off her but couldn't find it. She hesitated as she thought she heard her name being called from far off.

Yes, definitely someone calling her, demanding she wake up. Wake up? Did it look like she was asleep, laying here fighting whatever giant had smashed her to the ground like this? Did this look like sleep?

"-nda! Wake up, sweetie, and stop fighting us!"

Who in the hell was that? And she wasn't fighting anything except the weight that kept her pinned. Did that voice sound familiar at all?

"Amanda!"

Definitely sounded familiar. She knew that voice from somewhere.

"Wake up, Mavis!"

Amanda Lowery's eyes snapped open, then closed as the brightness of the lights overhead dazzled her vision.

"Why in the hell are you calling me Mavis for?!" she demanded. Or tried to. All she produced, however, was a croaking sound.

"Hang on, Amanda," she heard a woman's voice say. "Open your mouth, dear. Take the straw and get some water. You're dry after all this time."

She did as she was ordered, sucking at the water greedily once it started, realizing that she really was starving for hydration. She drank as much as she could as fast as she could it seemed, until she heard the sound indicating she had hit the bottom of the cup.

"Better?" the voice asked, and Amanda recognized it as Patricia Sanders.

"Much," Amanda's voice was more than a croak this time. "Now who in the hell called me Mavis?"

"Is that all you can think of?" Petra Shannon rolled her eyes, moving to look straight down at her friend. "Damn, girl. You need to adjust your priorities a little."

"Where am I?" Amanda ignored the advice. "Wait…I got shot. Jesus, Mary and Joseph, I got shot!" it finally hit her, and she struggled to get up.

"Hold up, there, Bonnie," Patricia pushed her back down. "I'm afraid you aren't going anywhere for a bit. Yes, you were shot. In the abdomen in fact, right near where your appendix would be had you not had it removed. You weren't wearing the plates for your vest and the bullet went right on through and hit you. You lost a lot of blood, and you can expect a progression of ass-chewings I'm sure, but you're going to recover."

"I took them out because they rubbed," Amanda mumbled. "I shouldn't have done that. I just thought since it was a holiday that things would be quiet."

"Anyone who ever worked an emergency room anywhere would assure you it wouldn't be," Patricia snorted. "Holidays and full moons are always interesting."

"How much trouble am I in?" she asked, looking at Petra.

"Not up to me," Petra was shaking her head. "I don't know. You scared a lot of people, though. Me included, you silly bitch," she leaned down and gently hugged Amanda close.

"Sorry," Amanda promised. "I didn't mean to."

"We know," Petra assured her. "Someone is already trying to fix problems like yours," she added, and Amanda blushed a bit. "Don't worry about that now, though. I don't think you'll be in a position where you're going to need a vest or anything else anytime soon."

"No, definitely not," Patricia was back, this time taking vitals. "I'm afraid you're down for the moment, kiddo." She stuck a thermometer to Amanda's head, then grabbed her wrist to check her pulse. She checked both wrists and then both ankles.

"How long, do you think?" Amanda asked, thinking about her lessons with Xavier Adair.

"Depends on your healing ability, really," Patricia explained. "How fast your body recovers. You had a hunk of metal moving at a high rate of speed tear into your body tissue. It will take a few minutes for that to heal, and that was before we had to open you up to repair the damage and find the bullet. At a conservative guess, a minimum of two months before you can get around without aid or difficulty."

"Two months!" Amanda almost wailed.

"You got no one to blame but you, girl," Petra reminded her. "Might as well get used to hearing that."

"I'm afraid that is true as well," Patricia agreed.

"Two frigging months, just trying to avoid some chafing," Amanda sighed, laying back and closing her eyes. "I can't imagine what they said."

"It wasn't all bad," Petra shrugged. "Honestly, I think they were more scared than mad, except for Tandi Maseo. He was mad."

"He's also a medic," Patricia reminded them both. "He's had to patch up people before. One of his friends was killed even though he was wearing his vest, plates and all. Another nearly met the same fate not long ago. Your injury would have been much less severe had you been wearing your plates."

"I know," Amanda nodded. "It was just the one time, and this had to happen."

"Try not to worry about that now," Patricia told her. "I've already sent for-
"

"I see Sleeping Beauty has awakened!" Greg Holloway said as he entered the clinic. He did not look as if he had rested all that well, but his cheery disposition went a long way to hide it.

"Ha, ha," Amanda said in way of greeting. "Sorry," she added immediately after.

"Me too," Greg nodded, moving to stand beside her. "You were hurt pretty bad, Amanda, and it could have been a lot worse. You were very lucky. We were very lucky. Had Tandi Maseo not happened to have been along with us, you might not have made it."

"What happened, anyway?" she asked him. Greg gave her an abbreviated version of events, concentrating only on the parts that had included her.

"Damn, I really screwed us up good, didn't I?" Amanda almost moaned.

"The only part of this that was your fault was not wearing your safety gear," Greg replied at once. "That ambush was laying there for days, waiting for us to come by. Had you not removed the plates from your carrier, you would have an ugly bruise instead of a nasty scar, but we would still have faced the ambush."

"Yeah, and without having to take care of my bleeding ass, you could have caught the guys who did it, too," Amanda snorted. "Damn. The one frigging day I screw up, too. It's like there's some higher power watching for that kind of shit."

"His name is Murphy," Greg nodded, smiling. "As in Murphy's Law. The military edition is somewhat different from the civilian one. Helpful gems such as 'if the enemy is in range, so are you', for instance. In this case, the one day you leave behind that unneeded equipment, you're sure to need it."

"No shit," Amanda snorted. "Patricia says I'm out for at least two months, and that's just until I can get around on my own. At which point I will be sorely out of shape."

"I'm afraid that is true," Greg nodded. "But your job is still there if you want it. It will wait for you to heal. You need to concentrate on that more than anything right now." He paused, looking at her so directly that she began to flush slightly under his scrutiny.

"From now on," his tone grew much more serious, "when you have a problem, and I don't care what kind of problem it is," he held a hand up to silence her before she could object, "then tell me. No one will think less of you. Guys have chafing problems too, you know. Just in different areas. They can be debilitating and require a visit to the medic and being scrubbed from a patrol. If you tell me you're having problems, then all anyone else needs to know is that you're on sick call and can't make the patrol. Understand?"

"Yes, sir," Amanda nodded, her face red.

"Make sure that you do, Amanda, because you only get one free screwup, and this was yours," Greg was dead serious now. "Rest up. Do what the doctors tell you. You'll be on your feet and moving again before you know it."

With that he departed, leaving Amanda once more with just Patricia and Petra.

"He's a pretty good guy, isn't he?" she asked Patricia suddenly, and the older woman smiled as she nodded.

"He is indeed," she agreed. "He, Clay and Jake Sidell have been friends since they were old enough to understand the meaning of the word. Got into all manner of trouble when they were younger," she laughed. "Painted Greg's girlfriend's name on the Jordan water tower, and then Jake's future wife's name on the one in Peabody."

"Katie?" Amanda asked suddenly. "With a heart over the 'I'?"

"That would be the one," Patricia affirmed. "Used John Deere Green paint because of a song by Joe Diffie. Who apparently did some research because the water department painted over it at least three times and her name just kept bleeding through it."

"That is so cool," Petra sighed. "Where are the guys like that now?" she lamented.

“There are a few of them still around,” Patricia promised. “But no more water towers these days. And paint is scarce as well. We’re back to carving initials into tree trunks, now.”

CHAPTER FOURTEEN

"Well, I see someone is awake and once more part of the land of the living," Xavier Adair's voice sounded airy. Amanda looked toward the door to see her…mentor? teacher? walking toward her, geared up to stand watch.

"Another joker," Amanda smiled. "And yes, I'm awake. I may not be part of the land of the living until tomorrow, though," she added.

"I understand that you will be sidelined for a good few weeks due to your injury," Xavier nodded his understanding.

"At least two months before I can even start getting back into shape," she confirmed, long faced. "No telling how long I'll be just laying here. And you can forget keeping any dignity, too," she added, her face reddening.

"I'm familiar," Xavier assured her. "At any rate, I am pleased to see that you will survive and be able to return to duty, assuming of course that is your desire. Listening to your litany of complaints, however, I believe that to be a safe assumption, no?"

"Yes," Amanda nodded firmly. "I'm not quitting. Now, I may get thrown out," she raised her hands in a gesture of helplessness, "due to excess stupidness, but I'm not quitting."

"I don't believe you'll be in danger of being cast aside, either," Xavier smiled slightly. "You can expect a serious lecture, what my less cultured friends refer to as an 'ass-chewing', followed by a guilt trip, something which Clayton excels at, I assure you. But I believe it is safe to say that when you are ready to return to the game, your position will still be there, awaiting your arrival."

"Thanks," Amanda smiled for the first time since waking up. "I suppose Kim will be way ahead of me by the time I can get back into the swing of things," her smile lost some of its shine. "I was working hard to stay ahead of her, too."

"Then you shall have to work just as hard to catch up, will you not?" Xavier returned her smile. "I must go and check in for watch. I had heard you were awake and wanted to wish you a speedy recovery. Chin up, dear girl," he actually used an index finger to flip her chin up. "It could have been much worse. Accept the good things and cast the bad aside. Get some rest." With that he departed, leaving Amanda smiling still.

-

Her next visitor was Zachary Willis, still munching on a sandwich as he entered the clinic.

"Zach, don't eat that in here!" Patricia complained, though smiling as she did so.

"She eats in here, don't she?" he pointed to Amanda.

"She doesn't have much choice in the matter," Patricia reminded him.

"Neither do I if I want to see her while I'm supposed to be at lunch," Zach shrugged. When Patricia gave him 'the look', he hurriedly shoved the remainder of his sandwich into his mouth before holding his empty hands out as if for inspection. Rolling her eyes, Patricia returned to work and let Zach go and visit.

"'ell, 'ou 'ook 'ike 'shi'," he told her around a mouthful of food.

"I would say thanks, but I'm fairly certain you just told me I look like shit," Amanda looked at him with a raised eyebrow of her own.

"Ah 'id," Zach nodded, eyes twinkling. He made a great show of swallowing and then drained his canteen of water before speaking again.

"I meant it in the nicest way," he promised with a grin. "Seriously though, how are you? You look better than I expected from the way things sounded yesterday. I about half expected to see you laying here on a monitor with tubes running in and out of you."

"Well, I got the tubes part, anyway," Amanda's face reddened a bit. "Some you can see, some you can't."

"I hear ya," he nodded without pressing her or making fun. "Are you in a lot of pain?"

"Not as much as I'd feared," she admitted. "It does hurt, and I mean all the time, but unless I move a wrong way or too fast, it keeps to a dull ache for the most part. It could be worse."

"Yeah, you could be dead, stupid," Zach didn't pull any punches the way Xavier had. "Hell is wrong with you, leaving your plates out like that? You could have died, Amanda."

"I know," she held up a hand as if to ward off his pronouncements. "I've had this lecture from more than one source and expect it at least once more today. It was a stupid thing to do, which I have acknowledged from the outset. I took something for granted, and I paid for it. I'm lucky it was just me paying for it and not someone else."

"I'm glad to hear you say that," Clay's voice caught her by surprise. She looked to the door to see him standing there, just inside. "At least you've learned something from all this."

"Well, that's my cue to leave you behind, Mavis," Zach shot her a grin. "Good luck with all this," he winked.

"Damn you, Zach," Amanda muttered, but couldn't help smiling at the departing teen. Clay nodded to him as they passed one another, then stopped at her bed side.

"I'd ask how you feel, but I already know," he told her simply.

"How?" she asked, frowning in confusion.

"I've been shot before," he told her with a shrug. "More than once. It hurts."

"Like a bitch," Amanda agreed. "Is there a merit badge for this or anything?" she tried to go for lighthearted.

"It's called a Purple Heart," Clay didn't smile. "Too many of them are awarded posthumously. Yours could very easily have been the same."

"I know," she looked down at her hands, all she could do for the moment since she was stuck in bed. "I'm sorry. Doesn't really help, but it's all I can do at the moment. I thought it was just another patrol and then we'd have the holiday…damn, it's Thanksgiving!" she interrupted herself.

"It is indeed," Clay nodded. "And thanks to you, the medical staff will have to rotate through here in shifts rather than join the festivities for the entire day."

"Clayton," Patricia sent a warning his way without looking.

"I doubt you even understand how lucky you are right now," he sighed, rubbing his face. For the first time she noticed how tired he looked. "That was a dumb thing to do, and it was made worse by the fact that you knew it. How many times were you warned in training about your safety gear?"

"More than enough that I should have known better," Amanda replied, taking it without dodging. "Like I said before, I took something for granted. And I did know better, Clay. I just didn't think about it. I made that terrible mistake of assuming something."

"They tell me you'll recover fully," he changed the subject suddenly.

"I've been told that, yeah," she nodded.

"Do you want to continue on in this line of work?" he asked her flatly. "You don't have to answer now, and you can change your mind if you want. I'm just wondering if this has soured your outlook on working in security. Or working for Greg."

"No, it hasn't," she said firmly. "And yes, I want to continue, just as soon as I can get back on my feet and back into shape. I just don't know how long that will be, exactly."

"I'd estimate twelve weeks, give or take," Clay said at once. "If they're saying you can be on your feet moving on your own in two months, then I would wager another month and you'll be back to battery enough to return to duty. Six weeks at most, depending on how fast you recover. You'll be on light duty almost until Spring," he chuckled. "Start coming off it just as it warms up a bit."

"Well, at least there's that," she sighed. "If that's the only silver lining I get, I guess I'll have to take it and run with it."

"Do not let this happen again," Clay turned deadly serious in the blink of an eye. "This or anything else like it. You could have died or caused someone else to be wounded or killed working to save you. We can't afford a single loss, let alone two. If there is a next time, Amanda, and you don't die, then you're out. You can pick vegetables and learn to sew. We don't need any more funerals. We need live, alert and prepared troopers ready to defend this farm and the people who depend on it. Greg needs live deputies he can depend on being able to help him return at least some form of law and order to this county. People who decide not to wear their gear because it's uncomfortable are a risk to themselves and everyone around them. You're too smart for that. Don't do it again."

"I swear, Clay, I won't," her voice was solemn as she held up her hand. "And I promise you I'd never done it before, either. I…I just had some problems, that's all."

"I'm aware of the problem and I've already told the seamstress circle to put aside whatever they needed to in order to make sure that you and the others are taken care of in the future," he told her, nodding. "Don't ever be ashamed or afraid to come and tell me, or Greg, that something like that is wrong. No one will give you any shit for it, and if they do, I will land on them like an airliner. But I can't deal with problems if I don't know they exist. Do you read me?"

"Yes, sir," Amanda nodded. "I'm sorry," she said yet again.

"Stop being sorry and start getting better," he suddenly reached out and ruffled her hair. "Enjoy your convalescence. If you need anything, send word and I'll see what I can do."

"Thank you, Clayton," Amanda said to his back, as he was already on his way out.

"You bet," he called over his shoulder as he went through the door.

-

There had been a slight hesitation on the part of some about going ahead with the planned Thanksgiving festivities considering the ambush and Amanda's being wounded, but those were quickly cast aside. If anything, the fact that Amanda was the only one injured, and would recover fully, was more than enough reason to be thankful.

Gordon had decreed that if they were going to do this, they would do it properly. A yearling cow had been cut from the herd, and along with two feeder size pigs were slowly cooked over a hickory fire on spits. The smell permeated the farm until everyone there was almost leaning that direction, mouths watering in anticipation.

Bread, potatoes, and corn, the major staples of the farm for the time being, were cooked in vast amounts, a good deal of the work being done outdoors with cast iron cookware. 'Just like the old days' more than one had laughed. Those old enough to remember the old days didn't laugh much, realizing even if the younger crowd did not that the 'old days' were not some kind of great time, and worse, knowing that the 'old days' were rapidly returning. But they allowed the younger crowd their fun while they could have it.

They would know soon enough.

Clay and Jose had talked to Gleason, extending the invitation to his troopers to join them for the planned celebration. All the men under his command had behaved extremely well at the small harvest festival celebration they had enjoyed on Halloween, so it was a unanimous decision to invite them again.

Gleason gladly accepted and offered to have at least two of him men join the farm's watch during the event. Clay informed him that it was covered for now, but that he would keep the offer in mind, in case it was needed.

Everyone who had any areas of responsibility spent the early afternoon ensuring that those responsibilities were met and covered so that everyone could enjoy a good time. Building Two would again serve as the dining area as well as the gathering for cards, dominoes, and various board games.

The younger set would dine at Leon's club, assuming they wanted to, with everything powered and ready for a night of entertainment. He had also broken out his soda maker and had mixed enough of the 'elixir', as it had become known, for anyone who wanted it. It was usually a big hit for the smaller kids, especially.

Ladies once more delved into their recipe books and produced cookies, brownies and hard candies for the young as well as the young at heart, to be enjoyed once the meal was over.

Grateful soldiers walked the buffet style line with their plates, taking only modest amounts of food, all on their best behavior and offering their thanks at being included in the gathering. None of them were in any way out of line or anything less than courteous. As the evening wore on, they would relax a bit and mingle, several of them ending up as participants in the various games being played. Three of the very young men, all still teens, ventured over to 'Deuce's Place' to play video games and mingle with a younger crowd that was closer to their age. All three were very well behaved, almost as if they believed that Gleason could still see them, somehow.

The night did not end until the wee hours of the morning, everyone having a good time and reluctant to stop. In many cases, they didn't stop and were still playing when the sun began to peek over the eastern horizon.

That was fine, as there were plans for a three-day celebration. Breakfast food was prepared for that morning, with a warning that only leftovers would be available from there on out. Everyone expressed their thanks to the ladies who had worked to provide such good meals and spent the rest of the time waiting on them in any way they could. The soldiers surprised several by forming a line to wash and dry any cookware and dishes that were dirty, which bought them a great amount of good will from the most important people on the farm.

The cooks.

-

"Okay, gentlemen," Jose informed the collected group. "Rules are quite simple. From here to the interstate, back, through the obstacle course and back to starting line. Crowding is not allowed and is grounds for disqualification. If someone gets to the course before you, you may pass them so long as you don't interfere with them. If someone tries to pass you, impeding them is grounds for disqualification. No teamwork. This is not qualifications. This is a competition. Teamworking will be grounds for disqualification. Are there any questions?" A single soldier raised a hand.

"What is the prize for winning?" the young man asked, clearly just curious.

"You get to say you're the baddest mofo on the place until someone beats you," Jose chuckled. "Anyone else? In that case, ladies and gentlemen, please take your places. Get set…go!"

A group of five National Guard troops, six of the 'Amazons' group, and Corey Reynard took off, racing for the highway.

"You didn't want to race?" Kim Powers asked Zach as they watched the group running down the road and out of sight.

"Nah," Zach shook his head before taking a bite of roast beef. "I do that pretty regular, anyway. No need to torture myself."

"I kind of had the same thought," she admitted. "Are you standing watch again?" she asked, noting his gear.

"I'm about to start, yeah," he nodded. "I have the Ground Watch from ten until two. I think I have response from eight to midnight, but I'll have to check. I offered to take someone's place that wanted to have the time with their kids or significant others."

"That's nice of you," she smiled at him. "You're always doing nice things like that."

"I never thought of it as nice," Zach looked thoughtful. "I just figured those with family ought to have time with them. Well, family or else someone close to them."

"You don't have anyone like that?" she asked him.

"Nah," he shook his head. "I mean, me and the guys are close. Have been all our lives. But that's a bro thing, so to speak."

"I thought you and Vicki-,"

"I'd rather not get into that," Zach interrupted her gently. "Gone and done. No offense or anything," he added.

"None taken," Kim promised. "I shouldn't have said anything. Truth is I was just fishing a little," she admitted suddenly, blushing slightly.

"What for?" Zach asked, looking at her.

"For you, stupid," she laughed gently. "I was checking to see if the coast was clear, so to speak. To see if there was someone you were seeing."

"Oh. Well, no. No, there isn't," he assured her.

"That's good," she leaned forward suddenly and touched her lips gently to his. It lasted only a second, with her pulling away almost as soon as she reached him. "Damn. I wanted to do that forever," she smiled.

"Shouldn't have waited so long," Zach had just a hint of a smile. "Definitely shouldn't have started as I was going on watch," he added with a small laugh.

"Zach, I'm not looking for a playmate," Kim warned him. "I really, really like you. A lot. If you don't think you can return that then we can stop here and still be friends. Maybe starting when you were going on watch wasn't as bad an idea as you thought," she moved away, still smiling. "You can think about what you might want, too. I won't be mad if you don't think of me like that, or else don't think you can in the future. I'll be disappointed, but I've been disappointed before. I'll live through it. And we'll still be friends, regardless."

"But if you think you're ready for something more meaningful, something deeper than just a physical roll in the hay, then I just might be your girl. I just wanted to give you something to think about."

"I'll definitely be thinking about it," Zach promised the former cheerleader.

"Good," she nodded her head once, firmly. "Well, you go and do your watch. Come find me when it's over. I'll be around, somewhere."

"I'll just do that."

-

Gleason was frowning as his five men finished the course. The fastest of them had finished in fourth place behind that one teenager and two of the women. Two of them were dead last.

"Well," he told them, walking down the line as the five tried to catch their breath. "I have a feeling that you thought you were going to wipe the floor with these civilians, didn't you?"

"I never seen anything like it," one man replied. "Even during basic. Hell, even AIT."

"Remember that they're trained to Recon standards at the least," Gleason reminded them. "Even the women, before you say anything," he laughed. "You did good, despite your placement. All of you finished well under the time limit. Good work. I will expect at a minimum a top three finish if we do this competition again, however," he warned.

"Yes, Sergeant!"

-

"I can't believe he beat us," Petra Shannon grumped as she plopped down onto the ground. "I was sure we'd beat him."

"Why?" Devon Knowles asked.

"He's such a...a...I don't know," she finally gave up. "Joker," she continued after a second. "That's it. He's such a clown all the time. Been shot up twice according to some of the others."

"Both times defending this place," Devon reminded her. "Clown or not, he's basically a veteran at this stuff, Petra. All of them are. We're getting there, but we haven't seen any real action other than working with the Sheriff. He's been off the farm on no telling how many operations."

"Okay, that's true," Petra allowed. "My mistake was underestimating him, I guess. Still," she lay back, looking at the sky. "I just really wanted to beat one of them."

"We will," Devon promised. "We just have to keep working. They didn't start out where they are. We can't either. If we want it, we have to work for it. That's all."

-

"Thought you might like a plate," Greg smiled as he entered the clinic to see Amanda sitting up very carefully in her bed. "Assuming you can have, like, real food?" he glanced over to Jaylyn Thatcher.

"She's okay," the doctor promised. "Don't overdo it, but she's fine to eat."

"Yay!" Greg's fake enthusiasm was funny as he set the plate down on her small table. "Here ya go, Deputy Dawg!"

"Deputy Dawg?" she looked at him askance. "Really?"

"You prefer Mavis, then?" Greg teased.

"Deputy Dawg it is," she laughed carefully. She wasn't so touchy about the subject of her name anymore. Any teasing she received now was sincerely good natured and not malicious. That made a real difference she had learned.

"Anyway, you can't grow up all big and strong without eating properly," Greg chuckled, adding a large glass of tea and some utensils to the tray. "Never let it be said that I do not take care of my men. Women. Deputies," he finally settled on a neutral word.

"I get it," Amanda chuckled, picking up her fork. "I definitely want to get big and strong so I can kick the ass of the people who put me here," she growled as she stabbed at the food on her plate. She was hungry.

"Ah," Greg suddenly turned serious. "I guess I thought you already knew."

"Knew what?" she looked back at him; fork raised halfway to her mouth.

"Didn't X and Zach visit you earlier?" Greg asked her rather than answer.

"Yeah. Why?" She had lowered her fork back to her plate, food still impaled on the tines.

"Amanda, there's no one left for you to get even with," Greg told her simply. "Xavier and Zachary found them and killed them all, the same night you were wounded. You were probably still in surgery when they left. Pushed an old truck to the interstate before starting it so no one could stop them."

"Really?" Amanda looked stunned.

"Really," Greg promised. "Burned the bodies, freed a woman and four girls who were being held prisoner and looted the place. They were just finishing up when we got there. I can't believe they didn't tell you," he shook his head. "They may not have wanted you to know. Sorry."

"Hell, don't be sorry!" Amanda exclaimed, then grabbed her incision. "Wow," she added, more softly. "I owe them big time for that."

"I doubt either of them would agree," Greg shook his head again. "In fact, had I not told you, I don't know when you might have found out."

"I can't imagine Clay was happy about that," she mused. "Or you either, comes to that," her eyes rose to meet his.

"I didn't care either way so long as they didn't get hurt," Greg shrugged. "Clay was a little miffed, but Zach pretty much told him 'tough' and 'get over it'."

"Oh my God," Amanda almost whispered. "What did Clay do?"

"He got over it, I guess," Greg huffed out a little laugh. "He hasn't said anything else about it and helped them load up their loot. Anyway, the problem of who shot you and why has been dealt with. So, all you have to do is get better. Which starts with a good diet!" he smiled and pointed to the plate he had brought her.

"Yeah," she nodded thoughtfully. "Thanks again, boss."

-

"Not a bad throw down, aye?" Jose told Clay as the two sat watching the outdoor part of the day's festivities.

"Nope," Clay agreed, drinking from a cup that smelled suspiciously of alcohol. "Not at all."

"This will be a good break for everyone, I think," Jose continued. "And a big deal for the young Guardsmen as well. They seem to be getting along just fine," he nodded in their direction. Clay could see several of the young men interacting with farm residents, including, he saw, a handful of the Amazon squad.

"I'm really going to have to stop calling them that," he muttered to himself.

"Calling who, what?" Jose asked, lowering his own cup that had a similarly suspicious smell.

"I keep calling the girls the 'Amazon Squad'," Clay told him, shaking his head. "It stuck in my head back before they started training and I keep using despite trying not to. Sooner or later I'll say it in front of them and probably make them mad. I don't want to do that. They've worked too hard to think that they're being disrespected in some way."

"Who's to say they'll be disrespected by it?" Jose asked with a shrug. "Amazons were badass women warriors, man. Those girls are definitely heading in the right direction. Come to think of it, maybe 'girls' is wrong, too. But 'young women' is a mouthful and sounds as if we're talking down to them or about to chew them out. Ladies seems derogatory to me, almost mocking, to be honest. So, I try to treat them the same way I treat the boys. By which I mean, I call them boys, so I call the girls, well, girls." He lifted his cup to take another drink.

"Sounds as if you got it all worked out, don't you?" Clay laughed.

"Not even ten percent of it," Jose shook his head.

"I'll think of something."

-

"What do you think they're talking about," Danica Bennet asked, using her chin to point to where Clayton Sanders and Jose Juarez sat. She was currently standing in a group that included Talia Gray, Kim Powers, Freda Fletcher and Jena Waller.

"Probably about us," Freda said, her voice indicating what she thought the topic of their conversation would run to.

"Not those two," Talia said at once, shaking her head. "Not like that, anyway. If they are talking about us, and I'd say they are, they're talking about what to do with us. Or else just what to call us," she added with a little laugh.

"What makes you think they aren't just looking at us like those others did?" Freda challenged.

"They aren't like those others," Talia replied evenly. "Neither are the guys stationed here now. None of them are. That sergeant of theirs looks like he could eat glass. I promise you none of them will ever get out of line so long as he's around."

"You talk as if you're sure none of the guys on the farm will get out of line already," Freda snorted. "There's no guarantee of that."

"Yeah, because they gave you that rifle to make it more challenging," Kim shot right back. "Give it a rest, Freda. Yeah, there are bad people in the world. Some closer than others. Those guys in uniform that you're so disdainful of? Been fighting the bad since almost day one of all this. The guys on this farm have been, too. Wasn't for them, we'd all be in a world of misery about now. You might want to keep that in mind when you start bad mouthing them."

"You're just sweet on that ball player is why you're saying that," Freda snapped. Kim's face turned red but before she could reply, Danica Bennet spoke up.

"You need to get a grip or else go home, Freda," her voice was flat and cold. "First off, it doesn't matter and ain't a damned bit of your business who Kim may or may not be sweet on. Second, every single man on this farm has been nothing but polite to all of us since we got here. Third, I haven't seen you turn down a single meal or suit of clothes they've given you. You got a hell of a nerve to even insinuate that anyone on this farm is less than they appear. You'd do well to remember where you were when they found you."

"No shit," Jena Waller was nodding emphatically. "Remember that it was only four of them who snuck into town to get us, and that was after a hell of a shootout right here on this farm just hours earlier. They could have left us where we were and been justified in doing it."

"They did talk about it," Talia nodded.

"See?" Freda seized on that.

"See what?" Jena demanded. "See that they had lost six people, one of them killed, defending their homes and families? See that they had no idea what they'd find in Peabody, assuming they could get there? See that they didn't owe us jack-shit nothing? I can see a lot of things, Freda. Including an ungrateful and disrespectful-,"

"Hold on, hold on!" Talia raised a hand as she cut the younger woman off before she could hurl an insult. "Freda, what is really in your craw?" she demanded. "You haven't said anything like this until today, of all days. What has set you off like this, and especially on our benefactors?"

"Nothing," Freda muttered, looking at the ground. "All of you…none of you see it."

"See what?" Talia demanded. "If you see something we don't then point it out. Don't just stand there and mumble. If there really is a threat, then you need to share it."

"They're men," Freda almost spat. "It's all they think about."

"Oh, boy," Kim murmured.

"I need a witness," Talia said suddenly, looking around her. "Jena, I need you to come with me," she chose randomly.

"Where?" Jena asked. "Witness to what?"

"Just trust me, please, and come with me," Talia shook her head as she started walking away. "We'll be back in a minute. Stay right here," she told the rest over her shoulder.

-

"Did I say Amazon too loud?" Clay asked suddenly, cutting Jose off.

"What? Why?" his friend turned to look at him, then followed his gaze. "Oh."

"I didn't, did I?" Clay asked, turning to look at Jose.

"I barely heard it myself," Jose shook his head. "I got nothin'," he admitted as Talia Gray and the Waller girl, he couldn't remember her first name, walked up.

"I need you to do us a favor," Talia said without preamble.

"Uh, I'll try," Clay promised. "Depends on what it is."

"I just need you to settle an argument for us. A disagreement more than an argument, I suppose," Talia assured him. "We saw you looking at us a few minutes ago, and the conversation turned to what you were talking about. I said you were either considering what to do with us, or how to refer to us.

Someone else had another idea, which we'll just keep to ourselves. So, what was it? Assuming we were right, and you were talking about us."

"Well, actually, you're right," Clay told her. "Mostly right, anyway. We were talking about all of you, really, rather than just you five. I keep thinking of you, as a group I mean, as the 'Amazon Squad'. It was a name that got tossed around when you first started training and it sort of stuck. We've not used it since it might seem disrespectful, but I still think of it because, honestly, it just stuck in my head like that. So, when I saw you standing over there among the group that's been talking with some of the Guardsmen, I thought of you as a group using 'Amazon Squad', which led me to say out loud that I had to quit doing that. Jose asked what I meant, and I told him."

"He didn't want to say it where you could hear it, assume it was a diss, and make you angry," Jose added. "Said you had all worked too hard for that."

"True," Clay nodded. "So, anyway, you were right, for the most part. It was you five that made me think of it, but I was thinking of the group. No offense meant or anything," he shrugged carefully. "It really is just something that stuck in my head."

"I don't think I mind that, actually," Jena said, having forgotten her role was to observe. "I kind of like it."

"I kind of do, too," Talia nodded. "Well, thanks for settling an argument for us," she smiled. The two moved away, talking among themselves.

"Well," Clay watched them go before turning to Jose. "Busted? I guess?"

"I think something else is going on besides this," Jose shook his head, eyes calculating. "If I had to guess, which I do, I'm going to say that one of the other three is suspicious of us, all of us men I mean, mostly due to her bad experience before. We sort of expected that as far as having the Guard contingent here, but maybe one or two of them are concerned about the rest of us?"

"Could be," Clay agreed. "But no one I know of on this ranch would say a word out of line, let alone do anything. And if they have, not a word of it has reached me. If you're right, then it's just someone soured on men in general. I really can understand that being the case, considering all they went through."

"True that," Jose raised his glass. "We'll see what happens now."

-

"What did you do?" Kim asked as a grinning Talia and openly smiling Jena returned.

"I went to the source and asked them, flat out, what they were talking about," Talia replied. "I was mostly right, it turns out," she smiled coldly at Freda. "They were talking about us. First of all, that we would be over here having anything to do with the Guard soldiers, and second of all," she giggled, "the fact that some of them have referred to us as the 'Amazon Squad'."

"Seriously?" Danica asked, her face showing her shock. "Amazons?"

"Seriously," Jena nodded, smiling broadly. "Clay thought of us as a group using that term, but then remarked to Jose that he had to try and stop thinking of us like that because he was afraid he'd say it aloud and some of us would get angry. He felt we had all worked too hard to hear something we might find insulting," she glared at Freda when she said the last part.

"Jose backed him up without prompting," Talia nodded. "That's what they were talking about when they were looking over here at us."

"Well. How about that?" Kim all but smirked. "Sounds like someone needs to be hunting up a little crow for supper," she told Freda. "I kinda like that Amazon tag, by the way," she turned her attention back to Talia. "Just, you know, for size and what not."

"We kind of do too," Talia laughed. "I certainly don't take offense to being compared to badass warrior women. That would tickle Amanda plumb pink, wouldn't it?"

All but Freda laughed at that, while she continued to scowl.

CHAPTER FIFTEEN

Zach had drawn the short straw on patrol, or in this case, the long straw as it were, being assigned the 'round the world' check as they often called it. He would use an electric cart to ride the entire perimeter of the farm, looking for any signs that they had been visited.

As he rode along, his thoughts returned to Kim Powers. Not just to her, but to what she had said. She was looking for something more than just a physical relationship, and Zach wasn't sure he was able to do that. Wasn't sure he was capable of it, in truth. Sure, he could pretend, at least for a while, but he wouldn't do that to anyone, let alone someone like Kimmy, who had been completely upfront with what she wanted.

He was attracted to her of course. No girl made four years as high school cheerleader without being attractive. She was almost as tall as he was and athletic to the core. There was nothing about her that he knew of not to like. But like was a lot different from what she was looking for. What she was wanting. And he honestly didn't know if he could do that.

It took almost his entire watch to make his round of the ranch, finding nothing out of place or any indication that trouble was lurking about them. As he neared the Troy farm headquarters, he had decided that all he could do was be as honest with her as she had been with him. After that, whatever happened, happened.

-

Zach grabbed himself a sandwich from the table of food in Building Two before venturing out into the front where the main festivities were taking place. He had ridden by them on his way in but had not stopped, returning the cart to the charger first. He had contemplated returning his gear to the Bunkhouse but eventually decided against it. He might need it to be close by, so he stored everything but his side-arm and rifle in the room across from Operations that was used by the Response watch.

Eating as he walked outside, he ambled in the direction of the huge teepee of wood that had been erected in the center of the field before Building Two; a bonfire for later in the evening. He could see people playing horseshoes, lawn darts, cornhole and various other outdoor yard games, all seeming to be enjoying themselves. Music was playing farther over toward the Troy House, with a few people even dancing. Kids were running and playing under several sets of watchful eyes, though colder temperatures and two heavy frosts should have put the snake threat to bed for good this year.

Truthfully, Zach was surprised they were doing this at all. While it wasn't frigid by any means, it was definitely on the cooler side, with the temperature not quite reaching sixty even at sun high. Thankfully, there was no wind, so the cool temperature wasn't quite so bad as it might have been, otherwise.

He had just caught sight of Gordy and the rest lining up for the cornhole tournament when he felt someone grab his arm. Stopping himself from reacting for a second, instead he simply looked to his right to find Kim Powers latched onto his right arm, smiling.

"Hiya," she waved comically, and he had to laugh a little.

"Hi, yourself," he replied. "Having a good time?"

"More than less," she nodded with only a slight frown. She explained their earlier problem, wondering what his reaction would be. To her surprise, he merely shrugged.

"Everyone reacts to stuff differently," he told her. "That may be her way of dealing. Or it could be her natural disposition. I don't know her, so I can't really say. It's not my business either way."

It was a much more mature answer than she had expected, and it caught her by surprise. He either missed that or ignored it in favor of finishing his sandwich. He noticed her appraising him and raised an eyebrow at her even as he lifted his water bottle to wash down the last of his late lunch.

"What?" he asked her as he put the bottle away. "I got something on my face?" he wiped his mouth with his sleeve, which for some reason made her laugh.

"No, you don't," she promised him. "I was just surprised at your reaction to Freda's issues, I guess. I honestly assumed you might take offense, or even get angry."

"Take more than that to do either," he shook his head slowly. "I can see where you might think it, though."

"Did you think about what I said?" she changed the subject to what she really wanted to talk about, leaning into his arm as she did.

"Yeah, I did," Zach nodded, looking at the ground in front of them as they walked. "You were honest with me, so I'll be honest with you. I think you're hotter than a July afternoon, to be honest, and any man who doesn't find you attractive can't be looking at you." He wasn't looking at her so missed a furious blush at his country boy compliments.

"You want something that I don't know if I can give you," he dampened that reaction almost at once. "It's not that I don't like you, because I do, and I already just said I was attracted to you. But you're wanting an emotional commitment, or at least that's what it sounded like. Yeah?" He looked up at her, waiting.

"I hadn't thought of it as an emotional commitment," she admitted, clearly mulling over what he had said, and what she had said to him earlier. "I suppose, long term, that would be right, though. But what I meant was a little simpler, to be honest. I meant that I wasn't just looking for a quick tumble like some might be, and then go our own way. I know cheerleaders get a bad rap sometimes, but I am not that kind of girl."

"Never heard anything like that about you when we were in school," Zach shook his head. "Not even from jealous girls."

"Well, that's something, anyway," she laughed lightly. "I meant that I want to try and get to know you better, and to see if there is some a connection we can build on. We might find out we can't stand each other, you know," she reminded him.

"That is true," he nodded. "And I had thought of that, as a matter of fact. The thing you need to understand, though, is that I'm maybe not-,"

She stopped him with a hand gently covering his mouth. He looked at her with one raised eyebrow, waiting.

"Why not let me learn what you are, or aren't, as we go?" she said quietly. "I'll do the same for you. We can form our own opinions of one another based on what we learn. All I ask, and offer in return, is not to lie. Whatever is, just is. So far as I'm concerned at this point, a lie would be the only deal breaker, other than you are seeing someone else. If you want to go another route, all I ask is that you tell me to my face instead of me having to hear it through the grapevine. I promise you the same in return."

"I can work with that," Zach promised. "And I agree."

"Great!" she smiled brightly. "So, tell me. Can you play cornhole?"

-

Amanda was almost asleep when she heard the door to the clinic open. Looking up, she found Xavier Adair observing her and tried to sit up. An upheld hand from him stopped her.

"Don't get up on my account," he instructed, walking to her bedside. "I simply wanted to check on your wellbeing before I begin my watch. I have to make the ground watch circuit tonight and thus will be gone for most of that time. How are you faring this evening?"

"I'm hurting, but I'm also breathing," she smiled wanly. "Both are preferable to being dead, so I'll take them."

"Well said," he almost smiled. "Do have need of anything? Did someone think to bring you part of the bountiful harvest for which we are demonstrating our thanks?"

"Greg brought me a plate earlier," she nodded. "He also told me quite a tale while he was here," she added, eyeing him closely.

"He is known for exaggeration, our dear Sheriff," Xavier nodded. "I shudder to think what embellishments and fabrications he shared while here."

"He told me that you and Zach went and killed everyone related to the man who shot me," Amanda said bluntly. She noted Xavier's smile freeze for perhaps a second before it returned.

"Yes, well, Zachary and I agreed it needed doing, and neither of us were occupied at the moment," his reply was as calm as still waters.

"Really?" she raised an eyebrow at him. "That's it?"

"We've both been told we needed a hobby," he shrugged easily. "That is something we're good at. Seemed like a win-win scenario to us."

"And here I thought you guys were going soft and had done that just for little ole me," Amanda laughed carefully.

"Well, it was what happened to you that brought them to our attention, so I suppose you could say that." She thought for a second that he had winked at her, but decided it was a trick of the lights.

"Well, whatever the reason, I appreciate it," she told him plainly. "Just makes me feel all warm and gooey inside," she added, trying to needle him a little.

"I would have thought the bullet in your abdomen would be responsible for that feeling," he didn't quite smile. "Still, you are quite welcome. For both the revenge and your…gooey insides…thing," he waved his lack of terminology away with a flourish of one hand.

"Now, I'm afraid I must take my leave," he told her. "I'm off to circle our little slice of heaven and make sure there are no threats upon us." He was already moving toward the door as he spoke.

"Be careful the Boogieman don't get you!" she called playfully. He stopped, hand on the door, and looked back at her over his shoulder.

"My dear girl," his smile would have frozen lava, "I would have thought you had figured it out by now."

"Figured what out?" she frowned, puzzled.

"That I *am* the Boogieman."

He was out the door and gone before she could frame a reply to those chilling words.

-

Gordy and Sam were dancing to the music around the bonfire, both smiling after a long day of merry making.

"This has been so wonderful," Sam almost sighed as she leaned on Gordy's shoulder.

"Has been pretty cool," he agreed.

"When was the last time we were able to do something like this?" she wondered aloud.

"Um, Halloween?" Gordy replied lightly. She hit him lightly on the shoulder with her small fist.

"I mean something so broad and big, like this," she clarified. "Even with Amanda in the clinic this has been a major celebration. And still has a day to go, too."

"It has been a shindig sure enough," he agreed once more. "We've been really lucky with the weather, too. You can't tell it this close to the fire, but the temperature has really dropped since sundown."

"When did you check it?" she asked, looking up at him.

"Didn't have to," he shook his head. "I can see the breath of every person that isn't close to the fire. It's cold tonight. Won't be long until we're looking at a hard freeze."

"Sounds like we'd better make the most of this, then."

-

"*Operations, this is Red. Please respond.*"

It took Leon a second to realize where the sound was coming from. The radio, all the radios, had been stone quiet for hours as the celebration continued.

"Go for Operations," he managed to scramble to the microphone from where he had been reclining with his feet up, reading.

"*I am currently at the eastern boundary, near the road,*" Xavier's voice was hushed. "*There is movement on the road, inbound. Multiple noise sources. I have not yet moved to take a closer look and check for weapons.*"

"Roger that, Red," Leon was all business. "Stand by one." Leon leaped from his chair and ran to the door. With all the commotion outside, no one would hear that radio message, or any he tried to send.

Bursting out of the door, the first person he saw was Corey Reynard, walking with Terri Hartwell.

"Corey, we got inbounds on the road from the interstate!" Leon told the older teen. "Red is at the property line, about to look them over. No one can hear us on the radio!"

"I'll take care of it," Corey promised, taking off at a run without even an apologetic look to Terri.

"Sorry," Leon offered before returning to the radio.

"Red, I've sent someone for Boss. Please stand by."

"*Roger that.*"

In less than a minute Clay was standing in Operations, Corey and Jose behind him.

"Red, this is Bossman," Clay took the radio. "Say threat."

"*Unknown threat at this time,*" Red replied quietly. "*There are at least ten people in this group, making their way steadily, albeit slowly, toward the farm. There is zero noise discipline among them, and the only light appears to be some sort of small lantern. Unable to confirm if they are armed or not.*"

"Roger that. We'll be ready in two minutes. I'll contact you again when we're ready to challenge them."

"*Roger that. Standing by.*"

"Gear up," he told Jose and Corey. "Spread the word, quietly, for everyone to gear up or take cover. I want everyone who can be there on the pad in two minutes."

Two minutes and thirty seconds later thirteen people were assembled on the pad with their gear, or at least most of it. Zach and Titus had been on the response team and were the first to arrive. Gordy had stored his gear in Operations with Leon and had grabbed it, then suited up as he moved to the pad. The rest were moving as quickly as they could.

"Situation is as follows," Clay said quietly. "Red has encountered a group of people moving toward the farm along the road, from the interstate. No idea if they're hostile, or even if they're armed. We'll move down the road, hit them with the handheld spotlight, and challenge them. I want three with me on the road, the rest divided north and south of the road. Your men are yours to command, Sergeant," he told Gleason, who was already geared up along with three of his men who had been on what they called a 'soft watch'.

"We'll back you on the road," Gleason had already made his mind up about that.

"Everyone else, as they assemble, will take defense positions," Clay ordered, looking toward Jose, who would remain behind. "This may be nothing, it may be some kind of hit. We can't know until we go see. Move out."

-

"Red, we're about to hit the lights."

Clay and the others had moved silently down the road until they could hear the noise that had alerted Xavier to the presence of intruders. Night devices were turned to stand-by or else the wearers were careful to be far from them as Clay made his call.

"*Roger*," Red whispered in Clay's ear.

"Hit it," Clay said simply. Gordy and Titus activated the handheld one million candlepower spotlights, shining them down the roadway to illuminate a ragged group of people, all now trying to shield their eyes amid panic.

"Stop and stay where you are," Clay called, his voice at a conversational level rather than a shout. "You are surrounded and have nowhere to run to. Raise your hands, empty, above your head and you will not be harmed."

"Who are you?" a voice from the crowd demanded. "This is a public road!"

"The road may be public, but the property to either side is private, and remains that way for five miles," Clay responded, keeping his voice reasonable. "Unless you can give us a good reason for your being here, I'm afraid you'll have to turn around and head back the way you came."

"There's nothing back there!" the same voice stated. "And there's something up ahead because we can see it!"

"There are homes ahead, yes," Clay agreed. "What you see is a simple pallet fire. Burning wood scraps. Now again, unless you can name a specific reason for being here, we'll conclude our conversation and ask you to return the way you came."

"We're hungry," a new voice chimed in, a woman this time whereas the first had been a man. "Give us food."

"We don't have it to spare, ma'am," Clay replied evenly. "I'm sorry about that, but it's just the way it is."

"This is farm country!" the male voice broke in again. "Don't tell us there's no food here!"

"We're past the harvest, friend," Clay said firmly. "We'll be lucky to get through the winter with what we managed to put back. As it is, we'll be hungry ourselves before the next harvest. Now, I'm done explaining myself to you. Turn around and head back. If you stay on this road once you cross the overpass, the town of Jordan is about ten miles or so that way. There's a National Guard contingent there as well as Constables and Militia. Maybe they can be of help to you, but we don't have the help to offer. While I'm sorry for that, I can't change it."

There was a grumbling discussion among the group, which Clay estimated to be around twenty-five people, give or take.

"You promise they'll help?" the woman's voice asked again.

"I can't promise something for someone else, ma'am," Clay said kindly. "I'm just saying they'll be more likely to be in shape where they can help. We've just got too many mouths to feed as it is."

"You know, we ain't the only people moving this way," the man's voice claimed, even as some of the group began to shuffle back toward the east, and Jordan. "There'll be more coming. We were just among the first to get out. We'll be sure and point them your way."

"I killed the last man who threatened me with that," Clay's voice was like ice. "I guess I need to make an example here as well." He made a show of racking a round into his rifle.

"No, no, no!" A woman's voice cried, different from the first. "He's just a loudmouth, that's all. Don't pay him any mind. I know he seems useless, but he's my son's father!"

"Then take your baby daddy away from me before he threatens my family again," Clay ordered coldly. "I'm sorry he's no good for you, but that is not my burden to bear. Neither are you. While I am sorry for your plight, there's nothing I can do to change it."

Technically, that wasn't true, and Clay felt a twinge of conscience as he said it. While the farm could provide meat, though at great expense to themselves, vegetables for so many was another matter. And he had to stick to the plan that had been set up by those who were experts in their field. If they wanted beef and pork for the morrow, then they had to preserve and conserve today. It was just that simple. In eighteen months, two years at the outside, the farm would have more than enough beef to feed many more than they did currently.

But not if he cast that plan aside in a bout of conscience, or out of fear from one loudmouth.

"We're going!" the woman's voice assured him. "I'm sorry! We're going!"

There was a great deal of grumbling within the crowd, and no small amount of literal crushed hope as the group had been moving toward what they had thought was a good meal. They had been right, for the most part, but unfortunately for them that meal was meant for others.

"Kill the lights," Clay ordered. "Lights are going out," he called over the radio. Seconds later the two spotlights began to dim, it taking a few seconds for such a bright light to go completely out.

"Heading back your way, Red," Clay called softly. "Grumbling."

"*I have them*," Xavier's whisper came back. "*Are they headed to Jordan, then*?"

"That's where I pointed them," Clay admitted. "Where they go is up to them."

"*I believe I shall remain here for a bit*," Xavier said after a pause. "*To ensure no others make this same trek*."

"I'm sending Zach to join you," Clay informed him. "We're doubling the watch tonight, after this."

"*Affirmative. Advise him I am on the south side of the road, roughly fifty yards from you*."

"Got that Zach?" Clay called.

"*Already on my way*," Zach assured him.

"We can help with the watch, Lieutenant," Gleason said gently.

"There's an OP buried near here, stocked and with a field telephone," Clay said after a minute. "If you want to man it, that would be a help."

"We can do that," Gleason nodded.

"Corey, take whoever the Sergeant assigns and show them to the OP, and where everything is."

"Got it, Boss."

"Everyone else, back to the barn," Clay called. "We need to regroup. It may be a long night."

-

The party was officially over. No one really liked it, but it was necessary considering the new development. The bonfire was extinguished even as personnel moved to assist with the doubled watch.

Down the road, Xavier and Zach sat with an electric cart, just off the road on a small field road entrance.

"How much charge does this thing have?" Zach asked.

"A bit over three-quarters," Xavier replied. "Why?"

"I…I can't explain it, exactly, but I got a feeling we need to go look at the interstate," Zach was hesitant, as if he didn't truly understand it himself.

"Is this a hunch or just something you think we should do?" Xavier asked carefully.

"It's a feeling is all," Zach waved his hands a bit. "If I could explain it, I would. I guess hunch is as good a word as any."

"Get on," Xavier said at once, turning the key to turn the cart on. In seconds they were on their way east toward the interstate.

-

"Have we got everything covered?" Clay asked as he entered operations. Leon had been joined by Millie and Leanne to help cover all the radio traffic with people checking into position.

"We do," Leon nodded without looking up. "This is straining the hell out of the watch schedule, though," he warned.

"Can't be helped," Clay shook his head. "Tomorrow, when we can see, we can get a better handle on this, maybe. Tonight, though, we can't see what or who's out there. That bunch could have walked right up on us if X hadn't just happened to be over that way at the right time. That was sloppy. I was sloppy," he amended. "This rests on me, tonight."

"Well, now that you've immolated yourself, you may want to look over who is where," Millie told him with a raised eyebrow. "Everyone has checked in somewhere, but almost no one is where they should be. I don't think it's a problem, but I can't swear to that."

"*Bossman, this is Red. How copy?*" Xavier's soft whisper was almost lost amid the noise.

"Go for Bossman," Clay replied, resisting the urge to swear.

"*You will want to very quietly make your way to the interstate,*" Xavier informed him. "*I really must stress the word quietly. Perhaps take one of the electric carts. You may want to bring Gleason with you as well.*"

"X, what the hell is going on?" Clay demanded.

"*You'll need to see for yourself,*" Xavier replied. "*Both of you. And Gleason may well want to make a radio call to his superior in Jordan. I suggest you hurry right along, by the way.*"

"Roger that."

-

Clay had taken one of the newer model electric carts that had been taken from the state park before the National Guard had taken over and stopped at the barracks to see if Gleason did want to go, explaining that Xavier had recommended it. Gleason was not only willing but eager to see what the commotion was.

The two rode mostly in silence, occasionally exchanging comments about how to secure the area if need be. Through his night vision device, Clay was soon seeing Xavier and Zach standing in front of the golf cart they had been on, looking north down the interstate. Parking perhaps twenty yards behind them to avoid the noise, Clay and Gleason moved stealthily to join them.

"What are we-," Clay started, then stopped as Zach raised a hand, pointing northward. Following that point, Clay looked down to the interstate. He could see blobs that indicated cars that had never been removed from the road, but noth….

Suddenly, Clay was aware of movement. Not from the cars, but around them. Not just one of them, but all of them. Everywhere.

It took him a minute to figure out that he was looking at refugees streaming down the interstate. Individuals, groups of two or three, occasional groups of a dozen or more. Some pushing shopping carts or pulling wagons or game carts, a few riding bicycles with weak lamps on the front, others pushing bicycles because it was too dark to ride safely.

"How many do you think?" Gleason whispered to Xavier.

"It has been steady since we arrived here some…twenty-eight minutes ago, now," Xavier informed him, checking his watch carefully. "A stream of them. Some have taken the road to Jordan, while others simply continue south. If I were forced to give a count, I would estimate at least five hundred, counting those we can see now."

"And no end in sight," Zach added from the dark. "As far as you can see, there's people."

"What happened to cause this sudden migration?" Clay asked out loud, without thinking about it. "Why now, of all times?"

"Lack of food, getting colder, bandits and lawlessness, take your pick," Gleason shrugged. "I told you this was coming. I'm surprised that it's taken this long. If I was to make an educated guess, I'd say that the gangs in Nashville have moved out of their hovels and begun attacking places like Murfreesboro. Which probably means we'll be leaving," he sighed.

"Going back?" Clay asked and the older man nodded.

"I doubt we'll surrender the town without a fight, and that fight will have to include our group," Gleason confirmed. "If it doesn't, I just don't see a way to make it happen. I should probably get back and make that call to the Captain."

"Yeah, me too," Clay agreed. "You guys hang here and stay back out of sight," he told his two men. "I'll send some help your way soon as I can, but things are a mess for the moment. We've got people all over the map right now."

"We'll be fine," Xavier assured him. "Though if you can find someone to bring us some food and water that would be appreciated. Warn them not to use the lights and to stop about where you did. We'll go to them."

"Will do," Clay promised. "You guys watch out for yourselves."

"But of course."

CHAPTER SIXTEEN

Dawn found most of the farm still awake. All the security members were on a rotating watch, four hours on, four hours off. While the rest had been allowed to return home, everyone was warned to be constantly prepared for the alert to be sounded. There was no way of knowing what kind of threat might emerge from the southerly flow of refugees.

In hindsight, Clay should have known better than to send that first group to Jordan. If he'd had more than a minute to think, he would have sent them on south, toward Lewiston. But, he hadn't, and now Gaines was arriving in a Hummer, her face red with anger.

"What do you mean telling all those people I could help them?" she demanded without so much as a hello.

"I didn't," Clay replied with a shrug. "I did mention that there was a Guard contingent stationed there, and that *maybe* you could provide them assistance, but I didn't know that for certain. All I knew for certain was that we could not."

"Yeah, right," Gaines snorted derisively. "This is a farm! You could have fed those people if you wanted to!"

"And have them ask to stay here?" Clay returned her scoffing. "No, thank you. We don't have the room, nor do we have the food to spare to take on so many new mouths for the winter. You may believe what you like, Lieutenant, but those are the facts. We will not allow people that we are not certain will be safe to be around to take up residence on this farm, where our homes and families are. Period."

"You're lucky Adcock is in charge of this area and not me," Gaines growled. "If it were me, I'd-,"

"Be dead," Clay interrupted gently, his voice now soft and frosty. "That's what you would be, Lieutenant Gaines. Dead. Because you were about to threaten me with seizing my family's property, weren't you? And I assure you, that is a grave mistake indeed," he leaned forward slightly as he finished, forcing Gaines to move back.

"Are you threatening me?" Gaines tried to sound incredulous, but it merely came out as more afraid.

"Yes," Clay nodded once. "I'm glad we understand each other. That will lessen any chance of miscommunication in the future, should you find yourself *in charge*, as you put it. This land has been in my family for well over one hundred years. We have worked our asses off to pay for it, and for everything we have. I will not have some half-wit, half-cocked, half-trained imbecile with a bar on her collar and chip on her shoulder threatening my family. That's you, by the way," he added snidely as another Hummer was making its way up the road.

"I'll have you-,"

"Have him what?" Greg Holloway asked from behind her. She whirled to see the Sheriff standing there, looking at her.

"I asked a question out here," Greg's voice took a harsher tone as he seemed to channel the Old Man. "Have him what? Because it almost sounded like you were going to threaten to arrest him. Which, I promise you, will be a mistake." Even as he spoke the new arriving Hummer stopped behind the first.

"Gaines, what the hell are you doing here?" Adcock demanded, almost angrily. "You should be back in Jordan, managing the humanitarian crisis there!"

"I came here to make sure that Mister Sanders knows who is in charge," Gaines informed him.

"That would be me, Lieutenant," Adcock's voice dropped to a near murmur. "This is twice you've tried to use or imply authority that you don't actually have. A third time will result in your removal. Just why is it that you felt that *Mister Sanders*," he stressed the words, "needed your input?"

"He sent all those civilians for me to deal with!" Gaines erupted. "Sir," she remembered to add just barely in time.

"And?" Adcock waited.

"And, he should have done it himself!" Gaines retorted. "Not sent them to me!"

"It is *not* his responsibility to 'deal with' the crisis that has developed here, Lieutenant Gaines," Adcock spoke very formally. "And it *is* yours. Events of this nature are exactly why you are posted in Jordan to start with! He did exactly the proper thing by sending those people to see you. Someone who is supposed to be there to provide support in time of need. Clearly you've managed to forget that while you sat in your cushy table job at the Headquarters."

"Now," he didn't allow her time to respond. "I suggest you get your ass back in that Hummer, and you return to your post. And that you do so before I decide you are disobeying me in the field, where I am the ultimate authority. Do I make myself clear to you, Lieutenant?"

Gaines clearly wanted to argue, but as Adcock's words hit her, she wilted. His threat may have been well dressed and polite, but vague or no it was still a threat. She was on the verge of being shot.

"Sir," she straightened to attention.

"I'm sorry, Lieutenant. I couldn't hear you. What was that?" Adcock cupped a hand to his right ear in what would have been a comical gesture under other circumstances.

"Yes, sir!" Gaines replied, stiffening further.

"That is moderately better," Adcock told her, his voice betraying his anger. "Get out of my sight."

Without a backward glance Gaines climbed into her Hummer, yelling at her driver to turn them around and take them back to Jordan.

"I really miss Flores, now," Clay said calmly.

"No shit," Adcock shook his head, then realized what he'd said. "Not that it matters, now," he added hastily. "Thanks for having Gleason let me know what was going on. I'm afraid I'll have to pull him and his men, though."

"He anticipated that," Clay nodded. "Know where you're going?"

"Not as yet," Adcock shook his head. "Still waiting on The Word. Meanwhile, I need a favor. A rather large one, I'm afraid."

"You need food," Clay stated rather than ask.

"Yes, I do," Adcock agreed. "I was going to ask if you could spare maybe two head of cattle to be slaughtered and cooked for the people in Jordan. I've already gotten three head from a place south of Lewiston for the people there. It's all we have for now other than what is left in the fields or in nature."

"Yeah, we can do that," Clay agreed. "But I want an escort into town when we do. We'll carry two cows and maybe four pigs that are feeder weight. I think it's four, anyway," he amended. "I'll have people start getting that together right now. We'll slaughter them here so we can keep the hides. That will mean we'll need Gleason's men to help load the sides."

"I'll escort them myself," Adcock nodded. "And helping load won't be a problem, either. I'll be taking Gleason and his detachment with me when I go."

"You'll need him if Gaines is anything to go by," Clay snorted.

"Isn't that the truth?"

-

"I want to make it plain that I am not complaining," Alicia said as the family sat around the table. "But I thought we had said we weren't going to dip into the herd anymore until the new crop of calves started to come of age. What happened to that?"

"A stream of refugees from the north," Clay replied with a shrug. "Hundreds of them. Maybe thousands by now, I don't know. Adcock asked me to spare something for the people that landed in Jordan, noting that other outfits had already done the same in Lewiston. So, I sent what we could and maybe a bit more than I normally would have. But Adcock has been good to us, all things being evened, so I decided to help him out."

"I noticed they were leaving," Gordon stated.

"Adcock took Gleason and his men when he left," Clay nodded. "He is escorting Cliff and Moses as they deliver the meat and ensuring their safety in returning. Adcock feels certain that the entire Guard contingent in this area will move north to engage whoever is pushing these refugees south. Which means we are alone. Again."

That declaration fell like a guillotine on the family.

"I didn't want them here, and now I don't want them to go," Alicia was shaking her head as she spoke first. "Wonder of wonders, huh?"

"It's easy to get used to being safe and protected by someone else," Clay agreed. "We got sloppy the last two days. If not for X, we would have been blindsided by that first group, and likely inundated by some of the others before daybreak. We got lucky."

"How many people are we talking about?" Robert asked, concern clear in his voice.

"No idea," Clay admitted. "They're still moving down the interstate, and not all of them are stopping, even in Lewiston. Adcock said before he left that fully half of the people on the road, if not more, are continuing south rather than stop. Seems as if they're more afraid of what lies behind them than they are of being hungry," he shrugged.

"What do we do now?" Angela asked carefully.

"We bottle up the road and we stay put," Clay told her. "It's all we can do. Greg has already said he can take the back way out, or even cross the branch on the tractor bridge and head overland to whatever they call that road to the north, now. Used to be Germany Hollow, I think?"

"It still is, but there's no ramp there," Ronny nodded.

"In a Hummer that really won't matter," Clay told him. "But I assumed he'd use that road to get somewhere he could use a ramp. He's already gone in fact, but he headed out with Adcock and the others. When the Guard leaves, Greg's work will really pick up. He dreads it, but it's his responsibility now."

"We are going to help him, aren't we?" Gordon asked, looking at his youngest son carefully.

"We already are," Clay promised. "But remember; every person on patrol with him is someone who isn't here to stand a watch or defend this place. We've lost the Guard detachment as well. So, expect long hours and a lot of grumbling about it. I don't blame them, but it's just the way it is. Try not to be angry at people who are, well, angry," he finished a little lamely.

"Meanwhile, I'd imagine there's work to be done," Gordon stood. "Things just got a lot more difficult, I'd wager."

"You can almost bet on it," Clay agreed. "We're going to be forced to make some hard and ugly choices soon. Be prepared for that, up here," he pointed to his temple. "Ask yourselves how badly you want your children to have a decent life, and not end up like those folks on the highway. What you're willing to do in order to make that happen. Because that is exactly where this will end."

"The easy ride is over as of now."

-

"Easy ride?" Alicia almost whispered as she and Ronny returned home. "He's saying things have been easy for us so far?"

"They have," Ronny looked distracted even as he replied. "Very easy, compared to others. We've worked for it, no mistake, but it's still been easy. But he isn't talking about the work, Ally. He's warning us, trying to prepare us. The ugly things he's warned us about time and again? They're about to start in on us in a big way. People turn vicious when they're hungry. Parents turn vicious when they see their children suffer."

"Yeah?" Ally still didn't see it.

"Ally, what would you be willing to do in order to feed our kids?" Ronny asked her, turning his full attention to her now.

"Anything I had-," she stopped short. "Oh."

"Oh," Ronny nodded. "We're about to be faced by people who will want to swarm this place like locusts and take every scrap of food they can find. What we've faced so far was nothing. An irritation at best." He took a deep breath.

"We're about to be in a position where we may have to kill some parent for doing the same thing we'd do if we found ourselves in their place in times like these."

-

"You need to take a break, Cowboy," Lainie said gently. She had been standing in the doorway of his small office for two minutes and he hadn't noticed her.

"Can't," he shook his head as he continued looking at rosters. "There's too much to do."

"Let some of the others take some of that," Lainie insisted, her voice still gentle; soothing. "You've done a great deal in the last day. You need to eat and rest at least a little. We need you to be up and functional when we need you, Clay."

That seemed to get through to him as he tossed the papers on the table and leaned back in his chair, looking at the roof above him.

"Because I've done such a great job up 'til now?" he snorted. "We almost got overrun last night, Lainie. I mean, it was close. Those people were attracted to the noise, and the light of the fire. Once they got in here, we'd have had to kill them to get them out. And if we didn't kill them, they would have come back and brought more with them."

"I know," was all she said. Stepping behind him, she began to rub his shoulders gently.

"This is going to be so bad," Clay lowered his head as her hands worked on him. "So terribly ugly. You're about to see things that usually only happen in Third World nations. Or in First World nations when they crumble. That's what has happened out there while we were insulated and isolated from it in here. The Greeks believed that Prometheus gave fire to man, to help him build civilization. Now, that fire has been snuffed out, leaving nothing but ashes behind. That great civilization, destroyed in a matter of minutes."

"I know," she said again. "There's nothing you can do about that, Clay. Your job is here. Adcock and the others have the job of trying to clean up the mess. Your job is to keep our small fire burning for us, and for as many as we can help."

"We're going to end up killing people who are just hungry," Clay told her, his voice mournful. "Killing people for following their instincts to find food and survive. Just to protect our homes."

"Probably," she agreed simply. "And it's a shame. A terrible shame that it has to happen. But Clay, what happens to us if we allow those same people to swarm over this place and take everything? What do we do after that?"

"We suffer," Clay sighed. "Which I can't allow. Even with the herd, I have to say no, because so much is riding on it for the future. Once we can get that first calf crop in, then we'll be in a real position to help rebuild at least our area. To help the Guard while they try to put things back together, planting acreage to feed them while they work. Maybe enough to feed extra if we're lucky."

"And that's why you have to do whatever it takes to save this place and the people on it, Clay," Lainie told him softly. "Because you may be the only one in a thousand miles who gives a tinker's damn about anyone but themselves and the people around them. Thinking about the future, about trying to rebuild. You've done it since before this even happened and continued doing it right up to now. I know it's hard, I do," she moved to the side of his chair and knelt down, her hand trailing down his jaw.

"I know, and I understand," she all but whispered. "But we've come this far, Clay. We can't quit now or else it's all been for nothing. The only way through is forward."

"You really are smart, you know," Clay smiled weakly, reaching up to take her hand in his. "I don't know what to credit for having you. I really don't."

"Well, you cut a pretty swell figure in that cowboy hat," Lainie smiled. "Got a nice truck. And a nice ass, too," she winked, almost giggling this time as she laughed. It made Clay laugh, which made him feel a tiny bit better.

"C'mon, Cowboy," she stood, pulling him from his chair. "Get off that nice ass of yours and let's go home for a little while. You need to eat, take a shower, and get some rest. I'll be right there with you to make sure you get it, too."

"You've talked me into it."

-

"How bad was it?" Corey asked, looking at Zach. All five of the former teammates plus Kurtis Montana were huddled together in the Bunkhouse, discussing the events of the night and day.

"I mean, nothing actually happened other than challenging that bunch on the road," Zach shrugged. "But if you mean the interstate…man, there were people fumbling in the dark as far as the NVD would let me see. Hundreds, maybe thousands of them."

"Did any of them get off at the exit?" Gordy asked.

"A few, here and there," Zach nodded. "They all headed toward Jordan, though. Without the fire going here, there was nothing to lead them our way."

"I just don't know about this, man," Titus was shaking his head. "This just ain't…ain't right. Why now? After this long everybody up and decides to see the sunny south? That don't sound right to me."

"It's not," Corey agreed.

"Gleason said something, or someone was pushing them, or else they were running from that someone or something," Zach told them. "He expects it to get worse, not better."

"I imagine it will," Kurtis spoke for the first time. "And you boys better be ready for some nasty days ahead, too."

"Some of them will get off here and want to come our way," Gordy agreed. "And no matter how desperate they seem, we can't allow it," he told the assembled teens. "I hate it. Worse than I can put into words, I hate it. But we cannot lose this place. It's all we have, and our futures are built on it. If we lose it, we lose everything."

"That's what I mean," Kurtis nodded in agreement. "You're gonna face some ugly decisions before long. Might as well set your mind to that now and be preparing to do what you have to."

"Just us?" Titus asked. "What about you?"

"I already did it," was the simple reply. "I faced this kind of thing before, on a smaller scale. And while it does suck, it is imminently preferable to the alternative," he settled back on his bunk. He offered nothing further and no one pushed him about it, sensing his unease.

"So, someone comes at you, holding a baby, and expects to walk right on in," Corey said it out loud. "What then?"

"You got two choices," Kurtis told him, hands folded behind his head as he stared at the ceiling. "You take care of their babies, or you take care of your own. There ain't no third choice." With that he turned his back to the rest and placed the edge of his blanket over his face to block the light. The others fell silent at that, each running things over in their minds. One thing was apparent to them all, however.

There would be no winners here.

-

"This will be a very bad scenario," Brick said softly as he sat on the front porch of what had been Leon's house.

"Most definitely," Xavier nodded in agreement. The two had taken to having these talks once or twice a week since they had met with Beverly and worked through their issues. There were still areas where the ice was thin, but the two were working at it. That was honestly more than Beverly had ever expected.

"It is my opinion that your former teammates will be of the same mind as yourself, when it comes to protecting this place and the people they care for?" said Brick before taking a drink from the cup of tea in his hand.

"They will," Xavier confirmed. "None of them are squeamish. They will regret it. They will hate themselves for it and will never grant themselves forgiveness, taking the guilt for it to their graves intact. But they will do what is necessary."

"I thought so," Brick mused. "I have no issues doing what is needful to protect this place or it's inhabitants, though I myself have only two people other than you that would concern me."

"Me?" Xavier's surprise showed on his face and in his voice. "You're professing concern for my wellbeing, brother? Be still my heart!" he feigned a fainting spell.

"Your humor is no better now than when we were children," Brick snorted. "Of course, I am concerned for you. It's obvious that you cannot look after yourself," he chuckled. "But I am also concerned about Lainie Harper, and Janice, of course. I promised Leon I would watch over both when he was gone."

"I doubt Miss Harper needs a guardian angel any longer," Xavier scoffed. "If it can get by Clayton, there will be no stopping whatever it is."

"That is my opinion of him as well," Brick agreed. "I do not believe the betrayal will come from within," he changed the subject suddenly.

"Nor do I," Xavier didn't question that there would be a betrayal. "I therefore must assume it will come from the lovely town of Jordan. Those in town who have lusted after this place for so long will see these masses as an ideal battering ram to push us aside and take what they want."

"Indeed," Brick nodded. "I have considered-,"

"No," Xavier cut him off. "No, let Clay make that decision. If he wants the old man dead, he is more likely to make the kill himself than order it done. That said, he would not hesitate to order it done if it became necessary."

"Very well," Brick didn't press the issue. "When the time comes, I will most likely fight from here unless Clayton wishes me somewhere else. This hill commands a good view while the leaves are gone from the trees. My rifle will travel a long way from here."

"Let's talk about that rifle," Xavier looked at his brother with a smirk. "Last I looked, that particular rifle was still in development. How did you come to have one?"

"Someone who had been asked to try one owed me a favor," Brick shrugged. "He offered me the rifle as a gift. I took it."

"Of course, you did," Xavier scoffed at the very idea of not taking such a beautiful rifle. "That must have been some favor you were owed, brother. I should very much like to hear about that."

Brick looked at his brother for a few seconds, then took a deep breath.

"I was in Bahrain, working…."

-

Clay was almost home when his radio came to life once more.

"*Bossman, this is Operations*," JJ's voice came through the earbud.

"Go for Bossman," Clay sighed tiredly.

"*You are needed in Operations ASAP*," JJ said flatly. "*Area Commander on the line for you with urgent traffic*," JJ added.

"Roger that. Bossman, on the way."

Clay looked longingly at his house. Lainie was probably putting supper on the table right now. He had promised to follow her home as soon as he made sure all the watches were set and everything was covered. Sighing tiredly, he turned around to head back down the drive to Operations.

-

Jaylyn Thatcher was in Operations when Clay got there, microphone in her hand.

"Have they been separated from the rest of the group since you arrived?" she was asking, holding up a finger at him for patience.

"*Affirmative*," Adcock's voice replied. "*Exposure will be limited to myself, and Lieutenant Gaines. Neither of us are sick nor exhibit symptoms currently. The men with Gleason unloaded the meat, but had no contact with anyone else here, including the rest of our unit*."

"Copy that," Thatcher responded. "Send them back. All of them. Tell Gleason to isolate in the barracks and we will be in contact."

"*Affirmative*," Adcock replied again.

"Bossman is here now, Captain," Jaylyn added, handing the microphone over. She looked worried.

"Come see me when you're finished talking to him," she almost ordered as she walked past him. "I'll be in the clinic."

"Go for Bossman," Clay said on instinct, watching Thatcher's departure with puzzlement.

"*This is Adcock*," the Captain replied. "*The threat is viral, repeat viral. That is what has sparked this…exodus, for lack of a better term. Some type of influenza-type illness has swept through Nashville and people are fleeing ahead of it spreading, or at least the threat of it spreading. We are all exposed as of now,*" his voice sounded tense.

"Understood," Clay replied, though it wasn't. "Are we sure it's the flu?"

"*Negative,*" Adcock replied. "*Only that the symptoms are similar. Nothing more. We lack the necessary equipment to check for sure. I am sending a blood sample back by way of Gleason, for Doctor Thatcher to examine. She may be able to discover what it is.*"

"What about Gleason?" Clay asked. "What about my two men? Are they exposed?"

"*Negative,*" Adcock replied at once. "*They have had no outside contact other than myself, and I am not symptomatic. Gaines is not symptomatic either, currently. Hopefully, we will remain that way, but for now, we're in isolation. Gleason and his men, and your two men, will have to isolate in the barracks for at least three days. I must ask you to take care of them for me, Lieutenant, at least for now. Hopefully, this will pass, but until and unless it does, they will have to fall under your command.*"

"Understood," Clay replied. Adcock's use of his former rank was the Captain's way of ensuring that Clay would look after Gleason and the others.

"*Understand, Lieutenant, that you must take every and all precautions to protect yourselves, and your command. Isolate yourselves and do not, under any circumstances, allow anyone to enter your AO. Send them this way and we will do all we can for them. I repeat, use any means at your disposal to ensure that your area remains isolated. And inform the Sheriff that he is to suspend patrols until further notice, or until this has passed in the event there is no notice forthcoming. I will include a written order confirming this with Gleason.*"

Adcock was slipping into formal speech as the pressure of his situation began to bear down. It was something that the military trained their men to do in order to keep them focused on their jobs. Clay had slipped back into it more than once, himself.

More than that, Adcock had just authorized Clay to do whatever he had to do to protect himself and the many people that lived on the farm. As Area Commander, Adcock had that authority, and his using it here would prevent Clay from being lynched if he had to do anything ugly to protect himself or the people that depended on him.

"Get Doc on the line and get him up here," Clay ordered JJ. "Then, call Greg and tell him to avoid all contact and return to base at once." As the teen turned to the local radio net, Clay keyed the microphone in his hand.

"Orders received and understood, Captain," he said formally. "Godspeed, sir. We are always standing by," he reminded the man.

"*Roger that. Good luck to us all, Lieutenant. Hopefully, we'll be in touch.*"

Clay set the microphone down, digesting what he had been told. He could hear Greg replying to JJ.

"He wants to know why," JJ informed Clay. Clay took the microphone JJ was using.

"Five-oh, this is Bossman. Be advised we have learned what the threat is. Viral, repeat viral. Highly contagious and spreading. Return to the barn by order of the Area Commander, avoiding any and all contact on the way in. Have you been exposed during this patrol?"

"*Negative*," Greg replied calmly, though Clay could tell his mind was racing. "*We've not been in contact with anyone today except by radio.*"

"Then come home. Now," Clay ordered. "Don't stop for any reason. Please acknowledge."

"*Roger that. Order acknowledged.*"

Clay handed the microphone to JJ.

"Not a word of this leaves this room for now," he told the teen. "Not until I've talked to Thatcher and know more about what's happening. I do need you to have someone on the watch take an FRS radio to the barracks, though. And lay a fire in the fireplace and get it going. We need to do that and get out before Gleason and the others return. Also, see if the Troy House has anything in the way of food they can send down in the next twenty minutes or so. Tell them to call anyone they need to for help. Remind everyone that they have to be out of the barracks before Gleason and the others get back."

"Yes, sir," JJ said solemnly, turning to the radio.

"And call someone down here to help you," Clay ordered over his shoulder. "Gwen didn't work today, did she?"

"No, sir," JJ replied. "I'll call and ask her to come in."

"No, you'll call and tell her I *told* her to come in," Clay corrected. "It isn't a request. Make sure she understands that."

"Yes, sir."

-

"There's very little reason for us to have any isolation protocols for the farm residents, aside from poor Cliff and Moses," Jaylyn Thatcher told Clay. "The simple truth is, if either Gaines or Adcock is infected, then it's already run through the farm today. If they weren't, then we're clear, again other than Cliff and Moses." She paused, chewing on her lower lip.

"We can't let anyone through to the farm," she sounded almost distraught as she said those next words.

"I know," Clay nodded. He heard the door open before he could say more and looked to see Tandi Maseo walking in.

"What's up?" the little medic asked, noting the pensive looks on their faces.

"They're running from some kind of virus," Clay told him. "The people on the highway are running from a virus that has already run through Nashville."

"Oh, shit," Tandi murmured. "That means we have to isolate ourselves right now," he added without thinking, then looked at the doctor.

"Sorry, ma'am," he smiled weakly. "Force of habit."

"Not necessary, Tandi," Jaylyn smiled. "You're right in any case. We were discussing it when you came in."

"You two get Patricia and Kaitlin over here and get them caught up on what's happening," Clay ordered. "Doc, take the ATV and get Patricia. Maybe the Webb girls as well, with their knowledge of herbal medicines and home remedies. We may have to treat the symptoms if we can't fight the disease. You guys put a plan together and I'll see to it that it's carried out," he told Jaylyn. "One way or another."

"Will do," she promised. "As long as we're careful, we can do this," she promised.

"As long as we're careful and can keep from being overrun," Clay amended, and she nodded silently.

"I have to go. If you need me, call me. I have a feeling I'll be awake."

-

"So, they're all sick," Jose sighed. "That's just great."

"They aren't sick at the moment," Clay shook his head. "And they aren't our concern, honestly. There's nothing we can do for them. We have to concentrate on saving this place. We were already putting the girls onto the roster, yes?"

"Yes," Jose nodded. "It helped replace the manpower that Greg is using."

"You're getting that back, as of tonight," Clay informed him. "Per Adcock's orders, Greg is to stand down until further notice. Also, per his orders, we are to use whatever means are at our disposal to protect this place and the people living here. Whatever it takes."

"That gets into some pretty ugly territory, Boss," Jose said softly.

"It does," Clay agreed. "But if this is even half as bad as they fear, then we don't have any other options. Rework the roster, figuring everyone back and standing watches. Go ahead and figure another one with Gleason's men added to it. If they're clean after three, maybe five days, we can use them, too. They'll be here, under our care as Adcock put it, until further notice."

"All that will help," Jose nodded slowly, mind already working. "We…we may need to think about sending a vehicle up the road to block anyone heading this way. Up to the interstate, or near it, I mean. They can use the P.A. on the rigs to send anyone that heads our way back toward Jordan. That alone will stop a lot of them."

"Do it," Clay agreed. "Do whatever you need to do to make us secure. Don't neglect the back approaches, either. We built the new barracks and dorm to be used as security posts, so use them. Gleason's men can help stand a watch on that side even while they're isolated, if it comes to that."

"Yeah, that will work," Jose mused, writing on a piece of paper. "I wish that briar hedge was finished," he chuckled darkly.

"Same here," Clay replied. "That would simplify our problems greatly. But it isn't, so we have to cover up. There is still the fence along the interstate, however. Most people won't climb that hill just to have to climb a fence and cross into an empty field. It looks barren, so there's no need to go through there looking for help, right? At least we can hope that's what they think."

"Maybe," Jose nodded absently. "We can definitely hope."

"Thanks for making me believe that," Clay said sarcastically.

"Sure thing."

"I'm going to rest a bit and get a bite to eat," Clay said, shaking his head as he moved to the door. "Call me if you need me."

"Will do."

Clay stopped at Operations to see Gwen Paige sitting with JJ. She saw him and waved, though she didn't smile. She looked worried and Clay assumed JJ had filled her in.

"Remember to keep this in here until the Doctor is ready to talk to everyone," he reminded them.

"Will do," both said, echoing each other. Clay nodded and made his way outside. He stopped for a minute, standing in the dark save for a handful of solar lights that would work for a few hours each night. As he stood in the quiet, trying to let his mind settle down, he felt something hit his face. As his hand moved to investigate, the mystery resolved itself in the form of a small, white crystal falling right before his face.

It was snowing.

-

"Hey, it's snowing!" Lainie sounds exuberant when Clay walked in. The house smelled delicious. She had probably made some dessert of some kind from the scent in the air. She literally skipped over to him and kissed him lightly. "And you're late!"

"It is," he nodded, unable to match her exuberance. "And I am. Sorry."

"What's wrong?" she was instantly guarded.

"I just learned why there is some kind of mass migration on the interstate in this weather," he sighed, ditching his gear as he spoke.

"What is it?" she asked, suddenly wary.

"It's the flu, or something similar," he didn't sugar coat it, mainly because he didn't know how. "They're running from a viral infection that has already run amok through Nashville. They're trying to outrun it by heading south, even in this weather."

"Didn't some of them go to Jordan?" Lainie stopped short. Her grandmother was in Jordan. They weren't on good terms at the moment, but Marla was still her grandmother.

"And to Lewiston, and still moving southward in many cases," Clay nodded tiredly. "Gleason and his men are returning, but they will have to be isolated for three to five days. So will Cliff and Moses, since I sent them in there to carry the damned meat we gave the town." He sat heavily in his seat at the table. Lainie took the seat next to him.

"I'm sorry," he said gently.

"It's not your fault," Lainie tried to smile but wasn't quite able to. "It was her that did it, Clay. I love my grandmother, and I always will, but she did this to herself. Chose it for herself. She had it just fine living here, and Leon would have made sure she was taken care of. She chose to put herself into the situation she's in."

"That doesn't make it hurt any less," he told her softly.

"No, it doesn't," she agreed. "But it does mean that you aren't to blame. I assume we can't go into Jordan until this is over?"

"We can't even allow anyone onto the farm until it's over," Clay shook his head. "Orders from Adcock personally. Protect this place with any means necessary. No one not already a resident here is allowed in until the virus runs its course."

"That sounds a lot like-,"

"Yeah, it does," Clay didn't make her finish. "Because it is." He looked down to see a bowl of chili in front of him, with fresh homemade bread on the side.

"Thanks for this," he smiled at her. She tried again to smile back but once more she didn't quite make it.

"I hope you like it."

CHAPTER SEVENTEEN

Word went out the next morning for everyone to gather at Building Two for an emergency meeting. No reason was given beyond that, but the word 'mandatory' had never been used when announcing a meeting. That alone was enough to start tongues wagging.

The snow hadn't stopped yet, either, which just made things a bit more complicated. Ronny had taken a small blade attached to an ATV and cleared the Hill off so that the old school bus could be used to give people a ride down to the pad before Building Two, rather than having to travel in the snow.

Titus Terry drove another ATV up the Hill to get Marcy George. Marcy grinned broadly when he arrived in front of her house specially to get her. Her smile faltered when she got in, seeing the grim look on Titus' face. She tried to ask him what was going on, but he just shook his head and told her to put on her seat belt.

When they arrived at Building Two, Titus motioned for her to follow, which she did, concerned now. Titus led her to Clay's office, but stayed with her as she walked in.

Quietly, Clay explained what had happened in Jordan. Marcy was crying by the time he finished, worrying about her family, especially her younger siblings. She had asked if it was possible to get them to her, and Clay had to admit that it wasn't. Not now. There was no movement allowed on or off the farm, by order of the Military Commander of their area, and all movement in and out of Jordan was being strictly controlled for now to try and limit the exposure of the rest of the area to any infection.

Marcy nodded her understanding, wiping her eyes. Clay motioned to Titus, who wrapped an arm around her shoulders and pulled her to her feet. Suddenly, she turned and buried her head in Titus' shoulder, sobbing. Clay rose to his feet and softly made his way to the door, patting Titus' other shoulder as he stepped out and shut the door.

Once outside, Clay rubbed his face with his hands, trying to get rid of the fatigue and hopelessness that suddenly threatened to overwhelm him. First Lainie, now Marcy. And the rest still to go.

The security personnel had been the first to be briefed on what was happening and what to expect. More importantly, on what was expected of them. Clay didn't pull any punches, knowing that the time for that was gone, now. Instead, he was blunt to the point of ruthlessness, a hint of the former hunter that he still was beneath the veneer of civility that he wore like a cloak.

"I'm sorry," Clay told them once he had explained the virus threat. "I know this is worse than horrible, but we have no choice. We cannot allow this farm to be infected. Nor can we allow it to be stripped bare. This is no longer about us. This farm and the food it will produce next year and in years to come may be all that sees us through. The things we've set up here, like the medicinal plants we're growing, the seed garden and other greenhouses, all of that has to be protected." He paused for a minute, looking at each one in turn.

"Most of you have heard of the Library of Alexander," he said finally. "You're read or been taught about the knowledge it contained, and how it was lost to fire, primarily during Julius Cesar's Civil War. It's a famous tale of lost knowledge, some of which we have never been able to recreate or reproduce, or so the legends say."

"But there was a place called Alamut Castle, in Southern Persia, in what is now Iran. Alamut Castle was a stronghold fortress of the Ismaili Movement among the Shia Islamists. Why am I telling you this? Simple. Alamut was the site of one the most impressive and yet relatively unknown libraries of the world. Ismaili doctrine believed in knowledge and equality, among other things that we don't normally associate with Islam today. Their library, believed to have been constructed during the rule of an Imam named Hasan, was thought to contain priceless scientific knowledge. And this library, and its fate, are not legend or clouded in mystery."

"During the Mongol invasion of Persia, Alamut Castle was ordered to surrender. The leader did so, and the Mongol Horde proceeded to dismantle and destroy that library of priceless information. Science, medicine, theology, the list could go on, but you get the picture. All that knowledge, gathered over centuries, lost to a horde of people who were too stupid to make use of it. Not because they themselves lacked intelligence, but because they had no forethought. They believed the Shia followers to be a nest of evil, and therefore the library must be evil as well. I doubt they ever cracked open a book before destroying them."

"Two years later, in 1256, those same Mongols destroyed another great library in Baghdad, Iraq, called the House of Wisdom. Again, full of centuries of advances, again, ignored in favor of 'cleansing' the area. You may have heard of the Baghdad Battery? It is, or was, in a museum, unearthed in an archeological dig, and believed to be around two thousand years old, or thereabouts. And it still works. For all we know, this was just one simple example of the knowledge lost in these two great libraries."

"The reason I told you all this is simple. We face a similar threat now. Not because we have a library of rare books, but because we have some of the last, functioning equipment capable of producing a large amount of food over the next three to five years. Because we have reams of knowledge stored on computer drives that will still be here, provided we protect it, when civilization tries to dig itself out of the ashes of this ruin."

"Because we have the means of producing seeds for the foreseeable future. Seeds that can reproduce themselves, unlike the modern seeds that some may can still find now. Yes, those GMO seeds will still produce, but they won't reproduce, not like ours will. Because we have a garden of medicinal herds and the know-how to use them to recreate at least some of the medicines we've lost access to."

"But only, *only* if we can protect this place. If we allow it to be overrun by the sick, the criminal, or even the hungry, then we can lose it all. Not only do we lose our homes, and our future, but we also lose the ability to be of any help to our fellow man in the years to come."

"With that understanding, the Area Commander under the Martial Law provision, Captain Adcock, has ordered me, a former military officer and now an officer of the unorganized militia, to protect this resource with whatever means are available and necessary. With any and all means at our disposal, we are to prevent anyone from entering this farm during the present emergency."

"It's a great deal to ask of you," he admitted. "I am beyond sorry to be the one to ask it of you. And, if any of you simply cannot in good conscience take part in defending the farm against all comers that way, I understand. Let me know in private once this meeting is over, and I will see what can be done. Just remember; your family, your friends, are depending on this place. If we lose it, we lose everything we've worked for. Pray for this to pass quickly, and for God to spare us from this ordeal. Dismissed."

To their credit, no one had asked to be relieved of duty.

-

The crowd gathered in Building Two talked among themselves, wondering why they were here. Though most spoke softly, the number of people meant that even that low discussion was loud when taken in total. All talking ceased, however, as Clay entered the room, followed by Jose Juarez and Jaylyn Thatcher. Clay decided not to beat around the bush.

"You'll note that most of the security personnel are not with us," Clay pointed out. "That's because they're either out on the line, or trying to rest for holding that line tonight, in the dark."

"What line, you may ask? Simple. You all know that there is a horde of people moving down the interstate and has been for at least two days. Last night we received word from Captain Adcock why that is. There has been a viral outbreak in Nashville, and they are trying to outrun it. Fleeing in all directions, apparently, including ours. The virus may already be present in Jordan, and in Lewiston, as refugees have flocked into those areas as they left the interstate. Others have continued south to other areas, probably hoping for better weather."

"Last night, under the Martial Law state of emergency, Captain Adcock ordered me to seal this farm. No one is allowed in, or out, until the present emergency is passed. We are to use every means we have to prevent this farm from being overrun. And yes, before any of you ask, that includes by those who are hungry, sick, or that have children. It means anyone. Period."

"Captain Adcock has declared this farm and others like it that are still functioning to at least some degree to be vital resources that cannot be risked. He knows what he has ordered us to do, and he regrets it as much or more as anyone here. But he had no choice. We are a unique operation that stands to be a great resource to this entire area in years to come. That can't be lost. It may be that the food, medicine and supplies that this farm produces in the next five years are all that prevent our area from sliding completely into barbarism. That can't be allowed to happen, so this farm has to be kept safe. The resources here must be protected at all costs. No matter that may be."

"Be prepared to work long hours in support of our security detail. Be prepared to support them directly, and to take over their everyday chores since they will not be available. Everyone who has been trained will be armed at all times from here on out. I see too many of you this morning who left their rifles and kit behind. Don't do it again. You may be called upon at any time to protect yourself or the people near you. Be ready to do so."

"I'm now going to turn this over to Doctor Thatcher, who has worked through the night trying to gather information on the virus, and any precautions we can take. Please listen to her. She knows more than any of us do at this point, and as of last night, that included the National Guard contingent. Doctor," he said to Jaylyn and stepped aside.

"I wish I could soften what Clay just said, but I can't," Jaylyn said sadly. "While we haven't been able to identify exactly what virus this may be, there is ample evidence that it is completely viral, with both airborne and fluid exchange contagions. Realize that all of this is reported symptoms by people fleeing the sickness, so there has to be some leeway in our interpretation until we can…."

Clay didn't hear the rest as he stepped outside into the snow. There had to be three inches of snow on the ground now, and it was still falling. Slowly, but steadily. He didn't know whether to be happy or sad. He didn't know anything at the moment except how tired he was.

"God help us," he whispered softly as he turned to head for home. He had to get something to eat, and some rest. Whether he had time for it or not.

-

To say things were tense would have been a massive understatement.

Everyone left the meeting with Doctor Thatcher's warnings ringing in their ears. Yes, the flu was potentially deadly considering their lack of access to modern medicines to combat it. Yes, it was highly contagious and could be spread with something as simple as a sneeze or a cough.

Yes, people who had been exposed to it had already visited the farm before it was known that there was a reason to avoid it. There was the potential now that some of them could begin showing symptoms.

This led to most everyone watching those around them closely for signs and symptoms of being sick. It also led to most everyone constantly worrying that any sort of cough or sniffle they had meant that they were sick.

Topping that was the danger of the farm being overrun by hungry, angry, and potentially very sick people, endangering their lives, their children's lives, and their homes. Even the most merciful of residents were unwilling to go that far.

After the meeting, everyone went about their work, those who had to work outside bundled up extra carefully to avoid any sickness that the cold, wet weather might cause. No one wanted to be mistaken for having the flu.

It was a nerve-wracking situation for the entire population of the ranch. The sound of gunfire shortly before noon did not help at all.

-

Zach was sitting in the turret of *Thug Life*, the four-wheel Cougar that Mitchell 'Thug' Nolan had named. The engine wasn't running so the entire crew was bundled up against the cold.

Devon Knowles was in the passenger compartment, moving from one side of the vehicle to the other, using binoculars to search for anyone who might be trying to gain access to the farm. Shane Golden, commanding the vehicle, sat in the front passenger seat, doing the same thing to their front. Petra Shannon sat behind the wheel of the Cougar, having learned to deftly handle the smaller Cougars while serving as a driver for Greg Holloway's patrols. While she helped keep a lookout as well, her primary job was to be ready to start the rig up and move it at a few seconds notice.

It had been quiet so far, the snow that blanketed the area seeming to insulate them from any noise.

In the wee hours of the morning, Roddy Thatcher had used the quietest truck available to them to carry a logging trailer near the interstate and wedge it across the road roughly fifty yards from the ramp. Fencing that ran parallel to the interstate on both sides of the small backroad, overgrown by heavy briars and bushes, met at each end of the heavy trailer, effectively closing the road down to all traffic. The fencing that provided limited access to the interstate was still intact, which added another barrier for people to cross before they reached the farm fencing if they tried to avoid the road.

No one believed that a simple roadblock and set of fences would stop someone who was determined to gain access to the farm. All it was intended to do was slow down any type of assault, giving time to the defenders to do what they would have to in order to protect the assets of the ranch, along with their homes and families.

To that end, the small MRAP was sitting in the middle of the small backroad roughly twenty yards from the log trailer, engine off to avoid noise. Other vehicles and personnel were spread across the line to either side of the Cougar, fulfilling the same job. All of them hoped that nothing would happen. That they would not be called upon to fire on people who were trying to find food and shelter.

It was not to be.

"Movement front," Shane's voice broke the silence. Zach had spotted the movement at the same time and straightened in the turret. For this particular job, the Cougar was carrying an M240 machine gun in the turret. No one anticipated needing the heavier M2 Browning for something like this. Below him in the passenger compartment sat an M249 as well, along with two very nasty 12-gauge shotguns.

Movement in the swirling snow that was still falling resolved itself into a medium sized group of what Zach estimated to be thirty people. Some were pushing shopping carts, others pulling game carts or even small wagons. It reminded him of the stories of pushcarts used by people moving west in the 1800's. He could hear some of them coughing even at that distance.

"Estimate thirty people," he said quietly into his microphone.

"*All units, this is Rattler. Be advised we are facing a group of roughly thirty people, approaching the roadblock. Stand by*."

Zach could hear Shane on the radio, which monitored the main frequency even while being set to transmit only in the vehicle. He could change it if he had to, but as vehicle commander it was Shane's responsibility to handle communications. It was also his job to try and discourage the people hoping to cross the roadblock.

"ATTENTION! THIS IS A RESTRICTED AREA, OFF LIMITS TO CIVILIANS! IF YOU ARE IN NEED OF AID, HEAD ACROSS THE INTERSTATE TOWARD THE TOWN OF JORDAN. THEY ARE SET UP TO RECEIVE AND CARE FOR REFUGEES! I REPEAT, THIS AREA IS RESTRICTED, AND OFF LIMITS TO CIVILIANS! PLEASE TURN AROUND NOW AND DEPART THE AREA!"

"We need help!" Zach heard someone shout. Hadn't Shane just told them that Jordan was set up to receive them?

"I REPEAT, THE NATIONAL GUARD IN JORDAN IS ALREADY SET UP TO CARE FOR ANY REFUGEES! PLEASE TURN AROUND AND HEAD EAST, CROSSING THE INTERSTATE AND CONTINUING ON THE ROAD UNTIL YOU ENTER THE TOWN OF JORDAN! THIS IS A RESTRICTED AREA! IF YOU ENTER THIS AREA WITHOUT AUTHORIZATION, YOU WILL BE FIRED ON!"

"You won't do it!" another voice yelled. "There are children in this group!"

"ASSISTANCE FOR BOTH ADULTS AND CHILDREN IS AVAILABLE IN JORDAN! PLEASE TURN AROUND AND HEAD EAST, ACROSS THE INTERSTATE! CONTINUE DOWN THE HIGHWAY UNTIL YOU ARRIVE AT THE TOWN OF JORDAN, WHERE THE NATIONAL GUARD IS DEPLOYED TO ASSIST YOU! SIR, IF YOU ATTEMPT TO CROSS THE ROADBLOCK, YOU WILL BE FIRED UPON. THIS IS YOUR FINAL WARNING!"

The last part of that comment had been directed at a man wearing a heavy long coat who was attempting to climb across the log trailer. Others were looking for a way around the trailer, even through the briars.

The man ignored Shane and climbed up onto the trailer.

"Zach, give them a warning shot," Shane's voice was grim.

Zach took his M4 from the rack insider the turret and fired a single shot which hit the trailer itself, making a ricochet sound that all could hear. He didn't want to shoot anyone either.

"That could have killed me!" the man screeched.

"YES SIR, IT COULD HAVE! YOU HAVE BEEN WARNED FOR THE LAST TIME. THIS IS A RESTRICTED AREA AND OFF LIMITS TO CIVILIANS. LEAVE NOW. THERE IS NOTHING HERE FOR YOU, BUT THERE IS ASSISTANCE FOR YOU IN JORDAN!"

The man continued crossing the trailer, heedless of the repeated warnings. Shane's voice was bitter as he called to Zach.

"Put him down, Zach," Shane ordered. "Use your M4 and try to make a single shot. I'd like to avoid hurting anyone we don't have to."

Zach propped his M4 on the turret and peered through his optical sight. He had hoped to avoid this. Sighting on the man who refused to listen, Zach slowly pulled the trigger. He didn't even blink when the rifle fired.

The man on the trailer fell back, hitting the pavement on the inside of the trailer. He didn't move after that.

"Damn you!" he heard from the crowd. "You killed my husband!"

"NO MA'AM, HE KILLED HIMSELF WHEN HE REFUSED TO HEED OUR ORDERS! PLEASE, ALL OF YOU, HEAD FOR THE AID MISSION IN JORDAN AND LEAVE THIS RESTRICTED AREA! PLEASE!"

Shane was practically pleading with them to leave.

Suddenly, three men in the crowd made a run for the trailer. Zach could not imagine what they were thinking but aimed his rifle at the one to the right of the group, waiting on Shane's orders. Shane waited until the three had moved past the body of the first man and were inside the cargo area of the trailer before giving that order.

"Zach, take them. All three." His voice sounded as sad as anything Zach had ever heard.

From his right to his left, Zach swept the three with his rifle, putting all three men down with a single round. As the last one dropped across the beam of the trailer, Zach could hear more screaming from the group. Likely from loved ones, he imagined.

Those in the back of the group had already started moving away and now began to move faster, not wanting to be caught in the gunfire. Zach watched as others dragged three women away from the bodies of the men he had just killed. They were finally successful, but at least two of the women hurled curses at them all in general, and him in particular, damning him for his actions. None of this meant anything to Zach, who replaced the magazine in his rifle and returned it to the rack inside the turret.

"Attention all units. Group is departing. Operations, this is Thug Life. We need a truck and some help with four bodies. Station is secure."

"*Roger, Thug Life. Operations copies all. We'll have someone moving that way ASAP.*"

"Thug Life clear."

-

Wearing MOPP specialty gear to protect themselves, Clay, Greg, Corey and Kurtis arrived to police the bodies. It had been decided early on that no bodies would be brought inside, the protocol being to drag the bodies clear of the roadblock and back toward the interstate. It was ghoulish work, but it was necessary in order to protect themselves. All four bodies were left in a neat line on the side of the road, near the interchange. The bodies we placed carefully straight, with their hands folded over their torso. If their next of kin wanted to come and claim them, they could.

The four returned to Building Two in the back of a truck driven by Tandi Maseo, who had not left the cab. Once there, they were decontaminated with steam laced with Lysol before removing the MOPP gear. Each immediately went and showered, their laundry being done immediately using the same decontamination practices they had used for the clothing pulled from empty houses.

Clay and Greg trooped to his office after making sure Corey and Kurtis were okay. Corey was sad but determined while Kurtis just shrugged and said, 'they made their choice'. Clay nodded in agreement and told the two to get some rest.

"I thought, for some reason, that it wouldn't start right away," Greg admitted. "That it would take a day or two, at least. Instead, first day out the gate and here we are."

"Here we are," Clay nodded. "I don't want you out on the line during all this," Clay told him.

"What? Why?" Greg was stunned.

"Because you're the Sheriff, now," Clay replied. "Last thing you need is to be accused of having been part of any 'massacre' or 'slaughter'. So, you'll stand a regular watch here, and not work the line."

"Clay, that ain't fair to everyone else," Greg pointed out.

"Nothing about any of this is fair," Clay snorted. "I'm asking teenagers to kill potentially unarmed people who try to access this place. Yes, I have a legitimate reason, and even orders to do so, but that doesn't make it better. We need you where you are, Greg. I know you don't like it, and I know this is just another reason for you to hate it, but this is how it is. We need you to be the Sheriff, and not just because you're the best man for the job. We're on the edge, here. Having the High Sheriff on our side will help. So, we need you clean and clear of any of this and in your position of Sheriff once this is over."

"I get it," Greg said slowly, then snorted with laughter. "Old Man would be cackling like a hen to hear you talk like that."

"Wouldn't he though?" Clay grinned sadly. "I admit I thought of him when I made the decision."

"You're moving toward replacing him, man," Greg told his friend.

"I've thought of that myself," Clay's grin fell at that.

"It ain't a bad thing, Clay," Greg told him. "Really it's not. Someone has to do it, and Leon wanted it to be you. Most of the rest of us want it that way as well."

"Most?" Clay raised an eyebrow.

"Well, I was against it, your lordship, but just on principal, you understand," Greg fought to keep a straight face. "My vote was for Leon the Lesser, but he already had a job-,"

"Get out," Clay ordered, pointing at the door.

Greg was still laughing as he walked away. Behind him, Clay waited until he was sure that Greg couldn't hear him before laughing himself. Imagining 'Leon the Lesser' running things just made him laugh harder.

-

Marcy George was sitting at one of the many rough outdoor tables that had been constructed since the Storm. Each table had from two up to six chairs, depending on how large it was. This one had two. She was staring out at the fields behind the Square.

"Hey, Marcy," Titus Terry said softly as he walked up behind her. He was geared up for his shift on the Line, a name that had stuck when Clay used it and was now considered a proper noun by most.

"Hey," she replied softly, reaching up to grasp his hand when he placed it on her shoulder.

"You okay?" he asked gently.

"That's a stupid question, Titus," she answered sadly.

"Well, you tell me how you want me to check on you, Miss Emancipated Teenager, and I'll use that next time," he shot back, squeezing her shoulder gently. "I care more about how okay you are than how smart I might sound."

She snorted a laugh at that and pulled his hand to her lips and kissed it softly before clutching it to her chest.

"I have no idea what I'd do without you," she told him, her voice so soft that he had to strain to hear her speak. "Without you, I'd be all alone."

"You're surrounded by people who care about you, Marcy," Titus scoffed at the idea. "Just cause none of them are as pretty as I am don't mean they don't care about you," he joked. She laughed outright this time, hugging his arm to her.

"You're a mess, boy," she shook her head. "And no, I'm not alright. I wish my brother and sister were here with me where I could keep them safe. My parents can fend for themselves, but with the state their mind was in when they left, I don't trust them to take good care of Malcom and Bernetta. But I can't do anything for them except pray right now."

"That ain't no small thing, girl," Titus turned serious for a minute.

"I know," she sighed, turning to look at him for the first time. "You're on your way out to the line?"

"Yeah," he nodded. "Got maybe ten minutes or so."

"Please be safe," she all but whispered. "Don't make me cry over you, too. Not again."

"I will do my dead level best," he promised seriously. "Promise."

She stood on her toes and kissed him quickly before fleeing to her house, afraid to watch him go. Titus waited for a minute before shouldering his rifle and heading for his post.

-

Heath Kelly had moved from the tower behind the Sanders' home to the rear cupola of Building Two. From there he could watch the back approaches to the ranch proper. The post was comfortable, and heated, with a telescope and a pair of night vision binoculars for use by the night shift. He had relieved Nate Caudell a few minutes before, and knew that Kurtis Montana was relieving Jody Thompson by now, if he hadn't already. The two of them would be on watch through the night.

Heath knew that Zach had shot and killed four men earlier in the day who wouldn't take no for an answer. Heath hoped he would not be put in that position but felt that to be a forlorn hope at best. No one had said it openly yet, but everyone knew that today was just the start. He checked his rifles before settling in behind the scope, using it until the light was gone for the day.

He had been there less than ten minutes when he heard someone on the steps beneath him and shook his head, smiling gently. He opened the trapdoor to reveal Leanne Tillman standing on the landing below, fist cocked back to knock on the door.

"How do you do that?" she demanded. "You always know when I'm around."

"I always will, too," he promised, standing aside to allow her entrance before closing the door again, this time throwing the bolt to secure it. "Not that I'm unhappy about it, but why are you up here?" he asked when he turned to look at her.

"Leon and I are splitting the duty in Operations," she told him. "I drew the night shift for the first week. Lucky me," she added sourly. "Anyway, Gwen and JJ have another hour to go before Janice and I relieve them. So, here I am," she smiled brightly.

"Here you am," Heath chuckled. "Have a seat," he told her, dimming the light in the cupola so he could see.

"Trying to get me in the dark, Mister Kelly?" Leanne teased as he began to slowly move the scope across his horizon.

"Always, Miss Tillman," he replied airily, knowing it had made her blush even though he couldn't see it. "Having you alone and in the dark is like a dream come true."

He smiled as he heard her behind him, spluttering and calling him stupid, her answer for anything he said that even came close to embarrassing her.

"Is it true about Za-," she began, but he cut her off gently.

"Yes, it's true," he told her. "Four of them, trying to force their way through the roadblock. Refused to stop even when faced with one man already down."

"I just don't understand," Leanne sighed. "No, that's not true. I do understand, at least in a way. But why throw your life away when there is actual help just a few miles in the other direction?"

"All I've got is a guess," Heath admitted. "They thought since this was a restricted area, that must mean there was something worth having down here somewhere. Technically, they're right of course. But in this case, this place has been sealed off until further notice, and that was done at Captain Adcock's command. It's not up to us anymore."

"I know," Leanne agreed. "It's really not even about just us, anymore. This place and a few others like it are all that remains in this area of the things we need to pick ourselves up and start over. We must preserve it. Protect the farm, the herd and everything else until we can start producing more food, more medicine and maybe rebuilding some technology."

"That is true," Heath nodded, sitting back from the scope for a minute. "You're really very smart for someone so vertically challenged," he teased, darting into her personal space to quickly kiss her lips before she could explode.

"I am smart regardless of my…my vertical challengedness," she stammered, her face blooming red after he had kissed her.

"That's true," he nodded. "You really are incredibly smart for someone so pretty," he winked at her, sending her into a further fit of blushing as she once more murmured 'you're so stupid' at him. It seemed to be her only defense.

Laughing very softly, Heath began to scan the horizon one more time with the scope as the light began to fade away completely.

-

"Think we'll get through the night without being challenged again?" Greg asked Jose Juarez. Jose was the night shift commander for now while Clay commanded during the day.

"I have no way to answer that," Jose admitted. "We don't have any eyes on the interstate directly, so we can't estimate how many are passing, or what shape they're in. Other than a few drone passes in the light, we're just sitting here, pretending to be a big old knot on a log."

"You know, one thing that's not helping is that there's no signage with that trailer we're using for a roadblock," Greg mused.

"What do you mean?" Jose frowned. "We need a big 'restricted area' sign or something?"

"No, I was thinking more of a 'bridge out, road closed,' sign, honestly," Greg shook his head. "Something like that. Tells them why the road is closed off. It might deter some of them from even heading down this way."

"You mean those who aren't discouraged by the four dead bodies at the interchange?" Jose asked dryly.

"I would estimate it as very likely that those bodies will be gone in the morning," Greg's tone darkened. "There are scavengers of all kinds roaming this area anymore."

"I hadn't considered that," Jose grunted. "Some of that bunch on the interstate just might see that as a free lunch, disgusting as that may be."

"It may be all they've had for a while," Greg shrugged. "I…I can't bring myself to judge too harshly until I know the circumstances. It's easy for me to say I won't do something. I have no wife, no children, no aging parents. Nothing to worry about but myself. And I'm completely capable of living off the land, even in winter. I have a feeling that most of the people we're seeing right now are not so capable."

"I would not disagree," Jose nodded slowly. "Those four today were very well dressed for refugees from what I've heard. Their clothing was dirty, and damaged, but was obviously high quality. That speaks to me of someone living the city life and being used to getting whatever he or she needed or wanted on the way home with just a swipe of a debit card. Clearly that isn't working anymore."

“Clearly,” Greg nodded. “I can under-,” He stopped suddenly as gunfire shattered the quiet for a second time that day.

CHAPTER EIGHTEEN

Gordy Sanders had relieved Zach in the turret of the small Cougar blocking the road into the farm. He knew that other vehicles were arrayed to his right and left, but his responsibility was here. He was currently huddled up against the cold, the hood of his jacket pulled up to keep the snow off him. While not falling as hard or as fast as it had been that morning, the snow was still going, and it was a cold and wet snow. That, plus a slight but steady wind that had come up near dark combined with cold temperatures and taunt nerves to create a miserable atmosphere to be stuck in.

Stacey Pryor was commanding the vehicle now, having relieved Shane Golden when Gordy had relieved Zach. Jenna Waller was in the passenger compartment monitoring their flanks while Janessa Haynes sat behind the wheel.

Gordy had almost committed the cardinal sin of drifting off to sleep when he noticed a slight motion through his goggles.

"Arrow," he whispered into his throat mike, trying to limit his movement.

"I see it," Stacey replied at once. "Good eye, kid." Seconds later Gordy heard Stacey calling the others spread across the defensive line.

"*All units be on your guard. Thug Life has movement front. Movement has not resolved itself sufficiently for identification. Stand by for updates*."

"What can you make out, Chip?" Stacey asked softly, back on the vehicle communications. Gordy studied the movement carefully before answering.

"I can make out at least five individuals, even from here," Gordy informed him. "They know they aren't supposed to be here, judging from their movement. They're trying to be stealthy, but in the dark, and with the snow, it's difficult for them to move quietly."

"Right. Stand by, then. I'm going to challenge them," Stacey told him. "I'm not going to use the light just yet, but if I do, I'll call 'lights, lights, lights', just like that, before I hit them, to give you enough warning to slip your gear to standby. Copy?"

"Got it," Gordy assured him. "Standing by."

"ATTENTION! SNEAKY PETES TRYING TO GET THROUGH THE ROADBLOCK! WE CAN SEE YOU CLEARLY AND KNOW YOU'RE THERE! THIS IS A RESTRICTED AREA AND OFF LIMITS TO ANY TRAFFIC FOR ANY REASON. REPEAT, THIS AREA IS QUARATINED FOR THE TIME BEING AND IS OFF LIMITS! NO TRAFFIC IS ALLOWED IN OR OUT! IF YOU REQUIRE ASSISTANCE, PLEASE MOVE EAST DOWN THIS ROAD TO THE TOWN OF JORDAN! THE NATIONAL GUARD HAS PEOPLE IN JORDAN WHO ARE SET UP TO RENDER AID!"

There was no response, but Gordy caught the sudden movement he had missed before.

"Arrow, be advised there are at least five more zombies on the south side of the road!" Gordy hissed urgently. "They started to move in the open after your warning. They weren't visible until then."

"Roger that. Try to keep track of them," Stacey warned. "We'll try to help from here." Seconds later he was on the radio again.

"All units, all units, this is Thug Life. Be aware that we now have a minimum of ten, repeat ten tangoes moving on our front, refusing to heed warnings. They were using the dark to hide their movements until we broadcast our warning. You may well see individuals moving on your front, so take care!"

As soon as he finished that radio call, Stacey was back on the P.A.

"ATTENTION! ATTENTION! WE CAN SEE YOU CLEARLY ATTEMPTING TO ACCESS THE ROADBLOCK. PLEASE CEASE YOUR ACTIVITY AND LEAVE THIS AREA! THIS ENTIRE AREA IS OFF LIMITS TO ALL TRAFFIC UNTIL FUTHER NOTICE! REPEAT, THIS AREA IS BEING HELD IN ISOLATION UNDER THE AUTHORITY OF THE MARTIAL LAW DECLARATION AND IS CLOSED TO ANY TRAFFIC, IN OR OUT! IF YOU CONTINUE TO MOVE THIS WAY, YOU CAN AND MAY BE FIRED UPON WITHOUT FURTHER WARNING! REPEAT, WE WILL OPEN FIRE IF YOU CONTINUE TO TRY AND ACCESS THIS AREA!"

"Rush 'em fellas!" a voice called from the dark. "They can't see us all! Once we're inside, we're golden! He already said no one in or out!"

"Gordy, you're cleared to fire as soon as they hit the roadblock," Stacey said at once, having heard the intruder's call to his compatriots.

"Copy that," Gordy's voice was flat. Dull. He had hoped not to have to do this. With so many targets moving toward him, he opted for the machine gun mounted on the turret rather than his rifle. He watched the trailer in front of him without blinking, counting each man who began to try to scramble over it in the dark. When the number hit five, Gordy took a deep breath and slowly squeezed the trigger.

The M240 was loaded with a tracer for every fifth round. The glowing points of light formed a chain across the distance between him and the roadblock, showing the rounds from the machine gun tearing into the trailer and the men trying to cross it. He couldn't hear the men crying out in alarm at the machine gun firing. They had been so sure that the guards would not fire on them that they had apparently decided it was a fact rather than a guess.

Gordy reminded them it was more than just a possibility.

The view from his goggles showed four men down from his first round of fire. He waited for a slow count of three before turning the gun on the remainder when they didn't flee. Two more down, then three, then four. He stopped again, waiting. Eight of at least ten were now down hard, not moving. Surely that was enough.

'Damn you!" a voice full on anguish yelled from the dark, though thanks to his goggles Gordy could see the figure shaking a fist at the vehicle. "Damn you for this! We were just looking for help! You just murdered *innocent men*!" The speaker had to stop then as he descended into fit of coughing, a sound that made Gordy's skin crawl and sent a shiver down his spine that had nothing to do with the cold.

"YOU WERE WARNED NOT TO CONTINUE TO ADVANCE! THIS REMAINS A RESTRICTED AREA, CLOSED TO ALL TRAFFIC IN OR OUT! YOU FORCED THIS ON US, NOT THE OTHER WAY AROUND! PLEASE, MOVE BACK AND TURN BACK TOWARD THE EAST AND THE TOWN OF JORDAN! THERE IS NO HELP AVAILABLE FOR YOU HERE AT PRESENT!"

"That's a damn lie!" the same man coughed his way through the accusation. "We know damn well there's food down there, and a doctor! We need both!"

"I REPEAT, THERE IS NO ASSISTANCE AVAILABLE FOR YOU HERE! PLEASE MOVE EAST, DOWN THE ROAD BEHIND YOU, TO THE TOWN OF JORDAN! THEY ARE ALREADY SET UP TO RENDER ASSISTANCE TO ALL REFUGEES THAT STOP HERE! WE LACK THE RESOURCES OR MANPOWER TO ASSIST YOU AT THIS TIME! PLEASE, I AM BEGGING YOU, DON'T MAKE US FIRE ON YOU AGAIN!"

"You might as well!" came another cough laced reply. "You've killed all but two of us, and we're dying without help you won't give us! You mangy bastards! I hope you burn in hell!"

Gordy noted that the sole remaining figure was checking those on the ground to see if they still lived. Apparently, they didn't, as he moved back to the speaker after checking the last one. Still screaming threats and curses, the two began moving toward Jordan, leaving their dead friends where they had fallen.

"Moving away," Gordy whispered, his voice steady despite the rumbling in his stomach. "I see no other intruders nearby."

"Nor do I," Stacey affirmed. He notified the rest of their situation, allowing the other vehicles to know that they were, for the moment, clear. Next, he contacted Operations to inform them that they eight bodies that would need to be moved once it was light, getting an affirmative response. Releasing the microphone, Stacey sat back, exhaling an explosive breath as he considered what had just occurred, and wondering what he could have done differently.

But he already knew the answer to that question; nothing. There were no other options available to them. No matter how dirty it made him feel.

-

"Where is Clayton?"

Startled, Jose looked up to see Jaylyn Thatcher standing over him, her face pensive and drawn. Her eyes showed real fear, something he'd not experienced from the good Doctor before.

"He's at home resting, ma'am," Jose replied, falling back on years of military courtesy to avoid sounding worried.

"Wake him," Jaylyn ordered tersely. "I need him down here as soon as he can make it. And call the people on the line. Tell them they are under no circumstances to make any physical contact whatsoever with any refugee. None. To consider that a standing order until further notice. They are to take every possible precaution and use any means necessary to prevent anyone, regardless of who it is, from crossing that line. Don't touch the bodies, either." Without waiting for an acknowledgement, she turned on her heels and returned to the clinic.

"Uh, did you guys get all that?" Jose asked Leanne Tillman and Janice Hardy, sitting in Operations and watching in stunned silence.

"Yes," both nodded slowly.

"One of you call Clay, apologize for waking him, and tell him Thatcher needs him in the clinic right away. Can you remember her orders for the others?"

"I can," Janice nodded again, her face still showing her stunned surprise.

"Then go ahead and send that message out to them," Jose told her. "Maybe we'll know soon what this is all about."

"Yes, sir."

-

By the time Clay got to the clinic, he was grumpy and very unhappy. He had gotten no more than two hours of sleep at a time for the last several days and it showed. He had been asleep for less than three hours when his phone rang, his niece telling him about Doctor Thatcher's 'orders'. He had gotten dressed and almost stomped to the hospital, intent on giving Thatcher a piece of his mind.

That feeling didn't survive a full three seconds once he got a look at her face.

"What's wrong?" he asked, tempering his anger.

"Gleason brought me three blood samples," she said without preamble.

"Yeah." Clay knew that.

"Two were from people who were clearly sick, with a list of every symptom they could recognize and as much medical history as they could retrieve from them. The third was from a blind draw, with no information whatsoever provided."

"You need that information?" Clay asked. "Is that it? We can call-,"

"No, I don't need it," she cut him off gently, her voice very subdued. "I don't have the equipment I need to do an exact breakdown of the blood I was sent, but I do have a microscope. I've been working all this time trying to identify what the infection is, hoping we could find an old treatment that would help at least some of the sick, and maybe protect us as well."

"No luck?" Clay asked, starting to wonder why she had called him down here. Almost nothing she had said so far made any sense to him.

"Wrong kind of luck," she replied bitterly. "I identified it, alright. I examined all three samples. All of them contain the *Yersinia pestis* bacterium. They're all-,"

"Wait," Clay held up a hand, to stop her. He felt a headache forming. "Pestis. I've heard that word before. When I was deployed." He wracked his memory, fishing for the definition of the phrase.

"Plague," Jaylyn helped him out. "They all three have plague. In this case, pneumonic plague."

"Plague?" Clay was stunned. "Like, black death, plague? *That* plague?"

"That plague," Jaylyn nodded. "One of three strains, and the only one that is spread through the air, and from person-to-person. Of course," her voice was bitter.

"Pneumonic," Clay repeated. "So…it's pulmonary."

"Exactly," Jaylyn confirmed. "Which is how it has spread so fast. Pneumonic plague infects the lungs, settles in them, and then with every cough, sneeze or drop of blood, spreads it like, well, the plague," she shrugged helplessly.

"I don't get it," Clay was still confused. "How do we end up with plague here of all places?"

"A year of shitty hygiene, for starters," Jaylyn told him. "A year of bad hygiene and lack of pest control. Plague can be contracted from fleas found on rats, squirrels, chipmunks, bats and other animals in those genus groups. And guess what hungry people eat when they don't have anything else?"

"All of the above," Clay groaned, leaning against the bench he was standing beside. "You're sure, I guess," he stated rather than asked.

"I discovered this several hours ago," she nodded. "I've spent every minute since then trying to disprove it. Didn't work. There is no question that it's plague. Bubonic plague is bad enough, but it at least isn't transmitted through aerosol. Pneumatic plague most definitely is. As for how? Here, I mean? No idea. It shouldn't be possible, especially with pneumatic plague, which is ridiculously rare."

"How rare?" Clay asked, more to give him time to process than anything else.

"Maybe three known cases in the United States in the last hundred years," Jaylyn declared flatly. "One in the last fifty years or so if I recall right. All I can figure is that somewhere, probably in Nashville, there was an outbreak of bubonic plague. At some point, it had to settle somewhere, in someone I mean, in their pulmonary tract and then into the lungs, where it transmuted into the pneumatic variant. Once that happened, it became highly infectious from person-to-person contact and began to spread. I would suspect that it spread rapidly. Onset from exposure can be anywhere from a few hours upwards to a week. How many days walk is it from Nashville to get here?"

"I…I don't actually know," he admitted. "A week? Ten days? But that assumes decent weather and reasonably good health.

"None of which we've had," she was nodding before he finished. "By now it's so contagious that there's almost no way to avoid it if we're exposed. Thank God you used MOPP gear to move those bodies earlier."

"I…it was just instinct," he admitted. "Something we've done before."

"Well, your instincts served you well in that case," she promised. "Probably saved your lives. You'll have to keep using them, too. And no more leaving the bodies to lay on the road, either. Burn them. Soak them in oil, moonshine, anything that will burn them completely up. And never, *ever*, be around the bodies without protection. Be sure to always go through decontamination when you return."

"I thought plague was a spring and summer thing," Clay almost sounding as if he were lodging a protest. "How is it here, now?"

"It's not just now," she told him. "I would imagine it started some time ago and has only just now reached what we'd call epidemic levels. But it will get worse. Remember that a lot of the refugees have moved on further south from here, if they bothered stopping at all. While many of them will be infected and die on the trip south, there will be others who are asymptomatic carriers and will be spreading it everywhere they go."

"Sweet Mother…I have to call Adcock," Clay declared at once. "He's got to know this right away."

"I agree, though there is exactly nothing he can do about it at this point," Jaylyn told him. "It's already taken hold and is moving with the Exodus. They're carrying it everywhere, Clay, and there isn't a damn thing we can do about it, now."

"God help us," Clay was still reeling.

"That's what it will take, I'm afraid," she nodded. "I'll go with you to call Adcock. You're right, he needs to know. It's possible that the cold will help protect him and the others so long as they limit direct contact with the sick."

"What about caring for the sick?" Clay asked as they moved toward the door.

"Most of them are already dead without proper treatment," she said mournfully. "Treatment we don't possess that we can give to them. When I said there wasn't anything we could do, I meant nothing at all. Some will likely recover, though they will probably be weakened to the point that something else might kill them, but...you can expect anywhere from fifty-to-sixty percent of the people moving south to...to die," she sighed. There was no way to soften the impact of her words. "That same percentage can probably be applied to anyone they come into contact with, as well."

"My God," Clay whispered. "There'll be bodies everywhere."

"And everyone who touches one without protection will be at risk of contracting the disease," she confirmed as they neared Operations. "This makes it more important than ever that we keep others out of here," she told him unnecessarily.

"By any means necessary," he whispered.

-

"*Home Plate, are you certain, repeat certain, of your diagnosis*?" Adcock's voice sounded even more tense after hearing Doctor Thatcher's explanation.

"Affirmative, Captain," Clay replied after seeing Jaylyn's nod. "There is no question. The virus is present in all three blood samples you provided us."

"*What do we do*?" Adcock asked. "*What* can *we do*?" he amended, almost resigned. Clay handed the microphone to Jaylyn.

"Captain, this is Thatcher," she said crisply, using what Clay imagined she called her 'Doctor Voice'. "There is no possibility of any kind of treatment at this point, at least not with anything we have available. The drugs we need aren't available anymore. As for those of you who are not yet sick, your only hope of protection is to limit your exposure to those who are infected. Avoid any bodily fluids of any kind, including spray from coughing or sneezing. Avoid touching exposed skin or any open wounds for any reason, including treatment. Keep all known infected isolated from others, and in an area that can be easily decontaminated or else destroyed entirely once there is no further need of it as a ward."

"*Doctor, that sounds as if you're saying to abandon the sick*," Adcock's voice revealed what he thought of that idea.

"That's exactly what I'm telling you, Captain," she surprised everyone who heard her sharp retort. "Understand me well, Captain. You have no personal protective equipment available to prevent your own infection. You have access to no drugs that will combat the disease or protect you from it. You have no vaccine that will prevent you from contracting the virus. Your people lack the necessary training for dealing with the infected safely. In short, your situation is completely untenable. You have no defense and no way to fight back. All you can do is withdraw and wait it out. Do you understand?"

"*Doctor...surely there is something*." He sounded almost desperate.

"I'm sorry, Captain," her voice softened slightly. "Sorry beyond words. But no, there's nothing you can do at this point. Spread your people out, so that if someone is infected it won't spread to everyone. Stay isolated for seven-to-ten days to look for symptoms. Do not assume that being asymptomatic means you aren't infected. It is a good sign, usually, however."

"*For how long*?" Adcock asked.

"Until further notice, Captain," Jaylyn told him flatly. "And if you have a way to contact those south of here, I suggest you do so now, and give them this information. They have a walking, talking, weapon of mass destruction entering their areas, right now. One they also will not likely have any defense against."

"As for you and your command, and the people in Jordan, begin now exercising every possible precaution. If you can find a still, use the alcohol as a disinfectant for hands, eating utensils and so forth. It may help, at least a little, in the long run. Other than that, fire will kill anything, including germs left behind by dying infected. Use it. But be extremely careful of coming in contact with bedding or any other cloth that might have bodily fluids absorbed into them. The disease will spread from there. And kill any fleas you see. Take as much care as possible to ensure that you don't have any of them on you. Use MOPP gear wherever possible to clear and clean areas that have been used to house infected. It will all but certainly protect you from infection but remember to decontaminate the gear after each use. As a last resort, boiling water to create steam will help in that regard, but again, the homemade alcohol is a better option simply by virtue of being able to kill almost anything."

"*Understood*," Adcock sounded weary. "*How long does this usually take to run its course*?"

"Captain, this isn't the flu, or a stomach virus. It doesn't run its course, not in the sense you mean. It will continue to spread even from dead bodies. So long as the bacterium can find a suitable host, it will continue to live, spreading through the simplest of contacts. Without access to modern drugs, all we can do is separate ourselves and wait. The 'course' will end when all the sick have recovered, or else expired and their remains destroyed completely, along with anything that might contain even a trace of the bacterium. And those who recover without drugs may still be able to infect others, so they will need to remain in isolation and be observed for any kind of symptomatic activity."

There was no reply from Adcock for well over a minute. Jaylyn looked at Clay in puzzlement, but Clay merely shrugged, shaking his head. All he could figure was that Adcock was digesting this onslaught of bad news and where it left him.

"*Understood, Doctor,*" Adcock finally replied. "*Be advised, other commands may try to contact you concerning your diagnosis and plan of action. We will implement your suggestions immediately. With this information, I am hesitant for you to continue sending people this way, but also hesitate to send them further south. At this point, I don't know what to do with them.*"

Clay reached over and took the microphone.

"Captain, remember that the schools in Peabody are still standing," he suggested. "Rather than letting people get this far, you can always send someone to the northern exits and direct them into Peabody, to the high school and elementary schools. I have no ideas what to do as far as caring for them, but both schools are listed as disaster shelters, so there may be blankets and other needs still in storage there, and might even be some foodstuffs there as well. It's not perfect, but it's better than what you have now."

Again, there was a long silence, presumably during which Adcock was contemplating this.

"*Roger that, Bossman,*" Adcock finally replied. "*That may be a workable solution, especially from the isolation aspect. If we do that, however, I'm going to need some assistance.*" He stopped short of asking.

Clay exhaled sharply as he closed his eyes. He knew what Adcock wanted, and was willing to help. But how to get that help to him without endangering his people any more than they had already been threatened?

"Understand your need, Captain, and we're willing to help with that," he said finally. "Suggest you send transport and manpower to the interchange. Give us twelve hours and then send two trucks and the manpower to our end of the interchange. Be prepared to have to clear the area of refugees as we've had several people leave the interstate at that exit. We will have what you need there, ready for pick-up, in twelve hours, Lord willing and assuming nothing goes wrong. Is there anything you need other than food?"

"*Negative, Bossman,*" Adcock's voice held true relief. "*Is the Doctor still there*?"

"Affirmative."

"*Will items sealed in containers be safe to use, Doctor*?" Adcock asked. "*Assuming the containers are cleaned before opening, would it be safe for the uninfected to open the crates and use the contents*?"

"So long as they've been sealed since before this started, then yes, Captain," Jaylyn replied after a minute of quick deliberation. "There should be no problem."

"*Will your opinion change if those containers are brought to the farm*?" Adcock surprised her.

"Negative, Captain," she replied evenly. "Assuming you are talking about containers that are meant to be weatherproof, then there would be no risk to whoever used the contents once the container is cleaned."

"*Roger that*," Adcock responded. "*Bossman, suggest you have two trucks of your own at the interchange, waiting for us to leave. I have a farewell gift for you. We'll see you in twelve. Adcock clear*."

"Home Plate, standing by." Clay returned the microphone to Leanne, who still looked stunned.

"I want everyone not on the line to be here at eight o'clock for another emergency meeting," Clay told Leanne and Janice. "No exceptions. You two take care of that. I have a lot to get moving on and not much time to do it. Leanne, before you get started, ring Kandi and tell her we need her down here ASAP."

"Got it," Leanne replied crisply.

"What do you suppose this farewell gift is?" Jaylyn asked as the two of them left Operations.

"I'm going to assume he has a load, or even two truckloads of gear and supplies that he hasn't opened yet and doesn't want to go to waste," Clay replied. He paused a minute, his face grim.

"He's preparing himself and his command for the eventuality of their not surviving," he said finally. "He's securing as much of his gear as he can in preparation for that."

"I suspected as much," she nodded. "I am so sorry that I can't do anything to help fight this." Her face betrayed how hard this had hit her. As a doctor, she was meant to stop things like this.

"This is in no way your fault, Doctor Thatcher," Clay said formally. "More than that, without your hard work over the last forty-eight hours we would have no idea what we're facing. A moment of weakness on our part could have doomed us all. Thanks to you, we at least know what we're facing. Personally, I'm grateful for that, and glad you're here. I'm also grateful for the many times since you've gotten here that you've patched up my men and women. We all are."

"Thank you, Clayton," she smiled softly. "That means a great deal, you know."

"You're very welcome, Doctor," Clay returned her smile. "If you'll excuse me, I really do have to get started on this."

"Of course. I need to get back to the clinic, anyway," she nodded tiredly.

"No, you need to rest is what you need to do," Clay was already moving to the door. "Get some rest, Jaylyn. This mess will still be here when you wake up." With that he was out the door and gone.

CHAPTER NINETEEN

"Plague?" The one-word question came from more than one place.

"Yes," Clay confirmed. "All three blood samples brought to Doctor Thatcher were from people infected with one of three strains of plague. That's the sickness that has driven people out of the areas to our north and sent them streaming in all directions even in this harsh weather. Our direction being one of them."

"There's no protection from that stuff, either. Is there?" Mitchell Nolan asked, face devoid of emotion.

"No," Clay admitted. "There are treatments for the sick that can help with recovery, but we don't have them and can't get them. All we can do is wait it out. In isolation," he added pointedly.

"So, we can't allow anyone access to the farm," Gordy said flatly. "For any reason."

"That's the verdict," Clay nodded. "Our only hope of survival is to keep ourselves isolated from the infected, or anyone who might be carrying the disease. There will be asymptomatic carriers in the Exodus who don't get sick but will be spreading the disease with every step."

"God help us," Gordon said softly. Prayerfully. "What will you do?" he asked his son.

"Whatever we have to," Clay shrugged. "We can't allow anyone onto the farm. We'll issue warnings and hope they're heeded. If they aren't, then we'll take whatever steps we have to in order to secure this place for our families and our children."

"There will be children in those crowds," Gordon noted, though not as a challenge.

"I'm far too aware of that," Clay managed to keep the bitterness from his voice. "It doesn't change anything. If we want to keep our own children safe, this is how we do it. Period." He turned his attention to the rest of the crowd.

"For those of you thinking you can't be a part of this, remember that all it takes is one person, be it man, woman or child, to spread this disease through the entire group. Just one. So, before you decide to render assistance on your own, remember that once you've come into contact with anyone outside our community, you become someone we have to be isolated from. There will be no exceptions made for that, either."

"As far as allowing someone through the line," Clay's voice turned darker, "anyone who does that will be shot. Considering the death waiting for the rest of us once we're infected, it will be more like mercy, but there it is."

"I don't like this any more than the rest of you," he continued. "Fact is, I hate it. But I can't change it. None of us can. So, when you think you can't pull the trigger, remember the children sitting behind you, counting on you to keep them safe. Their future is firmly in your hands, now more than ever."

"We'll be making a run to the interchange in a few hours to deliver some food supplies to Adcock and pick up some gear and supplies he's leaving for us. The few who go will be wearing MOPP gear which provides level four protection against infections, among other things. Once we return, the gear will need to be cleaned, as will the crates we're coming back with."

"We'll be taking two trucks, protected by the Guardian MRAPs. They can be made secure against something like this and will stay buttoned up for the duration. Those of us helping to unload our trucks, and then reload them, will ride in the trucks on the way back, decontaminate the suits and the crates when we return, as well as the trucks we carry the gear in. We have the chemicals needed for that to be carried out safely, so no one needs to worry about that."

"What are they sending?" Mitchell asked, leaning forward.

"No idea," Clay admitted. "Adcock just called it a farewell gift. I'm assuming it's gear that he had available and won't likely be called upon to use under the present circumstances." He looked over the crowd.

"Everyone, and I mean everyone is armed from this point forward. We've been allowing people to slide on that, but no more. If you see someone sneaking onto the farm, you will fire first and ask no questions. You will not approach the body under any circumstances. We will use the MOPP gear to move the bodies to a safe distance and burn them. It's the only sure way to kill the virus. If you think you can't do it, remember that if you let someone infected onto the farm, then every person who dies as a result is on your head. Harsh, but true." He paused for effect, looking over the crowd once more.

"Are there any questions?"

There were plenty of questions, but everyone recognized that Clay could not possibly answer them.

-

There was no contact between the two groups. The Guardsmen quickly offloaded the crates in their trucks before loading the meat and other supplies that Clay had spared for the refugees. He had gone over everything carefully with Kandi Ledford, supplying what they thought they could spare from their dwindling emergency stocks. Clay had steadfastly refused to part with any of their freeze-dried foods, as he had from the start. They were the groups only safety net.

As soon as Adcock's men were finished, they departed, leaving the men from the farm to load the crates, some of which were suspiciously heavy. It took some time to get it done, but by either good fortune or else Adcock's foresight, there was no one along the interstate at that moment to see them.

Finally finished, the six of them jumped into the back of the trucks, slapping the side to indicate to the driver that they could move. The drivers had stayed inside the trucks the entire time to avoid any possible exposure.

Once back to the farms, the gear was off loaded by the same people, still in MOPP suits, after which both they and the crates went through 'decon', which meant having the crates sprayed and scrubbed with bleach and disinfectant, then the scrubbers themselves finally being cleansed. Even watching the proceedings from afar made the skin crawl.

Finally, it was deemed safe to see what Adcock had left with them.

-

"Ammunition, web gear, magazines, spare parts, boots, looks like two dozen helmets," Jose was murmuring to himself as he picked over what had been left for them.

"There are twelve current generation night vision devices, and a surplus of batteries for them," Jody Thompson mentioned. "Also, three rifle scopes, nine lasers and fourteen holographic sights."

"Couple dozen standard issue combat knives," Mitchell Nolan added. "Holy shit!" he exclaimed suddenly, lifting one container lid much higher.

"What?" Clay asked, moving his way.

"There are four, no five, five crates of M18s in here," Mitchell almost whispered. "Thirty brand new Claymore mines!"

"Wonder why they had those?" Clay asked out loud, not really expecting an answer so much as just literally wondering.

"Sometimes for the mech infantry guys," Vicki Tully informed him. "But also, a lot of vehicle commanders will string M18s along their hulls to detonate from inside. They're useful for clearing out crunchies who get in too close, and for blasting IEDs that you can't disarm. It's frowned upon, but no one has ever tried to stop it from happening." The term 'crunchies' showed her armored roots, a less than caring name given to infantrymen by those in armor, especially tanks.

"Well, it seems that Adcock has repaid us plenty for the food we've sent them," Clay decided to cut the discussion short. "Get Kandi over here, Jose, along with one of the twins. Please help them get this stuff sorted and inventoried, and then get a crew from the civies to get it put away. The rest of you, try and get some rest. Most of you will be on the line later tonight."

-

"Nice of Adcock to send us some firepower," Mitchell noted as he walked next Clay, headed for the Troy farmhouse.

"It was," Clay agreed. "But the web gear, vests and NVD gear, in fact all the odd and end stuff he sent, is in some ways even better. We are sorely lacking there with the influx of new troops. This will help a lot."

"Sure will," Mitchell agreed. "This is a bad business, man," he added after a few moments of silence. "I never imagined-." A single gunshot cut him off, and he sighed.

"Neither did I," Clay agreed. "But we literally have no choice, Mitch. If we let an infected person on to this farm, it could wipe us out."

"Yeah, and plus you could get court martialed!" Mitchell jeered, trying to lighten the mood. "Lieutenant," he added with a slight punch to Clay's shoulder.

"That was kind of a low blow for him to do that," Clay shook his head. "Still, I don't blame a drowning man for grasping at any lifeline he can get. And he knew giving me those orders, in writing, would keep me out of trouble. Keep all of us out of trouble in fact, assuming there was anyone to be in trouble with after all this."

"Yeah, that took balls, man," Mitchell nodded his agreement. "Big time."

"Big time."

-

"*Bossman, Operations*," Leon's tone was clipped. He was starting to trim his messages down to something like what a police dispatcher might use.

"Go for Bossman," Clay replied tiredly.

"*Please come to Operations*," Leon requested. "*Traffic from AC*."

"Roger that. On my way." Clay started moving quickly toward Building Two. He hadn't expected to hear from Adcock again for a while. Now that he was, he feared it would be something bad.

Two minutes later he was in the radio room, accepting a microphone from Millie Long.

"Go for Bossman," Clay said simply.

"*Roger Bossman*," Adcock's voice came through strong. "*I'm in need of another favor, Lieutenant. My second in Lewiston, Lieutenant Gillis, was on patrol when all this started. He and his men have had no contact with the infected, in fact have had no contact with anyone in at least four days. I need a place for them to roost, so to speak. He has a patrol of eleven, including himself, with two Hummers and a small MRAP. I know it's a great deal to ask, but I have nowhere for them to go. Can you take them?*"

"You're sure, repeat sure they've had no contact with the infected?" Clay asked, stalling for time to think the request over.

"*Affirmative*," Adcock's voice rang with certainty. "*They have been on an extended patrol through backroads, searching for bandit activity. They have been out of the area for four days. Actually, today makes five days. They are tired and hungry and low on fuel. Outside Gleason's men, they may be the only troops I have left who haven't been exposed*."

"Roger that, AC. Send them our way. We'll take care of them."

"*Thank you, Bossman,*" the relief in Adcock's voice was apparent even over the radio. "*He's a good kid and has a solid NCO with him. He knows that he will be under your command until I recall him. By which I mean myself or Honcho personally. I really appreciate this.*"

"I'm glad to do it," Clay lied. "Anything else? How are you guys making it?"

"*We're getting refugees off the interstate and settled into the high school right now,*" Adcock replied. "*That was a good idea. Quite a few want to continue south, and I don't actually have a reason to stop them that won't end up with us in shooting engagement with civilians. We warn them not to attempt to leave the interstate at your exit or for Lewiston, but I'm sure some will try anyway. Anyone obviously infected or in the company of someone obviously infected we're stopping here, regardless. We've had to shoot more than a few to stop them moving on and carrying the disease with them.*" His voice sounded both strained and sad. No one in his position wanted to ever draw down on his own people, let alone actually shoot them down.

"I understand completely," Clay assured him. "We are maintaining our isolation here any way we can. Advise your field commander to use an alternate route, as we have blocked the road coming off the interstate. He should have no trouble understanding if he has a map."

"*Roger that. Will do,*" Adcock promised. "*I have seven troopers who are sick,*" he continued a second later. "*We were all exposed before we knew what was happening. There's nothing we can do for them. Let the Doc know we followed her instructions and passed the word south of the problem. Some of them are already calling it the Nashville Flu, even after I assured them it's not the flu. I don't think they want to believe it.*"

"I don't want to believe it either," Clay replied. "There's no explanation for it and no reason for it to be here. None. Yet here we are. The Doc is working the problem, but there is literally nothing we can do, even for ourselves. We don't have the means."

"*I know,*" Adcock sounded resigned. "*No one does that I'm aware of. It is what it is. We'll make it, or we won't. Thanks for taking in my wayward chicks, Bossman.*"

"Glad to do it," Clay said again, not lying quite as big, this time. "Take care, AC."

"*It may be too late for that, Bossman,*" Adcock tried to laugh, but it sounded closer to a cough. "*Very well. Area Commander clear.*"

"Home Plate standing by," Clay finished and handed the microphone back to Leon.

"Where are we going to put them?" Leon asked, returning the mike to the normal resting place.

"I don't know," Clay admitted. "Got a suggestion?" he asked the two. Both were silent for nearly a minute before Leon looked up.

"Is the Plum house empty?"

-

"As far as I know, Will and his wife were out of town," Gordon said when questioned about his old friend. "I've been by up there three times, and I'd like to think if Will was there, he'd have answered me. Nothing was moved and there was no sign of anyone being there or working to keep the place up. It's entirely likely that it's empty."

"Roomy enough for eleven people to isolate in for a week or so?" Clay asked, trying to remember what he could about the Plum farm.

"Well, yes," Gordon nodded after a moment. "Three bedrooms, two baths, a large den downstairs as well as a separate dining room. It will be cozy, but it will work."

"Wood heat?" Clay asked.

"He does have a fireplace, but he also had an infrared heater that used propane," Gordon said after another moment of thought. "If he had gas, and the tank has held on, then it's probably working. If the pilot was lit, then it may be out."

"Okay," Clay nodded, thinking quickly. "I need to get a rig up the road to stop them as they approach the house. We need to gather some provisions and firewood and get that moved up there as well. Thanks, Dad," he waved as he left the house in a whirlwind.

"You're welcome," he told his son's departing back. Closing his eyes, he leaned back in his chair and began praying once more. He'd done a great deal of that in the last few days.

-

"We are killing our food plan," Kandi noted as she helped load a truck with supplies for Gillis and his squad.

"Don't I know it," Clay nodded. "At this rate we'll be lucky not to have to break into the freeze-dried stuff."

"We'll do that carefully, if at all," Kandi told him. "Let me worry about that. Well, me and a few others who are trying to keep a healthy table set for everyone. Meanwhile, this will help them, and their presence will help us, will it not?"

"Yes, it will," Clay nodded, reminded once again that underestimating Kandi Ledford because of blonde hair and curves was a mistake. She was borderline brilliant at the least.

"I think that does it," Kandi interrupted his train of thought, stopping to stretch her back and then check her clipboard. "This should get them through their quarantine so long as they're careful. There are three dozen homemade brownies in a box, sitting in the cab. Might help pick them up a bit," she smiled.

"Might at that," Clay agreed with a much dimmer smile, but a smile, nevertheless.

-

Since he wasn't allowed on the defensive line holding people off the farm, Greg drew the duty of supervising the trip to check on and stock the Plum house. Jose Juarez and Mitchell Nolan had been dispatched ahead to meet the small incoming convoy and hold it up until preparations were complete.

Petra Shannon, Samantha Walters, Abby Sanders and Kurtis Montana joined the Sheriff on this small jaunt. The Plum farm was a 'mere' three hundred acres, a proverbial drop in the ocean compared to the Sanders' current holdings, but it was a lovely piece of ground, suitable for either the plow or for pasture. The home, having set empty for a year, needed dusting, and Abby applied a treatment of the Sanders' special remedy for insects, arachnids and other creepy crawlies as the others began cleaning.

Meanwhile, outside, Greg and Kurtis had the honor of unloading a truckload of wood for the fireplace. That finished, they moved to the back yard and checked the propane tank.

"Well I'll be," Greg almost chuckled. "A full fifty percent. How 'bout that?"

"Sounds like the pilot must have been off," Kurtis mused, fighting a yawn. He had been on the line the night before.

"Look, the heavy work is done," Greg told him. "Take the wood truck and head on back. Get some shut eye. We can handle the rest."

"You sure?" Kurtis asked, though the idea was clearly appealing to him.

"I'm sure. Go ahead, man. Get some rest."

"Thanks, Greg. I really appreciate it." With a slap on the shoulder, Kurtis did just that, heading to the Bunkhouse to get some much-needed sleep. Greg stepped inside to check on the heater. The gas had not been turned off inside, making it doubtful there was a leak or else they could have smelled it. Plus, the tank would have been empty.

He took a minute to study the large propane heater, made to look like a second fireplace near the middle of the house. There were simple directions for safely lighting the pilot light printed on the side, near the thermostat. Following those, Greg had the pilot going in about two minutes, with a warm flame blossoming over the fake logs three minutes after that.

"Nice," Petra noted, warming her hands. "That thing is pretty," she commented, returning to work.

"Hope it works good," Greg nodded. "But they can always burn wood. What can I do to help finish us up?"

-

Faron Gillis tried his best to hide his anxiety, but it was difficult at best.

For five days he and his men had maintained a patrol in the back areas of two counties, searching for any sign of the criminals responsible for a great deal of the violent crime in the area, particularly around Lewiston. There had been the faint hope that the elimination of the Bone family would put an end to the crime wave, but it was not to be. There was at least one more outfit, somewhere, preying on those who had managed to survive everything else so far.

Five days of MREs or jerky, water cleaned with purification tablets and bleach, camping on cold ground or inside cold vehicles hidden in dense foliage, all to try and stay hidden as they searched for the criminals. And all for naught as the last five days had netted them absolutely nothing in terms of success.

Then, he checks in with the Captain and finds out that the world has gone to hell, again, while he was out, having been out of contact in order to avoid anyone possibly overhearing their communications, or even just realizing that someone was transmitting.

Best decision he'd made, it appeared, since he was unable to be recalled and walk right into the Black Death.

Captain Adcock had spared no tact in informing his young lieutenant of the gravity of the situation they found themselves in. Everyone in Jordan and Lewiston could be considered as having been exposed. Some would not have been, of course, but there was no way to prove it. Since his men had been out since just before the first wave of the Exodus had arrived, they were considered clean.

Despite that, the squad would be quarantined for seven-to-ten days to ensure that no one was sick. There was exactly nothing that could be done for anyone who was sick, so isolation was the best thing in this case.

"Sir," Staff Sergeant Lowell shook the young officer from his thoughts, his hand pointing forward. A small MRAP like their own sat blocking the road. Gillis could see only two men at the moment.

"Stop," he ordered his driver, opening his door to get down even before the vehicle had completely stopped moving.

"Sir," Lowell began, but Gillis cut him off.

"Come along if you're of a mind to, Staff Sergeant," was all he said.

"Welcome to the end of the line," a semi-cheerful voice said over a low powered P.A. system. "We have a crew that is finishing up a housewarming, literally in this case for you guys. There's heat, wood and maybe propane, and we're stocking it with food. You guys will have to hang here for about ten days, give or take, and then if none of you take sick, well, that's good. I don't know what will be on the agenda next since this was laid on pretty quick like."

"That sounds pretty good after five days in the cold," Lowell muttered.

"Don't it, though?" Gillis replied. "Can you tell us anything that the Captain might not have known?" he called to the Sanders' MRAP. Before there was a reply, he heard a series of rapid gunshots, all on single fire.

"Nothing you'd want to hear or deal with at the moment," the P.A. did a good job conveying the man's sadness. "There are written orders waiting for you that will explain our situation in detail, and outline what's expected of you while you're at this location. We'll probably maintain a post here from now on as a guard on our back door, but I doubt they will keep all of you here just for that. Hold on," the man said, lowering one mike and retrieving another. They could just make out his voice as he had a brief conversation over the radio, and then he was back.

"Okay. They tell me the house is ready. Our people are on the way out so follow us, and we'll lead you there. The door is unlocked, and we left a couple of GMRS radios there with a small solar charger for you to use. In this terrain they will reach the Operations building, even if only barely. Try to keep one powered on and the other one charging so we can always communicate if we need to."

"Got it!" Gillis shouted back. "Back aboard, Staff Sergeant," he ordered Lowell. A minute later and they were following the leader to their new home.

-

"They're settled," Jose reported to Clay, thirty minutes later. "They are beat, too. Assuming they aren't sick, then the rest will do them good. They've been beating the bushes for five days straight, looking for people responsible for a lot of violent crimes south of here."

"House was in good shape," Greg added. "Bedding is good, though we stripped the bed clothes since they'd been there for over a year. Abby dusted the place for bugs while Sam and Petra cleaned and swept and what not. Kurtis and I left them a half cord of wood, too. Oh, and the propane tank was at fifty percent, so they can use the heater."

"Sounds good," Clay nodded. "They look okay, other than tired?"

"Gillis is worried," Jose replied thoughtfully. "And not a little scared, I'd imagine. He doesn't have the rank or time in grade, nor the age really, to be exercising an independent command, and he's smart enough to know it. He's leaning on his Staff Sergeant pretty hard, which is good. I'm sure they're worried about anyone they've managed to form an attachment to, whether in Jordan or Lewiston. Gillis is probably thinking about what may happen if the rest die and leave him and his few men alone, here."

"Well, he won't be alone, assuming none of them are sick," Clay reminded him. "Gleason and his troops are part of his command structure, too. We'll leave them together and issue orders for them through Gillis. With Gleason and Lowell both helping him, he should be fine."

"You're assuming any of us will be fine," Greg noted, his face stony.

No one replied to that.

CHAPTER TWENTY

It became a cycle. Those protecting the farm, usually on what was now simply called The Line, would rcport for duty. People from the Exodus would ignore the trailer across the road, ignore the newly erected sign warning of the plague and that the area was quarantined, and be shot.

Every day it was the same. One day became like any other. People ignoring the signs, the burning bodies, the warnings from the P.A. systems. Ignoring everything in favor of trying to bust through the roadblock or climb the fences or cross the creeks, overcome whatever obstacles that prevented them from invading the farm that they were sure had everything they needed.

Some were armed and tried to shoot their way through. Fortunately, they were usually not good shots, and after a year of apocalyptic living had little ammunition to spare. Facing trained and experienced soldiers with modern equipment was a losing proposition. None of the farm residents were injured by those attacks, protected by armored vehicles, or in some cases by the night itself.

For seven days it was the same. The Exodus down the interstate would thin for a while, then suddenly the numbers would swell. Adcock's last message, five days before, had indicated that the buildings they could use in Peabody were full, and a great many of those people were sick.

Adcock suspected that he was sick as well, and informed Clay of that. There was nothing for Clay to add, and the two had wished each other well.

Even more than the first days following the Storm, it truly felt like the end of the world.

-

Amanda Lowery managed to sit up in bed, wincing a bit as the action pulled on the stitching still present in her abdomen. Xavier Adair watched her from his perch on the side of her bed.

"Still hurting, I gather?"

She studied him closely before answering. He seemed to be genuinely concerned about her. She didn't know whether to be flattered or frightened. Xavier Adair just had that effect on people.

"Of course I'm hurting," she finally replied, allowing her normal sass to color her voice, and hopefully cover her pain. "I got shot, remember?"

"Oh, I do remember," Xavier assured her. "Everyone remembers that you were riding on patrol without your protection and as a result were horribly wounded. Be difficult to wear a bikini come summer, no?"

"Shut up," she muttered, her face flushing a bit. "I wear a one-piece," she added before she could help herself.

"Ah," he smiled. "I see. Well, that will help, I should imagine."

"Are you here just to cheer me up?" she growled at his good humor. "Because you really suck at it."

"I've been told that more than once," he admitted. "And no, I am not here to cheer you up. I'm actually here to check on your wellbeing. You were shot, after all," he just had to add.

"You're starting to scare me a little," she told him. "This is a bit out of character for you, ain't it? Being all…concerned and shit?"

"As ever, your word choice is amusing, if inappropriate," he laughed lightly. "I apologize if my concern…concerns you," he couldn't resist.

"Cheeky shit," she growled, but smiled as she said it.

"Indeed," he nodded. "Well, since you appear to be on the mend as well as regaining your usual sass and attitude, I shall be on my merry way," he stood. "As ever, if you have need of anything, send word to me or perhaps to Zachary. We shall see to it," he promised.

"I appreciate that, very much," she let her attitude die away to show real gratitude. "You guys are too good to me."

"We really are, aren't we?" he smiled. "Spoiling you, as it were. Still, you are one of our small group, and we take care of our own."

She was still staring at him when the door closed behind him on the way out.

-

"We haven't had word from the Captain in five days," Clay noted as he talked to Jaylyn Thatcher. "Or anyone else for that matter."

"This is all wrong," she was shaking her head, looking at her own scribbled notes.

"What do you mean?" Clay asked. "What's wrong?"

"All of it!" she exclaimed, tossing her notes on the table in front of her. "None of this makes a lick of sense, Clay! Pestis doesn't *occur* here! Especially the pneumatic strain! The very few times any of them have occurred in the U.S., it's been out west. This should not be happening here!"

"Well, I'll have to trust your expertise on that, Jaylyn, but…it is happening," he said carefully.

"I noted that myself," she snorted. "How are you all holding up?" she asked, looking at him cautiously.

"I doubt any of us will ever feel clean again," Clay admitted. "A few have had to be pulled, at Beverly's suggestion. Three days without the strain of the Line to see if it will help. But that just makes it more difficult on the others. We can't win," he said suddenly, a tiny chink in his armor allowing his depression and fatigue to show for just a second.

She examined him carefully while he stood there. Dark circles beneath his eyes, shallow respiration, face flushed slightly, fidgeting, all were signs of exhaustion. Which would lead to impaired judgement. Something they could ill afford.

"Clay, you have to get some rest," she ordered finally. "I want you to take twenty-four hours off duty. Get some hot food in you, cuddle on the couch, sleep the day away, whatever it takes, but you have got to get some rest. You are near the end of your rope."

"I know," he nodded slowly. "But there is so much to do and so few of us to do it," he shrugged.

"Jose can take over for one, or even two days, which would be better," she insisted. "He is the security chief anyway. Greg is the Sheriff. Let them handle things for the next forty-eight hours while you recover. It won't do us any good to prevent the plague from getting in here if we lose you to simple exhaustion or stroke. I want you to go home. Now. I'll inform Jose what's happening. I'll send a runner for Lainie as well. If something catastrophic happens, we can always call you on the phone. Go."

It was tempting, he admitted. So very tempting. Recline on the couch, have a hot chocolate and watch a movie. It was closing on Christmas, too. Still three weeks or so, but it was closer every day. Finally, he nodded.

"You know, that sounds good," he told her, suddenly so tired he could barely stay on his feet.

"You stay…no, you come with me," she ordered, not missing Clay's sudden weakness. She put an arm around his waist and guided him to the front of Building Two, where the response team sat, keeping warm. Gordy was sitting there, propped in a corner, trying to sleep.

"Gordy," Jaylyn spoke gently, and the teen's eyes immediately opened. He saw her standing there, essentially supporting his uncle, and was on his feet a second later.

"Doc?"

"Your uncle has reached his limit for a day or so," she said calmly. "Get an ATV and carry him home. Stop and see about picking Lainie up as well. She should be with him, I think. He is to rest and relax for the next forty-eight hours, after which I will evaluate him again. Tell Lainie she can call me on the phone when she gets things settled and I'll brief her in."

"Yes ma'am," Gordy took Clay's weight on himself, his uncle's rifle in his other hand.

"C'mon, Uncle Clay," he said softly. "Let's get you home."

"Sounds like a plan," Clay murmured, almost asleep even as he stood there.

"Please tell Leon I'll be back in a bit," Gordy told Jaylyn, who nodded. Once the two were outside, she headed for Operations to relay that message, and send one of her own to Jose Juarez.

-

"But you think he'll be okay?"

-

Lainie Harper had been sewing up a storm, in Angela's words, when Gordy had come in, walking quickly, though without panic.

"I need you to come with me," he'd told her flatly. Her eyes widened at that, but Gordy held up a hand to stop her panic.

"It's not like that," he assured her. "But he isn't well, and he needs you. Doctor's orders. And no," he added at her reaction to 'isn't well', "it's not the infection. He's exhausted."

"I knew it," she shook her head as she grabbed her coat and her gear, following him to the door. "*Dammit* I knew it. I've told him for a week that he had to take a break."

"Well, he's taking one now," Gordy promised. "Jaylyn has put him on forty-eight hours rest, barring some earth-shattering crisis. She said once you guys were settled to call her on the phone and she'd explain."

Lainie saw Clay sitting in the rear seat of the rig, leaning against the harness, clearly sleeping. She slid in beside him, wrapping her arms around him. She didn't say anything on the trip to the cabin, and Clay didn't speak either. Gordy helped her get Clay into the house and then get his gear off.

"I can manage, now," she smiled at Gordy. "Thank you."

"You bet," the teen nodded firmly. "Need anything, all of us are here for him. For both of you," he added pointedly, looking at her. "You're family."

"Thank you, Gordy," she said again. She set about to make Clay comfortable on the couch, placing a pillow beneath his head and spreading a blanket over him as well. That done, she had picked up the field phone and called the switchboard.

-

"I think he'll be fine with a couple days of rest and quiet," Jaylyn tried to sound reassuring. "He's exhausted. Pushed himself far beyond his limits and just kept going even when the tank was empty. He *must* have some rest. He needs to eat properly, too. A hot, hearty stew would be good for him. So would chicken noodle soup if you have it handy. But the stew would warm him as well as give him energy. Get him into a hot bath to relax him, and then get him into bed."

"He's on the couch now, asleep," Lainie told her. "I'm going to stay here with him and let him sleep until he wakes. After that I'll get him to eating."

"Sounds like an excellent plan," Jaylyn approved. "Call me at once if you need anything or if he seems worse."

"I will. Thank you."

"It's what I'm here for," Jaylyn replied. "Take care."

-

"Uncle Clay's down?" Leon asked as Gordy reported he was back.

"He's not down, he's just exhausted," Gordy shook his head. "He needs rest, that's all."

"That sounds like down to me, man," Leon objected, frowning.

"Well, it's not," Gordy said flatly. "He's been having all of us take time off but forgot to do it himself. It's caught up with him."

"That definitely sounds like he's down, dude," Leon insisted.

"Leon, just do your job and let Jaylyn do hers. Okay?" Gordy was tired also. Too tired to argue semantics with Leon.

"I'm doing my job!" Leon shot back, offended at the idea that he wasn't.

"Leon, for God's *sake*, give it a rest!" Gordy almost shouted, which shocked both Leon and Millie, who had stayed quiet during the exchange. The larger teen immediately caught himself, schooled his features, then continued in a calmer tone.

"We're all tired, and we've all had to do some ugly stuff," he told them both. "Enough. Worry about yourself and stop fishing for information I don't have." With that Gordy turned his back and walked out, leaving the two looking after him.

"I'd say Clay is not the only one who is exhausted, or near it," Millie said finally.

"Yeah," Leon agreed, still looking toward the door where Gordy had disappeared. "Guess not."

-

"Traffic on the highway has slowed," Shane reported to Jose later that night. "It hasn't stopped, but it has slowed."

"Can you give it a percentage?" Jose asked.

"Not an exact one, but if I had to spitball it, I'd say down by seventy to seventy-five percent," Shane shrugged. "Literally to a crawl right now and has been for over six hours. Closer to ten hours I guess, overall."

"We'll have some help tomorrow," Jose promised. "Gleason and his bunch are all but clear. Nine-and-a-half days and still clean. At this point it's almost a formality. That will let everyone get a little more time off."

"I heard Boss is down for the moment," Shane fished for news.

"You heard correctly," Jose nodded. "He's been on go all this time and it caught up with him. He's got a forty-eight from the gate by order of the Doc. Lainie is off with him, keeping an eye on him in case it's more than just exhaustion. Jaylyn seemed pretty sure, though."

"Some of the rest of us have been hitting it hard, too," Shane nodded. "But none of us have the stress of running things on us. All we have to do is show up for work."

"True," Jose agreed.

"You got it covered?" Shane asked.

"I do," Jose nodded.

"Well, call if you need me then."

-

Clay came awake very slowly, having to almost pry his eyes open. When he was able to get his eyes open enough to see, there was a mass of red hair in his face, attached to a head resting on his shoulder. No sooner had he moved than the head lifted, Lainie Harper looking at him with concern.

"How do you feel, Clay?" she asked him gently. He knew as soon as she called him 'Clay' rather than her usual 'Cowboy' that something was off.

"I'm hungry, and a bit tired," he admitted, slowly sitting up on the couch. She moved at once, flowing off the floor and taking his shoulder and arm to help him rise.

"What's going on?" he asked, suspicious. "Why are you so worried? What happened?"

"You're exhausted is what happened," she told him flatly. "I told you, time and again, that you had to rest. Had to eat. You didn't, and it caught up with you tonight. If Doctor Thatcher hadn't been there, there's no telling what might have happened."

"When was this?" he frowned, trying to remember.

"About six hours ago, give or take," she answered after looking at a clock. "Gordy came and got me, and we brought you home, got your gear off you and put you on the couch. You were out of it already. I put some soup on and sat down beside you as it simmered. I fell asleep too, but I knew if you moved it would wake me."

"I'm sorry you had to worry so much," Clay apologized, which surprised her. "Everyone is tired. We're tired and mentally exhausted as well as physically. I didn't think I was in any worse shape than the rest."

"The rest don't have all the other responsibilities of this place on them," Lainie fired back, though in no way harsh or unkind. "All they have to do is follow orders. You are doing much more than that. I told you we can't afford for you not to be at your best, and that was before this nightmare came to life. Dammit, Clay, you have got to take better care of yourself!" she insisted, tears brimming in her eyes that she refused to let out.

"Okay," his simple agreement surprised her yet again. "I have no memory of meeting Thatcher, or coming home, or any of the rest of it. I do remember being in Operations and being called to the clinic to see her. Nothing after that."

"Her diagnosis was exhaustion," Lainie repeated. "Fatigue that is so far advanced that it's threatened your health. You're on two days enforced rest, by her orders. Jose is in charge until you're back on your feet, and your father and brother will handle any non-security related matters for you, with help from Greg Holloway. Come on," she tugged on his arm, pulling him to his feet.

"Where are we going?" he asked, confused.

"I told you I made soup," she informed him, leading him to their small table. "There's also fresh bread. Well, mostly fresh," she amended. "It's left from yesterday but warmed up nicely. You're going to eat," she plopped him down in his normal chair, "take a hot bath, and then go to bed. Those are also doctor's orders, before you start," her hand came up like a traffic cop to start his objections.

"I wasn't going to," he told her. "In fact, all that sounds great. But maybe we can just curl up on the couch and watch a movie later?"

"We can do anything that keeps you out of the snow and the cold, and away from decision making," she promised. "First, you eat."

"Eating sounds good."

-

"Sounds as if just that small amount of rest helped him," Jaylyn told Lainie when the latter called to check in. "I'm not surprised he doesn't remember being here, but that in itself is a dire warning sign. If he gives you any trouble at all about the two full days of rest, call me. I can always make it three," she chuckled.

"I'd make it a week if we weren't in such a pickle right now," Lainie told her. "He's in the tub, with the water as hot as he could stand it. Once he's done there, it's straight to bed."

"Good," the doctor's nod was almost audible over the phone. "If he asks, everything is fine for the moment, and last reports I heard were that the Exodus was slowing. 'Petering out' was the actual term I heard used at one point. It's possible this is ending. At least our terrible part in it. Also, Gleason and his men are officially cleared, so they're helping hold the line now. Tell him to relax and let someone else do the lifting for two days. I'm sure most of our problems will still be here when he returns."

"That's what I'm afraid of."

-

"It is colder than a witch's tit out here," Gleason stated as he stood with Jose behind the roadblock. "That said, I am so glad to get out of that barracks that I don't care."

"It's a big help to have you guys able to be out here," Jose promised. "We're run ragged, and this has been a mess from the start."

"We heard gunfire at times," Gleason nodded. "I've spent this time talking to my boys, explaining what the situation is and how important this place will be for the survivors. They understand what's at stake, and what's expected of them. They're scared, hell they're horrified I think by what they may have to do, but I'd be worried if they weren't. I am dead certain of all but one man, and I'm reasonably sure of him as well. But he's in an observer/driver post for the time being, since I have that tiny doubt."

"Excellent," Jose nodded. "Boss is out for the next two days. Doctor's orders. He's suffering from complete exhaustion. Doesn't even remember seeing the Doc. Three others of our group are out as well. This has been a rough deal all around."

"The Lieutenant gonna be okay?" Gleason asked, concerned.

"He's already responding favorably with just a few hours rest," Jose informed him. "He should be fine in a couple days. Were you told about Gillis?"

"I was," Gleason assured him. "He's a good kid. Smart. Lowell is a steady NCO for him as well."

"They've got probably four more days in isolation, but so far they're fine," Jose told him. "They're in a farmhouse about three miles west of here, along the back side of the road. I think since we've opened the house, we're going to make it a post, too, but it won't need his entire group. Probably just a reinforced fireteam. Enough to blunt an attack and report in."

"Sounds like a plan," Gleason nodded. "I'm going to make a round and check on my guys. They're steady, but it never hurts to keep them on their toes."

"Good deal."

-

"*Pancho, this is Rattler. How copy?*"

"Go for Pancho," Jose answered, sleepily.

"*We haven't seen anyone along the interstate for two hours now,*" Shane reported from a hide they had established to watch the flow of traffic. "*Not a single soul. That doesn't mean we're clear, but it's good news. Right?*"

"It could be," Jose agreed. "Maintain your post for now. We can't afford to drop our guard. I'll have Operations try and raise Adcock again."

"*Roger that.*"

-

"AC, AC, this is Home Plate. Please respond."

Silence. Leon had tried every frequency available to them for ten minutes. No response of any kind from any source. He looked up at Jose and shrugged.

"It's not us," he informed the temporary Boss. "We're transmitting fine. No one is answering. Our main transmitter can reach Lewiston without breaking a sweat, let alone Peabody or Jordan. I know Gillis is here," he jerked a thumb toward the Plum farm, "but there should be someone down there. Right? The bulk of his command was there, wasn't it?"

"It was," Jose replied, grim. "Keep listening, but no more transmitting. Stick to the GMRS radios for now and keep the signal scrambled. Like we did when things first started. We may be on our own. Again."

"Got it."

-

"How are you doing, Zach?" a female voice asked. He turned to see Kim Powers coming up behind him, bundled against the cold and carrying her gear.

"I'm tired, I guess," he shrugged. "How are you? You guys making it okay?"

"We're all good, so far," she nodded. "But none of us are in spots where we have to shoot, either."

"That's good," Zach told her. "No reason for everyone to have to do it."

"I'm sorry you have to do it, Zach," she put a hand on his arm. "I wish I could help."

"No, you don't," he told her at once, shaking his head. "It's better like this. Limiting this kind of thing to just a few. It's going to be hell for some, I'm sure. No sense in adding to Beverly's workload."

"Have you seen her?" she asked, curious.

"Nah, I'm good," he said absently.

"Good?" she sounded startled.

"Good to go," he clarified. "I'm okay," he tried again. "No problem."

"How can you not have at least some issues about this?" she sounded incredulous.

"It's my job," Zach shrugged. "It's what I do for the farm, that's all. This place is our last line. We have to protect it. Period."

The flat sound of his answer almost stunned the former cheerleader, who studied him carefully.

"I tried to tell you before," he started, but she immediately shook her head.

"No, Zach," she raised a hand, her voice firm. "I told you. I'll figure it out for myself. You're stronger of will and mental fortitude than some of the others. That's commendable. But you should at least consider seeing Beverly, even if it's just to talk things out. Or, you can talk to me," she added softly. "I'll be here if you need an ear."

"I appreciate it, Kim," he nodded. "If I do, I'll call on you."

"Promise?"

"I promise."

She studied him for almost another minute before seeming to shake herself out of whatever train of thought she was in.

"I have to go," she sighed. "I'm due on watch."

"Things have slowed up for the moment," he told her. "Might not last, I don't know, but the break is welcome. Be careful," he warned.

"I will," she smiled at him. "See you later?"

"Sure thing."

-

"I don't understand," Gordy sighed, stretching out in the chair as he looked at Beverly. "They just keep coming. Burned bodies, signs, obstacles in the road, warnings from the P.A., and they keep coming. Almost daring us to shoot them."

"Some of them may be," Beverly nodded. She was keeping chats like this one very informal. "In law enforcement it's called 'suicide by cop'. People who don't want to take their own life, for whatever reason, will do something that forces a police officer to shoot them in the line of duty. They may have a religious deterrent to suicide, or else lack the nerve to pull the trigger. Some just want to make others suffer with them if they can, and a guilt trip over protecting your own family is a prime way to do that."

"That is just fu-, messed up," he caught himself.

"I've heard the phrase before, Gordy," Beverly laughed lightly. "You're okay. And yes, it is messed up, as you say. It's selfish, and wrong on a number of levels, ignoring the pain and suffering that you're inflicting on another human being. People still do it, even knowing that."

"Are we in the wrong, Miss Beverly?" Gordy asked suddenly. "Are we murderers now?"

Beverly took a minute to study the teen, taking in his posture, his eyes, the set of his face.

"Gordy, do you love Samantha?" she said finally, shocking him out of his fugue.

"What?"

"Do you love Samantha Walters?" Beverly repeated.

"I...yes," he didn't quite stammer.

"Do you love your parents?" she pressed.

"Of course!" he exclaimed.

"Sister?"

"Well...."

"Gordy," Beverly chided in a teasing way.

"Yeah, I guess," he admitted grudgingly.

"And the rest of your family as well, I imagine," she was nodding. "What happens when people who are sick, or who are carrying the virus, make it onto this farm and start spreading the disease among your loved ones?"

"I...I see," he nodded. "It's self-defense, isn't it."

"Absolutely," Beverly was firm in her reply. "It is a horrible thing to have to do, Gordy. It's terrible to have to ask any of you to participate. And yet, if we don't, then many of us will die and we lose what we need for the future. Those who challenge the quarantine really leave us no choice."

"It's their fault," Gordy nodded.

"I'm not placing blame, really, but rather responsibility," she told him. "Actions have consequences. There are plenty of warnings, signs included, and they ignore them. We have no choice but to defend this place, being literally backed into a corner. If they persist, then the responsibility for what happens is theirs. Whether we can call it blame or not isn't really up to me, but I can say that your actions are taken in defense of others and that means something not only here, but in God's eyes as well."

"I hope so," he sighed, his tone wistful. "I really do."

-

Charley Wilmeth and Gail Knight rode with Gordon Sanders, checking on the cattle and the fences. Charley was finally free of the cast on her arm and was likely the best pure horse handler on the ranch. Gail Knight was a former calf roping champion and had worked cattle through her teen years before her family had sold their operation. Both were good choices for helping the Sanders' patriarch check the pastures.

"Your cattle look good, Mister Sanders," Gail noted.

"I'm pleased to hear you say so, my dear," Gordon replied, eyes constantly moving as he checked everything. "It's been a bit of a struggle at times, since the Storm."

"I see that they finished separating the herd into smaller groups," Charley noted. "Good plan. We've done that with the horses as well."

"It mitigates the threat of any diseases," Gordon nodded, "but it makes caring for them much more difficult. And time consuming," he added. "That's the biggest loss really, is man hours. Woman hours, now," he joked and got two good laughs from the young women. He stopped abruptly and the two women reined in their horses as well.

"Is something wrong?" Gail asked softly, hand drifting to her rifle.

"That fence is loose," Gordon told her, reaching into the bags behind his saddle for a pair of heavy pliers. His assistants watched in silence as the old cattleman used the pliers to tighten the sagging line of barbed wire until it was taunt once more.

"Neat," Charley told him when he was finished. "Never saw that done before."

"No, I'd imagine you didn't use this kind of wire on horses," Gordon replied.

"We used it for our cattle when we still had any," Gail told them. "I've seen it done, but not for a long time, and never that easily and quickly. Our bunch would make a drama out of everything," she snorted.

"I try to avoid that kind of thing at my age," Gordon chuckled. "Too much excitement and agitation isn't good for an old man."

-

Abby was just finishing a run with an ATV and a blade, scraping snow and ice from walkways along the road and from house-to-house. Normally they wouldn't bother, but the snow had been fairly heavy and was still falling at times. Six inches of snow had accumulated so far, with a good bit of ice beneath it. It was much better to plow a little than treat a broken bone.

She pulled the small utility vehicle into the open tractor shed, lowering the blade and angling the rig so the blade wasn't in the way. She climbed out and was gathering her gear when someone spoke behind her.

"Just can't stay away from those blades, can you?" Greg Holloway teased. She jumped only slightly and turned to look at him, red-faced.

"Stop sneaking up on people!" she fussed, flustered at being caught by surprise, and flustered worse by it being Greg of all people.

"I wasn't sneaking," he managed to look affronted at the suggestion. "I saw you working and trudged over here through the snow to see how it was going. So…how's it going?"

"You jackass," she laughed at his humor. "It's okay. I've got walkways open down the hill and between all the buildings. Should be fine unless we get more sleet. If we do then I'll have to do it again. Last thing we need is someone breaking something."

"That is very true," he nodded. "And how are you doing?" he asked more pointedly. "How are you making it right now?"

"I'm fine," she said automatically. "Just working and trying to make sure I'm contributing to the farm, or wherever I can," she shrugged.

"You're doing that and more, Abby," Greg promised. "Don't worry about those who don't see that. Others do see and realize how hard you're working. You're doing fine."

"Thanks," she looked down, face heating. "I appreciate it."

"Keep your head up, kiddo," the Sheriff ordered. "You're doing your share and part of another hand. You got nothing to be ashamed of." With that he walked away, headed for her grandparents, where he was still staying for the moment.

She wasn't blushing due to shame, but she couldn't bring herself to tell him that.

CHAPTER TWENTY-ONE

Once more Clay came slowly awake, but this time it was easier, and without the effort to pry his eyes open. The only thing that was the same was the mass of red hair in his face. He smiled, laying still so as not to wake her.

Two days of enforced rest had indeed been just what the doctor had ordered. He'd eaten better than he had in two weeks, probably, and slept until his body said it was enough instead of just catching an hour on a cot or another hour in a chair, somewhere. He literally felt better than he had in weeks.

"Morning, Cowboy," Lainie was suddenly smiling at him sleepily. "How you feeling?"

"Better," he promised her. "Much better, in fact. I haven't felt this good since before Thanksgiving. It's amazing, really."

"Good," she crawled to where he was laying and kissed him. "I was worried for a minute, babe. You were having memory trouble in addition to almost passing out on your feet. Scared me."

"I am truly, deeply sorry for that," he wrapped his arms around her, kissing her gently. "I didn't realize how bad it was. I know, you told me," he pulled one hand back to raise a shield against an 'I told you so'. "And I wasn't ignoring you, I just had…there was just so much to do, and I thought I was okay to do it. That's all it was."

"Well, new rule around here, bud," she told him with mock severity. "When the woman warns you to take it easy for a bit, then you come sit down and take it easy. Eat and rest and then go back at it. Got it?" she poked his chest with her finger. She looked serious but her eyes were shining playfully.

"I got it, woman," he smiled and kissed her again. "Promise."

"Good."

-

"Well, Clayton, I am really rather surprised at how well you've bounced back with just two days of rest," Jaylyn said finally as she finished his exam. "You were very close to a total collapse, you know."

"I do now," Clay nodded. "Sorry."

"It's nothing to be sorry for, at least not to me," she shook her head. "Lainie maybe, but for the rest of us, you're trying to keep us safe and housed and fed and everything else. Still, where would we be if something happened to you? I know there are other competent military leaders around, but what about everything else? With your grandfather gone, you have become the glue that holds all this together."

"Hadn't thought of it that way," Clay admitted. "That would please the Old Man," he smiled faintly.

"Well, I doubt he'd be pleased to see you so run down," she frowned.

"No, he wouldn't," Clay agreed. "He fussed at me almost as much as Lainie to take better care of myself. And I thought I was," he shrugged, his hands out to his side, palms up. "I really thought I was. And I didn't think that I was hitting it any harder than anyone else was, either."

"Everyone else gets done with their work and goes home," she pointed out. "You go do something else, and then something else after that, and then get called back for yet something else before you can make it home. That's the difference, Clay."

"Yeah, that's what Lainie said," Clay was nodding. "I just didn't see it, that's all."

"That isn't surprising, and you aren't alone," she told him. "That's why you have to depend on others who can see what's happening to you, even when you can't. Lainie said she had been after you for at least a week to ease up, rest and eat better. She could see it even before I noticed. Listen to her when she talks, Clay," Jaylyn urged. "She cares about you a great deal, and you're the most important thing in her life. She worries over you because she loves you."

"I know," he nodded, looking at the floor. "It wasn't intentional. Worrying her like that," he clarified.

"I know, and I feel sure she does too," Jaylyn smiled suddenly. "But learn to listen when others tell you that you need rest. Another few hours, a day at most, and you might have been in severe trouble, Clay. And I don't have the medicines to treat that kind of problem the modern way. You don't need to develop high blood-pressure on us, or anything else. So learn to take better care, okay?"

"I promise I will. I promise."

-

"The Great One returns!" Jose smiled tiredly as Clay walked up to him, geared up for work. Jose was outside, about to go and tour the line on an ATV.

"I do, indeed," Clay chuckled. "Sorry about leaving you in a lurch, man," he added.

"It was worth it to see you finally get some damn rest, my brother," Jose shook his head. "I'm about to take a look around. Want to come along?"

"Sure."

-

"It's been thirty-two hours, roughly, since we've seen any traffic on the interstate," Jose filled him in as they made their way forward. "It slowed gradually to a trickle, stayed that way for maybe six-to-eight hours, then faded to nothing. We haven't had anyone try to break the quarantine in nearly two days. The downside of that is that we can't raise Adcock or anyone else by radio. I ordered us to go silent on all but the FRS and GRMS frequencies day before yesterday. We're monitoring, but not transmitting. I passed the same orders to Gillis, without letting him know they came from me," he flashed a smile at his Boss, who chuckled.

"Sounds like a good plan," Clay nodded. "When was the last time we had news from anyone?"

"Moving toward seven days, now," Jose replied. "Gleason and his men are out of quarantine, by the way, and have been a huge help holding the lid down, giving our guys a break they desperately needed. Gillis and his men are four days from being clear themselves and so far, reporting no illnesses of any kind.

"Sounds good," Clay nodded. Jose slowed as they neared the far left of their defensive line of vehicles, which was the Gray Ghost. Stacey Pryor saw them and waved from the passenger door. Dismounting, the two moved to where their friend stood, waiting.

"Greetings, Great One!" Stacey bowed deeply. "Welcome to our small and humble corner of the world!"

"What's the good news?" Clay laughed, shaking Stacey's hand.

"We are quiet along the…well, the northern front, I guess," Stacey amended his report with a smile. "That I've been made aware of, no one has challenged this area of the defense at all," he said more seriously.

"Sounds good," Clay nodded, looking toward the interstate, which lay beyond the tree line to their east. "Any problems of any kind?"

"Other than it's colder than a well digger's ass in a Montana winter?" Stacey replied. "Not a one so far."

"That's pretty cold, I guess," Clay laughed. "Okay, then. You got anything?" he looked at Jose.

"Nope," was the simple reply. "We'll move on, I guess," Jose told Stacey. "Remember to use only the local radio," he cautioned.

"Got it, brother."

Soon the ATV was traveling south to the next position, this one the Guardian named Cop Car One. Sienna Newell sat atop the vehicle with binoculars in hand, still scanning the tree line for movement. She slid down to the ground when the ATV stopped beside her rig.

"Well, look who's back with the living!" she smiled. "Good to have you back, Bossman!"

"Good to be back, too," Clay accepted her brief hug. "How are things going?"

For the next hour, Jose and Clay visited every post along the line, checking with vehicle commanders and ensuring all was well. By the time they were finished, both were pleased with what they had found. They discussed possible future moves on the ride back.

"We'll probably have to erect permanent posts out here," Jose sighed. "Maybe some hunting blind type structures that we can heat in the winter and open in the summer. Protection from the elements and what not."

"Not a bad idea," Clay nodded slowly. "We probably should have already done it instead of relying on a few foxholes to do the job."

"Well, we didn't have all this other crap going then, you know," Jose reminded him.

"That's true, but we knew we'd have problems," Clay sat back and crossed his ankles, relaxing in a way that Jose hadn't seen in a long time. "We can establish a watch line around us on probable threat vectors and then use Operations to do a check in every fifteen minutes or so."

"Lonely job, way out here in a phone booth, all alone in the night," Jose mused.

"I know," Clay agreed. "But we can't afford to be lax, especially now. Even with the flood down the interstate gone, we're still at risk."

"That is true," Jose agreed. "Well, we have Gleason and his guys, and hopefully we'll soon have Gillis and his men, too. That will go a long way toward helping us do that."

"Yeah."

-

"What's up, Buttercup?" Zach said as he propped on the side of Amanda's bed in the infirmary. Kim giggled quietly from behind him, hearing such a sentence from him.

"Buttercup?" Amanda glowered.

"You're right," Zach held up his hands in supplication. "Absolutely right. That was unforgivable of me. So…how are you, Mavis?"

"You shithead!" Amanda tried to hit him but failed to make contact, wincing with the effort.

"Swing! And a miss!" Zach tried to sound like a baseball announcer, smiling as he sat back down. "Okay, seriously now. How are you? Need anything?"

"To go back and not be so stupid," Amanda sighed, leaning back and trying to get comfortable. "That's what I need."

"Something we can get you, Amanda," Kim rolled her eyes playfully.

"They take good care of me," Amanda waved a hand toward Kaitlin Caudell, who had the duty in the clinic at present. "I don't have a thing to complain about that isn't my fault," she sounded almost dejected.

"Stop that," Zach and Kim said almost in unison, surprising one another.

"You made a mistake," Zach shrugged. "Not the end of the world. Could have been, for you at least, but it wasn't. Learn from it and move ahead."

"Yeah," Kim was nodding. "You're going to recover. Concentrate on how you will make sure it doesn't happen again, Sergeant Lowery."

"Oh, God, not that again!" Amanda almost wailed. "You try one time, just one time to build people up, and this is the thanks you get!" she told Zach.

"Yeah, I was thinking PFC Lowery myself," Zach nodded with mock seriousness. "Corporal Lowery at best."

"Oh, aren't you two a pair of cards," Amanda shot back. "The Jack of Asses and the Queen of Snarks."

"She doesn't look like a Jack to me," Zach eyed Kim, who smacked him in the arm, laughing.

"Are you saying you're a Queen?" Amanda asked him.

"Don't I look it?" Zach mimed primping his hair and then doing makeup, making Amanda laugh again.

"Stop making me laugh, idiot!" she cried, holding her abdomen. "It still hurts!"

"Well, stop giving me material," he chuckled, standing up and away from the bed. "I have to go, Amanda. But if you need anything, get someone to call me or X. We'll see to it."

"Hey," Kim complained. "I'm standing right here."

"Or her," Zach added, grinning. "I really do have to go. See you guys later." With that he made his way out, leaving Kim to lean against Amanda's bed.

"Well," Amanda leaned back, eyeing her friend. "What's going on there?"

"Nothing, yet," Kim's face reddened. "Still testing the ice, so to speak."

"He's a tough one to read," Amanda agreed. "And scary as hell, too," she added carefully.

"Scary?" Kim frowned. "How?"

"You really don't see it, do you?" Amanda asked softly. "I thought it was just Bad Boy Fever, but you really don't see it."

"See what?" Kim demanded.

"Kim, that boy is dangerous, with a capital D," Amanda kept her voice low. "And that isn't a criticism. I love him to death, and Xavier, too. But they are two of the scariest fuckers I have ever seen, in real life or in the movies."

"They don't seem scary to me," Kim protested.

"Then you aren't looking," Amanda replied. "I'm not trying to warn you off Zach, girl. I just want you to see what you're getting into. That's all."

Kim thought about that. Twice Zach had tried to talk to her about himself and she had stopped him, wanting to form her own opinion. Perhaps he had been trying to warn her?

"I'll see what happens," she said hesitantly. "I don't think he would hurt me," she added carefully.

"Of course not!" Amanda exclaimed at once. "He would absolutely kill someone that did hurt you! Just…be aware that he may have some issues. That's all."

"Okay," Kim nodded slowly, still clearly thinking. "Duly noted."

-

"Still nothing on the radio?" Clay asked as he stepped into Operations. Leanne and Janice both shook their heads.

"Completely quiet," Leanne stated. "Our own checkpoints are still checking in, of course, but from the others, nothing."

"Any of our spots having problems?" Clay asked.

"No. None of them are near the interstate and all were warned about the virus as soon as we knew what we were dealing with, so they've stayed isolated."

"I guess nothing from south of us, either," he stated rather than asked.

"Sorry," Leanne shook her head again.

"Sounds as if we're back to being on our own, huh?" Clay smiled at them, but neither smiled back.

"I had just gotten used to our not being alone and isolated," Janice almost whispered, she was so quiet.

"Well, maybe this won't last much longer," Clay tried to keep his tone light. "I hope the worst is over now and we can maybe start to recover." The look Leanne gave him let him know that she, for one, wasn't fooled.

"Well, if you need me for anything give me a call," he told them. "I've given Jose the day off for the next two days, making up for his having to cover for me. Greg will handle the night shift, but I'll be available. Try to let him make the call of whether or not to alert me, though, since he's in command for the evening shift."

"Will do," Leanne promised.

Clay left Building Two and started for home. He felt lighter than he had in a long time, working to let others take over some of the strain he had been handling alone. He had not been fair to Lainie, being so stressed out, and was determined not to do it again.

-

Faron Gillis stretched as he stepped outside into the cold. They were out of quarantine as of today. Once their blood tests had cleared, they were free to move around. Gillis had wisely decided to wait on Sanders to come to them, his written orders having instructed him to defer to Sanders as if he were still a First Lieutenant in the Army.

That suited Gillis just fine, in all honesty. There were things happening he didn't think he wanted to deal with if he could avoid it. Combat was one thing. Fighting a virus that could kill anywhere from six to eight people out of every ten was quite another. He'd stick to shooting, thanks.

"Lieutenant," Staff Sergeant Lowell said, pointing. Following the pointing finger, Gillis could see an approaching golf cart, two men on it. He recognized both, one being Sanders himself and the other being the Sheriff he had met what seemed like a year ago.

"Morning, gentlemen," Clay smiled as Greg brought their small ride to a halt.

"Morning, sir," both Gillis and Lowell replied at once.

"Rule Number One," Clay said with mock severity. "We do not refer to me as Sir, Lieutenant, or any derivative thereof. Okay?"

"Got it s-, Sanders," Gillis grinned as he caught himself.

"Call me Clay, or if you must, Bossman," Clay told him, rising from the cart and offering his hand. "I'm pleased to see you guys all made it clear. And we can definitely use the help if you're ready to rejoin the living. Or at least what's left of us," he added with a sigh.

"That bad, sir?" Lowell asked, not bothering to wince. He had been an NCO for a long time, and habits were hard to break.

"It's pretty bad," Clay admitted. "We've had to shoot…well, we've had to do a lot to keep this place safe. I doubt some of us will ever feel clean again, to be honest. But it had to be done. We may be all that helps us get back up and off the ground when the dust settles. We can't let this place be overrun."

"Those were in my orders from Captain Adcock," Gillis was nodding. "Though I suspect you wrote them for him while he dictated over the radio?"

"I did, yes," Clay nodded. "At the time, Adcock believed he himself was sick. We haven't heard from him or anyone else in over a week now, so he may well have been. We don't know, and we can't get into contact with anyone who does. We have contact with a handful of stations we set up right before this all started, but they are well away from the action and have remained isolated from this mess thus far."

"We had a little over company strength in all," Gillis said quietly. "We're less than a quarter of that between my patrol and the men with Sergeant Gleason. We can't be all that's left." He paused before looking at Clay. "Can we?"

"I would think not, but I have no idea," Clay admitted. "Those who didn't get sick may have fled. May have joined those going further south in hopes of escaping. I don't know if that will work or not. Doctor Thatcher seems to think not but admits she doesn't know. None of us knows much of anything right now."

"What do you want us to do, sir?" Gillis asked. "We're supposed to attach our command to yours."

"I want you to detail Sergeant Lowell to command this post with five men," Clay told him. "You will assume command of all Captain Adcock's forces on the farm and I will issue any orders through you. You and the rest will return to the farm proper, where we are trying to establish a screen of posts to protect us from trespassers. It's all we can do for now. I assume you guys have laundry?"

"Yes sir, we do," Gillis nodded. "A few days' worth."

"We happen to have a laundry," Clay smiled. "A real one. Bring all your dirty clothing down with you and we'll get it laundered and returned. Whatever else your men may need, we'll try and provide it, assuming we have it. Are you set for gear and ammunition?"

"Affirmative, sir," Gillis replied.

"Bring your vehicles down to have them refueled and let our mechanic look them over," Clay ordered. "Assuming they check out, we'll probably have your MRAP returned here to help with the watch. I hope they won't need it, but if they do then they'll need it in a hurry. Anything else we can cover back at the barn, where we can get out of this cold."

"Roger that, sir."

-

Clay had gathered everyone who played a role in decision making on the farm, assembling them in the area of Building Two that usually served as a group dining area for get togethers.

"Everyone, this is Lieutenant Faron Gillis," he introduced the newest member of their circle. "He was with Captain Adcock's command, stationed in and around Lewiston. His men have been through quarantine, and the Captain asked us to let them settle in here due to the emergency we're enduring. Introduce yourselves and then we'll talk a bit."

The introductions made the rounds of the tables, with everyone giving their name and a bit about the role they served. Finally, it was back to Clay.

"Well, we're in a mess again, and there's no doubt of that," Clay told them, not bothering to sugar coat anything. "We're pretty much isolated at the present, unable to raise anyone on the radio other than the few outposts we established back when Greg first took over as Sheriff. They're all keeping their heads down and staying isolated as well, hoping things will blow over without hitting them. So far, it has."

"Have we had any contact at all with Jordan?" Gordon asked.

"Not for several days," Clay admitted. "That almost bothers me more than not being able to contact Adcock, since there were about two thousand people in Jordan, and they had more than one working radio we had provided. Also, there was more than one radio in Lewiston, and even more people. Nothing from either town."

"So, we're alone, then," Robert said quietly, his face showing how he felt about that.

"Well, we're not completely alone," Clay told his brother. "Remember that I just said we're still in contact with our people in the radio stations we established. There are still people out there. But we don't know about places we can't contact. Not yet. And honestly, it's not worth the risk to go and investigate, either. Not right now, at least."

"How can you say that?" more than one voice protested, all of them civilian.

"I can say it because it's true," he held up a hand to stop their complaints. "Look, most of you don't realize it, but we've been attacked several times in the last two weeks. People, armed people, coming over our roadblocks and fence lines despite our warnings, determined to get at whatever we're keeping from them. Most believe we have a way to treat the disease, which we do not. Many assume we have food, which we do, but we can't feed everyone. We'll be hungry before the next crop comes in as it is. And that's assuming we get a good harvest."

"We've dipped deep into our own canned and stored food to help others, we've cut just as deep into the beef and pork we had held back for consumption, and we've taken on two dozen new mouths to feed," he ticked off the problems. "And our orders, my orders, were to isolate this farm and protect it at all costs. Allow no one onto the farm until further notice."

"If Adcock is gone, who will give that notice?" Ronny asked, curious rather than challenging.

"That's a problem, too," Clay admitted. "At some point I'll have to make a decision about that. But we are going to wait a good while before doing it. It's my hope that winter kills the virus, at least for the most part. Before we adjourn, Captain Thatcher will detail a report on what we can expect, but we'll get to that in a bit."

"The rule about no one getting in or out stands, for now," he continued. "Anyone who absolutely wants to leave may do so, of course, but they won't be allowed back, for any reason. We've been extremely fortunate to dodge this bullet, and we will not risk that by becoming careless at this late date."

"We'll be erecting permanent guard stations around the area to replace the vehicles that have helped hold the line up until now," Clay moved to a map of the farm and indicated a number of pencil drawn X marks. "These will be like hunting blinds, and we'll have to try and figure a safe way to heat them and build them so we can open them up in the summer to allow a breeze inside. These posts will be manned around the clock for the foreseeable future."

"That's a lot of manpower," Gleason mentioned, and several heads nodded.

"I know, but if we depend just on the towers, then by the time we see someone it may well be too late," Clay shrugged. "I don't want to do it either, I just can't figure anything else. This is what we can do, so we do it. We'll have a meeting for security personnel to hash this out further later, but just so everyone knows, this is the plan for now."

"Sooner or later we're going to start seeing people from Jordan who survived," Gordon noted. "They can't all have perished, can they?"

"The statistics say no," Jaylyn Thatcher stood when Clay motioned to her. "I guess this is as good a time as any for me to talk about this. Pestis is normally found…."

-

"Don't tell them I said so," Clay told Jose quietly a bit later on, "but I don't want the young women, the Amazons," he snorted, "working these isolated watch positions," he pointed at the roster for the new posts they were building. "Use them for internal security here around the buildings."

"Any reason why?" Jose asked, though he was sure he knew.

"I just don't want them isolated out on that arc, that's all," Clay replied as expected. "I don't want them where they can be taken by surprise and abducted."

"We could always have two people to a stand," Jose suggested, though he was not in favor of it.

"No," Clay shook his head. "No, that just invites conversation and letting your guard down. We'll rotate the guards every two hours or so. Maybe that will help. But remember that when you draw up assignments."

"Yes, Great One."

Clay ignored him as he moved on.

-

While he hadn't told anyone, Clay had expected trouble from Jordan long before now. Those who survived would blame the farm for not helping, even though the farm had helped them greatly. That assistance would, as ever, be overlooked as people in Jordan looked for someone to blame their sorrows on.

He had just finished breakfast when his radio came to life, requesting him at the roadblock as soon as possible. Taking his ATV, Clay headed that way. The snow had melted with warmer temperatures, leaving a muddy mess everywhere it had touched. Snow was good for farm country, but it still made a mess.

He arrived at the Cougar standing guard over the roadblock to see a single figure standing in the distance, holding up what looked like a bicycle.

"What gives?" he asked Shane, who was the vehicle commander for the morning.

"Showed up a half-hour ago, wanting to see you," Shane shrugged. "Said he had information for you."

Puzzled, Clay started forward slowly, giving him time to study the visitor. He looked familiar, and as he made it to the log trailer roadblock he finally realized where from.

"Constable Kelly," Clay spoke up. "What brings you out in such sloppy weather?"

"Weather is as good as it's going to get, Sanders," Tim Kelly shrugged, his hand moving to catch his rifle sling before it fell off. "I'm moving south, while I can." Clay noted that the bicycle had a basket in front and a rack behind the seat, and that it was towing a small touring trailer.

"Well, I hope you have a safe journey, Mister Kelly," Clay tried to sound optimistic.

"I was hoping to pick up some dried foods from you to help me make the trip," Kelly told him. "I brought you some information to trade for it. I'll tell you what I know, and you decide if it's worth any help to me or not. Fair?"

"Sounds like a deal," Clay nodded cautiously. "What's going on?"

"There are a lot of people in Jordan that are pissed at you," Kelly got straight to the point. "Clamoring about how you all should have done more to help. Mostly it's people that lost someone to the sickness, but some of them are just looking for a way to stir shit, if you know what I mean."

"I'm afraid I do," Clay sighed. "I'm going way out on a limb here and guess that Franklin George and those two that wanted to seize our homes are the ringleaders?"

"Got it in one," Kelly nodded. "George lost his wife, and his son," Kelly's voice softened. "He's grieving, but he was already hating on you to start with. Sutter and Wilkins just see this as a way to try and seize this place. Again."

"That I expected," Clay replied. "How did things go in Jordan, anyway? We can't get anyone on the radio at all and were starting to fear the worst."

"It was bad," Kelly admitted. "A few got sick and survived, but over half the town is dead, and about two-thirds of the soldiers, including their fussy little woman general."

"She was a second lieutenant," Clay snorted. "Long way from a general."

"Anyone ever tell her that?" Kelly laughed, though it was a bitter sound. "Anyway. Those three are stirring as hard and as fast as they can against you, and they've gathered about two hundred followers so far. Some of us ain't quite that dumb, but there's always a few in every crowd. They've got a lot of guns left from the militia, which has pretty much folded along with everything else. Pickett didn't make it," Kelly shrugged. "Dawson survived, but he was left weak and can't stand up to them."

"Any idea what they plan to do?" Clay asked, not daring to hope.

"Not supposed to, but I overheard some of them talking," Kelly surprised him again. "I'm not sure I wasn't meant to, though, so take that as you will. What I heard them discussing, though, was to infiltrate your place. Get inside and hit you before you knew they were here. It's a stupid plan, but then they're stupid people, so there ya go," he shrugged.

"I see," Clay sighed. "How many more do you think will follow them? You said they had a couple hundred already?"

"A little over that, I guess," Kelly nodded. "If I had to guess, there's going to be seventy-five to a hundred more before they hit a plateau. People that come to hear what's said but haven't seemed to decide as yet. They're leaning that way, though. I think it's just a matter of time, or a matter of George hitting the right chord."

"Any idea how long before they make a move?" Clay wanted to know.

"Some want to do it before Christmas, before it gets too cold," Kelly replied. "A few even wanted to do it on Christmas, since old man George told them you'd be celebrating out here, living high on the hog as you do. Them's his words, not mine. The rest want to wait until after the first of the year, and fight in the cold for some reason. It's almost as if they think you guys will just go to sleep like a bear, and not wake up until spring."

"I wish," Clay snorted. "Anything else?"

"No, not to speak of," Kelly said after a minute of thought. "I will say that old man George has a special hate for all of you, but you he really, really hates. He preaches against you every chance he gets, too."

"I don't doubt it," Clay admitted. "So, what do you want for your trip south?"

"What is all that I said worth to you?" Kelly shrugged.

"It's worth a good bit, but I don't know how you want to travel," Clay replied. "You wanted smoked beef, which I can supply in the form of jerky. I can also get you some dried fruit. You can either eat it like it is, or else drop it in some hot water and reconstitute it. It's not bad."

"Got any dried vegetables?" Kelly asked

"I do, actually. A few, anyway. I've not tried them myself, so I can't say how good they are."

"You think you can put me a pack together that will get me nine or ten days down the road, then?" Kelly asked cautiously.

"I think I can arrange that," Clay replied at once. "Wait here and I'll see to it. Deal?"

"More than."

-

"Had you asked me a year ago if Franklin George would be stirring up trouble against us, I'd have said no way," Gordon sighed. "I still can't quite believe it."

"I do," Clay told his father, face and voice both grim. "Look, I have to go and tell Marcy about her mother and brother," he stood up. "I just wanted to let you know what the deal was."

"Want some advice, Son?" Gordon looked up.

"Any time I can get it," Clay nodded firmly.

"Let Beverly and one of the other women go and talk to Marcy," Gordon said. "You go and talk to young Titus, let him know what's happening and then make sure he's not working for the next two or three days. Let him help her however he can."

Clay mulled that over before finally nodding, slowly.

"I admit that sounds better than me having to do it," he said at last.

"They'll do better at it than you can, Son," Gordon promised. "Likely had to do it before at some point. Be hard enough, you talking to Titus, I'd imagine."

"I imagine," Clay nodded. "Thanks, Pop."

"Welcome, Son."

-

While it might have gone better with Beverly, Martina and Samantha Walters going to inform Marcy George about her family, that didn't mean good. Already stressed and strained beyond measure, the young woman broke completely, collapsing on the floor as she learned about her brother, especially. Kandi Ledford and Sienna Newell, who shared the house with her, both agreed to sit with her, and Clay cleared their schedule for the next three days for them to do so. Samantha remained behind when the older women left, making a cup of now precious hot chocolate for Marcy to drink. Sam had always found warm chocolate to be a comfort and hoped that Marcy would as well.

Kelly had no word of Marla, and Clay hated to have to tell Lainie that. It had been the last thing Clay had asked, as he sat the basket with the food for Kelly on the ground and pushed it across to him with a rake. Kelly had seen Marla around a few times but wasn't sure if she had survived or not. Clay had thanked him and wished him safe travels. Kelly had put the food away and headed south on the interstate without another word.

Later that evening, Clay had gathered Greg, Jose, Gillis, Gleason and Lowell together, then added Virgil Wilcox and reluctantly called Sienna Newell away from Marcy for a short time. Mitchell Nolan was the last one to be added to the group as they sat down around a small table.

Clay outlined what he'd been told, and Greg had been able to vouch for Kelly, at least from what he knew of him before the virus. Anyone could change after going through something like that.

The small group stormed over plans and contingencies for a good two hours before agreeing that the changes they were planning would work for this eventuality as well as any others they had thought of. It was decided that the construction of the small hides would begin the next day, and that they would be hidden rather than sitting in the open as a deterrent.

Gillis was sorry to hear that so many of the men he had served with had perished, including Lieutenant Gaines. While he admitted he had never really cared for her personally, she had been a good soldier. Clay withheld comment on that, not believing for a minute that Gaines had been a good anything other than a trouble making ass-kisser. Not to speak ill of the dead, of course.

"Some of them will still be carrying the virus," Jaylyn Thatcher told them when asked to come and render her opinion. "If they survived having the virus, then it will still be in their blood, and possibly in their airways. They'll infect anyone around them that hasn't already been exposed and fought the infection off."

"That means that we have to keep them out," Greg told the others flatly. "No choice. We keep them at bay, no matter what."

"Maybe they won't come here," Gillis offered hopefully. Those who knew the people in Jordan better than he did quickly crushed that hope.

"They'll come, alright," Greg promised. "Just as soon as Franklin, Sandy and Myrtle get them to a fever pitch and are certain they won't get any more to join. They'll come."

"Kelly didn't have a time frame, just guesses on what others had suggested," Clay told them. "Based on that, we could see them tomorrow, or not until after the first of the year. Or, not at all," he added finally. When the others just stared, Clay shrugged.

"Kelly wanted food for his trip south," he mentioned. "I traded him for it because I decided it sounded plausible. But he could have made it up hoping to get that same food from me. I don't know."

"Possible, but I doubt it, based on what we know," Greg was shaking his head. "What I know," he clarified. "Kelly was a straight shooter and unlikely to lie. We also know that Franklin George, Sandy Sutter and Myrtle Wilkins were all against you, even way back when we were busting ass to help them get on their feet again in Jordan. I'd say his scenario is as likely as any other."

"Yeah," Clay nodded. "I do agree. Just was throwing that other out there, man."

-

"Well, that puts a damper on Christmas, now, doesn't it?" Lainie said when he got home. "We can't risk having everyone piled in, celebrating, if we're liable to be attacked at any moment."

"True," Clay agreed.

"So, what are we going to do?" she asked him, hugging a pillow to her as she sat next to him on the sofa.

"Whatever we have to," he told her honestly, putting an arm around her shoulders and drawing her to him. "Whatever we have to."

"Ashes," she whispered, not looking at him.

"What?"

"You said that the fire that had been America had burned out, remember?" she reminded him. "All that was left was ashes. So, here we are," she whispered mournfully. "Left sitting in a pile of ashes and surrounded by ruin."

There was nothing Clay could add to that. He did notice as he looked outside that it was snowing again. Large, heavy and wet flakes, falling like confetti that never stopped.

He noted idly that it looked like ashes, falling from a fire burning in the sky.

A NOTE FROM THE AUTHOR

(that's me, again 😊)

So, another chapter in the Sanders' Saga is complete. I owe many thanks to my family for their support of me as I write. For things that I forget to do, or else don't have time to do, for the times they have to call me for a third, or fourth, or even fifth time for something before they get through to me.

Thanks are due to Dan Edwards and Creative Texts Publishing for all their work. If it weren't for them, I'd lose about forty percent of my writing time, if not more. They really do take a lot off me, allowing me to concentrate on storytelling and making up stuff 😉

A very special thank you to all of you who read my books, and a huge thanks to those of you who have left so many reviews for the books I've written. As I've said before, reviews are important for many more reasons than the writer's ego. The number of reviews left figure into a search and recommendation algorithm that Amazon uses to recommend new books to their readers. That helps put books like this one in front of new readers that otherwise might never see my books. So, thank you for taking the time to leave a review of my work. Know, please, that I sincerely appreciate it, and ask you to please continue doing so. It really does help.

When I started this series, you would never have convinced me that I would be sitting here, typing an afterword for an eleventh novel in the series. It's staggering to my mind just to think of it. That, again, is due to you, the reader. The only appropriate way I can think of to thank you is to try and keep the Sanders' Clan as active as I can, for as long as I can entertain you with their story. As long as I can entertain you, as long as I can create an imaginary world that all of us can hide in, even for a few hours, then I've done my job. I can't take pride in my work until you, the reader, are satisfied that I did good. That's the greatest thing a storyteller can be told, folks. That we did good and you, the reader, were entertained by what we've created. Thanks for that, along with everything else.

The holidays are coming, and I hope all of you have a safe and happy holiday season. I wish only the best for each and every one of you, and offer you a humble thanks for letting me be a 'real' writer. If it weren't for you, none of that would happen. So Happy Thanksgiving, Merry Christmas and Happy New Year to all of you. May God bless you and keep you safe, especially in these troubling times.

From the banks of the Tennessee River,

N.C. Reed

More Books by Author N.C. Reed

Book Series

Fire From the Sky

Book 1: The Sanders Saga

Book 2: Brotherhood of Fire

Book 3: Trial by Fire

Book 4: Home Fires

Book 5: Friendly Fire

Book 6: Hostile Fire

Book 7: Hostile Fire

Book 8: Hell Fire

Book 9: Brimstone

Book 10: Damned Nation

The Black Sheep of Soulan

Book 1: Parno's Company

Book 2: Parno's Destiny

Book 3: Parno's Gambit

Book 4: Parno's Peril

Book 5: Parno's Gift

Stormcrow

Stormcrow: Book 1

Stormcrow: Book 2

Stand Alone Titles

Odd Billy Todd

Roland: Reluctant Paladin

Tammy and Ringo

Friggin Zombies

The Kid

THANK YOU FOR READING!

If you enjoyed this book, we would appreciate your customer review on your book seller's website or on Goodreads.

Also, we would like for you to know that you can find more great books like this one at www.CreativeTexts.com

Made in the USA
Coppell, TX
04 January 2021